WELCOME T

JULIE JAMES

"**A delicious, delightful read** that all hopeless romantics will enjoy."
—*Chicago Sun-Times*

"**Fueled by equal measures of seductive wit,** edge-of-the-seat suspense, and scorching-hot sexual chemistry."
—*Chicago Tribune*

"**A must-read for those searching for a smart romance** with great characters and a no-holds-barred plot."
—*San Francisco Book Review*

"**[Julie James] is a master.**"
—*Booklist* (starred review)

continued . . .

"You'll fall head over heels for *A Lot Like Love*."
—*USA Today*

"Julie James . . . is mastering the genre of romantic suspense."
—*The News-Gazette* (East Central Illinois)

"James writes characters so real you can almost reach out and touch them. A delicious blend of romance and suspense."
—*RT Book Reviews*

"Just the right balance of charm, love, action, and touches of humor and suspense."
—*Fresh Fiction*

"There's a whole lot to love about *A Lot Like Love* from Julie James. This is a superb read, plain and simple."
—*Babbling About Books, and More*

Something About You

"Smart, snappy, funny yet realistic. I can't count the number of times I laughed while reading the book . . . This is one book I can totally recommend."
—*Dear Author*

"From first impressions to the last page, it's worth shaking your tail feather over . . . This is a contemporary romance well worth savoring, and laughing over, and reading all over again."
—*Smart Bitches, Trashy Books*

"Just plain fun! James is a master of witty repartee."
—*RT Book Reviews*

Practice Makes Perfect

"A tantalizing dessert—a delicious, delightful read that all hopeless romantics will enjoy."
—*Chicago Sun-Times*

Just the Sexiest Man Alive

Love Irresistibly

JULIE JAMES

BERKLEY SENSATION, NEW YORK

THE BERKLEY PUBLISHING GROUP
Published by the Penguin Group
Penguin Group (USA) Inc.
375 Hudson Street, New York, New York 10014, USA

USA / Canada / UK / Ireland / Australia / New Zealand / India / South Africa / China

Penguin Books Ltd., Registered Offices: 80 Strand, London WC2R 0RL, England
For more information about the Penguin Group, visit penguin.com

LOVE IRRESISTIBLY

A Berkley Sensation Book / published by arrangement with the author.

Berkley Sensation Books are published by The Berkley Publishing Group.
BERKLEY SENSATION® is a registered trademark of Penguin Group (USA) Inc.
The "B" design is a trademark of Penguin Group (USA) Inc.

For information, address: The Berkley Publishing Group,
a division of Penguin Group (USA) Inc.,
375 Hudson Street, New York, New York 10014.

ISBN: 978-0-425-25119-5

PUBLISHING HISTORY
Berkley Sensation mass-market paperback edition / April 2013

PRINTED IN THE UNITED STATES OF AMERICA

10 9 8 7 6 5 4 3 2 1

Cover photo by Claudio Marinesco; image of satin background by Shutterstock.
Cover design by Rita Frangie.

ALWAYS LEARNING   PEARSON

For Ellery

Acknowledgements

As with all my books, I owe thanks to several people who, out of the kindness of their hearts, continue to answer every pesky e-mail from me bearing the words "Quick question" in the subject line. I'm particularly grateful to Kevin Kavanaugh for all his expertise and anecdotes that helped me create the world of Sterling Restaurants, and also to Andy Lansing, who graciously took the time to chat with me about life as a general counsel in the restaurant industry.

Continuing gratitude goes to John, assistant U.S. attorney extraordinaire, whose advice has been invaluable to the FBI/US Attorney series. I also owe a special mention to Diana Phung for getting me hooked on *Friday Night Lights*—which, in turn, inspired me to add a story line about a former football player to this book. Thanks as well to Chris Ernst and, particularly, Tom Fleming, for sharing their knowledge of the game.

I am truly fortunate to work with a fantastic editor, Wendy McCurdy, who understood what I wanted to do with this book and knew exactly how to push me to get there. Thanks to Erin Galloway, my fabulous publicist, and the entire team at Berkley, and to Elyssa Papa and Kati Brown, my awesome beta readers, who roll up their sleeves and do what they do even when working under some very tight deadlines.

Thanks to my friends and family for all their support, and to my husband, son, and daughter for putting a smile on my face every day.

Finally, thanks to you, dear readers, for the e-mails, the tweets, the Facebook posts, and the readers' choice nominations and awards. You guys are awesome, and I wish I could thank every one of you.

Oh, wait—I just did.

One

BROOKE PARKER STEPPED up to the bar at The Shore restaurant, ready to place her lunch order. The bartender, however, beat her to the punch.

"Hey, it's my favorite customer—Chicken Tacos, Extra Pico." He flashed her a grin. "That's my nickname for you."

Yes, she got that. "I suppose I've been called worse," Brooke said as the bartender moved to the cash register to ring her up. She was indeed a regular, and she took pride in that. The restaurant was only two blocks from her office, right on Oak Street Beach, which made it the perfect midday escape. And it had the best chicken tacos in the city. Not that she was biased.

Okay, maybe she was a *little* biased.

She handed over a twenty-dollar bill. "I'll take a strawberry-mango smoothie, too."

"Ooh, a smoothie. Getting a little crazy today, are we?" In his early twenties, with blond hair and a tanned face, the bartender had the look of a recent college grad who planned to spend a lot of time playing beach volleyball this summer.

He called Brooke's order back to the kitchen, and then

looked her over. "I'm starting to feel like I should know more about you, Chicken Tacos, Extra Pico." He winked. "Since we've been seeing each other on a weekly basis for nearly a month now." He took in the tailored gray suit she wore. "I'm thinking that you are a . . . lawyer."

"Good guess."

"I knew it. I bet you're one of those ballbuster types in court."

Brooke fought back a smile. Really, she should just spare the poor guy the embarrassment, but this was kind of fun. "Actually, I'm not a trial lawyer." She decided to give him a hint. "I'm general counsel for a company based here in Chicago."

He made a big show of being impressed. "Look at you, Ms. Thing. What kind of company?"

"Restaurants and bars."

"What a coincidence. We're both in the restaurant business." He leaned his elbows on the bar, giving her a smoldering, sexy look that likely helped him rake in big tips with the female clientele. "It's Kismet."

Or . . . maybe not so much. Brooke raised an eyebrow. "Are you supposed to be flirting with the customers?"

He brushed this off with an oh-so-cool smile. "Probably not. But for you, Chicken Tacos, Extra Pico, I'll break the rules. Just don't tell any of those stiffs in corporate."

Brooke had to bite her lip to hold back a smile at that one. Aw, she definitely couldn't clue the poor guy in now. Then a voice called her name.

"Playing hooky for the afternoon, Ms. Parker?"

Brooke turned and saw Kurt McGregor, one of the managers of The Shore. "Unfortunately, no. Just sneaking out for a quick break."

Kurt gestured to the bartender. "I hope Ryan here is treating you well."

"Ryan has been most charming," she assured him.

The bartender pointed between them. "You two know each other?"

Kurt chuckled at that. "You could say that. Ryan, this is

Brooke Parker from corporate. She's general counsel of Sterling."

The grin on the bartender's face froze, replaced by a look of panic. "Oh, shit. Sterling Restaurants. As in, the people who sign my paychecks?"

"The one and only," Brooke said.

The bartender looked like he'd swallowed a bug. "I just called you a stiff."

"And Ms. Thing."

"Please don't fire me," he whispered.

Brooke pretended to think about that. "It's tempting. But firing someone involves a *lot* of paperwork. Not something I want to do on a Friday afternoon. I'll hold off until Monday instead." She saw his eyes widen. "I'm kidding, Ryan."

Kurt cleared his throat pointedly. "Ryan, maybe this would be a good time to check on Ms. Parker's order?"

The bartender straightened up, clearly relieved to be dismissed. "Good idea. One order for Chicken Tac—uh, Ms. Parker—coming right up." With that, he bolted for the kitchen.

Kurt turned to her after the bartender left. "Okay, seriously. Should I fire him?"

"Nah. He sneaks me extra pico on the side. He's a keeper."

Kurt chuckled at that, then gestured to the terrace. "Are you sticking around? I'm sure I can finagle you a table with a view of the lake if you want to eat in."

Brooke looked out at the umbrella-covered tables on the sunny terrace, tempted by the idea. It was a gorgeous June day, and the view from the terrace was undeniably one of the best in Chicago: skyscrapers towering majestically against the shimmering blue of Lake Michigan. Today, however, duty called.

Actually, duty called every day. Duty had her on speed dial.

"Wish I could. But I've got a conference call in"—Brooke checked her watch—"yikes, twenty minutes."

Ryan the bartender came out of the kitchen with a carryout bag and a smoothie. With a sheepish look, he set both on the bar in front of Brooke and scurried off.

"By any chance would this conference call have anything to do with a certain deal you're negotiating with the Staples Center?" Kurt asked in a sly tone after Ryan disappeared.

Brooke's face gave nothing away. "I can neither confirm nor deny the existence of any such deal."

"Spoken like a true lawyer."

Brooke winked as she grabbed her smoothie and tacos and headed for the door. "Always."

BROOKE BRISKLY WALKED the two blocks from Oak Street Beach to the elegant eight-story building on Michigan Avenue that was home to Sterling's corporate offices. Tacos and smoothie in hand, she pushed through the revolving doors and waved hello to Mac, a retired Chicago police officer who manned the front security desk, as she passed through the lobby and headed toward the elevators.

When Ian Sterling, CEO of Sterling Restaurants, had approached her two years ago about coming on board as general counsel—or "GC" as the position was commonly called—he'd been very candid about his vision and plans. He'd started the company with one restaurant, an American bistro in the heart of downtown Chicago, and within eight years had opened six more restaurants that ran the spectrum from summer hot spot The Shore, to an Irish pub on the south side of the city, to Sogna, the company's "crown jewel" that had just this year earned a coveted three-star Michelin rating.

Many restaurateurs would've been satisfied there, but not Ian Sterling. He was aggressive, he was driven, and he had plans. Big plans.

A friend of a friend knew the owner of the Chicago Cubs, and Ian convinced the owner to consider letting Sterling Restaurants take over the food and beverage service for the Stadium Club and skyboxes at Wrigley Field.

"Should you choose to accept the position," Ian had said to Brooke, à la *Mission Impossible*, on the evening he'd formally offered her the job over dinner at Sogna, "your first task as GC will be to close the Wrigley Field deal."

"And then what?" Brooke had asked.

"You'll be part of a team that will build an entire sports and entertainment division of Sterling," he'd said. "Ballparks. Arenas. Stadiums."

Brooke had to admit, she'd been impressed with his ambition. She'd been working at a law firm at the time, in the corporate department, and had been the associate with primary responsibility over Sterling Restaurants' non-litigation matters. Having known Ian for several years by that point, she'd been aware that he'd contemplated hiring an in-house attorney. What she hadn't realized, however, was that he'd planned to ask *her* to fill the position. "You're not concerned that I only have five years' experience?"

"I've seen you in action many times, Brooke. You're tough when you need to be, and you can charm the pants off men who have three times your experience."

"Well, yes. Although I try not to take advantage of that too often. Very awkward negotiating with people who are sitting around in their underwear."

Ian had grinned. "I like your style—and just as important, I like you. So the better question is, do *you* think you can handle the job?"

A direct question. Luckily, Brooke had never been one to mince words, either, and Ian's enthusiasm and drive were infectious. It was an opportunity to take a chance, to get involved with a young company that was on the rise. So in answer to Ian's question, she'd looked him right in the eyes. "Absolutely."

Because Brooke Parker was a woman who was going places. She'd made that promise to herself a long time ago.

Two years later, she had zero regrets about taking a chance with Sterling. The company had grown steadily since she'd come on board as GC, most notably in their sports and entertainment division. After finalizing negotiations with Wrigley Field, Brooke and the other two members of Ian's "dream team"—the VP of sales and the VP of operations—had spent a lot of time schmoozing and wining and dining prospective clients. And when they'd landed a contract to take over the food service at the United Center—home of the Chicago Bulls and Blackhawks and the fifth-most-profitable sports venue in North America—they'd all partied like it was 1999 at the Sterling corporate office.

A few months after that, they'd headed down to Dallas, where Brooke and the two VPs had given their best sales pitch and negotiated a deal with the Cowboys. A short while later, they landed the contract for Dodger Stadium, too.

During the Dodger negotiations, the general counsel, a woman with whom Brooke had formed a friendly relationship, just so happened to let it slip that she'd heard whispers that the folks at L.A. Arena Company—who owned the Staples Center, aka home to the Los Angeles Lakers, Clippers, Kings, and Sparks—were also unhappy with their food and beverage vendor and looking to make a change as soon as their current contract expired.

So the dream team had struck while the iron was hot.

And now, assuming there were no hiccups in the deal Brooke was finalizing today with the lawyers representing L.A. Arena Company, Sterling Restaurants would soon be adding the Staples Center, the number-one most profitable sports venue in the country, to their roster.

In a word, they were hot.

Sterling was an exciting, demanding, absolutely exhausting place to work. Sure, that meant long hours for Brooke, but she believed in the company and her role there. Whether negotiating a multimillion dollar contract with the GC of the Dallas Cowboys, or investigating an internal complaint that one of their pastry chefs had a problem playing grab-ass with the waitresses, there was never, ever a dull moment.

After exiting the elevator at the third floor, Brooke turned down the hallway that would take her to Sterling's offices. She pushed through the frosted-glass doors and said hello to the receptionist. According to the clock on the wall, she still had fifteen minutes to eat lunch before her conference call. Plenty of time.

"I'm back," she told Lindsey, her assistant, who sat at the desk outside Brooke's office.

"A couple of calls came in while you were out," Lindsey said. "The first one was from Justin. He asked that you call him back as soon as you get in."

The message took Brooke somewhat by surprise. She and Justin, aka the Hot OB, had been dating for a little over four months now, and she could count on one hand the number of times she'd talked to him at the office. Both of them were always so busy during the day, it was simply easier to e-mail or text him on her way home from work. "Uh-oh. I hope he's not calling to cancel tonight. We've got reservations at Rustic House," she said, referring to a nearly-impossible-to-get-into restaurant on the north side that was *not* in the Sterling family.

"Traitor," Lindsey said with a grin. She handed Brooke a piece of paper with a phone number on it. "And you also received a call from Cade Morgan at the U.S. Attorney's Office."

Now that got Brooke's attention.

Just about anyone who followed the local news knew who Cade Morgan was. One of the top assistant U.S. attorneys in Chicago, he'd made a name for himself by prosecuting several high-profile government corruption cases—and, a little over a year ago, the famous "Twitter Terrorist" case that had garnered international attention. He had a reputation of being smart, disarmingly charming in front of judges and juries, and tough as nails against opposing counsel.

And what he might possibly want from Brooke, she had no clue.

"Did he say what this was in regards to?" Brooke asked.

"No. Only that he'd like you to call him back as soon as possible. He was very firm about that."

This unexpected message from the U.S. Attorney's Office had Brooke feeling a bit . . . uneasy. Cade Morgan was a prosecutor who handled big cases that got a lot of media attention. Whatever this was, it wasn't a social call. And as general counsel for Sterling Restaurants, her hackles were up.

"Thanks, Lindsey." Brooke went into her office and shut the door behind her, trying not to get too rattled by Morgan's message. She didn't know what he wanted, she reminded herself, so there wasn't anything worth worrying about. Yet.

Never a dull moment, she thought again to herself as she settled in at her desk and unwrapped one of the tacos. Double-tasking per usual, she took a bite while dialing Justin's number on speakerphone.

"Hey there," she said when he answered his cell phone. "I wasn't sure I'd actually catch you." She could picture him looking cute in his scrubs right then—an easy image to conjure up since she'd seen him wearing them a few times late at night after one of his shifts.

"I stepped out of the office for a short break," Justin said. His obstetrics practice was located a few blocks from Brooke's office, which was nice if they wanted to meet for lunch. Although come to think of it, they'd only met for lunch once, back when they'd first started dating.

He sounded apologetic. "I just sent one of my patients to the hospital to be induced. She's only a half-centimeter dilated, but she's forty-one weeks with gestational diabetes. Since it's her first baby, this could be a long night. Sorry to have to cancel on you like this."

"Darn babies. Somebody needs to explain to them about date night," Brooke said jokingly. While she was disappointed not to see Justin tonight, she understood that work conflicts sometimes came up. Heck, she'd had to reschedule two dates so far this month because of last-minute emergencies she'd needed to handle at the office.

"Yeah. Right." He cleared his throat as if hesitant about whatever it was he wanted to say next. "You and I sure seem to be missing each other a lot these days."

Aw, the Hot OB missed her. And he was right; it had been a busy month. She'd been in Los Angeles for nearly a week, working on the Staples Center deal, and then had been swamped trying to catch up with everything at work after that. Lately, it seemed the only times she and Justin were both free was between eleven P.M. and five A.M. "So let's not miss each other tonight, even if we can't do dinner," she suggested. "Why don't you text me when you're finished at the hospital and come over to my place?"

"That'll probably be around two A.M."

"I know. But since that's the only time we both seem to be available, it's either that or nothing," Brooke said.

"Yes, that certainly does seem to be how it works with us. Heaven forbid we ever go on an actual date."

When she heard the frustration in his voice, Brooke got a sinking feeling in her stomach.

Not again.

She tried to smooth things over. "Look, I know that things have been crazy for me with these back-to-back deals in Los Angeles. You're a doctor, you know how it is—your schedule is just as bad." Admittedly, she was feeling a bit defensive right then, and felt the need to note that for the record.

He sighed. "I know. Tonight is my fault. And then next time, something will come up for you."

"We talked about this when we first met." Given her less-than-successful track record with relationships, she'd been up front with him from the beginning about the demands of her job.

"You're right, we did," he said. "And frankly, back then I thought I'd hit the jackpot. It was great that you never got mad when I had to cancel plans, or when I forgot to call. And you never complain that I don't take you out enough. Hell, in some ways it's like dating a guy."

Alrighty, then. "I don't need to be wined and dined, Justin. I can walk into eight restaurants in this city and have every employee practically tripping over themselves to make sure I'm happy."

"I'm sorry, Brooke," he said contritely. "But this . . . doesn't work for me anymore. I like you. You're a great girl, and you have awesome Cubs skybox tickets. I love it when they bring that dessert cart around."

Glad she scored high when it came to the important things in life. "But?"

"But you seem to be really focused on your career right

now—which, don't get me wrong, is totally fine—except, well, I'm thirty-four years old. I'm starting to think about getting married, having kids, the big picture. And I guess what I'm trying to say is . . . I don't see a woman like you in that big picture."

Brooke blinked. Wow.

A woman like you.

That stung.

"Fuck, that came out harsh," Justin said. "I just meant that you're so independent, and I don't even know if you want to get married or have kids, and half the time I think you just like having a warm body to cuddle up with every now and then—"

"Hold on. This is the *non*-harsh version?"

"Sorry," he said, sounding sheepish. "I just think we're looking for different things. I want—"

"A big-picture girl," Brooke interrupted. "I got it." She definitely didn't need to have it spelled out for her any clearer than that.

When both of them fell awkwardly silent, Brooke glanced at the clock on her phone. "I hate to say this, since it's apparently what makes me a *small*-picture kind of girl, but I have to go. I've got a conference call with a bunch of other lawyers in Los Angeles that can't be rescheduled."

"I understand. You do your thing. Good-bye, Brooke."

After hanging up, Brooke stared at the phone for a long moment.

Another one bites the dust.

That was her third breakup since starting at Sterling. She seemed to be in a pattern with her relationships, where everything was great in the beginning, and then somewhere around the four-month mark things just kind of fizzled out. The men would give her some speech about not getting to the "next level," or about wanting "more" than hot sex at midnight after a long workday.

"Hold on. A *guy* said this to you?" Her best friend, Ford, had looked both shocked and appalled by this when they'd met for drinks after Breakup Number Two. "As in, someone with an actual penis?"

"Two guys now," Brooke had said, her pride admittedly wounded at being dumped again. "I don't get it. I don't put any pressure on these men, I'm happy to give them all the space they want, and the sex is good enough. What else could your gender possibly want in a relationship?"

"Beer and nachos in bed?"

"This is the advice you offer, your sage insight into the male perspective? Beer and nachos in bed?"

Ford had flashed her an easy grin. "You know I'm not good at the relationship stuff. Even other people's relationship stuff."

And, judging from today's turn of events with Justin, Brooke wasn't all that much better.

I don't see a woman like you in that big picture.

The intercom on Brooke's phone buzzed, interrupting her thoughts.

"I have Jim Schwartz, Eric Keller, and Paul Fielding on the phone for you," her secretary said, referring to L.A. Arena's in-house counsel and the two outside attorneys who represented them. "Can I put them through?"

Right. Back to work—no time for a pity party. As Brooke shoved her now-cold tacos back into the bag and reached for her phone, she spotted the note on her desk and belatedly remembered the call from the U.S. Attorney's Office. Well, Cade Morgan would just have to wait.

She told her secretary to put the call through and forced a cheerful note into her voice. "How are my three favorite Los Angeles lawyers today?" she asked.

As they said in Hollywood, the show must go on.

TWO

CADE STRODE UP to the lobby desk and presented his U.S. attorney ID to the security guard.

"Cade Morgan, along with Special Agents Seth Huxley and Vaughn Roberts," he said, gesturing to the two men in suits who stood behind him. "We're here to see Brooke Parker with Sterling Restaurants."

The security guard reached for his guest list.

"She's not expecting us," Cade said.

"O-kay . . ." The guard shifted uncertainly as he looked at all three men. Cade waited unconcernedly, knowing exactly how this would turn out. As he'd come to realize during the eight years he'd been an assistant U.S. attorney, there were very few places a man flanked by two armed FBI agents couldn't get into.

After a moment, the guard gestured to the guest book sitting on top of the gray marble desk. "I just need you to sign in."

"Of course." Cade grabbed the pen and quickly scribbled his name. "Cade Morgan. Plus two." After he set the pen down, he noticed that the guard stared at him curiously. He was familiar with that look of recognition; his was a name many people in this city recognized—often because of the high-profile criminal cases he'd prosecuted. Although, not infrequently, people still remembered him for his other claim to fame.

The guard pointed. "Cade Morgan. Quarterback at Northwestern, right?"

Bingo.

"That's right," he said.

"What was that, twelve years ago?" the guard asked. "I remember watching your last game." He grinned. "It's not like Northwestern goes to the Rose Bowl every year, right? You carried those guys there."

Cade brushed this off modestly. "It was a good team. We ran a really strong spread offense that year."

The guard gestured excitedly. "That last play was beautiful. Probably one of the best moments I've seen in college football. Really a shame about your shoulder, though. They said you would've gone pro."

This was true. Cade very well may have gone on to play professional football, if a two-hundred-and-thirty-pound linebacker hadn't taken him down hard in an attempted sack just a half second after he'd released the ball. When they'd hit the ground, the linebacker's full weight had come down on Cade's right shoulder, his throwing arm, and he'd known immediately that the situation was bad. A couple of hours later, after being rushed to the emergency room, X-rays had confirmed he'd suffered both a broken collarbone and a torn rotator cuff.

A career-ending injury, as it turned out.

Cade nodded in the direction of the elevators. "Which floor for Sterling?" he asked the guard.

"Oh. Right. Third floor. Offices are on the north side of the building, at the end of the hall."

After thanking the guard, Cade and the two FBI agents made their way to the elevators. Agent Roberts waited until the elevator doors closed. "How old does that get?"

Cade shrugged. "It's one of those sports moments people like to talk about." He eyed the Starbucks cup that Vaughn carried, deliberately changing the subject. "Did you get another chance to flash your badge at the cute barista?"

He and Vaughn had known each other for seven years, ever since they'd worked on their first case together, a simple single-defendant bank robbery trial. It'd been the first time both of them had been in front of a jury—Cade as the prosecutor and Vaughn as the testifying agent—and for the most part, neither of them had any clue what they were doing. Still, they'd somehow managed to get a guilty verdict, and afterward they'd gone out for celebratory drinks and had spent most of the time making fun of each other's courtroom screwups. They'd been good friends ever since.

In response to Cade's question, Vaughn shot a look at Agent Huxley, who'd been his partner in the white-collar crime division for the past year. "You told him about that?"

"Of course I told him about that. It was one of the least suave pickup moves I've ever seen." Huxley pulled out his badge, pretending to be Vaughn. " 'I'll pay for that skinny vanilla latte with my Starbucks card, which—well, look at that—just so happens to be right here next to my *FBI* badge.' "

"That's not how it went down. I told you, she *asked* to see the badge."

"How'd she know that you're an agent?" Cade asked.

"I may have mentioned it at some point." Vaughn grinned innocently. "What? The job impresses the ladies."

The elevator arrived at the third floor. "Right. I'm sure she thought you were a real badass with your skinny vanilla latte." Cade stepped out of the elevator, leading the other two men as they headed down the hallway. Quickly, the dynamic between them turned more businesslike as they approached Sterling's offices.

"How do you think Brooke Parker is going to react?" Huxley asked Cade.

Well, if Cade were a betting man, he'd hazard a guess that the general counsel of Sterling was going to be a wee bit ticked off at the sudden and unexpected appearance of an assistant U.S. attorney and two FBI agents on her office doorstep.

Actually, this was probably something that most people would not enjoy.

But unfortunately, time was of the essence. They had barely more than forty-eight hours to pull everything together, and he needed to speak with Brooke Parker before she left work for the weekend. He'd had no choice but to take things up a notch. "Once I explain the situation, I'm sure that Ms. Parker will see the value in cooperating with us."

Huxley raised an eyebrow. "And if she doesn't?"

"Then I'll explain it again."

Granted, Cade knew that what they were asking of Ms. Parker was a bit . . . unusual. For that reason, he had every intention of being gracious and polite during this meeting. At the end of the day, however, he harbored little doubt that she would agree to play ball with them. Some of this confidence stemmed from the fact that he generally believed—and maybe this was simply the idealistic prosecutor in him—that reasonable, law-abiding citizens understood the value of doing their civic duty when called to action.

And the more practical, cynical side of him said that even unreasonable people knew not to get on the bad side of the U.S. Attorney's and FBI offices.

Cade pushed through the glass door etched with Sterling Restaurants' name, and stepped into the office. It was a sophisticated space, modern and airy with cream marble floors and lots of natural light streaming in through the floor-to-ceiling windows. In front of him, a receptionist sat behind a frosted-glass desk, waiting expectantly. Presumably, the lobby guard had alerted her that they were on their way up.

"You must be Cade Morgan." Her gaze shifted as Agents Huxley and Roberts followed him into the office. "And there's the plus two." She picked up the telephone on her desk. "I'll let Ms. Parker know you're here."

Cade nodded. "Thank you."

The three men headed over to the waiting area, where Huxley and Vaughn took seats in adjacent cream leather chairs. Cade remained standing, hands tucked casually in his pants pockets. Catching sight of a row of framed photographs on the wall, he moved closer and saw that they were interior shots of Sterling's eight restaurants.

His eyes skimmed over the photographs until he found the one taken at Sogna, Sterling's flagship five-star restaurant located in the very building in which Cade stood, just one floor below the company's offices. Assuming all went according to plan, it was at that restaurant that he would get the last of the evidence he needed to nail a dirty politician's ass to the wall.

Last winter, the FBI had received a tip that Illinois State Senator Alec Sanderson had been accepting bribes in exchange for political favors. Given the politically sensitive nature of the allegations, the FBI had brought the matter to the U.S. Attorney's Office, and Cade had been assigned as lead prosecutor.

During a five-month investigation, Cade and the FBI had determined that the informant had indeed been correct. They'd gathered evidence that Senator Sanderson had accepted over six hundred thousand dollars in bribes, which he'd hidden via a shell company, in exchange for a virtual buffet of corrupt services: sponsoring or supporting legislation that would benefit various businesses, directing state monies to advance the interests of certain lobbyists, and lobbying other state senators and officials.

Cade was all set to bring the case to the grand jury—as soon as he and the FBI locked down one final piece of the investigation.

Via the wiretap the FBI had placed on Sanderson's phones, they'd learned that the senator had been in discussions with Charles Torino, CEO of Parkpoint Hospital on the west side of the city, who was extremely concerned that Parkpoint was on a short list of medical facilities that potentially were about to be closed by the state. During their discussions, Torino had suggested that the senator find a possible alternative to the hospital's closure, something that could "mutually benefit" them both. Then, last night, the FBI had intercepted another call between Torino and Sanderson, during which Torino had offered to take the senator to dinner on Sunday at Sogna restaurant to discuss the details of their "potential arrangement" in person.

Cade had a feeling he knew exactly what "potential arrangement" the senator and hospital CEO were going to discuss during that dinner. And he wanted *in* on that conversation.

One person—Brooke Parker—could help him with that.

Vaughn got up and moved to Cade's side to examine the interior photograph of Sogna. "Nice restaurant. A place like that is going to have security cameras." He kept his voice low so the receptionist didn't overhear them.

Cade was in synch with the agent's line of thought. "It'd be great if we could get the meeting on video." Even the smoothest-talking politicians couldn't talk their way out of a conviction when they'd been caught accepting bribes on camera.

Vaughn thought about that. "Depends on where the cameras are. We'll have to ask the GC."

"Assuming she ever shows up." Cade checked his watch and saw that Brooke Parker had kept them waiting for ten minutes. Fortunately for her, he'd planned to lay on the nice-guy routine real thick; otherwise he'd tell Vaughn to start flashing his FBI badge to get things moving.

Just then, he heard Vaughn speak under his breath.

"Oh, man . . . if we're doing good cop/bad cop as part of this, I so want to be the good cop this time."

Hearing his friend's appreciative tone, Cade turned around and got his first look at Brooke Parker.

Hmm.

Wearing a slim-cut gray skirt, cream silk shirt, and knock-out black heels, she strode confidently past the reception desk. Her hair, which she wore in a sophisticated knot, was the color of deep, burnished gold, and her stunning light green eyes were fixed directly on Cade as she walked toward him.

"Mr. Morgan," she said warmly as she held out her hand. "I could've saved you the trip over. I just wrapped up a three-hour conference call, and you were the next item on my agenda."

"It's no trouble at all," Cade replied, just as smoothly, as his hand clasped hers. "It's actually better that we meet in person." He gestured to Vaughn and Huxley, both of whom had stepped forward, seemingly very eager to make the acquaintance of

Ms. Brooke Parker of Sterling Restaurants and the Gorgeous Green Eyes. "This is Special Agent Roberts and Special Agent Huxley with the Federal Bureau of Investigation. If this is a good time, we'd like to speak with you for a few minutes. In private."

She shook hands with both agents, without so much as batting an eye over the request. "Of course. If you gentlemen will follow me, we can talk in my office."

She led them past the reception desk, down the hallway to a corner office. Brooke stood by the door and gestured for the three men to step inside. "Please make yourselves comfortable."

Cade walked in and immediately was struck by office envy. A large, rich mahogany executive desk stood in the center of the office, flanked by matching bookshelves. Being a corner office, there were floor-to-ceiling windows along two walls that overlooked Michigan Avenue and, beyond that, the sparkling blue water of Lake Michigan.

"Nice view," he said, taking a seat in one of the chairs in front of Brooke's desk. Vaughn slid a chair over from the small marble table in the corner of the room and sat on Cade's right while Huxley took the chair on Cade's left.

"Thank you." Brooke shut the office door and sat across from the three men, behind her impressive mahogany desk.

She folded her hands. "So, Mr. Morgan, now that it's just the four of us, let's dispense with the formalities. You clearly wanted to make a statement by showing up at my office with two FBI agents in tow. Whatever this is about, I'm guessing it's urgent." She got right to the point. "Is Sterling Restaurants in some kind of trouble?"

Hell, Cade had barely gotten comfortable in his chair before she opened with that salvo. Not that he denied her accusation—yes, he had wanted to make a statement. He could've asked only one of the agents to join him in this meeting, but had thought that bringing both along would help underscore the exigency, one might say, of the situation.

Or, one might also say, he was making a power move.

The clock was ticking on this sting operation, and Cade

wasn't afraid to flex a little U.S. Attorney's Office muscle to make things move faster. He answered Brooke's question with a similarly straightforward answer. "Sterling Restaurants isn't in any trouble."

A flicker of relief crossed her face. "Okay. Good." Then she cocked her head, as if something had just occurred to her. "Am *I* in trouble?"

Something about the way she had blown in like a storm with her knockout heels and take-charge attitude made Cade unable to resist one small joke. "I don't know," he said, raising an eyebrow. "Is there something you'd like to tell us, Ms. Parker?"

She glared at him.

Perhaps he should've tried a little harder to resist.

"It's been a long day, Mr. Morgan," she said. "Maybe we could fast-forward through the prosecutorial banter portion of this meeting?"

"But that's my favorite part."

She sighed. "So much for that suggestion."

Cade fought back a smile. He decided to skip the rest of the pleasantries—which weren't really going over so well, anyway—and cut to the chase. "We're here because we need your help."

This surprised her. "My help?" As the knowledge sunk in that no one from Sterling was about to be hauled out of the office in handcuffs, she relaxed a bit. "All right," she said, still maintaining a slightly cautious tone. "Tell me how I can I help you."

"There are two men who will be having dinner at Sogna this Sunday evening," Cade said. "We're anticipating that their conversation will be relevant to an ongoing investigation. With your assistance, we'd like to listen in."

Brooke looked confused. "I'm not sure I'm following."

"We want to bug their table," Cade said simply.

"Oh." Her lips curved at the edges in amusement. "I thought you guys only did that kind of stuff on TV."

"We're the FBI, Ms. Parker," Vaughn interjected. "We have all sorts of tricks up our sleeves."

"Of course. And how would this particular trick work, should I choose to assist you?"

Vaughn, along with Huxley, was in charge of the technical aspects of the sting operation. But when it came to dealing with lawyers, as the AUSA handling the case, Cade generally called the shots. Thus, the agent shot him a quick look, looking for the go-ahead signal before he proceeded.

Cade nodded.

Vaughn leaned forward in his chair as he explained. "You would need to give us access to the restaurant during a time when it's closed. We'll set up the bugs underneath the table, nothing that would ever be noticed by any of your servers or patrons. Then on Sunday evening, you'll just have to make sure that the targets are seated there."

"In addition, we'd like to station two undercover FBI agents at a nearby table, who will be there simply to make sure that everything proceeds smoothly," Huxley added. "I'll handle that, along with a female agent. We'll look like an ordinary couple out on a date—no one will ever be the wiser."

Brooke stared at them for a moment. "You're actually serious about this."

"Dead serious," Vaughn said.

"As part of some mysterious investigation, you want to bug one of the tables at Sogna, arguably the most exclusive restaurant in Chicago, and then you want me, the general counsel of the company, to make sure that these 'targets'—who I'm guessing are up to some very shady stuff—are seated there."

Cade, Vaughn, and Huxley looked at each other. Yep, that pretty much covered it.

Huxley held up a finger. "Oh, one other thing. You need to make sure that the female undercover agent and myself are seated nearby."

"Right. Wouldn't want to forget that part."

"The trickiest part will be getting the party to the table that's bugged," Vaughn said. "You should tell the hostess where to seat them, but without letting her know why. This operation has to be kept confidential. You tell the wrong person what's going on, and our whole cover could be blown."

Brooke leaned back in her chair, saying nothing for a long moment. "This is a lot to ask someone at—" she checked her watch—"four thirty on a Friday, don't you think?"

Cade sensed that it was time for him to jump back into the conversation. "We apologize for the inconvenience, Ms. Parker. We just learned of this opportunity last night. Although I do note that I tried to contact you earlier this afternoon."

Her gaze turned to him, and from the savvy gleam in her eyes, Cade knew that Huxley and Vaughn's part in this discussion was over. From this point on, he and Brooke Parker of Sterling Restaurants would have to lawyer it out.

Game on.

Three

"DO YOU HAVE a court order to do this?" Brooke asked.

"No." Seated across the desk from her, flanked by the two FBI agents, Cade appeared unconcerned with such pesky details. "But I can get one, if necessary."

From his self-assured tone, Brooke had a feeling that Assistant U.S. Attorney Cade Morgan was a man who was used to getting his way. He certainly looked the part, with his strong jaw, dark brown hair, athletic build, and cobalt blue eyes. He was remarkably good-looking—she would have to be a fool not to notice that—and had no doubt that this played very well for him both inside and outside the courtroom.

"You probably could get an emergency judge to grant you an order allowing you to plant a few bugs in the restaurant," she conceded. "But you would still need someone on the inside to make sure your target sits at the right table."

"True," he acknowledged. "It would be very difficult for us to pull this off without your help."

At least he could admit that much. "Before I'd even consider agreeing to this, I'd need to know who the target is and what that person or persons are being investigated for."

Cade shook his head. "I'm afraid the nature of the investigation is confidential. As for the identity of the target, *after* we have your agreement to cooperate, we'll provide you with that information at the appropriate time so that you know who to seat at the bugged table."

For Brooke, however, this point was not up for debate. "I have a responsibility to protect Sterling's interests, Mr. Morgan, and that includes the safety of its employees and customers. For all I know, the person you're after is an organized crime boss, a drug kingpin, or some other sort of dangerous criminal. What if these two men discover that the table is bugged? What if they identify Agent Huxley and his fake date as undercover agents and pull out guns and start shooting people? Can you imagine the liability I'd be exposing the company to if someone got hurt and I'd had advance notice that there was a potentially dangerous sting operation going down in one of our restaurants during regular business hours?"

Cade considered this point. "I can't reveal the nature of our investigation," he finally said. "But I can assure you that neither of the two men who will be at Sogna on Sunday night are considered dangerous. Nobody's pulling out guns and causing a shoot-out in the middle of your restaurant. This isn't the O.K. Corral."

"I'd still like the names."

His blue eyes held hers boldly. "You drive a hard bargain, Ms. Parker."

"I wouldn't be doing my job if I wasn't."

"Hmm." He stretched out in the chair, looking effortlessly handsome and every inch the successful trial lawyer in his tailored navy pinstripe suit. "Now, normally, this would be the point when I'd have to give you the tough-guy speech about how, if you were to reveal to anyone the confidential nature of the information I'm about to give you, you could be charged with obstruction of justice and face a possible felony conviction and imprisonment." He flashed her a dashing grin. "Luckily, though, since you're a lawyer and obviously know that already, we can skip over the tough-guy stuff. Which is nice, because that part of the conversation can get really awkward."

Maybe it was the fact that Brooke, admittedly, was having a bad day. She'd been dumped by the Hot OB, had just spent three hours on the phone haggling with the Staples Center lawyers over every tiny, miniscule part of their food service contract, and had done it all on two measly bites of a chicken taco and a melted strawberry-mango smoothie. She was tired, hungry, and, up until ten minutes ago, had been looking forward to the first Sunday in a long time when she did *not* have to work. So, yes—she was, perhaps, feeling extra-cranky because of circumstances that had nothing to do with anyone sitting in that office right then.

But Cade Morgan was seriously beginning to piss her off.

He'd come here, to *her* office, to ask for *her* help. Now he was threatening her with obstruction of justice charges—and most annoyingly, he was doing it with a smile.

So she returned the favor. "That is nice, Mr. Morgan. Because in response to your tough-guy speech, I, in turn, would've had to give you my tough-*girl* speech, about where, exactly, federal prosecutors who come to my office looking for assistance can stick their obstruction of justice threats." She smiled ever so charmingly. "So I'm glad we were able to sidestep that whole ugly business. Whew."

Although her attention was focused on Cade, out of the corner of her eye, Brooke could see Agents Huxley and Roberts looking at the wall and ceiling, seemingly trying to hide their smiles.

Cade looked momentarily caught off guard, the first time since he'd waltzed into her office, then his eyes flashed with something else entirely. Amusement, perhaps.

That annoyed her even more.

"Point taken, Ms. Parker." Then he clapped his hands, moving on. "All right. Here's what I can tell you. The reservation is for seven thirty, under the name Charles Torino."

Charles Torino.

Nope, Brooke had no clue who that was.

"I'll save you the Google search," Cade said, as if reading her mind. "He's the CEO of a hospital here in Chicago."

"And the other man?"

"State Senator Alec Sanderson."

Ah. Now Brooke was beginning to see what all the fuss was about. Based on the bits and pieces of information she had—the special agents from the white-collar crime division, the fact that Cade had previously prosecuted several high-profile corruption cases—Brooke would hazard a guess that the state of Illinois had yet another dirty politician on its hands.

Only one thing to say in response to that.

"I can get you into Sogna at seven A.M. on Sunday morning," she told them. "I realize that's early, but some of the kitchen staff will be arriving at ten o'clock, when deliveries for the dinner service start coming in. You'll obviously want to be done before then."

"That'll be fine," Vaughn said, appearing pleased with this arrangement. "After working for the FBI for seven years, a seven A.M. start feels like sleeping in."

"I think you can stop telling her that you work for the FBI, Roberts," Huxley muttered under his breath. "She's got it."

Brooke was trying to hold back a smile, thinking she rather liked these two special agents, when Mr. Obstruction of Justice had to chime back in.

"What about the other part of the deal?" Cade asked.

Brooke looked over. "Getting Torino, Sanderson, and the undercover agents to the right tables, you mean?" She shrugged. "I'll make it clear to the hostess where I want those two parties seated. I'm sure she'll be suspicious, but she won't say anything."

"You seem awfully certain of that."

"I'm the general counsel of this company, Mr. Morgan. If I ask an employee to keep something confidential, she will. Nevertheless, I'll plan to stick around the restaurant on Sunday evening, just to make sure there aren't any problems."

"Thank you," he said. "On behalf of both the U.S. Attorney's Office and the Federal Bureau of Investigation, let me say how much we appreciate your assistance in this matter."

"You're welcome." Brooke locked eyes with him, to underscore the significance of her next words. "And I trust that the

U.S. Attorney's Office will remember that appreciation, should Sterling Restaurants ever need a favor in return."

Cade cocked his head at that, regarding her with sudden suspicion. "What kind of favor?"

Brooke sweetly threw his earlier words back at him. "Let's just say that I'll provide you with that information at the appropriate time." She rested her elbows on the table, ready to get down to the nitty-gritty details of the upcoming task. "So. What else do you guys need from me?" she asked Vaughn and Huxley.

"Not much at this point," Vaughn said. "We might have some questions once we get into the restaurant on Sunday morning, but we're only bugging one table. That's a pretty simple job. For the FBI." He laughed when Huxley threw up his hands in disbelief. "Come on, I threw that one in just for you." Then he pointed, remembering something. "Actually, I do have one question. Do you have security cameras inside the restaurant?"

Although Brooke wasn't as familiar with the restaurants as a manager would be, she did happen to know the answer to that. Last winter, they'd caught a bartender on video who'd been swiping customer credit cards through a handheld device in order to steal the numbers. After firing the guy, they'd turned the evidence over to the police. "We do. I'm assume you'd like to catch Senator Sanderson and Torino on video?"

"As they say, a picture is worth a thousand words," Vaughn said.

"The security cameras inside the restaurant are typically focused on the bar area and the entrance, but I can tell our head of security to make sure that one of the cameras captures whatever table you select for that night," Brooke said. "Again, he'll probably have some questions, but I'll get around that."

Huxley and Vaughn exchanged looks. "That would be perfect." Huxley turned back to Brooke, his expression one of both surprise and gratitude. "Thank you."

Brooke turned back to Cade, all business once again. "One thing, Mr. Morgan: I'll need a subpoena for the video footage. Purely a formality, something we require anytime we turn over any sort of Sterling property to the authorities. I'm sure you understand."

Cade's tone was a touch dry, likely not enjoying the fact that she'd taken charge of "his" meeting. "I can get you a subpoena."

They wrapped up their meeting after that, making plans to meet at the restaurant at seven A.M. on Sunday. "I'll let the lobby guard know to expect you, so you won't have any trouble on that end," Brooke told them.

She walked them to her office door, where both Huxley and Vaughn shook her hand and thanked her again for her assistance.

Cade paused in the doorway. "I'll meet you guys in the reception area," he told the agents.

Brooke waited until the two agents had left before turning to face Cade. He was very tall—easily a good three or four inches over six feet—so she had to tilt her head back to hold his gaze. "Planning to threaten me with more federal charges, Mr. Morgan?"

He took a step closer. "You knew you were going to cooperate with us from the beginning, didn't you?"

Actually . . . yes. Or at least from the point in the conversation when she'd realized that Sterling wasn't in any legal trouble. Both the attorney and businesswoman in her knew that one did not lightly refuse to cooperate with the FBI and U.S. Attorney's Office. Cade Morgan may have irked her, but there was no doubt that he was a powerful man in this city.

"I negotiate multimillion-dollar deals for a living," she told him. "You may have your subpoena power and tough-guy speeches, but I'm not exactly a novice at the bargaining table. You got your bugged table at Sogna. All I wanted in exchange was an acknowledgement of the courtesies that Sterling Restaurants is extending the U.S. Attorney's Office."

Cade crossed his arms across his chest, the jacket of his suit pulling tighter around his broad shoulders. "For the record, I don't believe I actually agreed to this 'favor' you asked for."

"Nor did you disagree. Implied consent."

He gave her a long look. "I can't decide if you're irritatingly self-assured or just . . ." He seemed to ponder this for a moment, and then shrugged. "Nope, I've got nothing else. 'Irritating' it is."

Seeming to have settled this, he turned to go. "See you bright and early Sunday morning, Brooke Parker."

Then he strode out of her office just as confidently as he'd come in.

Most annoyingly.

Four

"WELL, I THINK that was a very productive visit."

Walking alongside Vaughn as the three men crossed the parking garage, Huxley concurred with his partner's assessment. "Assuming Brooke can deliver on getting the hostess to seat everyone at the right tables, this should go off smoothly."

Cade headed to the front passenger door of Huxley's Range Rover. So it was "Brooke" now, apparently. Not surprising, seeing how she'd practically had both agents eating out of the palm of her hand.

They all climbed into the SUV. As Huxley started the car, Vaughn spoke from the backseat, continuing to sing the praises of Brooke Parker of Sterling Restaurants and the Sarcastic Quips.

"I liked when she offered to have the camera directed at Sanderson's table. I would've suggested it regardless, but it's great that she's so willing to cooperate."

Cade fought the urge to roll his eyes. Okay, so she was hot. Whatever. And pleasant enough to people who didn't threaten her with obstruction of justice charges. Big deal.

"If only all lawyers were that agreeable to work with," Huxley said. "It would make our jobs a hell of a lot easier."

"So true," Vaughn agreed.

A silence fell over the car.

"Although she didn't seem to like you very much, Morgan," Vaughn mused.

Yes, thank you, he'd caught that. "Somebody had to be the bad cop. Clearly, it wasn't going to be either of you two." And in fairness, that hadn't been the role he'd expected the agents to play. Brooke Parker wasn't a witness, or a suspect—they'd been approaching her in her capacity as legal counsel for Sterling. Which meant she was his responsibility.

But he had to give credit where credit was due: there were very few people who could essentially tell an assistant U.S. attorney to kiss her ass with quite that exact mix of sarcasm and charm. She'd even had Vaughn and Huxley cracking smiles with that one.

Traitors.

"Does that mean you won't be asking for her phone number when this is all over?" Vaughn asked.

"Ah, *no*." When Vaughn said nothing further, Cade turned around in his seat to face him. "Don't tell me you're actually being serious."

"Well, *somebody* should ask for it. Smart, gorgeous, no wedding ring, no pictures of kids or a guy in her office. That is one very fine, very single woman." Vaughn held out his hands when Cade threw him a get-real look. "What? Like I'm the only one who noticed those things?"

"I don't think I'm comfortable discussing Brooke this way while she's assisting us in an investigation," Huxley lectured from the driver's seat.

Cade stifled a smile and turned back around to face the road. *Here we go again.* Huxley was a good agent—a very thorough, organized, by-the-book special agent—who hailed from Harvard Law School and was never anything less than immaculately dressed in three-piece suits. A direct contrast to Vaughn, who was far less interested in playing by the rules, frequently sported a five o'clock shadow and a wrinkled suit, and often looked like he'd just rolled out of some strange woman's bed. And probably had.

It was no secret that the two agents, partners for the last year, drove each other nuts. They bickered and bitched about each other like the Odd Couple of the FBI, yet Cade knew that deep down (perhaps deep, *deep* down) they respected each other's methods in the field.

"Fine. We can talk about something else," Vaughn said faux amiably. "Like your big date Sunday night, Hux. With Agent Simms."

Cade watched as Huxley's lips twitched in a slight smile at the mention of the redheaded female agent's name. Still, Huxley refused to rise to the bait. "It's an undercover op, Roberts. Not a date. Unlike you, I'm perfectly capable of having dinner with a woman without obsessing all night about getting in her pants." He shot Cade a look, clearly seeking to change the subject. "And why is he asking you about getting Brooke's phone number? Did something happen with Jessica?"

Crap. Leave it to Vaughn to bring that out into the open. Although Cade supposed the subject of the demise of his relationship would inevitably come up at some point. He and Huxley had gotten to know each other well over the last five months while working on the Sanderson investigation and were familiar with each other's personal lives.

Nevertheless, he kept his answer short and sweet. "We're not seeing each other anymore."

Huxley looked over. "Sorry to hear that." He treaded lightly with his next question. "Any particular reason?"

Sure. According to Jessica, the problem was that he was "emotionally unavailable." They'd been having dinner last Friday night at Sunda, a sushi restaurant located in the River North neighborhood, when she'd laid that one on him. They'd just finished dessert, and she'd said something about him being distracted, and he'd mentioned offhandedly that he'd had a crappy day at work. He'd had a cooperating witness go south on him that morning in a motion to suppress, a witness who'd already pled guilty and had cut a deal for a lesser sentence in exchange for providing complete and truthful testimony. On the stand, however, the witness—who'd been key to Cade's motion—had suddenly become hazy about certain important facts and deliberately evasive and uncooperative.

It had been a frustrating day, to say the least.

"Why didn't you say anything earlier?" Jessica had asked.

"Sometimes cooperating witnesses rise to the occasion, and sometimes they don't," Cade had said with a shrug. "It happens."

And somehow, that perfectly innocuous comment had led into a Whole Big Thing about how he *never* opened up and told her these types of things, and how she'd been feeling like she didn't really *know* him even though they'd been dating for three months, and how he *seemed* like this charming, easygoing guy on the outside but underneath that façade he kept himself closed off from any real, genuine intimacy and refused to let anyone in.

"I see," Cade had said when she finished with her speech. "Remind me never to mention that I had a bad day again." He took a sip of his Manhattan.

"That's all you're going to say?" she'd asked him.

Yep, that had been his plan. They had been in the middle of a crowded restaurant, and Cade didn't think it was necessary to entertain their neighbors with the numerous ways in which he was, apparently, an emotionally stunted Cro-Magnon. But from the stubborn look on Jessica's face, he'd sensed that leaving the restaurant without saying anything further wasn't an option. She'd wanted answers.

And, actually, there *was* something he'd wanted to say.

Frankly, he didn't think he was that bad of a boyfriend. He'd been raised by a single mother to be respectful of women, he never cheated, and if he said he would call a girl, he did. He had a good job, a nice condo, and could make a mean Denver omelette for breakfast. Nevertheless, he'd gotten this lecture from more than one ex-girlfriend about his so-called "emotional unavailability."

Normally in response, he simply apologized to the woman for not giving her what she wanted. But tonight? Screw it.

Come to think of it, it *had* been a shitty day. So for once, he'd decided to skip over the usual BS and keep it real.

He'd set down his drink and leaned in. "Fine. You want me to elaborate, I will. Here's the deal: I'm a *guy*. Generally speaking, we're pretty simple folk. I know women always want to think we have these deep, romantic, and emotionally angsty thoughts going on in our heads, but in reality? Not so much. You women have layers and you're complicated and mysterious and you say one thing, but you really mean another, and it's this whole tricky package that intrigues us and scares us and challenges us all at the same time. But men aren't like that. You talk about me not letting you in, but maybe what you don't realize is this: there is no *in*." He pointed to himself. "It's all right here on the surface, Jessica. What you see is what you get."

Jessica's expression had said she wasn't buying it. "I've talked about this with my friends, you know. They say you probably have a fear of rejection. I'm thinking it has something to do with whatever happened with your father. That thing you won't talk about."

Christ. And so the psychoanalysis began. "I think, by definition, one actually has to have a *father* in order to have father issues," Cade had said dryly. And he most definitely did not. Just an asshole of a sperm donor who'd gotten his mother pregnant.

Jessica had glared at him pointedly. "Nothing going on underneath the surface, huh? Right." She picked up her purse and stood up from the table. "I think it's probably best if you don't call me anymore. We obviously have different ideas about what it means to be in a relationship. For me, it's a little more than sex, having somebody to go to dinner with, and sharing the occasional interesting work story. It's about putting yourself out there, Cade. For your sake, I hope you give that a shot someday."

She'd stalked out of the restaurant, leaving Cade sitting alone.

He took another sip of his drink, ignoring the stares of the people seated around him.

Well.

That had pretty much sucked.

* * *

CADE REALIZED THAT Huxley was looking at him, waiting for an answer about why he and Jessica had broken up.

"It was a mutual thing," he said simply.

Huxley nodded. "Got it."

And, being men, they left it at that.

"You know, I think we should celebrate today's fortuitous turn of events with a drink," Vaughn suggested. "Come Sunday night, we'll have Senator Sanderson right where we want him, and to top it all off, Huxley miraculously has a quasi date with an attractive woman—granted, one who's being paid to have dinner with him, but we'll gloss over that part. All thanks to the lovely Brooke Parker."

Cade shook his head. *Enough already with the praises.* "She's just a girl, Vaughn."

"I take it that means you don't care if I ask her out on Sunday?"

Immediately, a pair of gorgeous light green eyes popped into Cade's head.

Because in response to your tough-guy speech, I, in turn, would've had to give you my tough-girl speech, about where, exactly, federal prosecutors who come to my office looking for assistance can stick their obstruction of justice threats.

All right, fine. So she'd almost made *him* smile with that one, too.

"If you want to ask her out when this is over, be my guest," Cade said.

"You hesitated," Vaughn noted in a sly tone.

"Not at all."

Huxley glanced over from the driver's seat. "Actually, you did. There was a definite pause there."

Cade sat back in his seat, shaking his head as he stared at the road in front of him.

Of course, *now* they decided to agree on something.

Five

LATER THAT EVENING, Brooke dropped by Ford's loft apartment. When he slid open the heavy steel door, she held out three tickets for Sterling's skybox at Wrigley Field.

"Cubs/Sox. Figured I'd see if you, Charlie, and Tucker want to go," she said, already knowing the answer to that. There wasn't a person in Chicago who would turn down free skybox tickets to the Crosstown Classic between the city's two baseball teams.

Ford grabbed the tickets without hesitation. "Skybox? Hell, yes. I love it when they bring in that dessert cart."

"One of my strongest selling points as a girlfriend, apparently," Brooke muttered as she stepped inside.

With its open floor plan, exposed brick walls, and raised ceilings, Ford's condo was nearly double the square footage of Brooke's high-rise apartment in the Gold Coast. Whenever Ford gloated about that fact, Brooke went into her usual spiel—the same one she'd given her parents when she'd bought her place—about how she wanted to be able to walk to work, wanted to be close to the lake, and felt safer, as a single woman, living in a high-rise building with a doorman.

Really, though, she just liked being near the fast-paced action of Michigan Avenue.

"I thought you were taking the Hot OB to the game," Ford said as he followed her into the kitchen. "Is he on call that day?"

"The Hot OB and I broke up earlier today."

Ford's arms fell to his side. "What? That's the third guy in eighteen months."

Brooke glared. "Thank you, I'm aware of that."

Right then, Tucker and Charlie stepped through the sliding glass door, coming in from the deck. They were Ford's former college roommates, and around a lot, seemingly never having any work to do—or anything else to do, really—and somewhere along the way Brooke had just sort of adopted them as friends, too.

"Hey, Brooke. Ford didn't say you were coming over." Charlie helped himself to a beer from the fridge and handed another one to Tucker. "Are you coming with us to Firelight?" he asked, referring to a popular upscale nightclub in the city's Gold Coast neighborhood.

She shook her head. "I just stopped by for a short visit. I have to get up early for work tomorrow."

"On a Saturday?" Charlie made a face to show his strong distaste for that notion, then pointed with his beer. "Hey, how are things going with the Hot OB?"

"He broke up with me this afternoon."

"Oh. Sucks." He paused for a moment, as if trying to come up with more, then threw Tucker a look for help.

"Don't look at me," Tucker said. "I'm still trying to figure out why she and Ford haven't hooked up."

"Never gonna happen," Brooke and Ford said simultaneously, probably for the five-hundredth time since they'd become friends over twenty years ago.

Ford reached into the refrigerator and pulled out two Amstel Light bottles. He held one out to Brooke. "Should we go to the Spot and talk?"

She took the beer from Ford, smiling despite everything that had happened that day at the reference to their childhood hangout, a shady bank next to a tiny creek that they'd nick-named "the Spot." Not the most creative of names, but then again, they'd only been ten years old at the time. "Sure. Although I'll give you the CliffsNotes version: it's pretty much the same story as the last two guys." She followed Ford outside and took a seat in one of the outdoor couches on his deck.

"So what happened?" Ford led in, sitting in a chair across from her.

A warm breeze blew Brooke's hair into her eyes, so she undid her ponytail and readjusted it. She'd changed into jeans and flip-flops before coming over—a far cry from her custom-ary high heels and pencil skirts, but it was *Ford*. She hadn't worried about what she looked like in front of him since . . . well, ever. "He said I'm not a 'big-picture' kind of girl."

Ford glared. "That's a dick thing to say."

Brooke appreciated the loyalty. But she'd done some think-ing ever since she'd left work and she'd begun to think there was a lesson to be learned here. "No kidding. But that doesn't change the fact that *something* isn't working with these guys. I keep investing four months of my time into these relation-ships, only to end up right back where I started. And you know what? It's not all that much fun to keep coming back here."

"Maybe you need a Plan B," Ford said.

"Cut back on my hours?" Brooke shook her head. "Not possible right now. With this sports and entertainment division I'm helping to build at Sterling, there's too much going on."

"Actually, I was thinking that maybe you should stop try-ing to shoehorn a relationship into your life. Especially since you're only halfway into these guys, anyway."

"Hey, that's not fair."

"Oh, right. The *Hot OB* was the love of your life."

Well . . . okay. Maybe not. But she'd enjoyed being with those guys in her downtime. All thirty minutes a week she had of it.

With a sigh, Brooke leaned her head back against the chair. "I think I need to go on a relationship sabbatical."

"It worked for me," Ford said.

That got a slight smile out of her. Ford, the king of casual dating, had been on a relationship "sabbatical" for years. Hopefully, hers wouldn't last quite that long. But after three breakups, it was time to face facts: in light of the demands of her job, relationships simply weren't a good fit for her right now.

And, come to think of it, she was tired of feeling like she needed to apologize for that.

She worked hard; she didn't deny that. Frankly, she'd worked hard her whole life—and she was proud of where that had gotten her. She and Ford had grown up in Glenwood, an affluent Chicago suburb that, with its elegant tree-lined streets and big, fancy houses with wide, beautifully landscaped lawns, looked like something out of a John Hughes movie.

Except, that is, for the part of town where she and Ford had lived, which was slightly more modest.

Actually, a lot more modest.

Nicknamed "the Quads" because each building contained four townhomes per unit, Brooke's childhood subdivision was considered a "hidden gem" because of the fact that it offered very affordable housing within Glenwood's school districts, which consistently ranked among the top in the state. Brooke's father, a butcher, and her mother, a day care instructor, had made the decision to leave the city of Chicago after the public school Brooke had been attending slipped to the bottom quartile in Illinois school rankings.

Brooke had always done well in school, had always *wanted* to do well in school—and, frankly, at the Chicago public school she'd previously attended, it hadn't taken a lot of effort for her to be at the top. But that all changed when she moved to Glenwood.

In Glenwood, the kids had private tutors. And nannies and stay-at-home moms who could help them with projects after school. Her classmates in Glenwood took piano lessons and dance lessons and every other kind of lesson imaginable from the top instructors in the area, and they learned foreign languages like German and Japanese in summer-break immersion programs.

When Brooke got to high school, things turned even crazier. She heard stories about parents who hired the most popular teachers in school to work with their children over summer vacation, and by her sophomore year all the parents and students had begun focusing on college, and the fact that the Harvards and Yales of the world would likely only take one or two students from Glenwood—the guidance counselors had repeatedly reminded them of that—no matter how accomplished they all were.

Brooke realized early on that, in many aspects, she couldn't compete with her far-wealthier classmates. Her parents couldn't afford a private tutor or a bazillion lessons in things that would look good on her college applications; in fact, at times they struggled to make their mortgage payments on their townhome. And, unlike many of the other students, her parents didn't have any "connections" with the top universities, or alumnae in the family who could help grease a few wheels. Which meant that if Brooke wanted to be a contender for those top university spots, she needed to do it the old-fashioned way.

By working her butt off.

As a result, she studied *a lot* in school. Her parents had given her the opportunity to attend one of the best high schools in the state, and she'd be darned if she didn't do her best to capitalize on that.

Fortunately, all her hard work had paid off, and to this day she could still remember the look of pride on her parents' faces when she'd received her acceptance packet from the University of Chicago. But what stuck with Brooke even more was the pride that she, personally, felt in knowing that she'd done it all by herself.

She was a competitive person, and that pride, that feeling of achievement, similarly pushed her to do well in undergrad and law school. By the time she'd graduated from University of Chicago Law School and began her legal career, that was simply a part of who she was. She gave one hundred and ten percent to whatever it was she was doing, and basically had one speed when it came to her career: full speed. And since she genuinely enjoyed working at Sterling Restaurants, she'd never minded that.

Her three ex-boyfriends, on the other hand, obviously had been less enthralled with the situation.

"You know, I'm not sure I'm feeling the proper level of sympathy here," she told Ford. "I think we need a little more rallying around the dumpee. If you were a woman and I'd told you that the third guy in eighteen months had broken up with me, right now we'd be drinking lemon drop martinis and giving each other female empowerment pep talks about how we don't need a man in our lives to feel complete. And then we'd watch *The Notebook* and drool over Ryan Gosling."

Ford flashed her a grin as he stretched an arm across the back of his chair. "Sorry, babe. But when they handed out best friends, you drew the straw with a penis attached. That means no Ryan Gosling."

"Just my luck," she grumbled.

A comfortable silence fell between them as they both looked out at the incredible nighttime view of the Chicago skyline.

"Do you ever take a moment to look at that," Ford pointed at the view, "and wonder how we got here?"

She smiled at that. "Not bad for two kids from the Quads."

"Any regrets?" Ford asked her.

She could tell that he was being serious, so she gave some thought to his question. "Not a one."

"Then screw all these guys," Ford said. "If they don't fit into *your* big picture, they're not worth your time, anyway."

Brooke looked over at her friend. Sometimes, penis and everything, he knew exactly the right thing to say. "Thank you."

He winked. "Anytime, babe."

Charlie opened the sliding door and poked his head out. "Is it safe yet for Tuck and me to come outside? We don't want to interrupt if you two are still making out or whatever."

Brooke and Ford shook their heads at each other. Make that five hundred and *one* times. They answered in unison.

"Still never gonna happen."

Six

PROMPTLY AT SEVEN A.M. on Sunday morning, Cade, Vaughn, and Huxley rode the elevators that would take them to the entrance of Sogna. A hostess desk, made of dark mahogany wood, stood empty before a set of wide etched glass doors—doors that were open.

"I guess that's our invitation," Cade said. He led the way inside Sogna and looked around curiously. He'd heard great things about the restaurant, but had never dined here himself. Sogna's signature, eight-course $210 prix fixe menu made it a "special occasion" kind of place for a man on a government salary, and none of his recent relationships had quite made it to the "special occasion" level.

The lights inside the restaurant were off, but the natural light coming in from the windows revealed a modern décor, with dark mahogany tables and booths offset by chairs covered in ivory fabric. A staircase made of glass and steel snaked its way to the second floor of the split-level dining room, which Cade knew, from the online research he'd done the night before, could accommodate nearly two hundred seats between the two levels. Striking floor-to-ceiling windows looked out

at Michigan Avenue, the Drake Hotel, and Lake Michigan—
the same view, on a much larger scale, as the one from
Brooke's office.

Suddenly, the lights came on, instantly brightening the
space and making it feel less empty. A moment later, Brooke
Parker of the Gorgeous Green Eyes, Sarcastic Quips, and Yep,
More Hot Shoes stepped out from a hallway behind the bar.
Her golden blond hair was pulled up in a knot again, and
she was dressed in a red skirt, crisp black shirt, and kick-ass
red heels. She carried a Starbucks cup in one hand, looking
every bit as sophisticated and professional as she had the last
time Cade had seen her.

He wondered if she slept in her high heels and tailored
clothes, too. "Good morning, Ms. Parker," he said in greeting.

"Mr. Morgan," she said with a nod. "Sorry if I kept you
waiting. It took me a few minutes to figure out where the light
switches are," she said with an easy smile.

Polite as ever, Cade noted. Despite the slight . . . friction
between them, they were both professionals who knew how
this worked. Business was business, and this morning they
had a job to do. "No problem. We just got here ourselves."

Brooke gestured to the restaurant with her coffee cup. "So
where do we start?"

"I think the first step should be to pick the table we want
Sanderson and Torino to sit at." Cade looked at Vaughn and
Huxley for confirmation. "Yes?"

With a nod of agreement, the two agents began walking
around the restaurant to survey the scene. Huxley explained
to Brooke the kind of table they were looking for in terms of
maximizing the audio quality of the bugs: one that allowed
for semiprivacy, so that Senator Sanderson and Torino felt
comfortable speaking openly, and one that also was located
away from any particularly noisy places like the bar or kitchen.

"Upstairs will be quieter, since it's farther away from both
of those spots," she said. "And the tables along the window
are considered the best seats in the house. I could always tell
the hostess that I heard the senator was dining with us this

evening and wanted to be sure we put him at a table with a nice view," she offered.

Huxley nodded. "We were going to suggest something along those lines. And Agent Simms and myself—we'll be dining under the name 'Carson' tonight—will take a window table, too. If anyone asks any questions, just tell them that I'm an old friend planning a special night for my date, and that I called you and asked if I could have a table with a romantic view."

"I've got it—maybe you're proposing tonight, Hux," Vaughn suggested. "We could get you a fake engagement ring and everything. Agent Simms can't say no, it'll blow your cover. This could be your one chance."

Huxley shot him a glare, but otherwise refused to rise to the bait. He turned to Brooke. "Do you feel comfortable with all that?"

Brooke nodded. "Carson. Old friend. Special occasion."

All four of them headed up the staircase to the second level. Huxley and Vaughn conferred among themselves, choosing the two tables they wanted to use that night. Brooke and Cade followed a few feet behind.

"So what's your role in all this?" Brooke asked him conversationally.

"Tonight I'm just an observer," Cade said. "I'll be in the van outside with Vaughn and the tech guys, listening in on Sanderson's conversation with Torino."

She studied him curiously. "Are prosecutors typically this hands-on at the investigatory stage of a case?"

"It varies," Cade said. "Some cases come to me after the investigation is complete and there's already been an arrest. But being in the special prosecutions division, it's not uncommon for me to get involved at the earlier stages. The investigations tend to involve more complex legal issues than, say, a simple drug bust or a bank robbery—and thus tend to be more of a collaborative process between the agents and myself. Oh, that reminds me." He reached into the inside pocket of his suit jacket and pulled out a folded document.

He handed it over to Brooke. "One subpoena, per your request."

"Thank you." She took the subpoena with her free hand, the one not holding her coffee, and flicked it open. She took her sweet time reading it, looking every bit the dutiful contract lawyer right then.

Cade waited patiently for her to finish. Then waited some more.

This woman seemed to enjoy keeping him waiting.

He looked her over as she reviewed the subpoena and couldn't help but notice that she looked rather . . . cute with her brow furrowed in concentration.

His tone was suddenly teasing again. Weird, how that kept happening around her. "Perhaps there's something you'd like me to explain, Ms. Parker?"

Two green eyes glared at him over the top of the subpoena.

"Or maybe I should just let you do your thing."

"Now there's an idea."

Fighting back a smile at her dry tone, Cade eased against a nearby table and folded his arms across his chest, waiting as Brooke turned the page over and continued reading. Then she flipped back to the front side and started all over again.

Come on. Cade held out his hands. "You can't be serious." The damn thing was only two pages long.

"Patience, Mr. Morgan." With a slight smile, she folded up the subpoena and tucked it under her arm. "It's fine."

She'd been messing with him again, Cade realized. Something else she seemed to enjoy. The lawyer in him thought back to his *irritatingly self-assured* comment on Friday.

The man in him was slightly more intrigued.

Good thing, then, that the man in him had no say in the matter. This morning was all about business.

As a reminder of that fact, Huxley called over right then. "Brooke, if you're ready, we've got the tables picked out for tonight."

She turned her gaze. "Absolutely. Just tell me what I need to do."

"Here's how this will work." Huxley set his hand on a back-corner table that was flanked on one side by windows. "First, you need to make sure Torino and Sanderson sit here. They have reservations at seven thirty, which means that Agent Simms and I will be here at seven o'clock, just to be safe." He moved two tables away from the one at which Sanderson and Torino would be seated, also in front of the windows. "The hostess should seat the two of us here."

They ran through the rest of the plan, and agreed that Brooke would get to the restaurant at six o'clock. That gave her plenty of time to speak to the hostess who was scheduled to work that evening and with the manager on duty, so she could give him, too, a heads-up that she'd made special arrangements regarding the seating of some of their guests.

After they'd run through the routine for the evening, and then had run through it again, Vaughn pulled out his cell phone and dialed. "Stand by to start the audio checks in five minutes." He hung up the phone.

Huxley set his briefcase on top of the table he and Vaughn planned to bug. Both agents smiled at Brooke expectantly.

She didn't get the hint.

Brooke looked at Cade. "Is somebody waiting for me to say something?"

He bent his head closer to hers. "This is the awkward part where I need to ask you to leave so that Huxley and Vaughn can do their secret-special-agent thing."

She raised an eyebrow at him. "You're kicking me out? This is *my* company's restaurant."

"I'm kicking you out."

She considered this, likely contemplating several sassy retorts, and then—surprisingly—acquiesced. "Try not to look so pleased about it, Morgan. I'll be in my office in case you need anything." Then she turned in her heels and strode off in the direction of the stairs.

Cade caught himself watching her as she left.

So it was "Morgan" now.

Tough to say whether this was progress.

* * *

TO KILL TIME while she waited, Brooke took a seat at her desk and caught up on e-mail. She saw that she had a new message from Ian, saying that he needed to cancel their weekly Thursday lunch meeting because he had "highly important CEO business to tend to."

In other words, he was playing golf.

She shot him back a quick response, updating him on the status of the Sanderson sting operation, which she'd informed him about on Friday, immediately after her meeting with Cade and Company.

She continued chugging through her messages, until roughly a half hour later, a knock at her door interrupted her. She looked up from her computer and saw Cade Morgan standing in her doorway, all cobalt blue eyes and thick dark hair and six-feet-plus of sophistication and lean-muscled confidence in a dark gray suit. She'd noticed earlier that he'd forgone a tie this morning, opting for a more casual look and leaving the top two buttons of his shirt undone.

It wasn't the *worst* look she'd ever seen on a man.

She cleared her throat.

"We're finished," Cade said.

Brooke checked the time on her computer. "That was fast."

"These guys know what they're doing."

Indeed. *And let's hope you do, too, Parker.* For the first time since the Mighty Morgan had shown up at her office on Friday, Brooke felt nervous. Everything was set and ready to go, which meant that she was next up at bat. Until now everything had seemed simple enough and, frankly, a little exciting and secret-agent-esque—make sure Senator Sanderson sits here, put Huxley and his fake date over there, trade a few barbs with Cade—but suddenly everything had become real. She, Brooke Parker, was about to participate in a federal sting operation that evening, and while she considered herself to be a savvy businesswoman and a great negotiator, this definitely was not her wheelhouse. And now several people—hell, basically every citizen of Illinois, all of whom deserved to be represented by honest politicians (she was still going with the corruption angle on this one despite Cade's vagueness)—were counting on her to get this right.

No pressure there.

"Okay, then," she said in a bright tone. Nervous or not, she'd be damned if she betrayed that in front of him. For Cade Morgan, prosecutor extraordinaire, this kind of intrigue and high-stakes drama was probably an everyday occurrence. "I'll just grab my stuff."

She packed up her briefcase, trying to ignore the fact that he was watching her. "Shoot," she said, remembering something. "I need to lock up the office and the restaurant." She turned back to her desk, holding her briefcase while she rummaged around with her free hand. "Keys, keys, I just saw those keys . . ." She'd borrowed a spare set to Sogna from their VP of security and had last seen them . . . somewhere.

She felt Cade at her side and looked up.

He reached for her hand. "These keys?" His blue eyes danced as he jingled something in her fingers.

She'd had the keys looped around her finger the entire time. *Crap.*

"Ah, yes. Thank you," she said, making a mental note to give herself a good, solid head-thunk as soon as she was alone.

He cocked his head, studying her. "You're nervous about tonight." A statement, not a question.

She shook her head. "No." She glared at his knowing expression. "Fine, maybe a little. If I threw you into a complex multimillion-dollar restaurant deal on less than forty-eight hours' notice, how well do you think you'd do?"

"I'd kick ass."

Truly, she wanted to *shake* him at times. "I swear, Morgan, you may be the most infuriating lawyer I've ever—" She stopped and collected herself. Rule Number One of any business arrangement: never let the other side see you rattled. "I'm locking up now." She gestured to the door. "That means you—*go.*"

He seemed to be fighting back another of his aren't-you-a-funny-one grins. "I'll walk you out."

Wonderful. "If you insist."

They walked side-by-side through the empty office, no conversation, just the same aggravating, pestering agitation that had been present since the moment they'd first met. Once outside, she locked the door to Sterling's offices and turned around. "Thank you, Mr. Morgan. I can take care of locking up the restaurant by myself."

He reached into the pocket of his pants and pulled out his wallet. He took out a business card and handed it to her. "That has my cell number. Huxley will be there tonight, but if anything goes wrong, or if anything concerns you, just call me. I'll be in the van with Agent Roberts." His gaze seemed to soften. "And for the record, I was a little hesitant about this sting operation at first, too. Normally in an undercover investigation, I've got a cooperating witness who's willing to wear a wire. Which makes things a lot simpler. So when Vaughn and Huxley came to me with this idea of bugging a restaurant table, I was a bit skeptical whether we'd be able to pull it off. Especially since the plan is so dependent upon the assistance of a civilian."

"You're telling me this *now*?" she asked. "Where was all this hesitation on Friday afternoon when you first approached me?"

"Gone." His eyes held hers. "Because I knew, ten seconds after walking into this office and meeting you, that we had this in the bag." With a nod in good-bye, he turned and walked off toward the elevators.

Brooke stood there for a moment, unable to move because her brain needed all its functional capabilities to process the fact that Cade had just given her an actual *compliment.*

This had been a most unusual morning.

Keys in hand, she headed in the direction of Sogna to lock up the restaurant. As she turned the corner, she glanced over her shoulder and saw Cade walking in the opposite direction.

At the same moment, he looked back over his shoulder,

too. Their eyes met for a brief second before they both turned back, going about their business.

CADE STOPPED IN front of the elevators, where Huxley and Vaughn waited for him.

"Guess that kills my chances of asking for her phone number," Vaughn said.

"No clue what you're talking about." Cade stepped inside the elevator when it arrived at their floor.

"Sure you don't." With a mischievous smile, Vaughn followed him into the elevator, along with Huxley.

And, being men, they left it at that.

Seven

BROOKE STOOD BY the bar in Sogna's dining room, thinking that she had quite an affinity for this whole FBI undercover business.

She'd spoken earlier to both Rochelle, the hostess on duty, and Patrick, the manager, and had explained the situation. In the most casual of terms, she'd made a joke about tonight being a "happening" night for Sogna and had informed them that there were two parties with dinner reservations that evening—Torino and Carson—for whom she'd arranged special seating. She'd laid out the tables at which each group should be seated, and then had made another joke about hoping it remained such a beautiful night outside since she'd gone to such efforts to personally ensure that the parties had a good view. Ha, ha, ha.

And then she'd followed that up with her toughest now-scram-and-don't-ask-me-any-questions stare.

Because, on the off chance that she was *not* quite as good as she believed she was at this whole FBI undercover business, she would get the job done anyway.

That had been over an hour ago, and in the meantime Agent Huxley and the pretty redheaded agent posing as his date, aka the "Carson party," had arrived and were already in position and seated at their table. Now all they needed was the last and most important piece of the puzzle: Torino and Senator Sanderson. From there on out, it would be smooth sailing.

"Excuse me, Brooke. We have a problem."

And . . . so much for that.

Brooke turned and saw Rochelle, the hostess, standing there.

"What kind of problem?" she asked.

"The couple at table twenty-eight is complaining that they'd requested a table with a view. I explained that we don't guarantee window seating, but they saw the open table you told me to set aside for the Torino party and asked to sit there. When I explained that the table was reserved, they demanded to speak with a manager." She took a breath, eager to provide a solution. "I talked to Patrick already. We've got another window table that should be opening up in a few minutes; the customers are just paying the bill now. He wants to know if we can move the Complainers at twenty-eight to the open table, and then put the Torino party at the other window table that's about to open up. It's only ten after seven; there shouldn't be any problem having it cleared and reset for a seven thirty reservation."

Normally, Brooke knew, that would be a perfectly acceptable solution. The Complainers would get their window table, and the Torino party could also be seated at one as soon as they arrived. Except for one teeny, tiny problem: the *bug* that the FBI and the U.S. Attorney's Office had gone to great lengths to plant at Sanderson's table.

Seeing Brooke frown, Rochelle was quick to backtrack. "Or I'm sure Patrick can just tell the Complainers that all the tables are reserved. No big deal."

Brooke had no doubt that Patrick and Rochelle could handle the situation—she was familiar enough with the goings-on at Sogna to know that they both were very capable at their jobs. But she'd inadvertently stuck them in the middle of this, without giving them any reason why, and on top of that she wanted to quell the problem as fast as possible before there was too much attention drawn toward the mysteriously "reserved" window table.

"It's okay, Rochelle," Brooke said. "Tell Patrick that I'll talk to the Complainers at twenty-eight myself."

Rochelle pulled back. "Really?"

Brooke couldn't blame her for being so surprised. As general counsel, she was arguably the second-most-powerful executive at Sterling Restaurants, behind Ian. She handled matters on a corporate level, while the managers had primary responsibility for the daily problems that arose at the restaurants. Which meant that Brooke personally did not get involved in customer complaints—ever—unless they turned into potential legal issues. So volunteering to interject herself in this particular situation was odd.

Still, she played it casually. "Yeah, sure," she said with a wave. "I've got it."

Rochelle paused at that, and her expression changed from one of confusion to curiosity. And suddenly, it clicked.

Something's going on.

Seeing the flicker of recognition in the other woman's eyes, Brooke held Rochelle's gaze unwaveringly. Yes, something was going on. But the beauty of being the second-most-powerful executive was that she didn't have to give any explanations.

After a moment, Rochelle nodded. "Of course." And no further questions were asked.

With that, Brooke headed toward the staircase that would lead her to the second level. The Complainers could fuss all they wanted, but they weren't getting anywhere near Sanderson's table. She, Brooke Parker, recently of the mad undercover skills, was on top of this.

She stopped, realizing something, and looked back at Rochelle.

"Um . . . which one is table twenty-eight?"

UPSTAIRS, BROOKE SPOTTED Agent Huxley and his undercover date, who were seated only a few feet from table twenty-eight. As the two agents chatted amiably, Huxley held Brooke's gaze briefly, as if to say he was aware there was a "situation" and was relieved to see she was on top of it.

Brooke's goal, as she walked toward the Complainers, was simply to resolve this issue as quickly as possible. By no means did she want Torino and Senator Sanderson overhearing any discussion about a table that had been reserved specifically for them. Since they had not, in fact, made any such arrangements, this would undoubtedly seem suspicious. And if that happened, they might get paranoid and clam up about whatever shady things Cade, Huxley, and Vaughn were all jonesed about, and Brooke would have a boring, anticlimactic ending to the really fantastic story she planned to tell someday about the time she was a key operative in a federal corruption investigation.

With that in mind, she threw on a smile as she approached the table and introduced herself. "Hi, there. I'm Brooke. Rochelle said you wanted to speak to a manager?" Conveniently, Brooke left out the fact that she wasn't one.

The Complainers were not what she'd expected.

Given Sogna's expensive prices, the restaurant tended to get more than its fair share of high-roller, high-maintenance types. Frankly, Brooke had assumed table twenty-eight was going to be a prime example of that: a wealthy couple, possibly a flashy investment banker sporting a thirty-thousand-dollar watch on one arm and his Gucci-clad, twentysomething trophy wife on the other—not that she was stereotyping here—who were offended by the notion that *they* weren't getting the best seats in the house.

Instead, what she found was a couple in their midfifties, *sans* Gucci and flash, who looked slightly embarrassed.

"Oh, thank you. But we're fine," the woman said. She threw a do-not-make-a-stink-about-this look at the man across the table from her. "My husband and I are having a wonderful evening. We're sorry to have bothered you."

The husband, not so easily appeased, turned to Brooke. "See, it's just that—"

His wife cut him off with a smile. "*Sweetie.* Let it go. I'm sure Brooke has a lot on her plate tonight."

Just helping the Feds take down a state senator. All in a day's work. "No apologies necessary. I'm told you were asking about moving to a table next to the windows?"

"Yes, because I arranged this *two* months ago," the husband said. He shrugged off his wife's glare. "What? She asked." He turned back to Brooke to explain. "When I made the reservation, I specifically mentioned that this was a special occasion for us, and from what I'd read in the *Tribune*'s review of this place—"

"It was the *Sun-Times*," his wife interrupted.

"We don't get the *Sun-Times*."

"We did when they gave us that free one-month subscription."

The husband paused, mulling that over, then turned back to Brooke. "Anyhow, I read the review in the *Sun-Times*"—he emphasized the words with a slight smile at his wife—"and it said that the view from this restaurant is one of the best in the city. So when I made the reservation, I'd asked if we could have a table by the windows." He pointed to the table being held open for Torino and Sanderson. "Like that one there, sitting empty."

The wife reached across the table and covered her husband's hand with hers. "It's fine, Dennis, really. Let's just enjoy the evening. The restaurant is amazing even without the view."

He rubbed his thumb over her fingers and lowered his voice. "You deserve to have the best, Diana. You've been looking forward to coming here for so long. I just want everything to be perfect for you."

Hearing that, Brooke knew two things. First, from their attire and accessories—Dennis's somewhat ill-fitting suit and inexpensive watch, and Diana's simple, modest diamond ring and slightly too-formal dress, possibly one she'd originally bought for a wedding and was glad to finally have the chance to wear again—she guessed that dining at Sogna was a splurge for this couple. Something they very possibly would do only once in their lifetime.

The second thing Brooke knew was that she'd just crapped on that once-in-a-lifetime experience.

Actually, Cade Morgan and Agents Huxley and Roberts had done the crapping, but since that whole crew was lollygag-

ging around in FBI vans or too busy smiling at cute redheaded
undercover agents, the fallout landed on Brooke's shoulders.
And even though it may not have seemed like it to an outside
observer, she understood where the so-called "Complainers"
were coming from. Back in the day, she wouldn't have been
able to fathom ever eating at a place where dinner cost $210
per person.

"If you don't mind my asking, what's the occasion?" she
asked.

"It's our twenty-five-year anniversary," Diana said.

"Congratulations. That *is* something to celebrate." Brooke
pointed to Sanderson's table. "So unfortunately, as Rochelle
mentioned, that table in the corner is reserved this evening.
But if you're interested, there'll be another window table
opening up in a few minutes. We could move you there as
soon as we've had a chance to clear it. And in the meantime,
as an apology for the glitch in your reservation, I'd like to
send over a bottle of champagne. My treat."

Surprised by the offer, Diana exchanged a look with her
husband. "That would be lovely. Thank you."

"It's my pleasure. Can't have an anniversary without champagne, right?"

Brooke chatted with them for a few more minutes before
heading toward the staircase to tell the waitress to charge the
bottle of champagne to her employee account. She paused at
the top of the stairs and looked back, just in time to see Diana
smile at Dennis. In response, Dennis picked up her hand and
pressed it to his mouth.

I love you, he said.

Even across the room, Brooke could read those three simple words, and she found herself unexpectedly moved by
them, by the couple's obvious affection for each other.

The sound of a loud cough cut into her thoughts, and she
saw Huxley, a few tables away, as he reached for his water
glass. *Time to get moving*, his pointed gaze said.

Brooke brushed off the sentimental feelings—not sure
what had happened there—and began descending the stairs.

All right, fine. Maybe she'd been suckered in, just a bit, by

Dennis and Diana's story, and perhaps had lingered too long chatting with them, but she was back on top of things now. The coast was clear for Sanderson and Torino, the FBI's sting operation was on track, and on top of that, a sweet older couple had a fun anniversary story to tell about the time a nice young woman with totally awesome red shoes—she'd taken the liberty of filling in a few details here—bought them a bottle of champagne at Sogna. All in all a very pleasant, rewarding evening.

Now everyone else needed to do their part, wrap this up, and get the hell out of her restaurant.

All this do-gooder sweetness was going to ruin her reputation as a tough girl.

LATER THAT EVENING, Cade sat in an unmarked van parked in the garage outside, wearing headphones and listening in on Sanderson and Torino's conversation. So far, they'd spent most of the dinner talking about nothing of importance: the food, the Cubs, and the TV show *White Collar*, of which, ironically enough, they were both apparently big fans.

Hey, dickheads, have you seen the one where the U.S. Attorney's Office and FBI plant a bug in a restaurant and catch a state senator accepting a large bribe from a hospital CEO? It's a good one. So let's say we cut through the chitchat and get down to it.

Seventy minutes into the conversation, after Cade had begun to wonder if this whole sting operation was going to be a bust, Torino and Sanderson ordered dessert and two glasses of port and finally turned to the subject of the hospital's possible closing.

Senator Sanderson sounded wholly at ease as he began.

"I poked around after we talked, and it seems like a few of my colleagues feel as though Parkpoint should be the hospital to go."

Torino, not surprisingly, sounded worried. "Do you think you could convince them otherwise?"

"I'm a pretty convincing guy. But you understand how

these things work, Charles. If I ask some of the other senators for a favor, then I owe all of them a favor in return. And for something like this. . . well, that's a lot of favors. I need to be sure this is a cause that's worthy of my support."

"I assure you, Senator. This would be a very worthy cause."

"How worthy?"

Cade exchanged a silent look with Vaughn, who sat across from him in the back of the van. *Come on, Senator,* Cade thought as the adrenaline began pumping. *Don't be coy.*

There was a pause, and then a soft thud, possibly the senator setting down his port glass. "Two hundred thousand."

The words were met with a long silence before Torino spoke again.

"Two hundred thousand, and you can guarantee that Parkpoint stays open?"

"I know you've got the money, Charles. I've seen photos of that four-million-dollar house of yours in Lincoln Park. So just think of this as a onetime state tax to keep you in that cushy CEO job of yours."

A short pause, and then Torino answered. "All right. Let's do it."

There was a rustle of clothing—as the video would later show, when the two men shook hands. A picture was indeed worth a thousand words.

The senator sounded pleased with himself. "You just bought yourself a hospital."

Hearing those magic words, Cade nodded at Vaughn. "We got it."

A SHORT WHILE later, Cade stepped into the empty offices of Sterling Restaurants. The space was quiet, and only one panel of lights was on in the reception area, likely to conserve energy since there was only one Sterling employee working right then.

Cade cut through the hallway that would lead him to Brooke's office. He'd texted her earlier from the van, asking if they could meet.

They had some unfinished business to attend to.

When he got to her doorway, he found her sitting at her desk, reviewing documents. *Nine thirty on a Sunday evening and still going*, he thought. This woman bested him in terms of hours spent on the job, and that said a lot.

The desk lamp gave her just enough light to work, casting the rest of her office in soft, dim shadows. She'd changed her hair since this morning; now it tumbled long and loose over her shoulders in dark golden waves. Cade knocked softly on the door with the back of his knuckles.

"I hear you have a soft spot," he said when she peered up from her papers.

It took her a second, then she blushed. "I assume you're referring to the champagne I sent over to the couple celebrating their anniversary." She stood up from her desk and packed the documents she'd been reviewing into her briefcase. "Just business. You needed me to get Torino and Senator Sanderson to their table without some big scene. I was simply upholding my end of the agreement."

Cade took a few steps into her office, not buying the "just business" routine. Huxley had reported in after he and Agent Simms left the restaurant, and explained how Brooke had handled the situation while simultaneously making the day for some couple celebrating their twenty-fifth anniversary. Which, naturally, had brought about another round of effusive praises from Huxley and Vaughn—*Oh, that was so sweet of her* and *Oh, Brooke's been so great to work with*, and, frankly . . . Cade was beginning to think there wasn't much he could say to disagree with that. "My office would be happy to reimburse you for the champagne."

She waved this off. "It's fine." She rested her hip against the edge of her desk. "So? Did you get your man, Mr. Morgan?"

"Now, Ms. Parker. You know I can't tell you that."

"I suppose I'll find out when I hear about Senator Sanderson being arrested in the news."

Cade leaned against the bookshelves across from her desk. "Hmm," he said noncommittally.

She threw him a look. "After everything I've done, you're really not going to give me anything else?"

Funny, how Cade was going to miss frustrating her like this. He'd rather enjoyed going a few rounds with Brooke these past couple of days. "Nope. But I am going to *take* something from you."

Her eyes flashed—with curiosity, perhaps. "That would be . . . ?"

"The video of Sanderson and Torino."

She blinked. "Right. I'd forgotten about that."

"I've arranged for an FBI forensic specialist to come by your office tomorrow," Cade said. "He'll need access to the computer where the security footage from Sogna is stored. He'll make a copy of the video, and then we will be officially out of your hair."

With that said, he held out his hand in farewell. And gratitude. All teasing aside, she'd been a tremendous help to him this weekend. "Thank you. For everything."

"You're welcome."

As her hand slid softly against his, their eyes met and held.

"About that favor I allegedly owe you . . ." Cade paused deliberately, his gaze still locked with hers. "Call me sometime. We'll talk."

Brooke's lips parted in surprise—likely trying to discern whether there was any hidden meaning in his words—before she answered. "I'll do that. To talk about the favor you *do* owe me. Not alleged."

Cade leaned in, the two of them standing close in the intimate setting of her dimly lit office. Behind them, the windows showcased a view of a vibrant city at night. His voice was suddenly husky.

"I look forward to it, Ms. Parker."

Eight

BROOKE HAD JUST finished reviewing the most recent bill they'd received from Gray & Dallas, the law firm they used to handle their employment and labor matters, when her secretary buzzed her.

"Keith is here to see you."

"Thanks, Lindsey. Send him in."

She set the bill on her desk, the businesswoman in her wincing at the amount. Unfortunately, it was a necessary expense, at least with the current setup of Sterling's in-house legal department—a "department" that consisted of herself, one paralegal, and her assistant. Because they were all so swamped, Brooke and Ian had made the decision that most employment and litigation matters would be farmed out to outside counsel.

Her door opened and Keith, Sterling's vice president of security, walked into her office carrying a file. He'd called her earlier this morning, saying that he wanted to discuss a confidential matter. Typically, that meant somebody at one of the restaurants was up to no good.

Hopefully not another employee stealing credit cards,

Brooke mused. Or any sort of headache-inducing "oops moment," like the time one of the restaurant managers called to ask if he could fire a line cook after discovering that the man was a convicted murderer.

"Jeez. How'd you learn that?" Brooke had asked.

"He made a joke to one of the waiters about honing his cooking skills in prison. The waiter asked what he'd been serving time for, and he said, 'Murder.'"

"I bet that put an end to the conversation real fast. And yes, you can fire him," Brooke had said. "Obviously, he lied on his employment application." All of Sterling's employees, regardless of job position, were required to answer whether they'd ever been convicted of a crime involving "violence, deceit, or theft." Pretty safe to say that *murder* qualified.

Ten minutes later, the manager had called her back.

"Um . . . what if he didn't exactly lie? I just double-checked his application, and as it turns out, he *did* check the box for having been convicted of a crime."

Brooke had paused at that. "And then the next question, where we ask what crime he'd been convicted for, what did he write?"

"Uh . . . 'second-degree murder.'"

"I see. Just a crazy suggestion here, Cory, but you *might* want to start reading these applications a little more closely before making employment offers."

"Please don't fire me."

Brooke had thunked her head against the desk, silently going all Jerry Maguire—*Help me, help you*—on the manager.

But she'd handled it, just like she would handle whatever it was that brought Keith from security into her office today.

"You sounded serious on the phone," she said as he took a seat in one of the empty chairs in front of her desk. "Should I be nervous?"

"No. But I do think you're going to be pissed. I sure am."

Brooke didn't like the sound of that intro. "Tell me."

Keith crossed his legs, settling in. "The other day, I got a call from our account representative at Citibank, letting me know that there had been a breach in our employee purchasing card online database."

Definitely off to a good start toward pissing her off. All corporate employees at Sterling, as well as the managers, assistant managers, chefs, sous-chefs, and wine sommeliers who worked at the various restaurants and sports arenas, were given a Citibank company purchasing card for business-related expenses. "Is someone charging extra expenses to that account?"

Keith shook his head. "It's not a theft issue. It seems as though somebody has an ax to grind with Ian. Someone hacked into his account and altered the descriptions of some of his expenses."

Brooke cocked her head, not following. "Just the descriptions? Why would anyone want to do that?"

Keith pulled a document out of his file folder and slid it across her desk. "Perhaps this will answer that."

She picked up the pages, a spreadsheet she was familiar with. Whenever a Sterling employee charged something to his or her purchasing card, they were required to enter into the Citibank database a brief explanation of the business expense, such as "Dinner with the L.A. Arena lawyers." Brooke skimmed through Ian's May expenses, not seeing anything out of the ordinary until she got to the entries for a business trip he'd taken to Los Angeles to look at some potential restaurant space, a possible expansion for Sterling now that the company had a presence in L.A. via the sports and entertainment division.

Then there was no missing the changes.

Dinner in L.A. with some of my faggot friends.
Picked up a queer dude in tight pants and bought him
    drinks before bringing him back to my pansy-ass
    hotel suite.
Cab fare to "Sperm-Burpers Anonymous" meeting.

And so on.
It was safe to say that Brooke had moved beyond pissed at

that point. "Pissed" was how she felt the time someone let their dog poop on the sidewalk in front of her building and she stepped in it while climbing into a cab wearing three-inch heels. But breaking into company records and writing homophobic slurs against her boss? That was whole different ball game.

She set the spreadsheet off to the side. "Do we know who did this?"

"No, although we at least know *how* he did it," Keith said. "As soon as I saw this, I talked to the managers about all recent terminations, anyone who might have expressed anger at Ian or Sterling in general. There was nothing in particular that jumped out at anyone. But what occurred to us is that only Ian or his secretary should have had access to his online expense files."

"I can't believe Liz would've had anything to do with this," Brooke said. Ian's assistant had been with him for years.

"Not intentionally, no. But as it turns out, she never changed her password from the default one we'd assigned to all employees back when we updated everyone's computers to the new software. She's still been using 'Sterling 1-2-3' all this time."

Brooke sighed. *Note to self: send out memo telling all employees to change their passwords immediately.* "Then this could've been anyone."

"Essentially, yes," Keith said. "I've been working with the folks at Citibank, and they provided me with a list of the date and times that Ian's entries were altered, as well as the IP address for the computer from which the changes had been made. Based on a Google IP search, I've been able to determine that the asshole in question did this from a computer in the Chicago area."

"That covers about eighty percent of all Sterling employees and ex-employees."

"Unfortunately, yes. And since that's the extent of what I can do, I contacted the FBI." Keith rolled his eyes in frustration. "The agent I spoke to said that because there was no actual loss of funds, and because this guy didn't technically hack into the bank's system—he used the default password and someone else's username—the matter would be viewed as 'low priority.' When I pressed him on *how* low of a priority, he said he'd have to get back to me. Frankly, I'd be surprised if I ever hear from him again."

And if that were the case, the jerk who'd done this would get away scot-free, still employed by Sterling. Luckily, however, Brooke knew someone who had the means to make sure that didn't happen.

Someone who just so happened to owe her a favor.

"Thank you, Keith," she said. "I can take things from here."

A FEW MINUTES later, she knocked on the door to Ian's office.

"Got a second?" she asked when he looked up from his desk.

Ian waved her inside. "Sure. Come on in." When Brooke shut the door behind her, he studied her serious expression. "Oh, shit. Don't tell me we've got another murderer."

Brooke smiled slightly at the joke. At least *now* they could laugh about that. But this new situation . . . not so much. She took a seat in front of his desk and came right out with it. "Someone broke into the Citibank purchasing card database and altered a few of your entries. Specifically, they changed the descriptions for the expenses you incurred during your last trip to L.A."

Ian looked at her in confusion. "The descriptions? Why would anyone do that?"

"To be malicious. We don't know yet if it's a current or former employee. We have determined, however, that this person took advantage of the fact that Liz was still using the default password." She slid the spreadsheet Keith had given her across Ian's desk. "I thought you should see this."

Ian took the document from her, clearly still not following, and began to skim. After a few moments, his mouth pulled tight. He finished reading, and then set the spreadsheet down. "'Sperm-burper.' I haven't heard that one since high school."

"We have the IP address of the person who did this, but Keith was only able to narrow the person's location to Chicago. The FBI is calling this a 'low-priority' matter, but I have a contact who might be able to help us out."

"It's not the first time I've been called a few bad words, Brooke. Do what you can, but I'm not asking you to make a federal case out of this. Yes, pun intended."

"It's possibly a current employee who did this, Ian. I'm not comfortable having some person working for Sterling who's malicious enough to hack into the CEO's personal account just to write these kinds of things. Regardless of whether the FBI makes an arrest, I want whoever did this out of here." Brooke paused, following his lead and making her tone lighter. "Besides, this is what you pay me the big bucks for, remember?"

Ian rubbed his jaw. "If I recall correctly, I pay you the big bucks because the last time you were up for a raise you gave me a sixteen-page report with charts and graphs of all the salaries for comparable GC positions."

Well, yes. Although in her defense, Ian had cheekily asked her to "prove" what she was worth. So she'd done just that— charts and graphs included. "So you're okay with my moving ahead with this?"

"You have my blessing to track this prick down, if you can, and give him the full Brooke Parker treatment."

That settled, she got up and headed for the door. Just as she was walking out of the office, Ian spoke.

"One last thing, Brooke." He held her gaze and nodded in appreciation. "Thank you."

Nine

AT THE DIRKSEN Federal Building, inside one of the court-rooms, Judge Reinhardt read through the charges in the nine-count indictment the grand jury had returned last week in the case of *United States v. Alec Sanderson, et al.* To the right of the center podium, in front of the lawyers' table, were five high-powered criminal defense attorneys with sober expressions. Behind them, the five accused sat stoically as the judge laid out the charges against them. Cameras flashed repeatedly from the gallery, which was filled to capacity with reporters, spectators, and a few family members.

Cade stood to the left of the podium, unfazed by the spectacle. Having been down this road before, he knew exactly the kind of defensive game these crooked politicians played. They hired the city's most expensive lawyers and PR firms, who would cry foul and righteously protest their client's innocence—*Justice will prevail! We will have our day in court!*—and then they would wake up one morning, have a nice dose of reality for breakfast, and start trying to flip on each other in exchange for a reduced sentence.

Along with Senator Sanderson, Cade had filed corruption

charges against Charles Torino, the hospital CEO who'd offered Sanderson a bribe at Sogna; as well as a real estate developer who'd paid Sanderson multiple bribes in exchange for his assistance in moving forward several major real estate projects; a lobbyist who had paid off Sanderson in exchange for allocating state funds to certain projects; and the financial consultant who'd set up the shell company though which Sanderson's bribes were funneled. Not unexpectedly, the indictment of the senator and four successful businessmen had been the top story in the Chicago media for the last week, and Cade's office had been flooded with calls from the press. Everyone wanted to know what kind of evidence the U.S. Attorney's Office had up its sleeves.

And in about two minutes, they were going to find out.

"How do the defendants plead?" the judge asked when she'd finished reading the charges.

One by one, the defense attorneys stepped up to the podium and responded "not guilty" on behalf of their clients. Sanderson's lawyer then immediately asked the judge for extra time to review the discovery materials before a trial date was set.

"We have no objection, Your Honor," Cade said. "Particularly in light of the fact that the U.S. Attorney's Office has over fifty-five thousand documents and roughly one thousand recorded phone conversations that establish our case."

And that would be the sound bite every one of those reporters would take out of this arraignment.

Because Cade knew how to play this game, too.

A low murmur rippled through the crowd at this revelation. Clearly unsettled by the news of the impending avalanche of evidence Cade soon would be dropping on them, the defense attorneys all fell silent for a moment. One of them, Torino's lawyer, literally broke out in a sweat.

Then four of them hightailed their high-powered asses up to the podium to request that their clients' cases be severed from the senator's.

And so it begins, Cade thought as the judge set a date for the lawyers to present their arguments for separate trials. It was only their first court appearance, and the four codefendants were already distancing themselves from Senator Sanderson. Given the substantial evidence, it was only a question of if, not when, their lawyers called him to discuss a possible plea.

After the hearing, he left the courtroom feeling satisfied that his case was off to a good start. He checked his watch. Three o'clock. Time for a coffee run. At the elevators, he nearly pushed the up button, thinking he'd make a pit stop at the office to see if Rylann, one of the other AUSAs in the special prosecutions group, wanted to join him—and then remembered that she was in trial this week.

Cade headed downstairs solo and cut through the lobby, past the metal detectors and the security guards. Once outside, he'd gone about a block when his cell phone rang. He pulled the phone out of the inside pocket of his suit coat and checked the caller ID.

Brooke Parker.

A slow smile spread across his face.

A jackhammer pounded away on the opposite side of the street, so Cade stepped into a Mrs. Fields cookie shop to get away from the noise.

He answered the phone. "Ms. Parker. What a pleasant surprise."

A throaty feminine voice. "I knew it was a corruption case."

Cade grinned. They hadn't spoken for two weeks, yet of course that would be her opening line. "So you're calling to brag that you were right. Imagine that."

"Actually, I'm calling about that favor you owe me."

Interesting. "I still don't recall ever agreeing to that."

"Give it a moment," she said. "I'm sure it will come back to you."

There was a long pause, until Brooke spoke again. "Hello? Are you there?"

"Sorry. I was giving it a moment. Nope, still no recollection."

She sighed. "I woefully underestimated how painful this conversation was going to be."

Cade laughed, realizing he really *had* missed bugging the

hell out of her like this. He could picture her, sitting at her desk with her hair pulled back, all long legs and high heels and sexy I-mean-business skirt.

It was not an altogether *un*pleasant image.

"What kind of favor?" he asked.

"The kind I'd rather not discuss over the phone, since it's a sensitive matter. Perhaps if you're free, we can meet this evening at Bar Nessuno on Grand? Say, six thirty?"

Admittedly, he was curious. For more than one reason. "Did you just ask me out on a date, Ms. Parker?"

"No."

"Are you sure? Because I—"

"Still no. I need something, and you're the one guy who can give it to me." She cut him off before he could even say the words. "Yes, thank you, I'm aware of how that sounded. I'm hanging up now, Mr. Morgan. Six thirty. Bar Nessuno."

With a smile, Cade hung up the phone, thinking that she'd sounded a little frazzled when he'd brought up the subject of their having a date.

Good.

CADE STEPPED OFF the elevator at the twenty-first floor of the Dirksen Federal Building, Starbucks cup in one hand, bag of Mrs. Fields Nibblers in the other. As he rounded the corner that led to the reception area of the U.S. Attorney's Office, a tall man with light brown hair bumped into him, seemingly in a rush.

"Oh, shoot. My bad," the guy blurted out.

Cade righted the coffee without spilling it—his shoulder might be shit, but having quick football reflexes still came in handy from time to time—then looked over and saw that the person who'd bumped into him wasn't a man, but a teen-aged kid.

The boy's blue eyes widened, then he swallowed. "Um, sorry. I wasn't watching where I was going." He shifted uncomfortably. "Obviously."

Cade gestured amiably with his cup. "No harm, no foul.

Just try to keep it under sixty in the hallways." Moving on, he made his way through the reception area and into the main office space.

The office was bustling, per usual, with the inner cubicles and desks occupied by secretaries and paralegals. The prosecutors' offices ran along the perimeter, with the largest corner office belonging to Cade's boss, Cameron Lynde, the U.S. attorney for the Northern District of Illinois. Cade made a pit stop at his secretary's desk before heading into his office.

He held open the bag. "Cookie?"

"Yum." Demi, his secretary, stood up and peeked inside. "Wow. How many did you get?"

"I was in the shop, there were all these good smells, and a cunning salesclerk mentioned something about a sale if I bought a dozen. I didn't stand a chance."

Demi looked at him shrewdly. She'd been his secretary during the entire eight years he'd worked for the U.S. Attorney's Office, and they knew each other well. "You're in a good mood this afternoon. I take it the hearing went well?"

"I had the defense attorneys sweating. Literally."

"Nice. By the way, Paul called to touch base with you," she said, referring to the office's media representative. "He said his phone's been ringing off the hook for the last thirty minutes."

"Thanks, Demi." Cookies and coffee in hand, Cade went into his office and settled in at his desk. He returned Paul's call, and briefed him on the arraignment. As soon as he hung up, Demi appeared in his doorway.

"Let me guess. Another cookie?" Cade said.

"Actually, the reception desk called while you were on the other line," she said. "You have a visitor. A Mr. Zach Thomas."

"Do I know a Mr. Zach Thomas?"

"Not sure. He says he's here because he has some evidence related to a case." Demi lowered her voice. "The receptionist mentioned that he's a teenager. And apparently, he's been acting a little odd. When she asked for a photo ID to sign him in, he got nervous and said he doesn't carry one. She wants to know if you'd like her to say that you're unavailable for the rest of the day."

Cade understood the receptionist's cautiousness—security was tight in the federal building. But he assumed this Zach Thomas was the same kid he'd bumped into earlier, and he was curious to find out why a teenaged boy would be interested in meeting with him. "Tell reception it's okay. I'll come out."

When Cade walked into the reception area, he saw the kid standing off to the side with his hands shoved into the pockets of his zip-up hoodie.

He went over, hand outstretched. "You must be Zach Thomas. I'm Cade Morgan."

Fifteen or sixteen years old, the kid had a firm grip, although his palm was a little sweaty. "Sorry again about bumping into you earlier."

"Trust me, I've taken a lot harder hits. My secretary said you wanted to speak to me about a case?"

Zach nodded. "Yeah, I have some, um, information. But I was hoping that we could, like, talk in private?"

Man, this kid was nervous. Quickly, Cade mentally scrolled though all his open cases—which, off the top of his head, wasn't an easy thing to do considering he currently managed about fifty of them in various stages of the litigation process. He tried to come up with one in which a sixteen-year-old kid might have evidence.

Then his jaw tightened. About a month ago, he'd gotten a conviction against a forty-year-old west suburban man, a junior high school gym teacher who'd secretly used his phone to videotape male students undressing in the locker room. The teacher had shared the images online with a circle of his Internet buddies who referred to themselves as the "Boy Lovers." Cade had flat-out refused to discuss a plea agreement— he didn't negotiate with people who produced and distributed child pornography—and had taken the case to trial and gotten a guilty verdict on every count. The defendant's sentencing hearing was scheduled to take place next week, and Cade was determined that the asshole would serve every day of the thirty-five-year maximum allowed under the Federal Sentencing Guidelines.

This kid, Zach—if that was even his real name—seemed older than junior high age, but perhaps he was a former student of the defendant's who'd read about the trial in the news and wanted to share some information in advance of the sentencing hearing.

Cade's gaze softened at the thought. "Sure, we can talk in my office. Follow me." He led Zach through the corridor and gestured to his office door. "Have a seat." With a quick glance at Demi, he signaled that she should hold any calls that came in. Then he shut the door behind them and sat down at his desk. "So," he began casually, careful not to go into cross-examination mode, "what case would you like to talk about?"

Zach exhaled. "This is really awkward."

"Take your time," Cade assured him.

"I wasn't sure I could go through with this. When they started asking me all those questions at the front desk, like my name and the purpose of my visit and for some kind of picture ID, I sort of panicked. I'd decided to bail, but on the way out I bumped into you and it seemed like, I don't know, a sign or something."

Cade cocked his head, catching something Zach had said. "So you recognized me?"

"Well, yeah. You're Cade Morgan."

Cade smiled at the slightly reverent way Zach said his name. "I take it you're a football fan." Either that, or he was strangely fascinated with criminal prosecutors.

"I get that from my dad—he's big into football, too." Realizing that the next move was his, Zach shifted in his chair. Then his eyes fell on the bag on Cade's desk. "Cookies. So that's what smells so good in here."

Clearly, Zach was stalling, but Cade went with it. No sense pushing the kid; he needed to do this, whatever it was, on his own time. "Help yourself. I got suckered into buying twelve of them."

Like any teenaged boy offered something to eat, Zach didn't hesitate. He reached for the bag and looked inside.

"Cool, there's one with M&Ms." He pulled out the cookie and inhaled it in one bite.

Cade smiled. "Those are my favorite, too."

For some reason, this seemed to strike a chord with Zach. He swallowed the cookie, his expression turning more sober. "I lied about my name. Actually, Zach Thomas is my first and middle name. I was afraid you wouldn't agree to see me if I gave the receptionist my last name."

Cade looked at him in confusion. "Why would I not want to see you if I knew your last name?"

"Because it's Garrity."

Cade's entire body went still. Whatever he'd been prepared to hear from Zach, it wasn't this.

Zach looked him dead in the eyes. "And I'm pretty sure you're my brother."

Ten

CADE SAID NOTHING for a moment—probably the first time in his life he'd been rendered speechless. "You think I'm you're brother," he finally managed.

"Is your father Noah Garrity?" Zach asked bluntly. He gestured at Cade. "I mean, I kind of know already. You look just like him."

Do I look like him, Mom?

Cade winced at the sudden flashback, a ten-year-old boy excited and desperately eager for information.

Quickly, he pushed the memory away. "Yes." It took a lot for him to admit even that much.

Zach smiled as if this was the greatest news in the world. "I knew it. He's my dad, too. That means we're half brothers."

"He's not my dad."

Zach's smile faded. "But you just said—"

"Biologically, Noah Garrity may be my father, but I don't have a *dad*."

Zach nodded, looking embarrassed. "Sorry. I didn't mean . . . I don't, like, know the whole story between you guys."

"It's a pretty short story. I met him once when I was ten, then I never saw or heard from him again."

Zach stared awkwardly at the ground. "So that probably makes this extra-weird for you."

Cade ran his hand over his mouth. *Noah Garrity.* Christ, he hadn't thought about the man in years. And, frankly, he would've preferred *not* to have thought about him for many more.

Given the sudden appearance of the teenager sitting across from him, that plan had just been blown out of the water. "I think we can safely classify this as extra-weird, yes." He took a moment to look Zach over, more carefully this time. The boy's hair was a lighter brown than his, but when it came to the eyes he could've been looking in a mirror. "How did you find me?" A thought suddenly occurred to him. "Don't tell me Noah sent you."

"No," Zach said quickly. "He and my mom don't even know I'm here. My dad . . . doesn't like to talk about you."

Glad to hear it's mutual. "Then how did you figure out who I am?"

"He told me once, a long time ago," Zach said. "I was four years old, and we were watching your Rose Bowl game. It's the first time I can remember watching a game with my dad. He was cheering and shouting at the TV, and in the last play, when you threw that awesome pass and won the game, he grabbed me and did this stupid little dance around the coffee table."

Zach had been smiling at the memory, but then his expression turned serious. "Then everyone realized you were hurt, and the sportscasters were talking about how you'd taken a bad hit and it could be a broken shoulder. I remember that the entire stadium was on their feet, clapping for you as the coach and trainer helped you off the field. And I looked over at my dad, and there were tears in his eyes. It was the first time I'd seen my dad cry, so I asked him if he was sad because the man on TV had gotten hurt. And then he turned to me and said, 'That man is your brother, Zach.'"

Cade stared at him, just . . . unable to understand any of

that. The kid might as well have walked into his office and told him that he was a time traveler from the future who'd been sent to save the planet from evil cyborgs, it was that surreal. He had *one* memory of Noah Garrity, and it ended with Noah walking out of his life for good. "Are you sure we're talking about the same Noah Garrity? From Hoffman Estates, dropped out of Conant High School?"

Zach seemed surprised by this. "He never told me he'd dropped out. I just knew that he'd played wide receiver and was some big star in high school." He switched gears, finishing his story. "I don't think he meant to tell me you were his son, because anytime I asked about you after that, he would change the subject. But it stuck with me, the fact that I had a brother out there. I always wondered what you might be like, and, you know, whether we might get along and stuff. Then I saw your name in the papers last week with the Senator Sanderson case, and I . . . guess I just wanted to finally meet you."

Cade ran his hand through his hair.

He had a *brother*.

Since Noah had written him off, Cade had never allowed himself to speculate about the rest of the Garrity family— especially since none of them had ever reached out to him.

Until now, apparently.

"Are there any more of you? Any siblings, I mean?" he asked.

Zach shook his head. "Nah. It's just me."

"What are you looking for, Zach? From me." Cade hoped the words didn't sound callous; he was just trying to wrap his mind around all this and be as direct as possible.

Zach shrugged. "Look, I get that I'm basically this total stranger to you, but I don't know . . . maybe we could grab a burger sometime or whatever. Just hang out."

Cade saw the eagerness in Zach's eyes, a look he understood. Because twenty-three years ago, he'd felt the exact same thing, and had put himself out there for a near stranger, just as Zach was doing now.

He didn't know jack squat about being a brother. And, no

doubt, he was wholly unprepared to have suddenly acquired one at 3:45 on a Friday afternoon. But he did know one thing.

He would not do to this kid what Noah Garrity had once done to him.

So he nodded. "I'd like that, Zach."

AFTER ZACH LEFT, Cade shut his office door and took a seat at his desk. The two of them had agreed to meet for lunch the following weekend at DMK Burger Bar. Cade had only one condition, and it was non-negotiable.

"Noah can't be there," he'd said. "I don't care what you do or don't tell him about the fact that you came to see me. That's your business with him. But he is *not* a part of this."

Zach had seemed a little surprised by his vehemence, but he'd nodded nevertheless. "Yeah. Sure. No problem."

Cade didn't know what it meant that Noah had been crying over his Rose Bowl game, and he didn't care. He was a lawyer; he dealt with facts. And in this case, there was one irrefutable fact, the only one that mattered: Noah Garrity hadn't bothered to contact him in twenty-three years. He wasn't a part of Cade's life, and never would be.

Cade knew enough of the story, although it had taken him years as a kid to piece it together. Noah Garrity got his mother, Christine Morgan, pregnant during their last semester of high school. Christine's parents had remained surprisingly level-headed that their homecoming queen daughter was going to have a baby; Noah, on the other hand, had freaked out. His older brother had flunked out of Illinois State University and decided to move to California with a buddy to open a land-scaping business. When they asked Noah to join them, he packed his bags for the sunny west coast, and broke up with Christine by leaving a note in her school locker. *Don't hate me, babe. I'm just not ready to be someone's father.*

Luckily for Cade, Christine realized that—ready or not—the arrival of a baby, one she'd decided to keep, meant that *somebody* needed to act responsibly. She finished high school and enrolled in the local community college. Cade, never one to cause his mother too much trouble, conveniently arrived during winter break, allowing Christine—with her mother as a babysitter—to resume classes by February. After two years, she received her associate's degree and transferred, with Cade, to Northern Illinois University where she earned a nursing degree.

When Cade was about five years old, right around the time he and his mother moved back to the Chicago area and she took her first nursing job, he began to ask questions about his father. Quickly, he realized it was a sore subject. His grandparents tried to skirt around the topic as much as possible, and his mother, only twenty-three years old at the time, talked about Noah exclusively in the negative: how he'd dropped out of school, how he'd flaked on them when she'd gotten pregnant, how he'd never tried to contact them once. Eventually, Cade just stopped asking.

Until the day, five years later, when his mother came to *him*.

He'd been in his room, playing *Super Mario Land* on his Nintendo Game Boy before bedtime, when she knocked on the door and said they needed to talk.

Cade knew exactly what *that* meant. Trou-ble. "It was Sean's idea to put the cricket down Mandy Franklin's dress during the assembly."

His mother folded her arms across her chest. "I hadn't heard anything about the assembly. But now I know what we'll be talking about next."

Oops.

She sat down on the bed next to him. "That phone call I just got, the one I took in the bedroom? That was your father."

Cade pushed the Game Boy aside and sat up. His. . . *father*? "What did he want? Did he say anything about me?"

"He did. He's back from California and he asked if he could see you."

Cade got an excited but nervous feeling in his stomach, like when he was waiting in line for one of the upside-down roller coasters at Six Flags. "What did you say?"

"I told him that it was up to you," she said.

When she said nothing further, Cade wondered if this was some kind of test.

"Will you be mad if I say yes?" he asked cautiously.

She shook her head. "I won't be mad, sweetie." She reached over and brushed a lock of hair off his forehead. "This is your decision to make."

Cade thought that over. "When does he want to see me?"

"Tomorrow."

"I want to see him."

His mom nodded, as if she'd expected that answer. "Okay. I'll let him know."

"You're making that weird smile," Cade told her. "The fake one you make whenever Mrs. Kramer comes over to remind us that our grass is getting a little long."

"Yes, well, Mrs. Kramer needs to find something better to do with her time than monitor the length of her neighbors' front lawns." She suddenly reached over and pulled him in for a hug. "I'll work on the smile for tomorrow, Cade. For you."

She'd tucked him in and then lay down on the bed next to him, something she only did when he was sick or on nights like the one when he was positive he'd heard a strange scraping noise in the closet after his friend Sean's older brother had let them watch *A Nightmare on Elm Street*. "Is there anything you want to ask me?" she said as they both looked up at the ceiling, her head on the pillow next to his.

"Maybe you can just tell me something about him?" Cade paused. "But, Mom . . . how about if you tell me something good this time?"

His mom swallowed, and wiped her eyes. *Uh-oh*, Cade thought. Maybe he'd pushed it with that one.

She turned to face him. "I haven't totally messed you up, have I?"

Cade pretended to think about that. "Even if you have, I probably wouldn't know it."

She smiled, just like he'd hoped. Then she tucked her arm under the pillow, getting more comfortable. "All right, three good things about Noah Garrity. He can make people laugh. Back in high school, everyone wanted to be friends with him.

Second, he was an awesome football player. Whenever he had the ball, the entire stadium cheered so loud you could probably hear it a mile away. And last," she stopped for a moment, as if this one was most important, "for the homecoming dance, he told me he'd spent an hour picking out the flowers for my wrist corsage. He said he couldn't find anything as pretty as me."

Cade parsed through these precious nuggets, the most information he'd learned about Noah Garrity in ten years. He thought the part about the flowers sounded a little mushy and lame, but the other stuff was good to know. And he couldn't resist one last question. "Do I look like him, Mom?"

She touched his cheek softly. "The spitting image."

All next morning, his stomach was doing the roller-coaster thing again. His mother seemed about to say something when he came out of his room dressed in his best button-down shirt, but then she bit her lip and went back to making their breakfast.

Just before noon—a half hour late, probably just because of traffic—Cade heard a car pull up in the driveway. Unable to help himself, he ran to the living room and looked out the front window.

It was *him*.

Cade watched as a man wearing a brown leather jacket climbed out of a black car with a few dents and scratches. Noah stared at the house for a moment, then shoved his hands into his jacket pockets and walked to the front door.

When the doorbell rang, Cade hung back, unsure what to do or say. His mother answered the door, said a few things in a low tone that he couldn't hear, and then, after ten years, his father was there, standing in his living room, looking very tall and cool in his leather jacket.

And suddenly, everything changed. Cade no longer felt nervous, or even excited.

He was angry.

Ten *years* it had taken him to show up.

"Holy crap." Noah shot a look at his mom. "He looks just like me."

She flashed him one of those fake Mrs. Kramer smiles. "That probably wouldn't come as such a surprise if you'd been around before this."

Noah pointed to Cade. "Are we going to do this now, in front of the kid?"

"The *kid* was thinking the same thing," Cade interjected defiantly.

Both Noah and his mom looked over at him. Cade braced himself for the lecture—no sassing, always be respectful to adults—but none came. Instead, she nodded. "Well. I'll let you two talk."

With a wink of encouragement at Cade, she left them alone. A moment later, he heard the clinking of bowls in the kitchen.

Noah shifted awkwardly. "Talk. Right." He gestured to the couch. "Maybe we could sit down? I bet you have a lot of questions for me." He laughed at that, like this was so funny.

Cade followed Noah to the couch, thinking that his mom should've mentioned a fourth thing last night—that his father was a *douchebag*.

He sat on the opposite end of the couch, determined to look tough. He had lots of questions, all right, starting with one in particular. "Why haven't you come to see me before this?"

Noah blinked. "Sure. Okay. I respect a man who says what's on his mind." Another laugh.

Cade glared.

Noah cleared his throat. "Um, well, it's complicated, Cade. I was just a kid when your mother had you."

"She was the same age, but she still wanted me."

Noah flinched. "Christ, you don't pull any punches, do you?" He sighed. "I needed to figure things out with my life, I guess." He glanced over. "I know you don't understand that, but maybe someday when you're older, you will."

"Is that why you're here now? Because you figured things out?"

"You're like a lawyer with all these questions." Noah smiled. "Your mom told me last night how smart you are. You get that from her, you know."

Cade thought it was best to keep silent on that one. But *duh*, obviously. "You didn't answer my question," he pointed out.

"I'm trying to figure things out, Cade. I'm really trying."

There was another long silence.

"I heard you like football," Noah finally said. "You know, I used to play myself."

Cade tried to seem disinterested. "Were you any good?"

Noah cocked his head and took him in, sizing him up. "How about I show you?"

Startled by the offer, Cade looked around. "Right now?"

"Yep. Go grab your football. I'll meet you in the front yard." As if that was settled, he got up from the couch and headed out the door.

Not sure what else he was supposed to do, Cade went into his room and got his football. He stepped outside and saw Noah waiting on the sidewalk, smoking a cigarette.

He exhaled, then nodded at Cade. "What position do they got you at?"

"Quarterback."

He took one last drag, and then tossed the cigarette into the gutter. "Let me see you throw." He positioned himself at the far end of the lawn, only about ten yards away.

Cade stepped back to the driveway and threw. Without having to move an inch, Noah caught the ball neatly at his chest.

"Not bad," he said. "Now hit me again while I'm running."

"Mrs. Kramer says we're not supposed to run across her lawn."

"Is that right? Well, let's see if I can get her to make an exception." Football tucked under his arm, Noah walked up the path to Mrs. Kramer's front door and rang the bell. A few moments later, she answered.

Cade watched from his driveway as Noah said something, then gestured to the football. Then there was some smiling, and more talking, and to Cade's shock, Mrs. Kramer actually *laughed*. He didn't even know that was possible.

Shortly after that, Noah walked off with a wave. He moved fast and fired the ball at Cade.

"We're good to go," Noah said after Cade caught it.

And with those four simple words, Cade found himself playing football with his father on a crisp, fall afternoon. A moment that was so simple—two people just tossing a ball around—and yet so perfect he thought his face might crack from smiling so much.

He didn't want to like Noah—well, not mostly—but the guy *was* really good at football. Sure, his mom tried to help him practice, and sometimes Grandpa Morgan, too, but both of them missed his passes so much they spent half of the time digging around in Mrs. Kramer's bushes for the ball. And neither of them could ever keep his calls straight, so the other half of the time his mom would be standing on the sidewalk for a skinny post when she was *supposed* to be running up the middle after a handoff. But Noah . . . well, he got it just right.

A couple of times, Cade saw his mom peeking out the window to check on them, and he waved to let her know he was fine. He figured she was probably secretly relieved seeing them—now that his dad was back she didn't have to worry about doing football duty anymore. Probably, there were other things Noah could teach him, like how to fix cars and leaky dishwashers and furnaces so they didn't always have to call a repairman every time something went on the fritz. He bet Noah knew a lot of things like that.

After a couple of hours, when they both were so tired they could barely walk, Cade collapsed on the ground next to Noah. Noah pulled a pack of cigarettes and a lighter out of the back pocket of his jeans and lit one up.

"Your mom was right. You are good." He reached over and ruffled Cade's hair. "Give it time, you might even be better than me one day."

Cade's chest squeezed so tight with pride, all he could do was nod.

Noah rested his arms on his knees, the cigarette dangling between his fingers. "So listen. I've got a buddy who has two tickets he can't use to next Sunday's Bears game. He offered them to me, and I was thinking maybe you'd like to go."

"With you?" Cade asked.

Noah laughed. "Yeah, with me."

In his excitement, Cade could barely get the words out. "That'd be great!" He paused, then something inside him, something tentative and awkward and yet hopeful, made him go on. "Thanks, Dad."

Noah's expression changed, a momentary falter in his smile, before he nodded. "Sure, kid. No problem."

On Monday, Cade bragged to his whole fifth-grade class that his father was taking him to the Bears game that weekend. Even Sean, who'd gone to a few Cubs games that summer with his dad and brother, was impressed. By Saturday night he was so excited he could barely sit still through his mother's bedtime lecture about how he and Noah weren't allowed to go anywhere—and she meant *anywhere*—except to the game and back, and how she'd stuck extra quarters in the pocket of his jacket so he could call her from a pay phone "just in case."

The next morning, he got dressed and wolfed down his breakfast. The game started at noon, so Noah had said he'd pick him up at eleven. At ten forty-five, unable to restrain himself any longer, Cade sat by the living room window to wait.

At eleven fifteen, he was still waiting.

"He was late last time, too. He'll be here, Mom," he told her.

By noon, when the game had started, he knew.

Noah Garrity had given him a tryout, Cade's one and only chance to have a father.

And he'd failed.

CADE EXHALED, RUNNING his hand over his mouth as he stared out his office window. He'd buried his issues with Noah Garrity a long time ago, and they needed to stay buried.

Luckily, it was Friday evening, which meant he could leave work, pour himself a stiff drink at home, and forget all about—

He suddenly remembered.

Friday evening.

Shit.

Cade checked his watch, and saw that he was ten minutes late for his meeting with Brooke Parker. He thought about sending her a text message to say he couldn't make it, but she was probably already waiting for him at the restaurant, undoubtedly thinking up all the sweet-as-pie sarcastic barbs she was going to hurl at him when he finally showed up.

He couldn't decide if that made him more or less eager to go.

He grabbed his briefcase and shoved in a few files he wanted to review that weekend, then headed out the door to grab a cab. Bar Nessuno, one of Sterling's restaurants, was an Italian pizzeria and wine bar just off of Michigan Avenue. The street was a one-way going the opposite direction, and traffic was as bad as always on a Friday evening, so Cade had the driver drop him off a block away to save time.

He walked briskly to the restaurant and pushed through the door. Against the warm exposed brick décor, the first person he saw was Brooke. She was chatting with the hostess, looking exactly as he'd imagined her that afternoon—sophisticated and all-around sexy in her skirt and heels.

He approached her. "I'm late. I know," he cut her off the second she opened her mouth. "Sorry. It's been . . . a strange afternoon."

She gave him a long once-over. Belatedly, he realized he'd loosened his tie and had yanked open the top button of his shirt while ruminating over everything Zach had dumped on him earlier that day. And he was pretty sure his hair was standing on end from running his fingers through it. Not exactly the way he normally presented himself in a professional setting.

Cade braced himself for the inevitable quip or comment.

"You look like you could use a drink, Morgan." Then, unexpectedly, her expression softened. She cocked her head in the direction of the tables. "Shall we?"

Out of nowhere, Cade felt a sharp tug in his chest—like a sailboat bobbing around in rocky waters that was suddenly righted by a warm, calm breeze.

As they followed the hostess to their table, he glanced sideways at Brooke. "Thank you."

She met his gaze with a slight smile. "I've had days like that myself, Cade. Plenty of them."

Eleven

ALMOST IMMEDIATELY AFTER they'd been seated, undoubtedly having been alerted to Brooke's presence by the hostess, a waitress stopped by to introduce herself and take their drink orders.

"I'll have a bourbon and bitters." Brooke caught Cade's look of surprise. "House specialty."

Cade turned to the waitress. "In that case, make it two." He pushed aside his drink menu, his eyes never leaving Brooke.

Something had changed. She didn't know if it had anything to do with this "strange afternoon" he'd had, or if it was the simple logistics of their meeting—a cozy bar on a Friday evening—but there was a new undercurrent in the air between them. Something bold in his look that said they were playing a different game now.

And sitting across from him, taking in his strikingly hand-some appearance—the finger-raked hair and devil-may-care loosened tie—Brooke wasn't entirely sure she objected to the new rules.

"Thank you for agreeing to meet with me on such short notice," she led in.

"This mysterious favor." Cade stretched an arm across the back of the booth. "What is it you need from me?"

"A name."

"Whose name?"

Brooke lowered her voice, careful to make sure that none of the restaurant staff could hear her. "The name of an employee who hacked into Sterling's expense account database."

That seemed to pique his interest. "I'm listening."

She filled Cade in on the details, pausing momentarily when the waitress brought their cocktails. He listened without interrupting, occasionally taking a sip of his drink, as she laid out the details of the investigation conducted by Sterling's VP of security, and then explained how they'd gotten stuck after determining the hacker's IP address.

"Keith talked to an agent at the FBI office, who said it could take a while before anyone got back to us. I was hoping, maybe, you could speed up the process for us."

She waited hopefully as Cade considered this.

He set down his glass. "I'm not going to talk to the FBI about this. It's—"

"—too insignificant of a case," Brooke finished for him. She continued on, undaunted. "Look, I understand that this is small potatoes in the grand scheme of investigations the FBI and U.S. Attorney's Office handles. This jerk—whoever he is—didn't take any money or steal anyone's identity or anything." She leaned in. "But nevertheless, he broke into company records with the sole purpose of humiliating my boss. And yes, I consider Ian a friend so that ticks me off on a personal level, but it's more than that. This hacker is a bully. Only instead of writing his homophobic crap on the bathroom walls like he probably did in high school, he's taken the twenty-first-century approach and spewed his insults via an online database." She locked eyes with Cade. "I'm not expecting you to press charges, or even make an arrest. But I'd at least like the guy's name so I can fire his ass."

When she was done with her speech, Cade rested his arms on the table. "If you would've let me finish my sentence, the reason I'm not going to bring in the FBI is because I think this is something the Secret Service should handle."

Brooke sat back in the booth. "Oh. The Secret Service. Of course." She cocked her head. "Because, in addition to protecting the president, the Secret Service has jurisdiction over . . . something I probably learned in law school but am totally blanking on now."

"Crimes involving U.S. financial institutions."

She snapped her fingers. "Yes. That."

"Your bully hacked into a Citibank database," Cade said. "It's not exactly a national security issue, but I'll ask a Secret Service agent friend of mine to look into it. You said you have the IP address?"

"Yes, right here." She pulled a piece of paper out of her purse and handed it over.

"Good." Cade slid the piece of paper into his briefcase. "Give me a few days. You'll be able to fire his ass soon. And the rest of him, too."

Brooke smiled at that, pleasantly relieved—and a little surprised—that it had been that easy. "Thank you."

"You're welcome." Cade pointed, suddenly changing the subject. "You've finished your drink."

"So have you."

"Another round? My treat this time."

As if sensing the nature of their conversation, or perhaps simply attuned to the fact that the—gasp—*general counsel* was sitting with an empty glass before her, the waitress stepped up to their table. "Can I get you both another drink?"

"We were just discussing that very question," Cade said, still with his eyes on Brooke.

Just say no. Brooke had gotten what she'd come for that evening, and now it was time to grab her briefcase, get up out of that booth, and walk away.

And from the daring look in Cade's eyes, she knew he was waiting for her to do just that.

Never one to back down from any challenge, at least not

one coming from the mighty Cade Morgan, she turned to the waitress. "Another round would be great, thank you."

Cade smiled slyly as the waitress hurried off. "You better pace yourself with that bourbon there."

Brooke eased back in the booth, not the slightest bit concerned. "I wine and dine people for a living, Morgan. You just worry about yourself."

OKAY, FINE. SHE may have been a little buzzed.

Just a smidge.

Clearly, that had to be the case, because she felt warm and good and—shockingly—was enjoying being around Cade.

They'd been at the restaurant for over an hour. A while back, the manager had come by to say hello to Brooke and had sent over a complimentary selection of antipasti. Brooke had ordered a glass of wine with that, and Cade had gone with another bourbon, and then somehow they'd just rolled into dinner—a hand-tossed pizza straight out of the restaurant's wood-burning oven.

"I have to give credit where credit is due," Cade said, helping himself to another slice. "You guys at Sterling know your way around food."

She took another piece herself. No disagreement there. "There are far worse places to work than for a restaurant company."

"Is this the way it is every time you eat at a Sterling restaurant?" Cade asked. "Everyone hopping around, making sure you're happy?"

"I don't know if I'd say *hopping*, exactly."

He threw her a look. "Please. You know you love it."

"This coming from a man who brags about having the Secret Service on speed dial."

"Don't forget the FBI, DEA, ATF, and IRS, too." He grinned before taking a bite of pizza.

"I rest my case." Brooke chewed thoughtfully for a moment. "Actually it's gotten better when I drop by the restaurants. In the beginning, I think everyone hated me. I was the first GC

Ian had ever hired, so when I came on board people didn't know what to expect. It took me about a year to convince them that I wasn't *looking* for problems—that my job is to help them when problems do arise."

Cade played with his glass, thinking this over. "I've been wondering something. Don't take this the wrong way."

"Never in the history of humankind has a man ever managed to *not* say something offensive after that lead-in, but if you want to take your chances, Morgan, be my guest."

The corners of his mouth curved in a smile. "Why are you single?"

Well, then.

Brooke reached for her wineglass and took a sip, making him wait before she answered. "Who says I'm single?"

"Vaughn. He deduced it from the fact that there aren't any pictures of a guy or kids in your office."

"You were talking about me with Agents Huxley and Roberts?"

"You may or may not have come up."

"I see. And what else did you three scamps say when you were gossiping in your little knitting circle?"

His eyes danced with amusement, but his gaze remained trained on hers. A prosecutor intent on getting his answer. "You didn't answer my question."

No, she hadn't. And while part of Brooke was tempted to move this conversation along to a different topic, there was another part of her that, admittedly, was a little curious herself.

She sat back in the booth, holding her wineglass with one hand as she faced off against him. "I'll tell you what. I'll answer that question if you will."

"How do you know that I'm single?"

"Because no man would ever ask a single woman that kind of quasi-flirtatious question if he was already seeing somebody. At least, not somebody he respected." Brooke took a sip of her wine. "So you're either disrespectful to women, or single."

The corners of his mouth curved. *Touché.* "I'm single." With that admission, he waited for her answer.

Brooke tried to appear nonchalant. "Apparently, I work too hard. According to the Hot OB, that means I'm not a 'big picture kind of girl.'" She saw Cade's jaw tense, but he said nothing as she continued. "Oh, and dating me is like being in a relationship with a guy, because I don't complain about not being taken out enough."

"No offense, but the Hot OB sounds like an asshole."

"He wasn't the first guy with that list of grievances." Brooke bit her lip, not having meant to admit that last part. Must've been the wine. "All right. Now it's your turn."

Cade took a sip of his bourbon. "I'm emotionally unavailable."

Brooke fought back a smile at the matter-of-fact way he said it. "Is that right?"

"According to my ex-girlfriends, yes. And I use sarcasm as a defense mechanism."

Brooke pointed to herself. "What do you know? Me, too."

Cade tipped his glass at her. "So if you and I got together, we could probably go our entire relationship without ever saying anything meaningful at all."

"Yes, although you and I would never get together since we don't even like each other."

"True." Cade gazed at her across the candlelit table. "Good thing we got that straight."

Brooke felt a few flutters in her stomach at the way he was looking at her right then. "It sure is."

WHEN THEY LEFT the restaurant an hour after that, Brooke was pretty sure they were *both* feeling warm and good. After the pizza, they'd had one last round of drinks while sharing lawyer war stories and, not surprisingly, trying to outdo one another with the funniest anecdotes.

At some point as he walked her home, Brooke realized that her non-date with Cade had been the most datelike evening she'd had in a long time. Granted, she'd met him for work purposes, but she felt more relaxed and at ease with him than she had since . . . she couldn't remember when. She hadn't been worrying about where things between them were going, or any of that other relationship rigmarole, nor had she been trying to impress him. And, given Cade's seemingly endless ability to irritate her, it was pretty safe to say he felt the same way. They'd just been two people, having drinks and sharing good stories and a pizza on a Friday night.

"Lucky you, being able to walk to work from home," Cade said in the elevator, heading up to her floor.

"Where do you live?"

"Lakeview."

"My first apartment in the city was in Lakeview. I still miss—" Brooke stopped, suddenly realizing something. "Wait. Why are you in this elevator?"

"Because . . . it's the one going up to your apartment?"

"And why are you going up to my apartment?" They'd been so busy talking when they'd walked into her lobby, she hadn't paid any attention to the fact that he'd come up with her instead of saying good-bye downstairs.

Cade contemplated her question. "Huh. That's curious."

With a *ding!* the elevator arrived at Brooke's floor. She stepped out. When he followed her, she knew.

"Which one is you?" he asked.

The butterflies in her stomach, the ones that had started fluttering around back at the restaurant, were now doing cartwheels. Still, she kept it cool, determined not to let him see that, yes, he had her a little flustered. "2506."

She led the way, digging around in her briefcase for her keys. When she got to her apartment, she turned around and faced Cade. "I'm not inviting you in."

He stepped closer. "That's not why I got on the elevator. You know that."

Yes, she did. Otherwise, she would've stopped him in his tracks before he'd gotten off. She raised her chin. "Then why?" she asked, even though she already had a feeling she knew the answer.

He closed the gap between them, his eyes dark blue and smoky. "I got on that elevator for this."

He lowered his mouth and kissed her.

Quickly, Brooke realized that despite any other faults, Cade Morgan *knew* how to kiss. He teased her lips open, his mouth seductively moving over hers in a way that left her tingling down to her toes. She slid her hands up his chest—*wow*, he had some serious muscles—and allowed herself one teeny, tiny moment to give in to this . . . whatever between them.

He reached up to cup her face, deepening the kiss as his tongue wound hotly around hers. He explored her mouth possessively, a low rumble in his chest when she responded by nipping playfully at his lower lip.

They heard a *ding!* down the hallway, as an elevator arrived at her floor.

Cade pulled back, his gaze heated as he traced his thumb along her bottom lip. "Good night, Brooke Parker."

He turned and left just as a middle-aged couple, Brooke's neighbors in 2508, passed by. Cade nodded at them with a pleasant "Hello," then strode off with the strap of his briefcase slung over his shoulder.

Brooke watched him leave, silently admiring his tall, broad-shouldered frame, and trying to muster up more irritation over the fact that he'd somehow managed to get in the last word once again.

Twelve

THE NEXT WEEK, not surprisingly, was a busy one for Brooke. On the first of the month, Sterling would be taking over the food service at the Staples Center, which meant she needed to work nearly 'round the clock to complete the employment contracts for the managerial employees they'd hired.

That was her project for this week. Next week, she would have to oversee the company's yearly anti-harassment and discrimination training, which was mandatory for all staff at Sterling's eight Chicago restaurants. After that, it would be something else—there was always something else. Not that she was complaining.

Well, not mostly, anyway.

Shortly after four o'clock that afternoon, Ford called to check in on her. "You're still planning on making it to the game tomorrow, right?"

Brooke balanced the phone against her shoulder, so she could talk while signing off on the expense reports that Lindsey had prepared for her. "I should be good to go. I'm trying to wrap everything up tonight so that I only need to work on Sunday this weekend."

"Do you want to meet for lunch before the game?" he asked.

"Yes. But not at Murphy's," she said. "I got two beers dumped on me last time we went there before a game."

"All part of the experience."

"She who giveth the skybox tickets gets to picketh the restaurant."

Ford grumbled at that. "Fine. But not Southport Grocery," he said, referring to a cute brunch spot a few blocks from Wrigley Field, one she'd dragged him to on several occasions.

"Come on. They do awesome egg-white omelettes."

"Remember that best-friend straw you pulled, the one with the penis attached? That straw does not do *brunch* before the Cubs/Sox game."

Lindsey stuck her head into Brooke's office, interrupting the debate. "You have a visitor. A Mr. Cade Morgan."

That was a surprise. Brooke had been expecting a phone call, not a personal visit. They hadn't spoken since their non-date last Friday, although Cade had crossed her mind a time or two. That kiss had been good—*really* good—but realistically, it wasn't as if things were going anywhere between them. Like her, he obviously had issues with relationships, given the things he'd told her the other night about his so-called "emotional unavailability."

"Send him in," she told Lindsey, before turning back to her conversation with Ford. "I have to run. I've got a business meeting to get to." Technically, that wasn't even a lie. She and Cade *did* have a professional relationship. Mostly. "I'll e-mail you later about lunch tomorrow."

She hung up the phone, then caught herself checking her hair in the window's reflection before remembering—oh, right—she wasn't trying to impress Cade.

"Here you go, Mr. Morgan," she heard Lindsey say, followed by a familiar rich, masculine voice thanking her secretary. Cade strolled into Brooke's office a half second later, looking dashing and handsome as ever in his gray three-piece suit.

Oh, Lord.

She'd always had a weakness for three-piece suits.

From the doorway, Lindsey smiled at Brooke. "If you need anything, Brooke, just let me know." Behind Cade's back, she silently mouthed one word: *Wow*.

"Thank you, Lindsey." Yes, fine, the man was hot. Brooke stood up from her desk, thinking it would be best to keep the door shut. She assumed Cade was there to talk about Sterling's hacker, which she'd been keeping on the down-low.

As soon as she shut the door, Cade flashed her that thousand-watt smile. "Ms. Parker. How good of you to see me."

She *so* was going to regret kissing him, she could already tell. Clearly, he felt that momentary indiscretion gave him leave to look her over, right there in her office, with a very bold, very familiar gaze.

"Mr. Morgan," she said, emphasizing with her tone that they needed to keep this *professional*. "I assume you have some information for me?"

He eased back against her bookshelf, making himself right at home. "I have that name you were looking for. Eric Hieber."

Eric Hieber. Brooke rubbed her hands together eagerly. Ooh, she so was going to fire his computer-hacking, homophobic ass.

As soon as she figured out who in the heck he was.

"Eric Hieber . . . that's not ringing any bells," she mused to herself, passing by Cade to look up the name on her computer.

"He's a waiter at Reilly's on Grand," Cade told her. "Twenty-four years old, no priors, been with Sterling for two years. Good friends with Darrell Williams, one of the tech support guys here in the corporate office, who let it slip about a month ago that he'd been bombarded with work doing a software rollout that, among other things, temporarily switched everyone in corporate over to a default password. Hieber insists that Williams has no idea that he'd hacked into the company's database. He claimed at first that the whole thing was just a joke, although, when pressed, he admitted that he waited on Ian Sterling and a male guest at Reilly's about five weeks ago, observed that the two men were openly affectionate with each other, and said he was shocked that, quote, 'A cool dude like Ian Sterling was into that homo crap.'"

When he'd finished, Brooke stared at him in amazement. "How do you know all this?"

"The Secret Service picked up Hieber this morning. I'm told he started crying during questioning when they mentioned the words 'federal charges' and 'bank fraud.'"

Brooke was still trying to catch up. "Hold on. Does that mean your office is taking on the case?"

"I've arranged for a junior AUSA in my group to handle the matter under my supervision," Cade said. "I suspect Hieber will end up with probation, but I'm guessing he'll think twice before ever again hacking into a bank's database as a 'joke.'" His eyes skimmed over her, abruptly changing the subject. "And for the record, you look hot as hell in that dress."

Brooke found herself going a little warm from his openly appreciative gaze. She'd put on a sleeveless red tailored dress that morning, mostly because she'd wanted an excuse to wear her red high-heeled shoes again. "This old thing."

At her coy tone, Cade's eyes flashed with undisguised interest. "Have dinner with me tomorrow."

His directness took Brooke by surprise. She'd expected more quips and quasi-flirtatious sarcasm, not to be asked on an actual *date*. "I'm not sure that's a good idea." Actually, certain parts of her were just fine with the idea of spending the evening with Cade. But other parts, the ones that were still thinking despite the blinding hotness of the cobalt blue eyes and three-piece suit, were remembering that she'd vowed to stay away from any emotional entanglements for a while.

"I was there when we kissed, you know," he said in response to her hesitation. "I'm pretty sure you liked it. A lot." He took a step closer, so that she was trapped between him and her desk.

She put her hand on his chest to stop him. "Easy there, cowboy. This is a place of busin—" she paused, pushing her palm against what was undeniably a very firm pectoral muscle. "Seriously, why *are* you so built for a lawyer?"

"I work out with Vaughn at the FBI gym," he said with a casual shrug. "The pool there is good for my shoulder."

"What's wrong with your shoulder?" she asked.

For some reason, Cade seemed surprised by her question. "Just an old college injury."

Before she could ask anything further, the phone on Brooke's desk began to ring. "I probably should get that," she said.

Cade remained standing right where he was. "You haven't said yes to dinner yet."

True. But she hadn't said no, either.

Yes, fine. Cade had grown on her a little. He was smart and funny, and he'd gone above and beyond with the Eric Hieber matter. But even if, for argument's sake, she was tempted to go out with Cade, she'd heard enough about Ford's endless string of hookups to know there were certain rules to the casual-dating dance. Like maybe she was supposed to suggest drinks instead, but then again they'd already had dinner on Friday. *But*, maybe it didn't count as an actual dinner if it had started off as a business meet—

Brooke's phone rang a second time. Too much to think through, too little time. "I really should take that. How about if I get back to you about dinner?"

Cade looked her over, the long, slow look of a man not accustomed to waiting for something he wanted. "All right. The offer stays open for twenty-four hours."

"What happens after twenty-four hours?"

"My fragile ego will be irrevocably wounded."

She couldn't help but smile at that. "I doubt that's even remotely possible."

"Maybe not. But it doesn't matter." He stepped closer and, with one hand, brushed Brooke's hair aside. He lowered his head and whispered in her ear. "You're going to say yes."

His eyes held hers as he pulled back. "Have a good afternoon, Ms. Parker."

THE REST OF the afternoon flew by with a steady stream of conference calls and e-mails. It was after six o'clock when Brooke finally came up for air again, having a few free minutes to scarf down an energy bar before jumping on yet another call.

This time, she would be speaking with a partner in the Los Angeles office of the firm they used for employment matters, to discuss some modifications they needed to make, per California law, to the contracts they had with two current managers they planned to move over to the Staples Center. Probably not the most fun way to spend a Friday evening, but Brooke planned to make up for it tomorrow at the Cubs/Sox game.

Sterling's offices were quiet, everyone else having gone home for the weekend. She liked the office when it was calm like this—it gave her an opportunity to think without the usual interruptions.

And right now . . . she was thinking about Cade.

You're going to say yes.

The man was too confident. Part of her found this irritating, but another part of her found it admittedly intriguing. In her daily life, as general counsel for Sterling, *she* was often the one making the decisions. So it was refreshing to be around someone who challenged her the way Cade did.

But.

Before she even considered accepting his invitation, she needed to figure out the ground rules. She hadn't done the casual-dating thing since college, and from what she'd gathered, it was a whole different world out there now that she was in her thirties.

With that in mind, she quickly dialed up Ford, the expert, thinking he was just the person she needed to talk to. Unfortunately, he didn't answer his cell phone. Brooke left him a message, then sat at her desk, staring distractedly at her computer. Her gaze sharpened, coming into focus as she realized what she had before her, literally at her fingertips.

The power of the Internet.

Quickly, she checked the clock on her desk and saw that she had ten minutes until her conference call. Plenty of time to do a little "research." She swung around in the desk chair and pulled her trusty iPad out of her briefcase—no way was she doing this on her work computer—then fired up the browser and quickly Googled "rules of casual dating."

3,730,000 results in 1.8 seconds.

Bingo.

She scrolled through the links until she found one that sounded like it got right to the point, from a popular women's magazine. "Ten Rules of Casual Sex." Brooke tapped on the link and began reading.

> 1. *Be candid about your intentions from the start. Make sure he knows you aren't looking for a serious relationship.*

Fair enough, she agreed. *Be honest. No problem.*

> 2. *Never go into a casual relationship with expectations. Remember that both of you are free to walk out at any time.*
> 3. *Keep it simple and stress-free. And have fun!*

Brooke rolled her eyes, beginning to think that this was really basic stuff, when the remaining rules caught her eye.

> 4. *In a casual relationship, all arrangements should be made only via text message. And the dirtier the message, the better!*
> 5. *Be sure to alternate text messages with him so that mutual interest is continually reestablished.*
> 6. *No personal gifts except for sex toys and massage oils.*
> 7. *A minimum of eighty percent of your time together should be spent naked or partially naked.*
> 8. *Don't call him just to say hi.*
> 9. *Never take a bath together.*
> 10. *Under no circumstances should you continue to hook up if one of you—and only one of you—wants something more.*

Brooke scrolled through the rules, not sure if she should laugh or be very, very afraid. *Eighty* percent of her time in a casual relationship should be spent naked? Did that include sleeping? Showering? But no baths, no sir-ee, because those were distinctly off-limits.

This had to be a joke. No personal gifts except for sex toys? Sure, because nothing said "I like but don't love you" like a "just because" vibrator.

Ridiculous. She'd save her questions for Ford—frankly, this advice seemed a little shady.

Brooke's phone started ringing. Time for her conference call.

Seeing that there was a three-page article following "Ten Rules of Casual Sex"—oh, now she *had* to read the rest, just for kicks—she decided to e-mail the link to her personal account, thinking she'd finish the article with a nice glass of wine when she got home. Not wanting to keep the guys in L.A. waiting, and a pro at multitasking, she answered the phone with an efficient "Brooke Parker," and—

Shit!—accidentally tapped the button to "like" the article on Facebook instead of sharing the link via e-mail.

Oh, no, no, no.

This was not good.

"Uh . . . hi. Hang on for a moment, guys," she stammered. So much for being a pro at multitasking.

A box popped up with her Facebook picture, prompting her to add a comment to the link for the "Ten Rules of Casual Sex."

She instantly hit "cancel."

And just like that, the whole thing went away.

Whew.

Now *that* had been a near disaster. No more multitasking at work, she vowed. Like texting while driving, trying to do a conference call while researching the rules of casual sex could only lead to big-time trouble.

With a deep, calming breath, Brooke went back to her conference call, where the L.A. guys were waiting. The call lasted just under a half hour, ending with a promise from the other lawyers to get her the revised employment agreements by Monday afternoon.

Afterward, she wrapped up a few loose ends, and then packed up her briefcase. Before shutting down her computer, she checked her work e-mail and saw, with relief, that no emergencies had popped up in the last half hour.

She was good to go.

It was a gorgeous evening, perfect for the five-block walk to her high-rise. She strolled along Michigan Avenue, thinking about her elevator ride with Cade the other night—and more important, that kiss at her front door.

Perhaps, per the rules, she should add in an eighty percent naked clause to his dinner offer. She smiled, thinking that certainly would make for an interesting evening.

As Brooke entered her building, she nodded hello to the lobby security guard before stepping into the elevator with five other people. Seeing that they had three stops to make before her floor, she pulled out her cell phone to check her e-mail.

She had fifty-two new messages to her personal e-mail account.

That was odd. Especially since every message was a notification that someone had posted a comment on her Facebook wall.

Quickly, Brooke began clicking through the messages. All from men.

I'M GAME IF YOU ARE, BABE!

LIKE! LIKE! LIKE!

TEN RULES EVERY WOMAN SHOULD LIVE BY!

PICK ME!!!!!!!!

Brooke's stomach hit the floor of the elevator.

Oh. My. God. She clicked over to her Facebook profile and saw the link right there in black-and-white on her wall, generously shared with all five hundred and twenty-nine of her closest "friends."

She'd favorited the damn "Ten Rules of Casual Sex."

Thirteen

FORD HAD ACTUAL tears in his eyes.

He was laughing so hard, he could barely get the words out. " 'Brooke Parker shared a link. *Ten Rules of Casual Sex*,' " he said, repeating the update that he had received on his Facebook home page last night, along with her five hundred and twenty-eight other "friends."

"Yeah, yeah. It's soooo funny."

"I should thank you for the advice," he said. "Because all along I'd only been spending *seventy* percent of my time naked when hooking up. Sounds like I need to start bare-assing it more often around the ladies."

Brooke gestured with a French fry. "Just so I know, how long can I expect the comedy routine to go on?" They were halfway through their lunch already and there'd been no sign that things were letting up anytime soon.

"Oh, you'll be hearing about this until we're old and gray." Ford went right back to it. "Brooke Parker wants everyone to know that you should never take a bath with a man unless you're ready to take his last name. Showers only, girls!"

"That's clever. Take a bath, take his name. I like how you

strung that all together." Brooke spread more mustard on her club sandwich. "You know, I didn't actually write the stupid rules."

"No, you just recommended them to everyone and their mother."

Yes, she was painfully aware of that. "I told you already, I hit 'cancel.'"

"All that means is that you posted the link without leaving a comment," he informed her, most belatedly. "But you still needed to go in and delete it if you wanted to remove it from your wall."

"Thank you, Mr. Tech Support. I realize that now." Last night, as soon as she'd gotten out of the elevator, she'd taken down the article. Unfortunately, that hadn't been soon enough, and her Facebook account had been hopping all night and morning. "Do you realize that I've gotten two hundred and thirty-seven friend requests since last night? All from men." Because the lascivious schmoes on *her* page had naturally "liked" her status, which meant that all of their other lascivious schmoe friends could see her original link and wanted in on the action. "I've been asked out on more dates in the last eighteen hours than I have in the last eighteen years."

"I can't fathom why."

She threw Ford a look when he started laughing again. "It really isn't funny."

"It really is." He smiled at her glare. "If I break out a few bare-chested pictures of Ryan Gosling on my phone, will that help take the sting off?"

Brooke thought that over. "It might."

"That was supposed to be sarcastic." Ford picked up his cheeseburger. "Why were you reading about the rules of casual sex, anyway?"

"I'd planned to ask you for some advice, but when you didn't pick up your cell I decided to kill some time on the Internet before a conference call."

"Advice on what?" Ford gave her a sly look, putting it together. "Wait a second . . . Brooke Parker, are you having sex with somebody?"

"A little louder, Ford. I'm not sure the people all the way in the back of the bar heard you." Luckily, the place was crowded and noisy, and half of the people there were already tipsy in advance of the big game. She lowered her voice. "And no, I'm not having sex with anyone."

"Ah. But there's someone you *want* to be having sex with."

"Let's say that I'm entertaining the possibility."

"Really?" Ford appeared intrigued. "Tell me more. Who's the guy?"

"Someone I met through work," Brooke said. "He asked me to have dinner with him tonight. I haven't said yes. Yet."

"But you're going to?"

She smiled coyly at that. "Perhaps. After making him wait another"—she checked her watch—"two hours and six minutes."

Ford looked confused. "Why two hours and six minutes? I don't get it."

"Sorry. Just an inside joke."

Brooke paused in surprise as soon as the words came out. Ford raised an eyebrow. For twenty years, *he* had been the guy she had inside jokes with.

"Interesting," he said.

"It's not a big deal," Brooke said quickly. "It's just dinner."

"Got it." Ford took a sip of his Diet Coke. He set it down, giving her a knowing look.

"Really, Ford. Just dinner." She watched as he simply nodded, still with the smug look. "I don't like you sometimes."

He laughed that off, having heard it for years. "I love you, too, Parker."

"SOMEWHERE ELSE YOU need to be?"

Cade glanced over at Vaughn, who'd caught him checking his watch. "Just debating whether I want to grab another beer now or wait until the next inning."

"Nice excuse. Except that's the second time you've checked your watch since we got here."

Huxley chimed in from the seat on Vaughn's left. "The third

time. He also checked when you were flagging down the hot-dog vendor."

Cade grumbled under his breath. Damn FBI agents—they didn't miss a trick. "It must be so exhausting for you two to have these amazing powers of perception that you can never turn off," he said sarcastically.

Vaughn grinned. "Yes. But it also makes us unbelievably cool."

"I'm okay with it, too," Huxley agreed matter-of-factly.

More grumbling ensued.

Admittedly, Cade was already a little on the prickly side. In just twenty minutes—not that he was counting—his dinner offer to Brooke would expire and he hadn't heard so much as a peep from her. Was she really not interested? He didn't buy it. Beneath all the quips, there was chemistry between them—he felt it, and she did, too.

Time would soon tell just how right he was about that.

Their professional relationship was over. The Sanderson case, the hacker at Sterling she'd asked him to track down—all of that had been resolved. They had no reason to see each other again unless, simply, they wanted to. He'd made his interest clear and now the ball was in her court.

Cade noticed Huxley and Vaughn looking at him expectantly, waiting for an answer. "I've got an offer on the table that expires soon. Just waiting to hear back from the other side," he said by way of explanation.

Vaughn seemed satisfied with that answer. Underneath the jokes, he was as committed to his job as Cade was to his. "Guess there's not much else you can do except sit back and enjoy the game, then." He gestured to the lush green outfield that stretched out before them, flanked by Wrigley Field's distinctive ivy-covered walls. Eighty degrees and clear blue skies made it the perfect day for baseball—although for today, the day that pitted Chicago brother against brother, the stadium would've been packed even in inclement weather.

Cade had scored tickets to the Cubs/Sox game months ago, and Vaughn was right—he needed to forget about Brooke and enjoy the afternoon. They had good-quality man stuff going on: baseball on a sunny day, cold beers, and hot dogs. With that thought, he flagged down a beer vendor and bought another round for all three of them. Huxley and Vaughn were off duty and unarmed that day—FBI policy prohibited agents from consuming alcohol while carrying—which meant they all could relax and bask in the pure, feel-good fun of America's pastime.

The inning was an exciting one, first with a base hit and then a two-run homer that made the crowd go wild. Cade was on his feet amidst the screaming and cheering, beer in one hand and high-fiving Vaughn and Huxley and the perfect strangers sitting in the row in front of them, when his cell phone vibrated in the front pocket of his shorts.

He pulled out the phone and saw he had a new text message from Brooke Parker. One word.

YES.

Cade noticed the time of the message and realized she'd conveniently accepted his dinner invitation one minute before it expired. He couldn't decide if that made him want to laugh out loud or throttle his cell phone—perhaps both—but he did know one thing.

This woman drove him crazy.

Standing beside him, Vaughn tapped him on the shoulder. "So?" He raised his voice over the crowd's roar and gestured to Cade's phone. "Good news?"

Cade tucked the phone back into his pocket. "She said yes."

Vaughn blinked—clearly having expected Cade to say something else—then threw out his hands. He had no clue what they were talking about, but right then everything was a cause for celebration. "She said yes! Hell, yeah!" He grabbed Huxley and pointed to Cade, shouting over the crowd. "She said yes."

"Sweet," Huxley said, tapping his beer to Cade's. "Who said yes?"

"Brooke Parker. I'm seeing her tonight."

"Fuck you," Vaughn said, somewhat in awe. "I *knew* it. You've been digging her from the moment she told you to shove your obstruction of justice threats up your ass."

"What can I say? I'm a sucker for the shy, quiet types."

"When did all this happen?" Vaughn asked.

"We met for drinks last Friday to discuss a criminal matter related to Sterling. Things progressed from there."

"Is that right?" Vaughn looked at him slyly. "Just how far did they progress?"

"Still not comfortable talking about Brooke this way," Huxley interjected.

Cade held back a smile, grateful for the excuse to change the subject. For whatever reason, he didn't feel like engaging in locker room talk about Brooke. "Huxley's right. Try to keep it classy, Vaughn."

Vaughn studied him for a moment. Seven years they'd been best friends, and they knew each other well. "You like her."

Cade took a nonchalant sip of his beer. "Just watch the game."

"Evading the question," Huxley said under his breath to Vaughn. "I think we got our answer, Agent Roberts."

"We sure did, Agent Huxley," Vaughn said.

Cade shook his head.

He really needed to get some non-FBI friends.

IN THE STERLING skybox, Brooke smiled when Cade's response came in a few minutes after her text message.

ABOUT DAMN TIME.

Quickly, she wrote back. WAS I CLOSE TO THE DEADLINE? OOPS.

OOPS, MY ASS. I'LL BE AT YOUR PLACE AT 7:00.

7:30, she texted immediately.

OF COURSE YOU'D SAY 7:30.

Brooke laughed at that, perfectly able to hear him saying the words. NEED TIME TO CHANGE AFTER CUBS/SOX, she explained. NOW STOP DISTRACTING ME—I'M TRYING TO WATCH A BASEBALL GAME.

There was a pause, then he texted back, WHERE ARE YOU SITTING?

Brooke shook her head. Such a guy thing to ask, wanting

to know how good her seats were. SKYBOX, she wrote. TO THE RIGHT OF HOME PLATE.

She'd just hit "send" when Ford's voice came over her shoulder.

"What are you acting all secretive about?" Sitting in the seat next to her, Ford tried to peek at her phone. "Sending dirty text messages to the mystery man, perhaps? Remind me again, which of the rules of casual sex was that? Number Five?"

"Still, with the rules?"

"This is payback," Ford said. "How many times have you mocked me for the time I accidentally drunk-dialed you instead of Cara Patterson my sophomore year of college?"

From the row behind them, Charlie let out a bark of laughter. "Man, I love that story."

Brooke held her cell phone to her ear, doing an imitation of Ford's drunken slur that night. "Hey, babe—my roomatez wen' to after-hours. Got the ho' plaze to myself. How 'bout you come over for some strawburry margaritas?"

Charlie cracked up, while Tucker, who sat in the seat next to Charlie, chimed in. "Did we ever figure out why it was strawberry margaritas?"

Ford waved off their laughter. "The TV was on when I called . . . I think I'd seen a commercial for Chili's . . . it seemed like a good suggestion at the time." He pointed at Brooke. "And you didn't exactly help the situation."

Brooke feigned innocence. "Why? Because I pretended to be Cara and told you that I'd be right over?"

"No, because you pretended to be Cara and told me you wanted to pour the margarita all over my body and lick up every drop."

"Certainly explains why Tuck and I later found you passed out cold on the kitchen floor, buck-ass naked, with one hand wrapped around a bowlful of strawberries," Charlie said.

"I don't think we even had a blender back then," Tucker mused.

"No, we didn't. Something I figured out after I was already naked, waiting for 'Cara' to show up," Ford said with a dirty look at Brooke.

"Poor Ford," she said. "Naked and cold on the kitchen floor, with nothing but a bowlful of strawberries and X-rated, tequila-soaked dreams. Truly tragic."

He put his arm around her. "And this, Parker, is why the Facebook story will never die. Ever."

Just then, Brooke's phone rang with a new text message.

"The mystery man chimes again," Ford said as Brooke reached for her cell.

Brooke read the text message Cade had sent her, and pulled back in surprise.

HOPE THE GUY IN THE STRIPED SHIRT KNOWS YOU ALREADY HAVE PLANS TONIGHT.

"He's here," Brooke said out loud.

"Who's here? The mystery man?" Ford asked.

"He can see us." Brooke leaned forward in her seat and peered over the skybox railing to the crowd below. There were thousands of people in the lower deck of the stadium.

Her phone rang, and she saw that it was Cade.

"To your right," he said when she answered her phone. His voice was husky in her ear. "Who's the guy?"

"Just a friend." Brooke stood up and leaned against the railing, her eyes skimming the stands.

"Farther down the first base line. Nope, not that close to the dugout."

She looked farther to her right. Still no sign of him. "You're enjoying this, aren't you?"

"Definitely. You're getting warmer now. Warmer . . . Look for Huxley's glaringly white polo shirt."

That should help, considering most of the crowd was dressed in Cubs and Sox T-shirts. A few rows back, Brooke finally spotted them, first Huxley—wow, that really was a white shirt—then Vaughn, who waved at her, and finally Cade.

He was too far away for her to see his eyes, but she felt his gaze on her nevertheless. It was a little strange at first, seeing him out of a suit and wearing a simple gray T-shirt and cargo shorts instead.

So this was what the mighty Cade Morgan looked like when he wasn't being a tough-guy prosecutor.

Not bad.

"If that had been a Sox shirt, I would've had to cancel dinner," he said in her ear as they faced each other across the
crowded baseball stadium, referring to the Cubs T-shirt she wore.

She smiled. Funny coincidence, them being at the same
baseball game on her one day off in ages. Perhaps it was a
sign. "How are those seats down there?" Cade and the two
FBI agents sat in the lower deck, in the sun, about halfway
up the first base line.

"Not bad. But not as good as the seats up there, I'd bet,"
he said.

Well, yes. Not to toot her own horn or anything, but the
skybox was pretty awesome. Eight seats overlooking home
plate, with a door that led to an air-conditioned private suite
complete with couches, a plasma television, and a kitchen
stocked with wine, beer, top-shelf liquor, and everything from
hamburgers and hot dogs to beef tenderloin and shrimp—all
courtesy of Sterling Restaurants.

"Although, now that you mention it, I am getting a little
concerned about Huxley," Cade added. "The poor guy's probably going to get a hell of a sunburn out here. Seeing how he's
pretty much the whitest man in America."

Brooke watched as Huxley, clearly having overheard the
comment, shot Cade a look and said something she couldn't
pick up over the phone.

"Well, I would really hate for Agent Huxley to suffer," she
said. "Especially since I happen to have a few extra seats in
this skybox."

"Is that an invitation?"

"I suppose it is."

"Good." Cade's voice dropped lower, adding one last thing
before hanging up. "And tell your friend in the striped shirt
that he's in my seat."

Fourteen

"ARE YOU GOING to tell us anything about this mystery man before he shows up?" Ford winked at Brooke. "If you want, I can give him the lowdown on your new approach to relationships. That the only gifts you're accepting these days are sex toys and massage oils."

"You mention those rules, and I'll have the Wrigley Field security team haul you out of this skybox so fast your head will spin."

"It would almost be worth it," Ford said with a chuckle. "Except then I'd miss the dessert cart."

"When is that coming, anyway? I *love* the dessert cart," Tucker chimed in from the back row.

"Hey now, we can't be wasting our time talking about dessert," Charlie said. "We need to start planning all the questions we want to ask the mystery man. Gotta grill the guy to make sure he's good enough for Brooke."

Brooke realized she needed to cut them off at the pass. Ford, Charlie, and Tucker tended to get a little weirdly protective of her whenever she brought a new guy around—which was bad enough when she was actually dating the man in question. But Cade was just a friend. Of sorts. Friend-ish. "I appreciate it, guys. But I think you can skip the interrogation this time. I haven't even had dinner with him yet."

"I want to play the part of the hard-ass friend today," Tucker said. "You know, just sit in the corner and glare at him the whole time. See if he crumbles."

"I've seen your hard-ass face, Tuck," Charlie said. "Mostly, you just look constipated. Ford, you'd better do the glaring."

"No glaring, and no hard-ass routines." Brooke said definitively. "No offense, but I doubt it would work, anyway. He's a prosecutor. He works with the FBI, DEA, and Secret Service all the time."

"Great," Ford said, rolling his eyes. "Now he's some hot-shot lawyer type."

"Hey. *I* am a hotshot lawyer type," Brooke said.

"Yeah, but it's different since you're a girl. It's cute."

She threw him a look. "You did not just say that."

"I don't think I like the sound of this guy," Tucker declared, out of the blue.

Brooke threw up her hands in exasperation. "You haven't even met him. Besides, you three don't like any of the men I introduce you to. You didn't even like the Hot OB."

"The Hot OB was a douche," Charlie said.

"This mystery man better not be another douche, Brooke," Ford warned. "I can't spend six innings trapped in a skybox with a douche."

Truly, she was losing brain cells just listening to this crap. "Seriously, if I were here with girlfriends, right now I'd be drinking daiquiris and talking about which of the players has the cutest butt."

Ford chuckled. "All right, we'll play nice. What's the mystery man's name, anyway?"

"Cade Morgan," she said.

"Get out of here," Charlie said in shock.

Ford pulled back in surprise. "Cade Morgan?" He looked her over for a moment, and then grinned approvingly. "Well done, you."

Okay . . . that was kind of an odd reaction. "You boys have a thing for assistant U.S. attorneys I never knew about?"

They all looked at her like she'd sprouted a second head.

"Cade Morgan used to play *football*," Ford said. "Quarterback for Northwestern. Won the Rose Bowl in 2001. How do you not know this? You deal with people in the sports industry all the time."

"Not back in 2001," she retorted. She'd been a sophomore in college back then. "Are you sure this is the same guy? Tall, looks delicious in a three-piece suit, annoyingly adept at taking a woman right to the edge of frustration and then—bam—sneaking in with a surprisingly sweet word or two?"

The three of them stared at her.

"Um . . . I would've gone with 'brown hair, six-foot-four, two hundred and ten pounds, but we can use your description if you like," Ford said.

Hmm. It sounded suspiciously like the same man. Brooke couldn't decide if she was irked that she'd never known this about Cade, felt foolish, or was intrigued. Perhaps all three. "He mentioned something about a shoulder injury. Is that a football thing?"

"My God, woman. It's only one of the most famous moments in college football history," Ford said.

Charlie jumped in. "See, Northwestern was down by four points."

"Which is a big deal to start with, because Northwestern barely ever makes it to the Rose Bowl," Tucker added.

"Right. But Morgan was awesome that year—everyone was saying he would go pro," Charlie said.

Ford picked up at this point. "So there's fifteen seconds left on the clock, and it's like, third and nine or something." He stood up and pantomimed, reenacting the scene. "And Morgan pulls back out of the pocket just as this huge linebacker charges at him full speed as he goes for the sack, and then he throws this perfect sixty-five-yard pass right into the hands of a wide receiver in the end zone. The whole stadium went absolutely crazy."

Charlie actually looked a little teary-eyed. "It was one of the most beautiful things I've ever seen."

Brooke was impatient to hear the rest. Screw the game. "What happened to Cade?"

Ford grimaced. "Took a bad hit from the linebacker and landed the wrong way, I guess. Northwestern was so busy celebrating, they didn't even realize at first that he was hurt."

"He broke his collarbone, and totally messed up his shoulder," Tucker said. "He never stepped on a football field again."

Brooke sat there, finding it hard to believe that they were talking about *Cade Morgan*, the successful assistant U.S. attorney who'd made a name for himself prosecuting corrupt politicians and other high-profile white-collar criminals. "I never knew that about him."

Just then, the door from the suite opened. *Speak of the devil.*

Cade stepped onto the skybox terrace, followed by Huxley and Vaughn. His eyes landed immediately on Brooke. Seeing his lips curve in amusement, she naturally opened her mouth to get in the first quip and—

—was cut off by a loud cheer from Ford, Charlie, and Tucker.

"Cade Morgan! Dude, we were just talking about you," Tucker said enthusiastically.

So much for the hard-ass routine.

Ford reached out to shake Cade's hand. "I was telling Brooke about your Rose Bowl victory."

"You've been keeping secrets," she said to Cade.

"Wait a second." Vaughn looked at Cade in mock surprise. "You played football in college? Get out of here." With a wink, he and Huxley joined Brooke at the railing, as Brooke's three friends circled eagerly around Cade, bombarding him with questions.

"We've heard the Rose Bowl story before," Huxley explained to her.

"I take it Cade likes to reminisce about the good old days," Brooke said.

Huxley thought about that. "Actually, he never brings it up. Everyone else does."

Brooke was surprised to hear that. Cade Morgan, being modest? Inconceivable.

She looked over at him, wondering if there was some kind of story there. She watched as he nonchalantly brushed off an effusive compliment from Tucker, something about how he'd put up great numbers at Northwestern despite not having an elite receiver.

Unfortunately, she wasn't going to get a word in edgewise with him right then, seeing how her friends were fawning over him like twelve-year-old girls who'd scored backstage passes to a Justin Bieber concert. So instead, Brooke fell into an easy conversation with Huxley and Vaughn, talking a little about work, and then about the game.

At one point, she peeked over just as Cade said something that made the group laugh. She watched as Ford grinned and spoke animatedly, clearly into the conversation, and she couldn't deny that it was a little heartwarming to see her best friend getting along so well with a guy she'd introduced him to. Maybe a lot heartwarming.

Luckily, Charlie's voice rose above the fray before that line of thought went any further. "Probably, we should all hate you," he was saying to Cade. "Illinois played against Northwestern that year for our homecoming, and you totally slaughtered us—" He broke off at the sound of a knock on the interior door to the suite.

A woman in her early twenties, dressed in a skirt and a black T-shirt with "Sterling Restaurants" in red letters, walked into the suite pushing a three-tiered dessert cart.

"Sweet Jesus, it's here," Charlie whispered reverently.

Brooke fought back a smile. The dessert cart was something Sterling Restaurants had introduced a year ago, as a perk for all of the skyboxes and luxury suites at the sports arenas they collaborated with. Needless to say, it had been a huge success. Four kinds of cake (chocolate with toffee glaze, carrot cake, traditional cheesecake, and a pineapple-raspberry tart), three types of cookies (chocolate chip, M&M, and oat-meal raisin), blond brownies, dark chocolate brownies, lemon squares, peach cobbler, four kinds of dessert liquors, taffy apples, and, on the third tier, a make-your-own sundae bar with all the fixings.

"*Wow*. That is some spread," Vaughn said, wide-eyed.

Simultaneously, the men sprang forward, bulldozed their way through the suite door, and attacked the cart like a pack of starving *Survivor* contestants.

All except for one.

Cade stayed right there, on the terrace. He leaned back against the railing, stretching out his tall, broad-shouldered frame. "Whew. I thought they'd never leave."

Brooke walked over, joining him. There was something she was very curious about. "Why didn't you ever mention that you'd played football?"

"It didn't come up," he said with a casual shrug. He saw that she wasn't satisfied with that answer and conceded. "It's nice, sometimes, not to have it be the first thing people ask about."

She supposed she could understand that. Her eyes traveled over him, easily able to picture him in a football uniform, especially given the way his T-shirt showed off his toned chest and defined, seemingly very strong arm muscles.

She gently touched her hand to his right shoulder. "Was it this shoulder?"

"Yes."

Brooke looked up and saw the undisguised warmth in his eyes from her touch. When she moved her hand to the railing, he covered it with his own, lightly brushing his thumb over her knuckles.

"How many innings do we have to stay before grabbing that dinner?" he asked.

She felt sparks of excitement in her stomach at the husky tone to his voice. "Leave the Crosstown Classic early?" she said teasingly. "Never."

"So that's how it's going to be tonight, is it?" His eyes held hers boldly. "Good."

Fifteen

"I REALIZED SOMETHING," Brooke said, in between bites of the chocolate chip cookie she'd snagged off the dessert cart. "I've seen you play football."

After the game had ended, they'd hung out in the skybox with the other guys while waiting for the crowd to dissipate. Cade had suggested the two of them walk to a casual sushi lounge just around the corner from his apartment—a restaurant *not* owned by Sterling where, as he put it, "no one would be hopping around like jackrabbits on crack trying to keep Brooke Parker happy."

She thought that sounded perfect.

It was a warm July evening, the air filled with the scent of backyard barbeques. Reveling in the Cubs' victory over the Sox—a bigger cause for celebration on the north side of the city than the Fourth of July—people sat outside on front porches, balconies, and back decks, and played cornhole on the sidewalks and in the alleys while drinking wine, beer, and mixed drinks from plastic cups.

A far cry from the Gold Coast neighborhood she lived in. Brooke smiled, thinking about the likelihood of her

Prada-clad neighbors ever getting together to drink beer and
a play a round of cornhole on the rooftop deck of their high-
rise building. Although, in fairness, they probably thought
the exact same thing about her.

"Must've been a televised game," Cade said. "Since we
never played the University of Chicago."

During their dinner at Bar Nessuno, Brooke had mentioned
where she'd gone to undergrad and law school. "Nope. I saw
you live and in the flesh. I was at that Northwestern/Illinois
game Tucker mentioned earlier. Ford had invited me down
that weekend for the homecoming festivities."

Cade flashed her a confident grin. "And of course you now
remember how impressed you were with my utterly brilliant
performance."

"Actually, I barely looked at the field. I was too busy flirting with this hot guy in Ford's fraternity." She smiled innocently when Cade's grin turned to a frown. "You asked."

They maneuvered their way through a crowd of people
waiting on the sidewalk in front of an ice-cream shop. "I take
it you've known Ford for a long time, then?" he asked.

"Since the fourth grade. We were neighbors," Brooke said.

"Where did you grow up?"

She paused momentarily. "Glenwood."

"I see."

Brooke had heard that tone before, and knew exactly what
Cade meant by that. It wasn't exactly a secret that Glenwood
was an extremely affluent suburb. In fact, *Forbes* had recently
rated her hometown the ninth-richest neighborhood in the
United States, something that had been repeated ad nauseam
in all the Chicagoland newspapers.

"I know what you *think* you see," she told him, as they
turned a corner onto a residential street.

"Really?" He regarded her mock-archly. "And what do I
think I see, Ms. Parker?"

"You see the pricey U of C education, the high-rise apartment off of Michigan Avenue, and then you hear that I grew
up in Glenwood—"

"—Don't forget those fancy red high-heeled shoes. As long as we're generalizing."

"—and you *think* you see somebody who grew up with a silver spoon in her mouth." She raised an eyebrow. "Am I right?"

He cocked his head in acknowledgement. "Okay, maybe I was thinking something along those lines. Tell me, then—what should I see instead?"

"Someone who has worked very hard to get where she's at," Brooke said, with no small amount of pride. That being all she needed to say about the subject, she kept walking, taking a few steps before she realized that Cade was no longer alongside her. She looked back and saw him waiting on the sidewalk. "What are you doing?"

"Just waiting for the rest of the story," he said.

"The rest of what story?" she asked.

"Oh, I'm sure you're used to throwing out some tiny little nugget about yourself, one small comment about your background that you can use to get your point across before moving on, but that's not going to cut it with me." He folded his arms across his chest expectantly, looking every bit the prosecutor despite his gray T-shirt and cargo shorts. "Tell me more about what I should see."

She gestured to their surroundings. "Right here?"

He shrugged. "You opened the door to this line of questioning."

Darn litigators, she thought crankily. They acted like the whole world was their courtroom. And he wasn't going to back down; she could tell.

Fine. Whatever. She could answer his question, no problem. "For starters, you should see somebody who grew up in the one part of Glenwood that *Forbes* magazine wasn't talking about. Someone who never could've afforded to go to a school like U of C if her undergrad tuition hadn't been covered almost entirely by merit scholarships and financial aid."

She saw a flash of something in Cade's eyes she couldn't read. But he said nothing, just began taking steps toward her.

"Someone who lived off campus for three years with an

aunt who had a apartment in the city, so that she could save money on rent and be able to afford her textbooks. Someone who . . . just kept chugging away, always trying to stay one step ahead of the pack, and probably didn't stop worrying that she might do something to screw it all up until she got her first paycheck as a lawyer. And truly, I have *no* idea why I'm telling you this stuff," Brooke finished, not having meant to ramble on like that.

She waited for Cade to say something. Anything. Instead, he was just standing there, looking at her. She squirmed, feeling very . . . exposed. "Stop staring at me like that. I'm not one of your witnesses, Morgan."

He moved even closer, still not saying a word, and then she realized that he was waiting for her to look at him. So she did. Peered defiantly right up into those amazing blue eyes of his. "Don't make me break out the tough-girl routine again," she warned him.

Cade touched her chin. "You don't scare me, Brooke Parker. Not even with the tough-girl routine."

Maybe it was because of the fact that she'd just oddly shared more about her background than she had in her last three relationships. But right then, as he peered down into her eyes, she felt as though he was truly seeing *her*, not the high-powered general counsel of Sterling wearing a suit and expensive high heels who handled whatever came her way without batting an eyelash. Just plain old Brooke.

She tilted her head up and kissed him.

Without hesitation, as if he'd been waiting for just this, his lips slowly moved over hers as his fingers fanned out to cup her face. He was such a *good* kisser—sexy and playful, and yet very much in charge.

Brooke wrapped her arms around his neck and pulled closer, and she felt his other hand move to the small of her back, pressing her against him. Her breath caught at the feel of his long, lean body against hers, his mouth hot and demanding, until he pulled back and peered down at her.

His eyes were dark. "Brooke."

She knew what he was asking. "Yes."

Immediately, Cade took her hand and led her—quite briskly—along the sidewalk.

"Thank God I'm not wearing the red high heels today," she said.

"In two minutes you'll be wearing nothing," he said in a low voice.

Well, then.

About halfway down the block, he led her through a wrought-iron gate and up the steps of an elegant gray stone building. From the mailboxes outside the front door, there appeared to be six units, including one for unit 3B, labeled "Morgan."

Cade unlocked the front door and pulled her inside. He led her up two flights of stairs, then they got caught up kissing against the door to his apartment. She sunk her fingers into his hair as her tongue clashed with his, while he simultaneously slid his keys into the lock and let them into the apartment.

She took a quick peek as the door shut behind them, curious to check out Maison de Morgan, and saw a nicely decorated place that was clearly a bachelor pad. A large black leather sectional and matching oversized ottoman took up most of the living room, facing a large plasma television mounted over a fireplace. She saw a small dining room, and a staircase beyond that, and was just wondering where the stairs led when Cade picked her up in a fluid, effortless move and carried her . . . somewhere.

"Your shoulder," she said, wrapping her legs around his waist.

"Oh, *crap*." He dropped her a few inches, making her gasp, and then winked when he caught her. "Kidding. I'll be okay."

Brooke smiled, not sure she'd ever before met someone who could simultaneously make her laugh while inspiring some *very* naughty thoughts. In response, she adjusted her position, deliberately settling his thick, hard erection between her legs.

Heat flashed in his eyes. "Actually, more than okay." He set her down on something cool—a glass table in the dining room—and quickly relieved her of her ponytail, tossing the band to the side and watching as her hair tumbled wildly over her shoulders.

"I'll be needing that hair tie later," she told him.

"Much later." Cade lowered his head and kissed her neck, his lips trailing an erotic path along her skin.

Brooke inhaled unsteadily, her head falling back. Oh, God, that felt incredible.

"There are two ways we can do this," he said. "Being a gentleman, I'll let you decide. Option A is nice and slow and fancy, and then there's Option B."

"What's Option B?"

He stepped back and yanked his T-shirt over his head.

Whoa, Nelly.

"I like Option B so far," Brooke said, awestruck as he stood before her.

Delights abounded everywhere she looked—smooth, summer-bronzed skin, toned chest muscles, broad, strong shoulders and arms, and a hard, flat stomach. She'd never been a woman who'd gone crazy over athletes before, or ex-athletes, but it was almost obnoxious how incredible he looked without his shirt.

She made a mental note to be aggravated about this later. Much later.

"Option B, it is." Seemingly pleased with this decision, Cade reached for her, and within seconds her shirt lay on the ground next to his. Then her jean shorts, too. He paused then, and took in the sight of her, nearly naked before him on his dining table.

She expected him to say something teasing and coy. Par for the course with them.

He reached out and ran his thumb over her lower lip. "I love the way you look when I kiss you," he said in a husky tone. "I—"

He stopped himself, suddenly looking uncharacteristically uncertain, then stepped forward and swept his hand in her hair. He pulled her closer, capturing her mouth in a searing kiss.

Brooke wrapped her hands around his neck, her urgency

matching his. No clue what he'd been about to say, but for once there didn't need to be any verbal dance between them. What she wanted right then was something far more primal and simple. She slid her hands over his firm chest and moaned when he pressed the steely ridge of his erection between her legs.

Yes. That. "Cade . . ." she said, her voice thick with need.

He moved against her in a slow, teasing motion. "Is this what you want?"

Since the day you walked into my office. "Yes."

He glided one hand down to her underwear and under the lace. He spread her open, then slid a finger inside. "Christ, you're like silk," he said in a guttural voice. "You're going to feel amazing wrapped around me."

She felt a throbbing heat between her legs and arched her hips. "If we ever get to that part."

"Sassy as ever." He yanked her panties off, and then undid the fly of his shorts with his gaze on her the entire time. "Last chance for Option A," he warned.

She reached up and undid her bra, letting it fall to the floor in answer.

Cade's jaw tensed, and then he was on her again, kissing her hotly as he reached inside his shorts. She felt his erection against her leg, hard and thick, and heard a rustling as he pulled out his wallet and removed a condom. There was the rip of a wrapper, both of them breathing heavily as their mouths battled, and then Brooke spread her legs—so, so ready—as he slid one hand underneath her bottom and angled her up.

He thrust into her with one hard stroke.

She cried out against his mouth with pleasure. Oh, *God,* he was big . . . everywhere.

He stayed still, giving her body a chance to get used to him, as his free hand tangled in her hair. He gently pulled back, forcing her to meet his gaze as he began to slide in and out of her.

"Have you thought about this?" he rasped. His eyes, dark with desire, held hers as he thrust.

"Yes." No games right then. "I want it hard," she breathed.

It had been a long time since she'd felt this sexy and hot and *good*.

From the flash in his eyes, he seemed to be just fine with that idea.

"Put your legs around my waist," he told her.

She did so, and he eased her down onto the table, the glass cool against her back. He took both of her hands in his and pinned them to the table over her head.

His blue eyes burned so hot into hers she was surprised the table didn't melt beneath them.

He thrust hard into her and she moaned.

He thrust again. Then faster and deeper, making her breasts bounce as he took her against the table. She closed her eyes, then whimpered when he lowered his head and sucked the tip of one of her breasts into his mouth. He flicked his tongue over the peaked nipple.

"That feels so good," she moaned, moving her hips to meet each of his thrusts.

"Good. Because I plan to fuck you like this all night." He reached down between her legs and teased her clit expertly.

He had her hands trapped against the table, and her lower body was pinned by his thick shaft as he took her hard. She opened her eyes and watched the bunch and flex of his arms, shoulders, and chest, and it felt so damn incredible to just surrender, for that moment, to him, to the strong, powerful body giving her so much pleasure.

"Cade," she said urgently.

He thrust against her, deep, possessive strokes. "You are so fucking sweet," he growled. He slid his hand underneath her bottom, tilting her hips up and holding her steady against his strokes.

That did it. Two more thrusts, and Brooke shattered. She cried out, her body trembling as wave after wave of her orgasm hit her. Cade released her wrists and flattened his palm against the glass, flexing his hips and pumping hard until he groaned deep in his chest. He rocked against her, his body shuddering against hers again and again, until he collapsed on top of her and buried his face in her hair.

Brooke felt his heart beating against her chest as they lay there, boneless. For two people who preferred to speak in quips and sarcasm, that had been unexpectedly . . . intense.

She wasn't quite sure how to feel about that.

Then Cade spoke.

"I think this is the first time I've ever used this table," he said against her neck.

Brooke began to laugh. My God, he was still *inside* her and she was already giggling. "I take it you don't do a lot of formal entertaining."

He pulled back, his dark hair falling across his forehead. "Were you not entertained, Ms. Parker?"

It was something about the playful way he said it, the affectionate way he gazed at her right then. Suddenly, she felt the urge to wrap her arms around him and never let go.

Careful, girl.

Easy and fun—that's all this was.

No problem.

Sixteen

CADE BLINKED WHEN he opened his eyes, not expecting his bedroom to be so bright with midmorning sun. Then again, it had been a really long night.

In every hot, hope-the-neighbors-didn't-hear-but-*damn*-that-was-some-great-sex sense of the word.

He looked over at Brooke, sleeping on her side next to him with her dark blond hair spilling over her bare shoulders. The sight brought a smile to his face, thinking how sweet and angelic she looked right then.

She'd probably skin him alive if she knew he was thinking that.

He'd begun to suspect that there was a softer, vulnerable side of Brooke Parker. She tried hard to conceal it underneath her dry-humored, nothing-gets-to-me exterior, but he'd seen a few glimpses of it here and there.

He got it. Lots of people—possibly everyone he knew—would describe him the same way.

It's all right here on the surface, he'd told his last ex-girlfriend. *What you see is what you get.*

But as he peered down at Brooke, wrapped cozily in his

bed, part of him couldn't help but think that he wanted more than just tiny glimpses of her softer, vulnerable side. He wondered what it would be like if she truly let him in. And if he was being honest with himself, that same small part would have to admit that he'd been feeling a little jealous ever since he'd met her friend Ford. Not because he thought there was anything going on between the two of them, but because Ford was clearly in the circle of trust while Cade—despite being the man who'd slept with her—was still standing on the outside, looking in.

The other part of him, however, thought he needed to stick his head under a faucet of icy water, or do whatever else it took to wake up out of this post-sex morning afterglow he was in.

Because to get *in* with a woman like Brooke, he would need to let her in, too. And that was something he . . . just didn't do. Wasn't sure he knew *how* to do, even if he wanted to.

But he did, at least, know one thing: he rocked the morning-after routine. He quietly got dressed, not wanting to disturb Brooke, and headed downstairs. In the kitchen, he grabbed the ingredients he needed to make a Denver omelette, the specialty of the house, and got some butter melting in a small skillet. He chopped up green peppers and onions and diced the ham, then tossed them into the pan. After that, he cleared off the small breakfast table at which he normally ate and set it for two, then got to work on the eggs.

A few minutes later, as the scents of the sautéed vegetables and ham filled his kitchen, he peeked up from the stove to see Brooke coming down the stairs. Her hair was tousled about her shoulders, her cheeks had a rosy, just-woke-up flush, and she conspicuously wore the same Cubs T-shirt and shorts she'd had on the day before.

"I can't believe I slept so late," she said, seeming rather abashed at the notion. She pointed to the stove. "What's all this?"

"Breakfast." He nodded at the table by the window. "It'll just be a minute, if you want to have a seat."

She seemed surprised by the offer. "Thank you."

Cade folded the omelette he had cooking on the stove, then slid it onto a plate. He immediately added more butter to the pan, then walked over and set Brooke's omelette in front of her. He pointed to the items on the table. "Salt and pepper, that's orange juice in the pitcher, and how about some coffee?"

"Um . . . sure."

Cade grabbed the pot out of the coffeemaker on his counter and poured her a cup. Then he added the rest of the egg mixture to the pan, expertly lifting the edges of the omelette and tilting the pan as it set. He added the ham and vegetable mixture, and then some cheese, folded the omelette in half, and—voilà—had breakfast for two.

He carried his plate over to the table and took a seat across from Brooke.

"This is quite impressive," she said.

So she'd noticed. *Good.* "It's no trouble," he said with a wink. He took a bite of his omelette.

Brooke dug in herself, chewing thoughtfully. "Let me ask you something. Do you tailor the breakfast to the woman you've just spent the night with, or is it always a Denver omelette?"

Cade paused midchew.

Oh, shit.

Continuing on before he could answer, Brooke picked up her coffee cup and cradled it in both her hands. "Don't get me wrong, I love a Denver omelette as much as the next girl. But I'm curious whether that's your thing, or if you try to change up the routine depending on the specific woman. You know . . . like, green pepper because I have green eyes, ham because I'm so funny, and onions for all the tears you'll shed after I leave."

She smiled cheekily when Cade threw her a look. Ha, ha.

"It's called a *gesture,*" he said. "One that other women seem to appreciate just fine." This was not the way the morning-after breakfast routine typically went. Usually, the lady in question saw him working at the stove and was pleased, possibly even a little touched by his thoughtfulness. Often high jinks ensued from there.

He should've known, however, that this woman would be tougher to impress.

Maybe he should've left his shirt off while cooking.

"So it is always the same omelette. Interesting." With a teasing expression, she took another bite. "By the way, it's delicious. I'm just usually more of a grab-an-energy-bar-on-the-way-into-work kind of girl." She checked her watch. "Speaking of which . . . I really should get going."

"You're working today?"

"Unfortunately, yes. Cinderella had her fun at the Cubs game and on the dining room table, and now she must get back to work." She glanced down at her plate. "Sorry about the omelette."

Screw the omelette. Cade was more curious about something else she'd said. "Interesting analogy—you as Cinderella."

She appeared surprised, as if she hadn't even realized what she'd said. Then she brushed it off. "I didn't mean it like that. It's just an expression." Quickly, she changed the subject. "What about you? Any big plans for the day?"

Cade tensed at the reminder. Actually, yes. Today he was meeting Zach for lunch, something he was both looking forward to and wholly dreading. He'd done a good job of ignoring the situation, of trying not to think about what the two of them would talk about, and pretending as though he didn't have questions for Zach about the man who, technically, was his father.

He saw Brooke watching him. "No big plans," he said casually.

"You have the same look you had the night we met at Bar Nessuno." She studied him with her light green eyes. "Is everything okay?"

Well, since you asked. . . . My father abandoned me before I was born, then abandoned me again when I was ten after deciding I wasn't worth the trouble. And for years, every time I stepped onto a football field, it was to prove how wrong he'd been about that. But I moved on. Until my kid half brother showed up at my office, stirring up all sorts of crap I really don't want to think about.

Oh, sure. Because *that* info-dump wouldn't leave her sorry she'd asked.

Brooke was a busy woman; she'd already said that she needed to get into the office. She didn't want to hear his maudlin, angsty tale. Frankly, if he had the choice, he wouldn't think about it himself.

"Everything's fine," he said. "There's just this thing I have to do today. No big deal."

Her eyes searched his, and then she nodded. "Well, I really should get going." She got up from the table, looked around the apartment, and then remembered. "No purse. Right." She patted the back pockets of her jean shorts. "Money. Keys. It's like I'm in college again."

Cade grinned. "I'll drive you home."

Brooke waved this off. "That's okay, I'll catch a cab. Just, you know . . . text me sometime."

Text me.

She didn't need to say another word; every single man and woman knew what those two words meant after a hookup. And if Brooke wanted to keep things casual, that was A-OK with him. Great, actually. He had a lot going on in his personal life right then and didn't need any more complications.

In the doorway, he smiled at her, charming as always. "Don't be a stranger, Ms. Parker."

He watched as she walked away, and then firmly, decidedly, shut the door behind him.

Seventeen

CADE HAD BEEN waiting at a table at DMK Burger Bar for ten minutes when Zach showed up.

"Sorry I'm late." Zach sounded winded, as if he'd been rushing. "There was some problem on the Blue Line and the train sat on the tracks forever."

"The Blue Line?" Cade asked. That didn't stop anywhere close to the restaurant.

Zach nodded. "I had to take that into the Loop and then transfer to the Brown Line. I'm starving after all that." He picked up the menu and began reading through it.

Cade felt like a jerk, hearing that Zach had taken *two* trains to meet him. He'd suggested DMK because he'd figured that a place with twenty different types of burgers would be a teenaged boy's wet dream. But he hadn't even bothered to ask Zach what neighborhood he lived in—mostly because he'd been trying to avoid hearing anything specific about the rest of Zach's family.

So many things he didn't know about his brother. And he was quickly realizing that if he was going to have a relationship with Zach, avoiding the subject of Noah Garrity would be impossible. "You should've said something, Zach. We could've gone someplace closer to you."

Zach shrugged. "I don't want to be a burden to you or anything."

Was that what he thought? Cade looked the teenager straight in the eyes, wanting to be sure they were clear on this. "You're not a burden. I want to be here. And the next time, you pick the restaurant."

Zach grinned, his face lighting up at the reference to them doing this again. "Cool. I'd really like that."

Glad that was settled, Cade picked up his menu. "So what looks good?"

"No clue. I've never even heard of half this stuff." Zach read out loud from the menu. "'Roasted hatch green chile, fried farm egg, Sonoma jack, and smoked bacon.' Or how about this one? 'Fresh goat cheese, pickled red onions, and blueberry barbeque sauce.' It says that's on a bison burger." He peered up at Cade. "That's, like, a buffalo, right?"

The waitress showed up at their table before Cade could answer. "Are you guys ready to order?" She turned first to Zach, who squirmed in his seat.

"Oh. I guess I'll have, um . . ." he trailed off while looking at the menu uncertainly.

In hindsight, Cade realized the place was a little trendy for a sixteen-year-old. What did he know? He hadn't hung out with a teenager since he'd been one. "While he's thinking, I'll have the number eight. Cheddar cheese, and let's do ketchup and mustard instead of mayo. Just a plain old, regular cheeseburger."

Zach looked relieved as he handed his menu to the waitress. "I'll have one of those, too. And a chocolate shake."

After the waitress left, Cade watched as Zach ripped open a straw and sucked down nearly half of the glass of ice water sitting in front of him.

"It's like an awkward first date, isn't it?"

"What is?" Zach pointed between them. "Oh, this? Yeah, I guess."

"Just with a man who's half my age and happens to be related to me."

"That *would* be awkward."

They both grinned, and some of the tension was broken. Cade fell back on lawyerly instinct—he was good at getting witnesses to talk, to open up and feel comfortable. With that in mind, he started with one of the few things he did know about Zach. "So you like football, obviously."

Zach toyed with the straw wrapper. "Yeah, I'll be on varsity this year."

"What position do you play?"

A voice from the past echoed in his head. *What position do they got you at?*

He really needed to figure out how to shut that voice up.

"Wide receiver," Zach said. "I've been running a lot of drills this summer, trying to shave a few hundredths off my forty. Coach is always saying that my hands are my strength, not my feet. But I'd still like to be a little faster."

"Have you tried overspeed drills?" Cade asked.

Zach shook his head. "What's that?"

"Training that reduces resistance when you sprint, allowing you to run faster than normal. Wrap a towel around your waist and have a teammate hold you back while you start to run. He lets go after a few steps, and you get a burst of speed, quicker than what your body normally can do. And you could also run sprints downhill."

They talked football for a while, with Zach asking enough questions to make Cade curious. "Noah played wideout in high school. I'm sure he's had lots of tips for you, right?"

"Oh, yeah. I've just, you know, been trying to come up with a few ideas on my own, too." The waitress brought Zach his chocolate shake, and he seemed grateful for the interruption. He took a long draw of the shake and smiled. "That's a really good shake."

Cade's prosecutor instincts were on alert, sensing that something was not quite right here. "Can I ask you something, Zach? Do you *want* to play football?" He could easily imagine

Noah, looking cool with his leather jacket and cigarette, trying to relive his glory days by pushing his son—the one he acknowledged, that is—into the sport.

Zach relaxed, as if he'd been bracing himself for a different question. "Heck, yes," he said emphatically. "I love the feeling I get every time I strap on those pads, the rush of adrenaline in the locker room, and then that smell when I first step on the field. It's like a combination of freshly cut grass, sweat—"

"And gasoline," Cade finished.

"Exactly." Zach studied him interestedly. "Can I ask *you* something? How did it feel when they told you that you couldn't play anymore?"

Cade had been asked this question many times, and normally, he just fluffed off the answer or made a comment about going out on a high note. He appreciated people's interest, and he understood their curiosity, but he saw no reason to let the whole world in on the fact that that had been one of the worst moments of his life.

But with Zach, for whatever reason, the usual answer felt like a cop out. "I'd *seen* myself going pro," he told him. "Pictured it in my head probably a thousand times since I was ten years old. To have that dream taken away from me was a really tough pill to swallow."

"So what'd you do?"

Cade shrugged. "Spent the next three months wallowing in self-pity, skipping classes, getting drunk, and generally being an asshole." He paused, considering his audience. "Not sure I'm supposed to be telling you things like that."

"I'm sixteen. I've heard the word *asshole* before."

"I meant the part about skipping classes and getting drunk in college." Cade pointed. "These stories are anecdotes, not advice. When you're older, don't do the things I did."

"Wow," Zach said. "You just sounded so much like my dad right then it was scary."

"Yeah, well, when your *dad* tells you not to do the things he did, that's damn good advice to take," Cade said dryly.

Zach paused. "You really do hate him, don't you?"

The blunt words, out of the blue, took Cade by surprise.

"Mostly, I try not to think about him, Zach. And that's how I'd like it to stay."

Zach nodded, disappointment etched on his face. "I'm not saying I blame you. I'd probably feel the same way if I were in your shoes."

There was one thing, however, that Cade did want to know. For Zach's sake. "He's a good father to you, then?"

Zach hesitated. "I don't know how to say this to you . . ." He stared down at the table for a moment, then back at Cade. "But, yeah. He's a great dad. He told me that he really settled down after meeting my mom, and to me he's always been just a normal, regular father. I mean, he's not perfect, and this past year he rode me nonstop about getting my English grades up, but he's my dad, you know?"

Cade looked away, focusing on a small crack on the wall. No, he didn't know.

The waitress suddenly appeared at their table, carrying two plates. "I've got two plain-old, regular cheeseburgers here."

"Thank God," Cade said, grateful for the interruption. *Whew.* Things had gotten a little intense for a moment there.

The waitress smiled. "You guys are hungry, huh?" She tossed her curly brown hair over her shoulders, looking appreciatively at Cade. "Anything else I can get you?"

He had a feeling she wasn't referring only to the lunch menu. And she was attractive, no doubt. But still . . .

"I think we're good for now," he told her.

"If you think of anything else, just let me know." She sashayed off in her short black skirt, all legs and shapely, early-twenties ass.

Zach stared, wide-eyed, ketchup bottle hovering midair above his plate.

Cade reached over and casually plucked the bottle out of Zach's hands, squirting ketchup onto his own plate for his fries.

"She is really nice . . ." Zach blinked, coming out of his daze. "Hey, you never finished your story. You said that after you got injured, you spent three months being pissed off. What happened after that?"

"I finally got tired of being angry," Cade said. "The spring after I got injured, I was having lunch with a bunch of my former teammates, and they were talking about gearing up for the next season. I realized that I could either bitch for the rest of my life about not being a part of that, or I could start working on a backup plan. Law school seemed like a good fit."

Zach seemed skeptical. "Sure, but, come on. Don't tell me you don't miss the smell of grass and gasoline and sweat."

Cade smiled. "Now it's the smell of a courtroom that drives me. The smell of leather briefcases and coffee and justice. Nothing quite like it, Zach."

Now Zach looked *really* skeptical. "Sure."

Cade laughed, having the sudden urge to put the kid in a headlock or something. "All right, I'm done being on the witness stand. Now it's your turn. What's this problem you had with your English grades?"

Zach blushed to the roots of his light brown hair. "It's nothing. I had a harder time concentrating in that class, that's all."

"Why only English?"

Zach shrugged. "You know, different environment, different people . . ."

Ah. "Different people. I see." Cade eased back in his chair, getting comfortable. "Judging from the fact that your face is about the shade of that ketchup bottle, I'd say we have one of two situations going on here: hot teacher or cute classmate. Which is it?"

"Cute classmate."

"We can work with that. What's her name?" Cade asked.

"Paige Chopra. She's got this long, dark hair, and these light green eyes, and she's really smart. Like, probably the smartest girl in my class," Zach said.

"Green eyes and really smart, huh?" Cade asked. It sounded like he and his brother had similar tastes in more than just cheeseburgers and M&M cookies. He rested his arms on the table, ready to come up with a plan.

His kid brother was getting this girl.

"Okay, so tell me what the problem is." He gestured to

Zach. "You're a good-looking guy, you play football. Girls like these things."

"Not this girl," Zach said, picking at his fries. "I'm pretty sure she thinks I'm just a dumb jock."

"Why would she think that?"

"Because whenever I'm around her, I act like a dumb jock." Zach threw up his hands in exasperation. "I can't help it, she makes me nervous. She sat next to me last year in English class, and every time the teacher called on me I could see Paige watching, and I wanted to say something insightful or whatever. But I choked. Every time. And since participation was forty percent of our grade, and I could barely, like, string a sentence together, I got a C. I've never gotten a C before."

Zach shook his head, continuing. "I thought I'd forget about Paige over the summer, especially with . . ." He hesitated, then gestured at Cade. "You know, me tracking you down and everything. But her dad owns the ice-cream shop in my neighborhood, and she works there over the summer, so I keep going in and buying all this ice cream and trying to think of something to say. But after twelve double-scoop cones, the most I've gotten out is 'Hi, Paige.' " He ran his hand through his hair. "It's a mess, dude. *I'm* a mess."

Cade sat across from his brother, the alleged mess, trying really hard to fight back a smile. In his entire life, he'd never felt so utterly smitten as Zach clearly was over Paige Chopra. He'd dated plenty of girls and women, but even as a teenager he'd been more guarded with his emotions.

Zach waited for him to say something. "You're looking at me weird. It's because I'm totally pathetic, right? I mean, you're Cade Morgan. You probably never have to worry about girls, right?"

"You're not pathetic. Actually, I envy you a little."

"Because I'm a mess?" Zach asked dryly.

"No. Because you're not afraid to be a mess."

"It's not exactly a conscious decision, you know. I'd much rather just be cool and get the girl."

"You want to be cool? Try *talking* to her."

Zach sighed. "Can't I just text her?"

"No." Cade pointed emphatically. "No texting. If two people like each other, they should be able to sit down and have an actual conversation, the way normal adults do when they want to get to know one another better."

Zach raised an eyebrow. "Dude . . . it's just texting."

Right. "Regardless, you're going to have to figure out some way to have a conversation with this girl. So if she makes you that nervous, you need a battle plan. Start off the conversation with something she likes. Something you know she's interested in."

Zach considered this. "I think she likes poetry. I once heard her talking to Ms. Stevens after class about how she's written some poems herself."

Cade clapped his hands. *Bingo.* "It's perfect. If you have trouble talking to this girl, find another way to let her know how you feel. Maybe get her a book of poetry."

"I'm a sixteen-year-old wide receiver. I know option routes and screen passes. I don't do poems."

"You will if you want Paige Chopra to like you. Sounds like you need to up your game for this one." Cade grinned as Zach made a big show of rolling his eyes. "Just keep it simple, tough guy. Try T. S. Eliot." He chuckled at Zach's look of surprise. "Don't look so shocked. I took a poetry class as an elective in college. I'd heard that the professor gave everyone who showed up an A." And he'd also heard from a fellow football player that the poetry chicks were hot and arty and got big-time turned on whenever a guy showed his "sensitive side" by discussing poems—all of which he could confirm as *very* true—but that was an anecdote for a different day.

"I'll think about it." Zach took a sip of his shake. "What about you? I know you're not married. Are you seeing anyone or anything?"

An image of Brooke sleeping in his bed popped into Cade's head. Then a second image came to mind, of her giving him the "text me" speech at his front door. "Nothing serious."

"Really? 'Cuz you paused there."

If one more person commented on these damn alleged pauses . . . "Just eat your lunch," Cade said.

With a grin, Zach threw Cade's words back at him. "If you're having trouble talking to some girl, maybe you need to find another way to tell her how you feel."

"I know how to talk to her just fine."

"Maybe you're not saying the right things, then."

"Can we change the subject?" Cade ran his hand through his hair. "You're sixteen years old. Trust me, relationships get a lot more complicated when you're an adult."

"Is this a friends-with-benefits situation?"

"Aren't you a little young to know about friends-with-benefits situations?"

"I didn't say I was partaking in them myself," Zach said. "But shockingly, yes, I have heard of scenarios in which adults engage in intercourse without riding off into the sunset together."

Cade tried to decide how best to sum up the situation with Brooke. "There is a woman. We are friendly. There have been benefits."

"Do you like her?"

Cade gestured with his burger. "Of course I like her. She's, like, the smartest, wittiest, woman I've ever met. And hot, too."

"Yeah, I can see why you'd be confused about that," Zach said. "Smart, witty, and hot. Sounds like a real complicated situation to me."

Okay, fine. To youthful, unjaded ears, it probably did sound odd. Cade tried a different way to explain. "She and I are on the same page. We're just keeping it casual."

"Hey, you're an intelligent guy, you obviously know what you're doing," Zach said. "But casual or not, if this girl's that great you probably need to follow your own advice."

"What advice is that?"

"Up your game." That said, Zach took a big bite of his cheeseburger.

Cade thought about that. Up his game? *Pfft*. If he had been thinking he might want to try to change Brooke's mind about their just-having-fun situation—which obviously he did not, since no man of sound mind and body ever messed with a just-having-fun situation—maybe then he'd worry about upping his game.

He scoffed. "You're a teenager. What do you know?"

"I'm wise beyond my years," Zach said, his mouth full of burger.

Cade laughed, a warm feeling spreading across his chest. Asshole or not, Noah Garrity had managed to do one thing right by him.

He'd given him this.

BROOKE BLINKED, REALIZING that she'd been staring out her office window for several minutes.

She sat at her desk, pen in hand, allegedly with the purpose of reviewing the revised employment contracts that Sterling's outside counsel had sent her. She still had six contracts to review, yet she'd been having trouble staying focused. Not usually a problem she faced.

It was just after noon, and outside her window she could see couples strolling hand in hand along Michigan Avenue, and women walking with oversized bags while enjoying a leisurely day of shopping. She couldn't remember the last time she'd had one of those. Normally she was so busy, she targeted a specific store and got in and out as fast as possible.

Behind Michigan Avenue, she could see Oak Street Beach. The sandy lakeshore was packed with people, all enjoying the sunshine and the waves.

Maybe she'd rushed out of Cade's apartment too quickly.

As quickly as the thought popped into her head, Brooke shoved it right back out. The contracts piled on her desk weren't going to review themselves, after all. Besides, she and Cade were keeping things casual—that meant no hanging around his place "just because," regardless of whether she had to work or not. They'd had sex—something lots of adults did. Sure, it had been hot sex, and there'd been a few laughs, too, but that didn't mean she wanted to pick out curtains with the man. And given his well-practiced Denver omelette routine, it was safe to say she wasn't the first woman to spend the night at Maison de Morgan. Nor would she be the last.

The thought made her feel a little . . . prickly.

Get over it, Parker.

This was exactly the way she wanted it, she reminded herself. Just her and her work, together on a Sunday afternoon. Daydreaming about her and Cade while staring longingly at the beach was pointless.

Even if it would be fun to imagine him all tanned and shirtless.

Brooke mulled that over for a moment.

Aw, hell. One fantasy wouldn't kill her.

She was lying on the beach, with no cell phone or laptop or iPad in sight—definitely a fantasy right there—listening to the sound of the waves breaking peacefully against the shore. Cade, of the aforementioned tanned shirtlessness, sat next to her while rubbing sunscreen on her back.

Brooke closed her eyes. She could practically feel his strong hands caressing her skin . . . then the light, teasing touch of his fingers brushing her hair off her shoulders as he leaned down, his voice husky and warm in her ear, and said—

"Brooke."

Her eyes flew open. Okay . . . she really *could* hear him. Slowly, she turned around in her chair, and saw, unbelievably, Cade standing in her office doorway.

This was one heck of a vivid daydream.

"You might want to think about locking the main door to the office when you're working here alone," he said, no hello or anything, just bossing her around.

Definitely the real Cade.

She ignored his lecture for a moment, since there was a more pressing issue at hand. "What are you doing here?"

He shifted awkwardly in the doorway, as if he wasn't sure of the answer to that himself. "If you have to work on a Sunday, the least you can do is eat more than an energy bar," he said gruffly. He held up a white paper bag.

Brooke stared in surprise. "You brought me lunch?"

"I was in the neighborhood."

She checked out the label on the bag. "DMK is twenty minutes from here."

"I was in *that* neighborhood, and now I'm here," he said in exasperation. "Seriously, woman, you are impossible to feed." He strode over and set the bag on her desk. "One cheeseburger with spicy chipotle ketchup and a side of sweet potato fries— chosen *specifically* for a certain spicy and sweet girl I know— and a green dill pickle for your eyes. So there." He crossed his arms over his chest.

Brooke studied him. "You seem very ornery right now."

"As a matter of fact, I am."

"Why?"

"I don't know," he huffed. "Just . . . eat your Brooke Burger. Stop asking so many questions. Sometimes a guy just wants to buy a girl lunch. Any objections to that? Good. Enjoy your Sunday, Ms. Parker."

He strode out of her office, gone as quickly as he'd appeared.

Brooke stared at the doorway and blinked.

No clue what that was all about.

Eighteen

A WEEK LATER, Cade sat across a conference table from Charles Torino and two of his defense attorneys. As the federal prosecutor who'd filed the charges against Senator Sanderson, Torino, and the other three defendants, Cade had made certain predictions to himself as to who the first defendant would be to approach him about a guilty plea. He'd gone with Torino, mostly because he'd guessed that a hospital CEO who lived in a four-million-dollar home would try to do anything to avoid serving time in a federal prison. And the fact that his lawyer had literally broken out in a sweat during the arraignment made Cade think that the Torino defense team wasn't feeling all too confident about their case.

His suspicions were confirmed that Friday morning.

"We'd like to talk about the charges our client is facing," said Owen Lockhart, the lead defense attorney for Charles Torino, who'd called Cade earlier in the week to request a meeting.

"Conspiracy to bribe a government official," Cade said matter-of-factly. "And as I told you on the phone, Mr. Lockhart, I'm afraid there isn't much for us to discuss."

Lockhart gestured. "My client is considering changing his plea."

"A wise idea, given the evidence," Cade said. "We can call the clerk's office and set up a change of plea hearing anytime you'd like."

"But what am I going to get in exchange?" Torino blurted out, ignoring the looks of his attorneys.

Cade rested his arms on the table. "I apologize if this wasn't made clear to you, Mr. Torino, but I've already told your lawyer that I don't intend to cut any deals with respect to the charges against you."

Torino's other attorney, James Wheeler, was younger and seemingly more aggressive than Lockhart. "We know your primary target is the senator, Morgan. You seem to have a hard-on for politicians these days."

"What I have a hard-on for, Mr. Wheeler, is making sure that justice is met against those individuals who willfully and flagrantly break the laws of the United States."

Lockhart jumped back in, quick to appease. "What my colleague means to say is that Mr. Torino is a small fish in the very big pond that is this case. According to the FBI reports, you guys have been building your case against Senator Sanderson for months. Perhaps we can assist you in getting your big fish."

Cade's tone remained polite, but firm. "With all due respect, gentlemen, I already have everything I need from Mr. Torino." He turned to address the hospital CEO directly. "I have recorded conversations between you and the senator, both on the phone and at Sogna. On top of that, we've got a video of the two of you at the restaurant, literally shaking hands as you agree to pay him two hundred thousand dollars in exchange for keeping Parkpoint Hospital open. That's more than enough for the jury, regardless of whether or not you testify."

Torino looked at the window and shook his head, as if he couldn't believe any of this was happening. After a few moments, he spoke in a subdued tone. "I made a mistake, Mr. Morgan. *One* mistake. I've already lost my job and a three-million-dollar severance package. But worst of all, I've lost my reputation. And now I'm facing twenty years in prison because of this." He swallowed hard, seeming to struggle to maintain his composure. "I have two daughters. Seven and nine years old. Even if the judge only sentences me to half the maximum sentence, I'll miss out on so much time with them."

Despite the fact that Cade heard stories like this all the time, he wasn't immune to them. And while he certainly felt sorry for Torino's two daughters, he'd learned a long time ago not to think about the families of the defendants he prosecuted. He had a job to do, one that he believed in, and he remained focused on that. "I'm sure those are factors the judge will take into consideration at your sentencing hearing, Mr. Torino." With an efficient nod, he stood up from the table. "I think, gentlemen, that we've covered everything we need to discuss."

"Hold on, Morgan." Lockhart glanced at Wheeler, then at Torino, who nodded.

Cade knew instantly that something was up.

"What would you say if I told you there was another big fish in the pond?" Lockhart asked. "One you haven't hooked yet."

"I'd say that you probably should stop using fishing metaphors if you want to keep me in this room."

"I'll put it a different way, then." Lockhart folded his hands on the table. "In exchange for certain guarantees, Mr. Torino could tell you about other . . . arrangements, shall we say, that he had with another government official."

"Arrangements I made solely to serve the interests of the hospital," Torino added.

Lockhart and Wheeler shot him a look, and Torino quickly shut up.

Cade kept his face impassive, but he'd be lying if he said he wasn't curious. Another corrupt politician. Imagine that. "Another senator?"

Wheeler shook his head, no. "State representative."

"How much are we talking about here?" Cade asked. This conversation wasn't even worth pursuing if all they were talking about was Torino trying to schmooze some state representative by buying him a few steak dinners.

"Enough for you to be interested," Lockhart said.

"Try me. I'm a finicky man."

Lockhart paused. "About three hundred thousand dollars."

Cade maintained his cool façade, but that was a heck of a big bribe. *If* this was good information, somebody in the Illinois House of Representatives was giving Senator Sanderson a run for his money in the sleazy-politician department.

Reluctantly, that meant that Cade wanted to hear more. Just as Torino's lawyers knew he would.

"You understand, of course, that we're telling you this solely in furtherance of plea discussions," Lockhart added.

Yes, Cade knew that. Which meant, per the Federal Rules of Evidence, none of this conversation would be admissible at trial should Torino decide not to plead guilty. He leveled his gaze on Torino, seeing the hospital CEO in a very different light now that he knew the man had spent half a million dollars buying off not one, but *two* members of the Illinois General Assembly. "A onetime mistake, huh?" he asked, not bothering to hide his sarcasm.

Torino shrugged. "Figured I'd try the sob story first."

Cade shook his head disgustedly as he pulled out his cell phone and dialed his secretary.

"Can you book this conference room for me for the next hour?" he asked Demi. "I'm going to need more time than I'd anticipated. And get a hold of Greg Boran from the Federal Defender's Office and let him know that I'll have to push back our call to later this afternoon."

After thanking Demi, he hung up and faced off against Torino and his lawyers.

"Does that mean we're going to talk?" Lockhart asked.

"No." Cade tucked his cell phone into the pocket of his suit jacket, and then retook his seat at the conference table. "But it means that I'm at least willing to listen."

"I'LL GIVE THE guy this: he'd covered his bases with both branches of the Illinois General Assembly."

Cade sat across from his boss, U.S. Attorney Cameron Lynde, and relayed the information he'd gleaned during his two-hour meeting with Torino. "He had Senator Sanderson in one pocket, and as we learned today, Representative Bill Fleiss in the other. Together, Torino paid them roughly five hundred thousand dollars in bribes. Of course, he'll tell you that this was all for the public good. He claims that because Parkpoint Hospital serves one of the lowest-income neighborhoods in Chicago, he was just doing what he needed to do to ensure that, quote "poor people had access to quality health care, too.' "

Sitting behind her desk, Cameron didn't look impressed with that excuse. "He's a regular Robin Hood out there in his four-million-dollar home."

Cade wasn't surprised by her sardonic tone. When Cameron had come on board nearly two years ago as the U.S. attorney for the Northern District of Illinois, she'd made it clear that she considered government corruption cases to be one of her top priorities. While likable and down-to-earth in person—characteristics Cade certainly appreciated in a boss—Cameron had earned a professional reputation of being tough as nails when it came to crooked politicians. As a result, she was well respected both inside and outside the office, and had quickly become a powerful woman within the Department of Justice.

"What are your thoughts on moving forward?" she asked.

Cade had been anticipating this question, and therefore had spent some time thinking it over before dropping by Cameron's office to discuss these new developments regarding Torino.

"We obviously need to talk to the FBI about launching an investigation into Representative Fleiss. And, reluctantly, I think it's in our best interests to cut a deal with Torino in exchange for getting his statements on the record." He wasn't pleased to see Torino get off with a lighter sentence, but sometimes that was how the game was played.

Still, he didn't intend for the hospital CEO to get off scot-free. "I told Torino and his lawyers that I won't drop the charge in the Sanderson case. I did say, however, that I would consider agreeing to petition the judge for a Rule Thirty-five reduction in light of Torino's cooperation and ask for eighteen months' incarceration in a minimum-security facility."

Cameron mulled this over. "It's sad, really. Torino served as chairman on two of the most powerful hospital lobbying organizations in Illinois. He could've used that influence for so much good instead of resorting to bribery."

"Even if we don't agree to the reduced sentence, Torino likely won't get more than four years," Cade said. "It's his first offense, and his lawyers can point to all the supposed good he's done in the community. This way, at least we get Representative Fleiss, too."

Cameron toyed with a pen, taking her time to think through the options. She sighed. "As much as it leaves a bitter taste in the mouth, I agree. Make the deal."

Cade gave her a nod. "Done."

Cameron leaned back in her chair, studying him. "You're making quite a name for yourself with these corruption cases. People are going to be watching you with even more interest."

"Good. At least it gives them something to focus on besides the damn Twitter Terrorist case."

Cameron laughed at the reference to the infamous computer hacking case, one that Cade had been assigned while working under Cameron's predecessor. It was something of an inside joke between them, a reference to the days when they'd been AUSAs in the special prosecutions division together, working for an egomaniac boss who'd turned out to be corrupt himself. Thankfully for Cade and everyone else in the office, things were much better now that Cameron was running the show.

"I think you've given people plenty to be interested in besides the Twitter Terrorist case," Cameron said. "Speaking of which, I'm glad you stopped by today. There's something I wanted to talk to you about."

She folded her hands on top of her basketball-sized stomach, using it as a shelf. "Assuming all goes according to plan, Baby Boy Pallas will be here in about eight weeks. Which is a good thing—if it went much longer than that, I think Jack and I would be blacklisted at every baby store in the Chicago area."

Cade chuckled. To say that Cameron's husband, FBI Special Agent Jack Pallas, was a bit protective of his pregnant wife and unborn child would be an understatement. "What did Jack do now?"

"In addition to returning our third baby monitor in a row for having 'questionable security controls,' this weekend he interrogated the guys who delivered the baby furniture for forty-five minutes on their 'training and special skills in the crib-installation arena.'"

Cade laughed at the image. He'd seen Pallas's interrogation face—it wasn't for the faint of heart. "Did they pass?"

Cameron shook her head. "Nope. So now I've got a box the size of a refrigerator sitting in the baby's room instead of a crib. Jack asked Nick and Sam to come over this weekend," she said, referring to two other FBI agents in the Chicago office. "Apparently, they're going to put it together themselves."

"What do McCall and Wilkins know about putting a crib together?"

"Exactly." Despite Cameron's wry tone, there was an unmistakable sparkle of happiness in her eyes. "Anyway, I've told the attorney general that I plan to take three months off for maternity leave, and we've agreed that the logical course is to name an acting U.S. attorney while I'm gone. The smoothest transition would be to temporarily promote someone from within the office, so the attorney general asked for my top recommendation. Which means . . ." she paused, with a sly expression, "that if you're interested, the position of acting U.S. attorney is yours."

Cade blinked. "I don't know what to say. Thank you."

"No thanks necessary," Cameron said. "You've earned it. You're an excellent trial lawyer, and we have the same agenda in terms of cleaning up Illinois politics. I'm happy—and, candidly, relieved—to know that you'll be holding down the fort while I'm gone." She pointed, her gaze firm. "But it's just for three months, Morgan. I will be back."

"Understood. I promise not to burn the place down in your absence."

"I appreciate that. And I wasn't being flippant when I said that people are watching. You've come up in more than one conversation between the attorney general and myself. I have a feeling this acting U.S. attorney position is going to open a lot of doors for you."

Cade worked hard as a prosecutor and enjoyed his job, but there was no denying that he'd begun to think about the next step in his career. Most AUSAs stayed on for ten years or less, with the majority going to lucrative positions at large firms afterward. Based on the assumption that he would want to continue on as a trial lawyer after leaving the U.S. Attorney's Office, he'd already put out feelers with two top-tier Chicago firms who'd expressed interest in bringing him on to lead their white-collar crime practices.

But, no doubt, this acting U.S. attorney position opened up even more opportunities. Assuming he didn't screw up the job—which was a safe assumption since he planned to kick ass for those three months—this could very well be a springboard to higher-level political positions should he choose to continue on in the public sector.

He and Cameron began to discuss the logistics of the transition, and agreed that he would begin sitting in on status meetings with the AUSAs who were handling more complex cases, as well as meetings related to all new matters that came in over the next two months. Cameron also suggested setting up meetings with the heads of the Chicago branches of the FBI, DEA, Secret Service, ATF, and IRS to give him an overview of the open investigations their office was working on with each agency.

"When do you plan to tell the others?" he asked at the end of their meeting.

"Soon. I know people have been curious about what's going to happen after I have the baby." She placed one hand affectionately on her stomach. "Actually, I'm a little curious about that myself."

"You know there's a pool going around the FBI office, right? First person to get a photo of Jack wearing one of those baby-carrier things wins."

Cameron laughed at that—then paused. "What's the pool up to?"

"Last I heard it was five hundred bucks."

"Hell, I want in."

On his way out the door, Cade thanked Cameron again. "One thing. Do you mind if I tell Rylann before you make an announcement to the office?" He had a feeling he'd be seeing the other AUSA, who was finally back in the office after a two-week trial and weeklong vacation, in a short while for their daily Starbucks run. He preferred that she heard the news about the acting U.S. attorney position from him directly.

Cameron nodded in understanding. "Of course."

WHEN HE *GOT* back to his office, Cade shut his door behind him, sat down at his desk, and soaked it in.

Acting U.S. Attorney Cade Morgan.

That had a real nice ring to it.

Deciding that a celebration was in order that evening, he scrolled through his options. There was Vaughn, of course—there was always Vaughn. And Huxley, too. He quickly ruled out any of his AUSA friends. Many of them were ambitious, like him, and he didn't want to rub this promotion, even if temporary, in their faces.

So Vaughn and Huxley it was.

Unless . . .

Perhaps a text message to Ms. Brooke Parker of Sterling Restaurants might be in order.

Admittedly, after that weird moment last Sunday, when he'd felt compelled to drop by her office with the Brooke Burger, he'd wanted to put some precautionary distance between them. Just . . . because.

But he was fine now. Back on his game. And if he wanted to celebrate this good news with a hot date, he saw no problem with that.

With that in mind, he pulled out his phone and texted Brooke. He infused a little flirtation in his opening salvo, just to feel her out. YOU NEVER THANKED ME FOR THE BURGER. INGRATE.

He checked his work e-mail and fired off a few quick replies. About ten minutes later, he got a text message from Brooke.

SOMEBODY WOULD'VE BEEN THANKED IN PERSON, IF HE HADN'T STORMED OUT OF MY OFFICE AS PART OF SOME CRANKY-MAN TIRADE.

He smiled while replying.

OUT OF THE KINDNESS OF MY HEART, I'LL LET YOU THANK ME IN PERSON OVER DINNER TONIGHT. GOT GOOD NEWS TODAY, NEED TO CELEBRATE.

JUST HOW GOOD IS THIS GOOD NEWS? she wrote back.

Cade thought about that. ON A SCALE OF MEH TO HOLY-SHIT-I-JUST-WON-THE-ROSE-BOWL, I'D SAY THIS COMES IN AT REALLY DAMN COOL.

A minute later, his cell phone rang.

"I was typing out my reply and realized it would be faster just to call," Brooke said when he picked up. "I'm intrigued by this 'really damn cool' news of yours." Her voice turned contrite. "But unfortunately, I can't do dinner tonight. I'm being wined and dined by the outside counsel we hired to assist with our EEO training sessions last week. Presumably, they intend to use this as an opportunity to hit me up for more business." She paused. "I'm sorry, Cade. Of course, I would be stuck working."

Like he was going to let her off so easily. "I can work around your schedule, Cinderella," he teased. "How about if we meet for drinks after your dinner?"

There was a pause before she answered. "I'd like that. I should be free by nine o'clock, if that's not too late."

Cade realized then just how much he was looking forward to seeing her that night.

Pfft. Obviously, for all the sex he'd soon be getting.

"Nine o'clock it is," he said. "I'll pick you up at your place."

"I'll have a Denver omelette waiting."

"That's cute."

She added one last thing before hanging up. "And, Cade, whatever this news is—congratulations."

With a smile, Cade tucked his phone into his suit jacket.

"From that grin, I'm guessing that some defendant, or his attorney, is about to have a really bad day."

Hearing the woman's voice, Cade checked his watch and saw it was three o'clock on the dot.

Starbucks time.

He turned around in his chair and saw a familiar face standing in the doorway. "Well, look who's back in town. How was the vacation?"

Rylann Pierce, one of the other AUSAs in the special prosecutions division, stepped into his office. "Much needed. If I never again see another ten-defendant, thirteen-count mortgage fraud case, it'll be too soon."

"I bet the week in Bora Bora helped," Cade said. "People are saying that Rhodes whisked you off as soon as the guilty verdicts came in, to a helicopter waiting on the roof of the building."

"People say a lot of things. And I don't think they allow convicted felons to park their helicopters on top of the federal building," Rylann said, referring to her boyfriend's colorful criminal history.

A year ago, she'd created a huge stir around the office by going public about her relationship with Kyle Rhodes, a wealthy network security entrepreneur who also happened to be an infamous ex-con known as the Twitter Terrorist. Initially, Cade had been particularly surprised by their relationship, given that (A) he considered Rylann one of his closest friends in the office, and (B) he, personally, had been the prosecutor who'd convicted Rhodes and had him sentenced to eighteen months' imprisonment.

Awkward.

However, despite the unusual circumstances, he and Rylann had managed to get past the fact that he'd once called the love of her life a "cyber-menace to society"—yep, awkward again—and had continued to be friends. Which was nice, because on top of being someone he enjoyed hanging out with, Rylann was an excellent prosecutor. As two of the most senior AUSAs in the special prosecutions group, they frequently talked shop, sought out each other for advice, and traded courtroom war stories. True, he and Rhodes weren't going to be drinking eggnog together and singing carols at the annual office holiday party anytime soon, but for Rylann's sake they kept a quiet distance from each other.

"So no whisking away, huh?" he asked her. "The office gossips will be crushed."

"No helicopter, but . . . there may have been a limo waiting outside the courthouse after I got my guilty verdicts," Rylann said. "With champagne chilling on ice."

Of course there was. Cade got up from his desk and walked to the door. "You know that I'm now required to make fun of you for that for at least the next two weeks, right?"

They walked side-by-side down the hallway to the elevators. "Yep." Rylann grinned cheekily. "And it's worth every moment."

AT STARBUCKS, CADE suggested they grab a table after he and Rylann got their drinks. He found an empty one in the corner of the café, where they could speak privately.

"There's something I thought you should know," he led in. "And I wanted you to hear it from me first. I had a meeting with Cameron this afternoon. She's asked me to step in as acting U.S. attorney while she's on maternity leave."

He wasn't sure how Rylann would react to the news. She was a great litigator, also in the special prosecutions group, and very dedicated to her job. He didn't want this temporary promotion to be something that caused friction between them.

Luckily, her response alleviated his concerns.

"Congratulations, Cade," she said enthusiastically. "That's fantastic. And well deserved."

He brushed this off modestly. "I suspect a lot of it came down to seniority within the Chicago office." Although he and Rylann had the same level of experience, she'd previously worked in the San Francisco office and had transferred to Chicago only last year.

She took a sip of her Frappuccino, and then brushed a lock of raven hair out of her eyes. "I appreciate you saying that. And yes, the fact that you've been in Chicago longer than me should be a factor that Cameron considered. But more important, Cameron picked you because you'll be great at the job."

"Thanks, Rylann. That means a lot."

"Don't get me wrong, I would've been great, too," she added. She swirled her drink, mixing up the ice. "But we both know that never could've happened. There's no way the attorney general ever would've signed off on an acting U.S. attorney who's in a relationship with a famous ex-con."

She said the words matter-of-factly, without any trace of bitterness. And while Cade wouldn't have said it as bluntly as she had, they both knew she was right. Rylann, however, had accepted a year ago that there would be limits to her career in the government sector in light of her relationship with Rhodes—and as far as Cade knew, she didn't have any regrets about that.

In fact, her comment provided him with the perfect lead-in. He gestured to the huge diamond making its debut on her left hand. "Judging from that rock on your finger, I think you and Rhodes are a little past the "in a relationship" phase. I assume congratulations are in order?"

She blushed, glancing down at the ring. "I wanted to say something earlier, but, you know . . . given your history with Kyle, it felt a little weird."

"It's not weird." Cade conceded when she threw him a look, "Okay, it's still a little weird. But come on—tell me the proposal story, anyway."

She raised an eyebrow. "Really?"

"Really. Just keep in mind that I'm a guy, which means I'm genetically predisposed to think that whatever mushy romantic tale you're about to tell me is highly cheesy."

Rylann laughed. "I'll keep it simple, then." She rested her drink on the table. "Well, you already heard how Kyle picked me up at the courthouse after my trial. He said he wanted to surprise me with a vacation because I'd been working so hard, but that we needed to drive to Champaign first to meet with his former mentor, the head of the U of I Department of Computer Sciences, to discuss some project Kyle was working on for a client." She held up a sparkly hand, nearly blinding Cade and probably half of the other Starbucks patrons. "In hindsight, yes, that sounds a little fishy, but what do I know about all this network security stuff? He had his laptop out, there was some talk about malicious payloads and Trojan horse attacks—it all sounded legitimate enough at the time."

"Remind me, while I'm acting U.S. attorney, not to assign you to any cybercrime cases."

"*Anyhow*. . . we get to Champaign, which as it so happens, is where Kyle and I first met ten years ago. And the limo turns onto the street where I used to live while in law school, and Kyle asks the driver to pull over because he wants to see the place for old time's sake. So we get out of the limo, and he's making this big speech about the night we met and how he walked me home on the very sidewalk we were standing on— I'll fast-forward here in light of your aversion to the mushy stuff—and I'm laughing to myself because, well, we're standing on the *wrong* side of the street. So naturally, I point that out, and he tells me that nope, I'm wrong, because he remembers everything about that night, so to prove my point I walk across the street to show him and"—she paused here— "and I see a jewelry box, sitting on the sidewalk, in the exact spot where we had our first kiss. Then I turn around and see Kyle down on one knee."

She waved her hand, her eyes a little misty. "So there you go. The whole mushy, cheesy tale. Gag away."

Cade picked up his coffee cup and took a sip. "That was actually pretty smooth."

Rylann grinned. "I know. Former cyber-menace to society or not, that man is a keeper."

Nineteen

BROOKE CUT THINGS closer than she'd intended that evening, and walked through the front door of her condo only five minutes before Cade was supposed to arrive.

I can work around your schedule, he'd said when they'd spoken earlier on the phone.

It was such a silly thing, but it had been a long time since any guy had said that to her. Basically, since she'd started working for Sterling.

It was just a casual comment, she reminded herself. It didn't mean a thing.

Focusing on the task at hand, Brooke quickly set up her surprise in the kitchen, finishing just as someone knocked at her door. She answered, still wearing her work clothes.

Cade stood in her doorway, dressed casually in a polo shirt and jeans. He raised an eyebrow, seeing her in her business attire. "How was the wining and dining?"

"Longer than expected." She gestured for him to come in. "Just let me change and then we can head out."

He looked curiously around her condo, taking in the view. "This is nice."

"Thanks." Despite the hefty mortgage she paid for the one-bedroom plus den, and the ridiculous assessments on top of that, she loved the place. Hardwood floors, a nicely sized master bedroom, and a small eat-in breakfast area off the kitchen with floor-to-ceiling windows that overlooked the city.

Cade walked through her living room, which opened to the kitchen. He stopped when his gaze landed on the champagne bottle that sat chilling in an ice bucket on the counter.

He looked at her. "Is that for me?"

Seeing his obvious surprise, Brooke suddenly felt awkward. When she'd swung by the wine shop around the corner on her way home from dinner, the champagne had seemed like a nice gesture, given that Cade had mentioned getting some really good news. But now she remembered Commandment Number Six of the "Rules of Casual Sex."

No personal gifts except for sex toys and massage oils.

Yes, fine, she got it now. Although, admittedly, she had to bite her lip to keep from laughing at the thought of handing Cade a congratulatory penis ring.

Surprise!

Covering quickly, Brooke waved her hand dismissively at the champagne. "It's a bottle someone gave me as a gift. I had it sitting around and figured that whatever your mysterious news is, 'really damn cool' on the scale of '*meh* to holy-shit-I-just-won-the-Rose-Bowl' merited some champagne."

Noticing that Cade still watched her interestedly, Brooke went into the kitchen and pulled a corkscrew out of one of the drawers. She opened the champagne, poured them each a glass, and handed one over to him. "So. What are we toasting to?"

"In eight weeks I'll be the acting U.S. attorney for the Northern District of Illinois."

Brooke's mouth fell open. "You're kidding. That's awesome."

"It's just while my boss, Cameron, is on maternity leave," he said.

"That doesn't matter. It's still awesome." Brooke clinked

her glass to his. "Congratulations." She took a sip, noticing that his eyes fell to her mouth after she pulled the glass away.

She swallowed, suddenly feeling as though the temperature of the room had shot up twenty degrees. One look—the right look—was all it took from this man, and here she was getting all hot and bothered.

"How is it?" he asked, holding her gaze.

"Not bad." She gestured to his glass of champagne. "Have a taste."

He set his glass on the counter. "I think I will." He hooked his finger into the waistband of her skirt, pulled her closer, and lowered his mouth hungrily to hers.

CADE HAD BEEN in a state—meaning the horny-as-hell kind of state—since the moment Brooke had answered the door in another one of her hot skirt-and-heels combos. He'd been thinking about getting his hands on her all day, ever since they'd talked, and now here she was, pressed against him, her fingers tangled in his hair as their mouths melded together.

You like her.

Ah, lovely. Another annoying voice in his head, this one sounding suspiciously like Vaughn.

Go away. Got my hands on a woman's ass here.

Cade turned his head to murmur wickedly in Brooke's ear. "It seems like such a waste, going out for drinks when we have an open bottle of champagne right here." He dipped his head lower to nuzzle her neck, which he'd discovered last weekend was her weak spot.

Her head fell back. "Well, when you put it that way . . ." she inhaled when he trailed his lips along her collarbone, "I'd hate to be a party to wastefulness."

Glad they were in agreement, Cade swept his mouth over hers in a hot, demanding kiss. Brooke wrapped her arms around his neck and pulled him closer, so he scooped her up and carried her to the closest piece of furniture he could find— the couch in her living room. He laid her down and climbed

over her, tugging at her shirt and sending a button flying in
his impatience.

"Crap. I think I might owe you a new shirt."

"I don't care about the shirt." She pulled his mouth back
to hers.

That decided, he yanked the shirt open the rest of the way.
She moaned when he tugged down one of the lacy cups of
her bra, and traced the tip of her breast with his finger. He
glided his other hand down, along the silky skin of her navel,
then reached underneath her skirt. When he pushed her panties aside, he nearly groaned. "You're so wet for me already."

"Probably because I was thinking about you during my
business dinner."

Oh, really? "What kinds of things were you thinking
about?" He eased two fingers into her, sliding them in and
out in a slow, smooth rhythm. "Maybe it started with me doing
this?"

She moaned, *yes*, and Cade shifted his hand to tease her
clit. She reached up and pulled down the other cup of her bra,
pushing her second breast up for his hungry mouth, and he
greedily sucked on the tight peak. He nipped her gently with
his teeth, his erection threatening to bust through his zipper.
He wanted all of her tonight, underneath him, on top of him,
on her knees—but first things first.

"I'm going to watch while you come," he told her. He loved
seeing her undone like this, and wanted to prolong that just
a little more.

She moaned softly, her lips parting as she breathed raggedly. He couldn't help himself; he bent his head and kissed
her. Her tongue wound around his just as she began to shud-
der in orgasm, and he groaned, feeling her body clench tightly
around his fingers, letting him know just how good it would
feel when he got inside her.

When she finally came down, he gathered her in his arms
and stood up from the couch. His voice had an edge. "Which
way to your bedroom?"

With a sly smile, she waved her hand. "Oh, no. I'm good
now, thanks. I think I'll just crash here and watch TV."

Yep, still as sassy as ever.

"We'll see about that," he growled.

She squealed in surprise when he shifted her in his arms and hauled her over his shoulder in a fireman's carry—business skirt and heels and all.

They passed by a den before entering what was obviously the master bedroom, given the four-poster, king-sized bed that was adorned with cream silk bedding and numerous pillows. Without discussion, he dropped Brooke onto it.

She put her hands down to steady herself and stared up at him in disbelief. "You did not just literally carry me in here over your shoulder."

"Oh, but as we saw, Ms. Parker, I just did." He got rid of his shirt, not wasting any time, then undid his zipper and kicked off the rest of his clothes. He stood before her, naked and hard as steel. "Move to the edge of the bed."

The teasing look was back in her eyes. "You seem very ornery again."

"Brooke," he said warningly.

The little minx just smiled.

She pushed her shirt off her shoulders and tossed it to the floor, then slid two high-heeled legs off the bed. She walked over to him and brushed her hands over his bare chest. "Maybe I can do something to change that." Without further discussion, she got down on her knees and took him into her hot, wet mouth.

"Oh, *fuck*," he moaned. He threaded his hands into her hair and tried not to explode right there.

Play-action pass. Bootleg. End-around. Quarterback sneak. Christ, this woman is blowing my mind.

He looked down and watched as the sexiest, smartest, most confident woman he'd ever met licked her tongue across the throbbing head of his erection.

It was the hottest moment of his life.

"Stroke your hand up and down," he told her in a guttural voice. He felt something raw tug at him, a primal need to make her *his*. He watched as she swirled her tongue over the head, then eased him further in and sucked. "Just like that. Take more of me, Brooke." She went deeper still, then moved her mouth over him. He closed his eyes, letting his hands fall to his sides as she used her lips, tongue, and mouth to bring him right to the brink.

He stopped her before he went all the way over. "Come up here."

She slid her hands up his body as she got to her feet. Her eyes widened as he guided her backward until she was trapped against the bed. He turned her around so that she faced it.

"You remember when we met, how you told me off in your office? Ever since then, I've wanted something." He smoothed his hands up her legs and pushed up her skirt. With one sharp tug, he ripped her lacy thong and tossed it to the floor. "You at my mercy."

He heard the excited catch of her breath and bent his head to murmur in her ear. "Good thing you still have those heels on." He grabbed his jeans off the floor, and removed a condom from his wallet. He rolled it on, then slid his hand up her legs and pushed up her skirt over her bare ass, exposing her to the cool air.

He palmed one of her butt cheeks, and she gasped and exhaled unsteadily.

She wasn't being sassy now.

In fact, judging from the quick rise and fall of her chest, Cade would hazard a guess that Brooke Parker of Sterling Restaurants was quite turned on right then. "Put your hands on the bed."

She did so, the raised bed making it so that she only had to bend a little. He gripped his cock in his hand and pushed the head into her—the high heels gave her just enough height to make this work—then he grabbed her hips and slowly eased into her.

Cade sucked in his breath as her slick passage clenched tight around him. He heard Brooke gasp and immediately stilled. "I'll stop if it's too much."

She shook her head. "No . . . I'm good." She arched her hips back. "Really good."

He clenched his jaw, and began to thrust slowly, moving

in and out of her in a smooth glide. After a few strokes, he increased his pace, his fingers gripping her tightly. His hips smacked against her bottom as her moans tangled in the air with his. He looked down, nearly going over the edge as he watched his cock thrusting in and out of her.

He reached around and slid one hand between her legs. She began to tremble, then she looked over her shoulder, her words a throaty whisper. "Cade. Kiss me."

With a low growl, he braced one hand against the bed, leaned down, and claimed her mouth in a deep, possessive kiss. Skin to skin, they moved together in a slow, erotic rhythm.

Something made Cade pull back and stare into her eyes. "It's so fucking perfect with you," he rasped. He thrust again and they both exploded, together, their loud moans filling the room until they shuddered to a stop and collapsed on the bed.

"ACTING U.S. ATTORNEY Cade Morgan. That ought to do wonders for your fragile ego."

Cade gestured magnanimously. "You are allowed to show your awe."

"And so it begins."

He laughed, taking a sip of his champagne. Normally, he wasn't the biggest fan of the stuff, but since Brooke had opened the bottle to celebrate his promotion, he felt rude not drinking it.

They were curled up on her couch, her legs stretched over his lap as she faced him. After their latest round of *damn*-that-was-some-hot sex, she'd changed into a tank top and pink pajama-looking pants and had snagged a bag of Chips Ahoy! cookies from the kitchen to go with her glass of champagne.

He found the whole combination rather cute.

"So? Tell me how this promotion came about," she said, looking genuinely interested.

Cade filled Brooke in on his meeting with Cameron, and also his subsequent conversation with Rylann. This last part seemed to particularly intrigue her.

"Hold on. You're *friends* with a woman whose fiancé you sent to prison?" Brooke asked, interrupting him.

"What, that doesn't happen every day?" he joked.

"Um . . . no." Brooke mused this over. "Do you think you'll be invited to their wedding?"

Cade blinked. Well, shit. "I hadn't even thought about that." He cocked his head. "I wonder if they make a card that says 'Congratulations and best wishes. So glad we've all gotten past the time I called one of you a terrorist in open court.'"

"Sure. I saw two of those at Hallmark last week."

They looked at each other and laughed.

Cade drained his champagne glass and set it down on the coffee table. Then he reached over and stole a cookie from the bag she held. "What can I say? You met me at a very interesting time in my life."

The words slipped out before he'd thought about them.

"Yeah? What else is going on in your life these days?" Her tone was casual, the words said between nibbles of her cookie, but her bright green eyes were keen as she studied him.

Cade actually debated for a split second.

I found out that I have a brother.

Then he thought, *Nah.* They were having a good time; he didn't want to ruin the mood by dumping his baggage on Brooke.

Luckily, he was saved by the proverbial bell when her cell phone rang.

She frowned, presumably anticipating some sort of work emergency. But when she grabbed her phone off the coffee table and checked the caller ID, her face relaxed.

She answered. "Hey, you."

Cade had a pretty good idea who the "you" was, and he wasn't sure how he felt about the guy calling at ten o'clock on a Friday night. He reached over and poured himself another glass of champagne, as if paying no attention to their conversation.

But he was listening, all right.

"Good," she said next. Her gaze shifted to Cade in response to whatever the caller said next. "Yes."

She smiled as the conversation continued.

"No."

"Don't know."

"Next question."

"Next question."

"Still, with that?"

"I'm going into the office tomorrow. How about lunch at The Shore at noon?"

"I'll keep that in mind. What are you up to tonight?"

"Is that the blonde who sounds like a goat when she orgasms, or the chick who makes you talk dirty in a Scottish accent?" She chuckled. "Good luck with that one. See you tomorrow."

She hung up and set the phone aside before turning back to Cade. "Sorry about that."

"I'll go out on a limb here. Ford?"

She nodded, turning back to her cookie. "Yep."

Cade waited for her to elaborate.

She didn't.

He raised an eyebrow. "Are you sure you two aren't—"

"Positive."

"And all this time, you never—"

"Not once." She waved casually at him. "You should understand. You just told me that you're friends with that Rylann woman. I assume you're not sleeping with her?"

"That Rylann woman doesn't call me at ten o'clock on a Friday night."

"Are you getting ornery again?"

"If I say yes, do I get another blow job?"

She laughed at that, blushing a little. "Nice try."

Cade found that blush even cuter than the pink pajamas and Chips Ahoy! cookies. "Had to give it a shot."

She smiled, and then went quiet for a moment. "Ford and I lived in the same neighborhood growing up. He . . . didn't like being at home very much, so my parents took him in whenever he wanted. He's basically like family."

Her expression said there was a lot more to that story, but since she didn't offer anything further, Cade didn't ask.

She cocked her head, clearly looking to change the subject.

"Do you really want to spend the whole night talking about Ford?"

"Not really." And based on what she'd just said, he already felt more comfortable with their relationship, anyway. Not that he had any *claim* on Brooke or anything. *Pfft.*

"Good." Brooke set down the bag of cookies and climbed over to straddle Cade's lap. Her voice was throaty and coy. "Maybe we can find something else to occupy our time, then."

"Scrabble?"

With a smile, she lowered her head and kissed him.

This was how it should be, Cade thought, sliding his hands under her tank top and caressing the bare skin of her lower back. Two people, having a good time and keeping everything right at the surface.

No need to go diving down into the deeper, murkier waters below.

Twenty

ON TUESDAY, IAN dropped by Brooke's office after she'd gotten back from the day's EEO training session. He appeared extremely pleased.

"I got your message about the meeting with Curt Emery." He gave her an approving nod. "Nice job."

"I wouldn't get too excited yet. It's a long shot," Brooke cautioned him. Although, yes, she was kicking ass and taking names these days. In addition to finalizing all the employment and service agreements for the Staples Center, *and* overseeing the anti-harassment training sessions at the restaurants, she had, in her few free minutes, taken it upon herself to call Curt Emery, the director of food service of the Chicago Bears, and left a message asking for the opportunity to meet with him to talk about Sterling Restaurants' sports and entertainment division.

He'd shocked her by calling back that morning to say yes.

Brooke had done her research, so she knew what she was up against. For the last fifteen years, Spectrum Group—the world's largest contract food service provider—had been in business with Soldier Field, home of the Chicago Bears.

Spectrum's North American division alone had revenues of nearly eleven billion dollars the previous year, providing food service management for everything from corporate cafés, college and university cafeterias, special events catering like the U.S. Open, and sports and entertainment arenas.

As it so happened, over the last two years, Brooke—along with Micah and Tony, the other two members of Ian's "dream team"—had snagged three of Spectrum North America's largest sports clients: Cowboys Stadium, the United Center, and the Staples Center. And while Sterling still didn't hold a candle in either size or revenue to the Goliath corporation that was Spectrum, Brooke had no doubt that people were paying attention.

Now that Sterling had contracts with both the Chicago Cubs and Bulls, it made sense for her to pitch to the city's football team, too. She'd heard through the grapevine that the Bears' relationship with Spectrum had started via a personal connection—somebody at Spectrum played golf with the cousin of one of the Bears' corporate directors or something—but she had no idea whether that personal relationship still existed, or whether Curt Emery, director of food service, might be willing to consider other options.

Only one way to find out.

Ian took a seat in front of her desk, stretching out comfortably. "What do you make of the fact that Emery asked to meet only with you?"

Brooke had initially paused over that as well. When the Bears' director had left his message, he'd specifically said he was willing to meet with her, but only her. Then again, it wasn't unusual for her, Micah, or Tony to take meetings alone—particularly when first meeting a potential new client. "I'm guessing it means that the Bears have another year, maybe two, left on their contract with Spectrum. So while Emery may be interested in making a change down the road, he wants to keep this preliminary meet and greet casual."

"Regardless, it's a great first step," Ian said. "When's the meeting?"

"Two weeks from Monday. At the Bears' corporate office up in Lake Forest."

"Ooh, you get to hang out at Halas Hall. Very cool." Ian rested his hands behind his head. "I'm already picturing myself in the Sterling luxury suite at Soldier Field, right above the fifty-yard line."

Both the lawyer and pragmatic woman in Brooke felt the need to manage her CEO's expectations. "You're getting way ahead of yourself here, Ian. In fact, I think you just lapped yourself."

"A man can dream, Brooke."

She chuckled. "Who are you kidding? You barely use our suites at Wrigley Field and the United Center."

He waved this off. "Yeah, but football's different. If we get this deal with the Bears, you better believe my butt will be at Soldier Field for every home game." He saw her fighting back a grin. "What?"

"I just wonder what it is about men and football," Brooke said. Sure, because of her job she could hold her own when it came to talking sports, but—*wow*—had her eyes been opened when she'd been down in Dallas, negotiating the Cowboys deal. Those men didn't just love football, they *lived* football. "Is it a warrior-metaphor kind of thing? The idea that the strongest, toughest men of the region strap on their armor and step onto the battlefield to face off against the strongest, toughest opponents?"

"As a matter of fact, that's exactly what it is."

"I see. And remind me: in what century did it become customary for one's army to be attended at the battle ground by hot girls with spanky pants and pom-poms? Was that a tradition Napoleon started?" Brooke pretended to muse. "Or maybe it was Genghis Khan."

"You scoff at America's sport. I have fired people for less."

Brooke threw Ian a get-real look. "No, you haven't. You don't fire anyone without trotting down to my office and asking *me* first whether you'll get sued. And then I'm always the one that has to fire them, anyway."

"Because you do it with such charm," Ian said with a grin. He knew she spoke the truth. "You know I'd never get by without you, right?"

"You remember that the next time I'm up for a raise and I hand you another sixteen-page report with charts and graphs."

"I can hardly wait." With a wink, Ian got up from the chair to leave. He paused in the doorway, and then turned back to her with a thoughtful expression. "It's because it reminds me of some of the best moments I've had with my father."

Brooke cocked her head, not following. "I'm sorry?"

"You asked what it is about football," he explained. "I knew I was gay by the time I was thirteen. And so did my father. But that wasn't something we could talk about back then. In fact, for about five years, we didn't talk much at all. But for three hours every Sunday, while watching a game, we could hang out and yell and cheer and just be a father and son again." He paused, with a slight smile at the memory. "I don't know about other men, but that's what football means to me."

IAN'S WORDS HUNG in the air after he left, giving Brooke plenty of food for thought. Admittedly, she'd never paid too much attention to football—possibly because she had a teeny, tiny bias against the sport. Growing up, like in many towns, the most popular kids in her high school had been the football players and cheerleaders, and since she definitely hadn't been part of that crowd, she'd dismissed the whole scene as too clique-ish.

But now she thought back to that day at the Cubs game, and the way Ford, Tucker, and Charlie had nearly swooned when Cade had walked into the skybox. They'd gone on and on about Cade's college football days, particularly his Rose Bowl victory, yet it was a part of his life that Brooke herself knew very little about.

And maybe that was a good thing. Since she didn't want to get too close emotionally, then it was probably better that she didn't know all about Cade's past experiences, the things that had shaped him to be the man he'd become.

That settled, she went back to work. But she heard Ford's voice in her head, distracting her.

It's only one of the most famous moments in college football history.

On the other hand . . .

She *did* work with sports teams all the time as part of her job. If Cade's Rose Bowl win was that big of a deal, then she probably should know more about it. It was research, really. Besides, it was *one* football game—it wasn't as if she was going to get weak in the knees from watching him throw a few nice passes.

That decided, Brooke got up from her desk and shut her office door. She grabbed her iPad out of her briefcase, then took a seat and fired up Google. She searched "Cade Morgan Rose Bowl," and clicked on "videos."

Voilà.

She scrolled through the various YouTube clips, clicked on the link that looked most promising, and settled in at her desk. It was a fourteen-minute highlight clip, beginning with all sorts of pomp and circumstance and an announcer talking over swelling marching band music: "We're live in Pasadena, where the dreams, the blood, sweat, and tears, the perseverance, and the anticipation, have all come down to this: the 2001 Rose Bowl, presented by . . ."

Blah, blah, blah . . . Come on people, I'm a busy woman, let's get to the good stuff.

Finally, things shifted to the actual game footage, and—

There he was. Twenty-one-year-old Cade, wearing his purple Wildcats uniform—helmet, shoulder pads, and all—with "Morgan" blazed proudly across the back of his jersey.

So cute.

Brooke watched a montage that covered the big moments in the first half of the game, plays in which Cade dropped back out of the pocket and dodged and weaved and ran and passed the ball, and then right before halftime he did this thing where he fought off one lineman and spun around and charged through another guy to get to the end zone and tie the game, and—

Holy crap, he was awesome.

In the third quarter, they cut to a shot of Cade standing on the sidelines, watching while the refs did a measurement to see if Northwestern had stopped a key first down. It was the first time during the highlights clip that they had shown him with his helmet off, and Brooke smiled when she saw Cade, all sweaty and dirty, with his dark brown hair mussed and shorter than he wore it today.

The video went on, featuring clip after clip of Cade in action. There could be no doubt that he was the star of the game—but as Brooke continued to watch, her heart began to beat faster with nervousness.

Because, unlike anyone who'd been watching that game live, she knew how it was going to end.

As the highlights from the fourth quarter flew by, her anticipation grew. Finally, with fifteen seconds left on the clock and Northwestern down by four points, that purple Morgan jersey got behind the offensive line for what Brooke knew was Cade's last time playing on a football field.

She held her breath as the center snapped the ball.

Cade dropped back, skillfully moving into position and setting up for the pass—no desperate Hail Mary here—and Brooke saw the linebacker charging around the line, heading right for Cade, and she had no doubt that Cade saw him, too, yet he never wavered as he pulled back and threw a perfect, beautiful, sixty-five-yard pass right into the hands of the wide receiver waiting in the end zone.

The crowd went absolutely wild.

What everyone failed to see at the time—the entire stadium's eyes had been on the ball and the wide receiver—but what Brooke saw in a slow-motion replay from a different camera angle, was that the linebacker had tackled Cade a split second after he'd released the ball. They hit the ground hard together, all that force and weight landing on Cade's right shoulder.

Brooke watched the replay with no small amount of awe as Cade used one arm, the one not injured, to shove the linebacker off of him so he could see if the pass was complete. The instant the ball dropped into the wide receiver's hands, he rolled onto his back on the field, one fist raised in victory.

Seconds later, a mob of his ecstatic teammates fell on him, one piling on top of the other in the excitement.

Brooke saw it in their faces, the moment his teammates knew something was wrong. The raucous celebration gave way to frantic shouts for the trainer and concerned expressions as everyone cleared out of the way to give Cade space. He remained on the field for some time, talking to the coach and the trainers as they looked him over. When they finally helped Cade up and he walked off the field, the whole stadium, previously quiet, broke into thunderous applause and cheers.

The video ended after that.

Brooke leaned back in her chair, blinking back an unexpected swell of emotion.

Probably, if she and Cade *had* been dating seriously, she would want to know what he'd been thinking while lying on that field. Undoubtedly, she'd also want to know why he never brought up the subject of football, and whether he missed that part of his life. And, if they'd been in a real relationship, it wouldn't just be the past she'd be curious about. She'd also want to know about whatever was going on in his personal life, and whether he was okay, and whether, maybe, there was something she could do to help.

Good thing, then, that they weren't serious.

Because that was a *lot* of questions for two people who, as Cade had once put it, could probably go their entire relationship without ever saying anything meaningful at all to each other.

Someone knocked at her door, interrupting Brooke's thoughts. "Come in."

Tony, the VP of sales, stuck his head inside her office.

"I heard about your meeting with the Bears," he said. "Nicely done. Got a few minutes to chat?"

"Sure." She clicked off her iPad.

Tony pointed. "I can come back if you're in the middle of something."

Brooke waved this off. "I was just messing around on the Internet." She shoved the iPad back into her briefcase, and then turned back to Tony. "So. Soldier Field. Given the gleam in your eye, it's probably best if I give you the same long-shot speech I just gave Ian."

Duty called once again.

Twenty-one

"ARE YOU SURE you should be doing this?"

Standing a few feet away, Cade brushed off Zach's question. Although, as a matter of fact, he probably should *not* be doing this. "Stop worrying about my shoulder. Focus instead on those slow feet of yours."

They'd commandeered a deserted field behind a warehouse, where Zach apparently scrimmaged during the off-season with his football buddies. Staying true to his word, Cade had suggested they hang out someplace closer to his brother's neighborhood this time—after not so subtly extracting a guarantee from Zach that Noah wouldn't be there.

Deep down Cade knew, as his relationship with Zach grew, that one day he would have to face his father. But that day was still a long way out. For now, he wanted to focus on Zach. His brother lived on the south side of the city, in a neighborhood of modest homes that had been built right after World War II. Cade was familiar enough with the area to know that it was relatively safe, and that the football team at the public high school Zach attended was one of the best in Chicago.

He'd bet that was one of the reasons Noah had chosen this particular neighborhood.

Cade stood midfield, waiting for Zach to take his place at the line of scrimmage.

"When's the last time you threw a football?" Zach asked worriedly.

Aside from the few times Cade had tossed one around casually with friends, a long time. "About twelve years."

Zach threw him a panicked look.

"I won't push it," Cade said. It wasn't as if his shoulder was entirely unusable; in fact, on a daily basis it didn't bother him at all. His rotator cuff simply couldn't withstand the repetitive stress of competitive football. "I just want to see what I can do." He pointed emphatically. "And if the answer is 'not much,' you better not tell a soul. I've got a reputation to uphold here."

Zach smiled, loosening up. "All right. I don't want to stand in the way of you reliving your glory days or whatever."

"Good. But in case this all goes south, my car keys are in the outside pocket of my duffle bag. When you drive me to the emergency room, if I'm too busy mumbling incoherently from the pain, just tell them I've got Blue Cross Blue Shield insurance."

Zach's eyes went wide.

"I'm kidding, Zach. Now get moving."

They started with shorter routes, with Cade faking the hike and dropping back while Zach sprinted for the pass. He pushed Zach hard that morning, just like every coach had ever pushed him, but he knew the kid could take it. He saw how good Zach was—so much so, that it got Cade's own competitive juices flowing. Luckily, he'd kept in shape over the years, lifting weights, swimming, and running, so he was primed to be back on that field, every muscle in his body ready and raring to go.

Save one.

After an hour or so, Cade felt the soreness creeping into his right shoulder. "Why don't we take a break?" he suggested to Zach.

They grabbed a couple of bottled waters from Cade's duffle bag and sat in the grass. The field they were playing on that morning wasn't much to speak of, with its view of the warehouse and the adjacent empty parking lot, but there was open space and lots of grass. Two guys playing football on a Saturday afternoon didn't need much more.

"How long have you lived in this neighborhood?" he asked.

"Since I was five," Zach said. "We'd been living in an apartment on the west side before that, but then my dad got a new job that paid enough for us to buy a house here."

Cade debated where he wanted to take the conversation from there. He looked across the field, keeping his tone casual. "What does Noah do for a living these days?"

"He's a night security guard at Water Tower Place. My mom also works, as a customer service rep for ComEd." Zach plucked at the grass. "I told her about you."

Cade tried to picture this unknown woman for whom Noah had apparently settled down. He felt a flash of protectiveness toward his own mother, who'd had to do everything on her own. "How'd that go over?"

"She thought it was great that you and I were spending time together." Zach paused. "She'd like to meet you."

Cade took another sip of water, grateful that the sunglasses he wore hid the uncertainty he felt. He deliberately kept his voice cool. "Does Noah know we're talking?"

"No. But I know he'd like to see you, too," Zach added quietly.

Cade looked out at the field again, having serious doubts about that one. He deliberately changed the subject. "How are things going with Paige?"

A flicker of disappointment crossed Zach's face. Probably, he'd been hoping to talk more about their father. But despite the fact that Cade was quickly growing closer to Zach, there were limits on how far he was willing to go when it came to Noah Garrity.

"I bought some book of poetry I saw at the bookstore. One that didn't look totally uncool," Zach said. "But it's been a busy week. I haven't had a chance to give it to Paige yet."

Busy week? The kid was on summer vacation. From the way Zach was squirming right then, Cade had a sneaking suspicion his brother was still nervous about talking to the girl. "You said she works at an ice-cream shop around here, right?" He made a big show of wiping the sweat off his brow. "Come to think of it, a nice double cone would really hit the spot in this heat."

Zach's expression was one of pure teenage mortification. "Yeah, because that's exactly what will help my inability to talk to her—my older brother watching and critiquing all my moves."

"I thought we'd already established that you don't have any moves."

"Now that's funny. Picking on someone half your age. Hey, here's an idea: I'll introduce you to Paige as soon as I meet this so-called smart, witty, and hot woman you're supposedly seeing. Sounds a lot like one of those made-up girlfriends who live in Niagara Falls."

"She's real. I'm seeing her tonight, in fact." They hadn't decided their specific plans yet, but Brooke had texted him last night, asking if he was free.

"Wow. You actually, like, *beamed* when you said that."

"Get out of here," Cade scoffed. "I did not."

"What's her name?"

Cade opened his mouth to answer, then paused.

Zach grinned. "Worried you can't say it without beaming again?"

Ridiculous. "Her name is Brooke." He deliberately maintained a straight face.

Zach made a big show of studying him, presumably looking for any sign of this alleged "beaming." He stepped closer and then, with a comically scrutinizing face, slowly looked at one side of Cade's face, and then the other.

Cade never cracked once.

Finally, Zach gave up. "Dude, I'm impressed. You need to show me that trick." His cell phone suddenly rang from the backpack he'd left on the grass.

"What trick?" Cade asked. His prosecutorial, I-*ask*-the-questions-I-don't-answer-them face? Just another trick in his trial arsenal, a close cousin to his equally impressive don't-bullshit-me face.

"How to hide your true feelings so well." With a sly grin, Zach reached across the grass and pulled the phone out of his backpack. "It's my mom. I should probably take this." He stood up and walked off a few feet to talk in private.

Cade watched as Zach answered the phone, his brother's words still hanging in the air. *How to hide your true feelings so well.* He knew Zach had made the comment in jest, part of his teasing about Brooke. But, in reality, it wasn't all that far off the mark.

I envy you, he'd told Zach the first time they'd met.

Because I'm a mess?

No. Because you're not afraid to be a mess.

Seeing that Zach was still talking to his mother, Cade reached over and pulled his cell phone out of the duffle bag.

He shot a quick text message to Brooke. I'VE DECIDED THAT I'M TAKING YOU OUT FOR DINNER TONIGHT, CINDERELLA.

A few moments later, he got a reply.

THE SOON-TO-BE ACTING U.S. ATTORNEY HAS COMMANDED, AND SO IT SHALL BE.

He laughed at that. She was a saucy one, all right. He wrote back. YOU ARE ALLOWED TO SHOW YOUR PLEASURE. PICK YOU UP AT 7:00.

She fired back a response. 7:30.

He smiled at the inside joke. OF COURSE YOU WOULD SAY 7:30.

Cade tossed his phone into his bag just as Zach walked back over.

"Sorry about that." Zach shoved his phone into his backpack and took a seat on the grass. "My mom needed to talk to me about a few things."

"No problem." Cade looked out at the field before them. He felt good right then, really good, which was probably what prompted him to look sideways at Zach and say what he did next. "I want you to do something for me."

Zach shrugged earnestly. "Sure. What?"

"Go long," Cade said, meeting his brother's gaze through his sunglasses. "Just once."

After a moment, Zach nodded. "Okay."

Cade grabbed the football and stood up. He walked to the

far end of the field, and watched as Zach took his place to the right of him, at the line of scrimmage.

"Blue Cross Blue Shield?" Zach called out.

"Yep." In the zone now, Cade mentally readied himself and called the play. He faked the snap and dropped back.

Out of the corner of his eye, he saw Zach take off at top speed, and everything else faded away. He could still perfectly envision the wall of purple Wildcats jerseys in front of him, could hear the roar of the crowd that day in Pasadena. Mere seconds left on the clock, but this moment was his, the adrenaline pumping through his veins as his wide receiver headed for the end zone. In his peripheral vision he saw the linebacker charging around the line, gunning for the sack, but screw him—victory was so close he could taste it and nothing was going to get in his way. He pulled back and threw hard, stepping back to watch as the football sailed through the air in a perfect spiral.

About seven yards short.

Readjusting quickly, Zach cut forward and dove for the ball. He caught it midair in his fingertips and landed in a sprawl on the field.

He held the ball up victoriously. "First down!"

Cade broke into a wide grin and headed over. If this had been a real game, he would've just thrown an embarrassing interception and probably been booed off the field. But he'd take the moment nevertheless.

When he reached Zach, he held out his left hand and helped him off the grass. "Now that was some fast footwork." He slapped him across the shoulders

Zach grinned, boyishly proud. "Thanks." He pointed to Cade's right shoulder. "We're done?"

Cade nodded, wincing at the sharp twinge in his shoulder. "Oh, yeah. We're done."

Twenty-two

THIS TIME, BROOKE was ready to go when Cade showed up at her apartment. With her schedule, she didn't get a date night often, so she'd spent a few extra minutes—okay, maybe a lot of extra minutes—on her hair and makeup and had slipped on a cute pair of jeans with her heels.

Cade eyes traveled over her when she answered the door, coming to rest on her shoes. "Are those the ones from Monday night?"

"They are."

He stepped inside her apartment and kicked the door shut. Well, then.

"I have good memories of those shoes." With a warm gleam in his eye, he reached up and cupped the nape of her neck, leaning in to kiss her.

Hmm. She might have to wear these shoes all the time around Cade, if they put him in this good of a moo—

He jerked back, cursing under his breath.

Brooke blinked in surprise, still feeling the warm press of his lips on hers. "Um . . . what just happened?"

He winced, rotating his arm gingerly. "I reached around to grab your ass."

"And . . . it electrocuted you?"

He chucked her under the chin. "No, sassy. My shoulder's a little sore after playing football today."

That was news to her. "I didn't know you still played football."

"I don't. I was helping out someone else and got caught up in the moment."

Someone who? Brooke nearly asked, then decided against it. If Cade didn't want to let her in on this mysterious thing going on with him, she wasn't going to pry it out of him. "Did you take anything for the pain?"

He brushed this off. "I iced it earlier. I don't need anything for the pain."

Men. "We can stay in and take it easy tonight, Cade. It's no big deal."

"I'm fine." He raised an eyebrow, as if daring her to contradict that.

"Okay," she said, with a shrug. If that was how he wanted to play this, she'd go along with it.

For now.

BROOKE HAD TO admit, Cade put on a really good tough-guy act.

If this had been a first date, she probably wouldn't have noticed that anything was wrong. Not surprisingly, he was nearly pitch-perfect in covering up the fact that something was bothering him. He was charming as ever, he asked about her workweek, made her laugh, and told several interesting anecdotes about life as an assistant U.S. attorney. But by now she knew him well enough to pick up on the little signs, like the way he'd reached with his left hand to open the restaurant door for her. Or how his jaw had tensed slightly when he'd needed to use his right hand to cut his steak.

Going along with the charade, she said nothing through

dinner, nor through their dessert of flourless chocolate cake, nor during the cab ride back to her building. Instead, she waited until they got inside her apartment.

"I have something for you," she said with a deliberately mischievous air.

He raised an eyebrow. "I like the sound of that."

She led him into the kitchen.

"More champagne?" he joked.

She shook her head. "Better."

She took out a glass and filled it with water. His expression was one of confusion at first, then he made a face when she reached into a second cabinet and pulled out a bottle of ibuprofen.

"That's my surprise?" He looked like a boy who'd been given socks for Christmas.

Brooke dumped two caplets into her hand and held them out. "Humor me."

After a big show of scoffing and grunts of disapproval, Cade popped the pills into his mouth and took a drink of water.

"Do you miss playing?" she asked.

She figured he'd most likely fluff her off with his answer, the same way he'd nonchalantly handled her friends' questions at the Cubs/Sox game. But it was something she'd been wondering about ever since watching the Rose Bowl video, and she just wanted . . . to ask.

Instead, he surprised her by looking at her for a long moment. "Yes."

That quiet, simple admission tugged at Brooke's heart. She'd seen his passion for the sport in the video, and his incredible talent, yet he hadn't given up when football had been taken away from him. Instead, he'd channeled that drive and confidence into his legal career and had made a name for himself as federal prosecutor.

In her business, she worked with successful men and women all the time. But Cade Morgan . . . impressed her.

She came around the counter and held out her hand. "Come with me."

His expression was skeptical. "What is it this time? A heating pad?"

"Not a heating pad," she promised. But he was on the right track.

She led him into her white-marbled bathroom and headed to the oversized shower. Without saying a word, she reached in and turned on both the rain showerhead and the jets.

"Now this seems more promising," he said.

"I thought you might see it that way." Brooke lifted her shirt over her head, and then toed off her shoes. She undid her jeans and slid them down her hips and off.

Her bra hit the floor next, and then her underwear.

Cade's eyes were on her the entire time. Instinctively, he reached for the buttons on his shirt, then grunted in pain and dropped his right arm in frustration.

Brooke crossed the room to him. "I'll get that." She stepped close and began to undo the buttons on his shirt.

"Just in case you were getting any tricky ideas, I still have one good arm to throw you over my shoulder."

She looked up at him. "I get the nothing-fazes-me routine, Cade. I really do. But tonight, let me take care of you."

She saw a flicker of emotions cross his face, before he answered huskily.

"Okay."

CADE WATCHED AS Brooke finished undoing the buttons of his shirt, then carefully eased it off his shoulders. She freed his good arm first and then, gently, his other one. She smoothed her hands down his chest, and he sucked in his breath when her fingers brushed across his stomach.

She moved her hands to the button of his jeans, and thankfully wasted no time in undoing his fly. He helped her out, using his good arm to push his jeans and boxer briefs over his hips. He kicked them off with his shoes, then stood before her, naked.

Brooke took his hand and led him toward the shower, her dark gold hair tumbling down her back. She stepped inside and leaned her head back under the spray, looking like a goddess with the water streaming down her body.

Cade didn't need an invitation. He stepped inside the shower and shut the door, closing his eyes as steam swirled around him and six jets pulsed against his skin. He growled low in approval when he felt Brooke press her warm, wet body against his.

"Keep your eyes closed and take a step back," she said.

"You're naked and wet. My eyes aren't staying closed for long."

"Trust me. You'll like this."

He couldn't resist such a promise. Cade stepped back and inhaled sharply when one of the jets hit his sore shoulder. Then he relaxed as the hot water slowly began to work its magic. He tipped his head back, giving in. "That feels great." He felt Brooke move around, then she stepped onto the marble bench behind him.

Her soft hands rested lightly on his shoulders. "Tell me if I do anything that hurts."

She slid her hands down his chest, her fingertips like silk against his skin as the water beat over him. His erection swelled as her hands began to caress him in a sensual massage, soothing the muscles of his chest, arms, and back.

It felt like . . . heaven.

For several minutes, Cade did nothing except enjoy the sensation of Brooke's hands and the pulsing water running over his body. He leaned back, his head resting against the lush curves of her breasts. She was careful around his sore shoulder, avoiding those muscles and letting the water, steam, and ibuprofen loosen him up. But then she lowered her mouth and kissed his neck, and by then he was so sensitized from the heat, the jets, and from her massage that he groaned.

She pulled back. "Does that hurt?"

"No." Needing more than just her hands, or a teasing kiss, he turned around and snaked his good arm around her waist. He lifted her off the marble ledge, crushing his mouth to hers. As they kissed, he slid her down his body, skin to skin, until her feet touched the ground.

She pulled back from the kiss. "I'm supposed to be doing all the work," she reminded him breathlessly.

Cade pressed her against the shower wall, the jets pulsing against his back as his cock pulsed against her. Unable to resist, he rubbed the tip of his shaft between her soft folds, fighting for control. "I need to be in you, Brooke."

She looked up into his eyes, and whatever she saw made her meld her mouth to his while fumbling to turn off the water. He pushed open the shower door with his good arm, and in a tangle of towels, hands, legs, and mouths, they landed on the plush oversized rug in front of the bathtub.

Brooke reached over, opened one of the drawers in her vanity, and pulled out a condom. She ripped it open and slid it over him, then she straddled his hips and slowly eased onto him, inch by sweet, heavenly inch.

Her eyes opened and met his just at the moment when he was fully buried inside. Cade's chest pulled tight at the intimacy of the moment, and he was filled with a sudden need for more.

He pushed up on his elbows, not giving a shit about the pain in his shoulder, and pulled her in for a kiss. He eased back to the ground, bringing her with him and holding tight, wanting to be as close as he could get as she began moving over him.

Twenty-three

ON MONDAY, CADE sat at the head of the table in a trial-prep room—a "war room" as they were called around the office—directing his team as they worked through the massive evidence database they'd put together in the Sanderson case.

The war room served a dual function: a place where the trial team could meet, since no AUSA had an office large enough to comfortably accommodate ten people; and it also served as the storage room where they would maintain the many boxes of evidence in the case.

Discovery would begin soon, and Cade wanted to make sure that they had everything in order and that all the evidence was accounted for. As such, he'd gathered the team he and Cameron had assembled: Rylann, who would cochair the case along with him; two midlevel AUSAs from the special prosecutions group; and two paralegals. Along with them were Huxley and Vaughn, as well as two other FBI agents who'd assisted them in monitoring the various recorded conversations throughout the investigation. They all sat around the table, everyone armed with either an open laptop or iPad as they worked their way through the database.

"And we've got all the records for wire transfers and deposits into Diamond Strategic Development's accounts?" Cade asked Vaughn and Huxley, referring to the shell company Senator Sanderson had created to hide the funds he'd collected as bribes.

Huxley nodded. "Boxes twenty-three through twenty-eight."

As the paralegals made notes to the database, Cade moved on to the next item. "I know we have the call index . . . speaking of which, what's the status on the audio recordings?"

"You have all of them," Vaughn said. "The only thing you don't have is the video of Sanderson and Torino's meeting at Sogna. The forensic lab has the original footage we took from the restaurant on a hard drive; they just haven't had a chance to transfer it to a DVD. I'll follow up with them next week if we still don't have it."

"They've had the video for four weeks. Tell them I want my copy by Friday or I'll drive over to the FBI lab and burn it onto a DVD myself."

"I'm pretty sure that would violate the chain of custody," Vaughn said, never missing a chance to be a smart-ass.

"You guys worry about chain of custody?" Rylann joked. "Wow. Such sticklers."

They continued that way for the rest of the afternoon, with everyone good-natured despite the fact that double-checking evidence logs was undoubtedly one of the most tedious parts of an AUSA's and special agent's job. They made it until six o'clock and finally called it a day.

Huxley pressed his forehead against the table. "That was mind-numbing."

Vaughn half-groaned in agreement. "I need a drink."

Cade concurred wholeheartedly with both those sentiments, so the three of them went to an Irish pub located a block away from the federal building. After they ordered dinner and a round of drinks, Cade quickly checked his cell phone.

Of course Vaughn, with his FBI superpowers of perception, had to comment.

"Got another offer on the table that expires soon?" he asked.

"Go away."

Vaughn grinned. "You're quite circumspect about this situation with Brooke. I find that very intriguing, don't you, Hux?"

No reply.

"Hux?" Vaughn looked to his right, where Huxley was reading something on *his* phone. With an unmistakable smile, he tucked his phone into the pocket of his impeccably tailored Ralph Lauren suit, and then noticed Cade and Vaughn looking at him. "Sorry. What were we talking about?"

"Just giving Cade crap about a certain sexy general counsel. But never mind that." Vaughn pointed suspiciously. "What's going on here, with the phone and the sneaky smile?" He studied his partner. "Don't tell me you actually have a hot date tonight."

"Okay, I won't tell you." Huxley took a sip of his beer, deliberately leaving them hanging.

"Look at you," Cade said. "With who?"

"Addison."

"Addison? Who's—" It took Vaughn a second, then his mouth fell open. "Agent *Simms*? When did this happen?"

Huxley swirled his glass, looking quite coy. "Things have been percolating for a while. But they shifted into high gear after our fake date at Sogna."

Vaughn threw out his hands in exasperation. "First Morgan, now you. Plus McCall's getting married next month, and Pallas is having a kid. Purposely. Am I the only one *not* getting laid as part of an FBI sting operation?"

Huxley pretended to muse over this. "Maybe you should take some time. Figure out what's gone wrong with your mojo these days."

"My mojo is perfectly fine," Vaughn assured him.

Cade was curious. "Is it serious?"

Huxley smiled. "Yeah. I think so."

Vaughn scoffed at this. "Come on. You've only been seeing her for, what, a month?"

Huxley shrugged. "I like her. She likes me. It's not that complicated."

Cade and Vaughn threw each other looks. *Right.*

"Amateur," Vaughn said, with a conspiratorial grin.

"Amateur, huh? I'll be sure to ask Addison tonight if she agrees with that assessment."

And if his confident smile was any indication, Agent Seth Huxley wasn't worried about the answer to that one bit.

"YOU REALLY DO impress me, you know."

Cade peered down at Brooke, who lay against his chest, curled up in the sheets of her bed. "Thanks. I even impressed myself with that one."

She chuckled. "I wasn't referring to that move you threw in at the end there. Although, yes, well done, you."

"Glad you approve."

"Actually, I was thinking about our conversation earlier, when you were talking about being out with Vaughn and Huxley."

"You're thinking about Vaughn and Huxley while we're lying in bed together? Not sure I like the sound of that."

She perked her head up and looked at him. "Oh . . . so that's not something you would ever consider? The three of you, you know . . . all at once? Because I kind of have this fantasy I was going to talk to you about."

Cade was about to laugh, but then she held his gaze so unflinchingly that for a split second he wondered if she was actually serious.

Okay . . . this definitely was *not* a conversation he'd ever expected to have with Brooke Parker of Sterling Restaurants, the Gorgeous Green Eyes, and Holy Shit She's Into Foursomes.

But then he saw the telltale sparkle in her eyes.

He exhaled. "You suck."

"Oh my God, you should've seen the look on your—" She

cut off, laughing when he beaned her with one of the pillows. Then he bonked her two more times for good measure.

She sprawled across the bed when he'd finished, her hair tousled about her shoulders. "So that's a 'no,' then?"

Cade smiled. The woman may have driven him crazy, but he had a grin on his face the whole way. He lay on his side, facing her. "That is definitely a 'no.' And you still suck."

She turned into him, absentmindedly trailing her fingers over his bare chest. "What I was referring to, when I said I was impressed, was the way you've managed to have so much balance with your job. You're obviously very successful. You have a great career at the U.S. Attorney's Office. Yet you still have time to play football and hang out with Vaughn and Huxley and just . . . have an actual life." She mused momentarily over this. "I haven't figured out that trick yet."

"I get busy, too, especially when I'm on trial." Cade paused, proceeding cautiously with his next words since he knew it was a sensitive issue. "But you do realize that your work schedule isn't exactly the norm, right?"

She thought about that. "It's just because we're building the company right now," she said, ready, as always, to defend Sterling. "Ten years ago, Ian owned one restaurant. Now, on top of seven additional restaurants, we're in ballparks and arenas across the country. Things will quiet down eventually, but for now I just have to keep chugging away."

"Have to?" Cade asked.

"Ah, I see what you're trying to do there, counselor. I *want* to keep chugging away," she quickly amended. "Look, I know the hours are a little crazy. But I worked hard to end up right where I am now. And when I walk through Sterling's doors every morning, I feel proud of what I've accomplished."

That brought to mind something Cade had been curious about. "Do you ever go back to Glenwood?"

She tucked her arm under her head. "I haven't been back there in years. My parents sold our townhome after I graduated from high school. In fact, they put it on the market literally the week after I graduated. After it sold, they moved three hours west of here, to a small town on the Mississippi River.

I remember being so perplexed by that at first—my parents had lived in Chicago for years, and then Glenwood, which was a decent-sized suburb. So I kept wondering when the desire to live in a small town had set in.

"They moved just after I started college, so the first time I saw the place was Thanksgiving break. It's a cute house, a little Victorian, and they have a big yard. On my first visit, my mom took me around the yard and told me about all these plans she had for a garden. I remember laughing a little, and asking her when she'd gotten so into gardening, since the most we'd ever had at our townhome was a few potted plants. And she said to me, half-joking and half-serious, something about being inspired by all the big, fancy gardens she'd had to drive by, every day, when we lived in Glenwood."

Brooke chewed her lip, thinking about that. "It was this strange moment, because, as a teenager, I'd really only thought about how it felt for *me* to live in the 'poor' part of town, and how much harder *I* had always had to work for everything. But then I kind of put it together, the fact that my parents had put their place on the market the week after I'd graduated, and realized that they'd probably been wanting to get out of that place for a long time. But they'd stayed for me, so that I could get the education they thought I deserved. That was . . . a little humbling." She looked at him across the bed. "I just don't want to let them down. It's like, sometimes I feel this weight, the pressure of everything everyone in the Parker family, including myself, has done for me to get where I am today."

She peered at him, appearing surprised. "I've never said that to anyone. Not even Ford."

"Why tell me?" he asked huskily.

"I don't know . . ." She studied him, then shrugged, deliberately teasing. "Maybe I just wanted to talk. And you happened to be here."

"I feel so used."

She laughed, just like he'd hoped. And when she curled closer to him, he felt it—that same tightening in his chest. He looked down at her, turning more serious. "I'm sure, more than anything, your parents just want you to be happy."

Brooke nodded, as if mulling this over. "Well, and I am happy, obviously," she said, almost as an afterthought. She changed the subject. "What about your parents? Are they in Chicago?"

It was a perfectly innocuous question. Cade started with the easy part. "My mom lives in Scottsdale. She got married after I graduated from college and moved shortly after that. It was kind of weird when she got married, because it had always been just the two of us, but I'm happy for her. Kent, her husband, is a good guy."

He paused, falling silent for a long moment before something drove him on. "Do you remember that night we met at Bar Nessuno, when I showed up late?"

Brooke nodded. "You said you'd had a strange day."

"The reason I was running late was because my sixteen-year-old half brother, who I didn't know existed, showed up at my office out of the blue."

Her eyes widened. "Oh, wow."

"That was basically my reaction at first."

"How did you not know he existed?" she asked.

Certainly a fair question, so Cade thought about where to go from there. He'd avoided talking about Noah for so long, it wasn't easy to know where to start. "I've only met my father once. My mom got pregnant when they were in high school and he bailed on us. I was ten when he finally decided to show up. He came to my house, and I was furious with him for not being around. But then we went out into the yard and played football, and it was good. Really good. Like, suddenly there was this person I barely knew who fit into my life so perfectly." Cade's tone turned dry. "Of course, it was all an illusion."

"What happened?" Brooke asked.

"When we'd finished playing football, Noah—my father— asked if I wanted to go to the Bears game with him the following weekend. He never showed up that day. Or any other day afterward."

Cade lay there, debating, before he continued. "I know the exact moment I pushed him away. It was when I called him 'Dad.' I saw the panic in his eyes, and I think, deep down, that a part of me knew right then that I'd blown it. For years, I wished I could go back and change that one moment, wished I could tell myself to keep it in check, and just not *care* so much. Because in the end, I was setting myself up for a huge disappointment."

After a pause, he looked at Brooke. "I've never told anyone that before."

She held his gaze. "What made you tell me?"

He pretended to think about that. "Maybe I wanted to talk, and you just happened to be here." When she smiled, he reached over and pulled her closer, their naked limbs tangling together as she rested her head against his chest.

Tomorrow morning he would undoubtedly start to sweat, big-time, thinking about why he'd decided to share more about his past with Brooke than he ever had with anyone else.

But right then, with her lying in his arms, he wouldn't change a thing.

Twenty-four

SAFE TO SAY, Friday was *not* a banner day for Sterling Restaurants.

Brooke spent the majority of her afternoon in her office with Keith, Sterling's VP of security, who'd received an anonymous call earlier in the week from a woman claiming to work at one of the restaurants at the United Center. She'd told Keith that the general manager of the restaurant had been stealing from the company for the last few months by voiding out cash sales from the point-of-sale machine at the end of the night.

At first, both Brooke and Keith had been skeptical.

"Dave's been with Sterling for seven years," she'd said, referring to the general manager in question. "He and Ian golf together all the time. He wouldn't steal from the company, let alone a friend."

"Could be a disgruntled employee or ex-employee trying to make trouble," Keith had said.

"We'll find out soon enough." They'd agreed that Keith would conduct an immediate internal investigation and report back to her.

And now they knew.

"I'd really hoped this one would go the other way," Keith said. Even the normally unflappable VP of security looked dejected after filling Brooke in on the results of his internal audit. Bottom line: the allegations against the general manager appeared to be true.

Brooke sighed, a mixture of frustration, anger, and disappointment. Firing some random homophobic jerk she'd never met was easy, but she *knew* Dave Lyons—he was a senior-level employee whose wife she enjoyed chatting with every year at the company holiday party. "I'll talk to Ian and bring him up to speed. He's going to be crushed."

"For what it's worth, I think Dave is in trouble financially," Keith said. "I'm hearing rumors about a gambling problem."

That certainly didn't make Brooke feel any better about the situation. "When do you plan to talk to him?"

"He should be at the restaurant now," Keith said. "Figured I would get this over with before the weekend."

Agreeing with that, Brooke counseled Keith on the various questions he should—and more important, should *not*—ask when he interviewed the general manger. When they'd finished, and Keith had left to head out to the United Center, Brooke went to see Ian in his office.

She knocked on his door. "Got a minute?"

Sitting in front of his computer, he waved her in. "Absolutely. Just checking out the Bears' schedule in advance of your big meeting and making sure I have all the home games on my calendar. Kidding." He paused when he saw her expression. "Oh, boy. I know that look." He turned in his chair and faced her, never one to beat around the bush. "Tell me."

"We think Dave Lyons has been stealing from the Stadium Club."

Ian's expression went from surprise to disbelief. "No way. Dave and I have known each other for years. He was the manager I hired to run my first restaurant." He shook his head. "There must be some mistake."

"Keith is heading over to the United Center now to talk to him. But he's already done an internal audit and it looks pretty incriminating," Brooke said. "I'm sorry, Ian. Keith said he's hearing rumors about Dave possibly having some financial issues, maybe a gambling problem. But that part is just speculation at this point."

"Aw, hell." Ian ran a hand over his face. "I knew about his gambling habit, but he never said anything to me about having money problems." After a moment, he looked at her. "How much do you think he took?"

"Roughly fifty thousand dollars."

Ian went silent, hearing that. "All right," he finally said, his tone having turned noticeably more businesslike. "Assuming this turns out to be true, what are our options? I can't believe I'm going to ask this, because I probably shouldn't give a crap what happens to Lyons, but . . . I don't know, if it is a gambling thing, can we have him resign quietly and then work out some kind of private arrangement? He gets himself into Gamblers Anonymous and agrees to pay the company back every penny, that kind of thing?"

And this was one of the reasons Brooke believed in Ian, both as a person and as a CEO. Even when he'd likely been stabbed in the back by someone he'd considered a friend, he *cared*.

Unfortunately, that didn't change the fact that their hands were tied in this particular instance. And, as general counsel, it was her responsibility to advise Ian of that. "If it were one of Sterling's independent restaurants, that might be something we could consider. But the United Center owns the Stadium Club, and as part of our contract with them we're obligated to report all known instances of employee theft to the police."

And the news didn't get any better as the afternoon progressed.

Two hours later, Keith called Brooke from the Stadium Club to let her know that he'd met with Dave, and that the general manager had broken down and admitted everything. Over the course of the last six months he'd lost a significant amount of money in gambling, a fact he'd kept from all his friends and family. Not knowing where to turn, he'd started pocketing cash from the restaurant's POS machine—small amounts at first, and then he'd grown bolder in his desperation.

Hearing the whole story just made Brooke feel . . . bad. For once, she thought she'd actually prefer another oops-I-hired-a-murderer moment. At least with that one, she'd been able to laugh eventually.

"Dave's in pretty bad shape," Keith said. "As soon as I confronted him, he started crying. *Sobbing*, actually. I think part of him is relieved to have gotten caught—he keeps saying he feels terrible for doing this to Ian. I assume you want me to call CPD and let the police handle this from here?"

Brooke tiredly ran a hand through her hair. That would be the normal procedure, yes. And she knew what would happen from there: two Chicago police officers—likely detectives from the financial crimes unit given the amount at stake—would show up at the Stadium Club, throw Dave Lyons in handcuffs, and then would very publicly escort him out of the restaurant.

Unless . . .

She debated for a half second, and then thought about whether she would pick up the phone and call Cade if they were simply friends and not sleeping together. When she decided that, yes, she would, that put an end to her hesitation.

"Hold off for a couple of minutes, Keith. Let me make one call before we bring in the cops." Brooke hung up with the VP of security, then dialed a now-familiar cell phone number.

"Ms. Parker," Cade answered, his voice low and rich. "An actual phone call instead of a text message—I'm honored."

"I have a favor to ask of you. Work related."

Instantly, he turned more serious. "What do you need?"

"We caught one of our general managers stealing," she said. "To make a long story short, he's confessed to everything and we're turning this over to the police. For various reasons, I'd rather not make a spectacle of the guy's arrest. I was wondering if maybe you had, you know . . . a guy at the Chicago Police Department who could handle this quietly."

Cade seemed amused by her question.

Of course he did.

"Yes, I have a *guy*," he said teasingly. "You're in the eighteenth district—you want to talk to Sergeant Joe Ross."

Brooke quickly jotted this down on a piece of paper. Secretly, she was in awe of the fact that Cade had come up with a name so easily, but given the already-quite-healthy size of his ego, she'd rather go jogging naked through Millennium Park in her red high heels before admitting that.

"I'll give him a heads-up that you'll be calling," he continued. "I don't know where the GM works, but if your goal is to handle this quietly, I wouldn't do the arrest at the restaurant. Your best bet would be to bring him to Sterling's corporate office. Sergeant Ross will be in plain clothes—if it's a voluntary surrender, and it sounds like it is, he can escort the guy out without handcuffs and put him in an unmarked car. Doesn't get much quieter than that."

No, it didn't. "This is very helpful," she said in all sincerity. "Thank you."

"Have I impressed you again, Ms. Parker?" he asked coyly.

She smiled for the first time that day. "Maybe. Then again, it has been a really strange afternoon." She exhaled raggedly, thinking about the not-so-fun task ahead.

"You sound tired," Cade said, his voice deepening. "Long day?"

The words slipped out of Brooke's mouth before she thought about them.

"Long year."

EARLY THAT EVENING, Brooke stared out her window, looking at the people below as they shopped, met friends for drinks, or headed off to dinner reservations. And then there were the couples, leisurely walking hand in hand, who seemed to be simply enjoying the Michigan Avenue scene with no particular plans at all.

She wondered what it felt like to be one of those people.

"I see that you're still leaving the front door unlocked when you're alone."

Brooke started, hearing the voice. She turned around and saw Cade standing in her office doorway, looking as handsome as ever in another one of his tailored suits. His dark brown hair was a little mussed, presumably from being outside, and her first thought was that she wanted to sink her fingers into it and get him mussed even more.

She cleared her throat.

"I see you're still sneaking up on people when they're working," she said. "And for the record, I'm not alone. Ian's here, too."

Appearing somewhat appeased by this, Cade stepped into her office and shut the door behind him. "I thought I'd see how things went with the arrest. Did everything go okay with Sergeant Ross?"

"Sergeant Ross was very professional and discreet. Thank you again, for that."

"Why the need for discretion?" Cade asked curiously. He sat on the edge of her desk. "I would've thought you would relish the idea of publicly setting an example of someone who stole from the company."

Normally, yes. "I heard the guy was *sobbing*. I've hung out with his wife a few times . . . I guess I just wanted to do something." She leaned her head against the chair. "I don't know how you hear these stories every day, Morgan. Clearly, I would make a terrible prosecutor."

"Probably." He reached out and ran his thumb along her cheek. "But I like your soft spot, anyway."

Their eyes met and held until Cade spoke. "You look burned-out. Maybe you should call it a night."

She looked at the clock, and then stared at him in bewilderment. "At six thirty?"

"At six thirty."

He held out his hand.

"It's not even dark out," she said. "I can't leave now, especially after the day we've had. It would be unseemly."

Cade's mouth curved at the edges, but he still said nothing.

She bit her lip, contemplating. "Can I at least bring work home for later?"

"Nope."

"You expect me to *leave* my briefcase behind?" Impossible.

"Yep."

Maybe she was out of sorts after having a rough day. Or maybe it was his matter-of-fact tone. But suddenly . . . going home sounded really appealing. "Okay."

With that, she slid her hand into his, grabbed her purse, and left.

She made it all the way to the reception area before panic set in.

"I forgot to shut down my computer," she remembered.

"It'll be fine in sleep mode for one night."

"I think I saw something in my mail inbox on the way out. It could be important."

"It was just the new *ABA Journal*."

Brooke exhaled as they stepped into the elevator. "Right. So, what's the plan for tonight?"

"You're going to relax and do nothing."

She laughed, then saw that Cade was serious. "Oh . . . see, I don't do 'nothing' so well."

"You're a smart woman. You'll figure it out."

She looked at him for a long moment. "Why are you doing this?"

"Why did you make me take the ibuprofen the other night?" he asked.

Still, with the ibuprofen? "Because you needed it. You were just too stubborn to admit that."

With a satisfied smile, Cade held her gaze.

"Exactly."

BROOKE STARED SKEPTICALLY at the rising water.

She was not a bath kind of girl, hadn't been a bath kind of girl since she was, oh, about *seven*. Baths were so . . . idle.

And, apparently, they were also part of Cade's "evening of nothing" plan.

She was not on board with this.

There was a knock at the door, then Cade stuck his head

inside and saw her standing there in her bathrobe. "Oh. See, you're supposed to get *in* the tub."

Ha, ha. "Can I at least bring my phone in with me?"

"No. But you can have this." He handed her a glass of wine.

"How long do you expect me to stay in there?" she asked.

Cade shrugged. "I don't know. Maybe twenty minutes? Now stop stalling and get in." He smacked her rear on his way out the door.

Stop stalling and get in, Brooke mimicked to herself as she slipped off the robe and climbed into the tub. *Pushy, bossy man, expecting everyone to just fall in line with whatever he—*

Oh my God, the water felt good.

She set her wineglass on the edge of the tub, sinking in deeper. Okay, fine. She supposed *maybe* she could survive twenty minutes of this.

She leaned back and rested her head against the basin. The hot water wrapped around her like a cocoon, relaxing her muscles as steam filled the air in the tranquil, quiet room.

So this was what it felt like to do nothing.

Brooke reached out with one hand and took a sip of wine. Then she set the glass back down and closed her eyes.

Maybe thirty minutes.

BROOKE BLINKED AWAKE, realizing that she'd dozed off in the bathtub. An actual *nap*. Something else she probably hadn't done since she was seven.

She was definitely off her game tonight.

She climbed out of the tub, and had just wrapped a towel around herself when she remembered—uh-oh—Cade. She'd left him . . . come to think of it, she had no clue where he was right now. She hurried into her bedroom and threw on a pair of yoga pants and a T-shirt. She spotted her clock on the nightstand and saw that she'd been in the tub for forty-five minutes.

Oops.

She walked down the hallway, expecting to find one of two things: either he'd be annoyed that she'd disappeared for nearly an hour, or he'd smile smugly, thinking he'd been proven right in his assertion that she'd needed to relax tonight.

But when she rounded the corner into the kitchen, she discovered something else entirely.

Cade stood at the sink, pouring a pot of boiling noodles into a strainer, while a second pot with some kind of sauce simmered on the stove.

The man was making her dinner.

Brooke leaned her head against the wall as she watched him, her heart suddenly squeezing tight in her chest. Something occurred to her then, something she probably should've noticed before with the inside jokes and some of the stories they'd shared, and the way he always made her smile even though he frustrated her like no other. But there was no denying it now.

Things were getting a little too close for comfort with Cade Morgan.

Twenty-five

BROOKE KNOCKED ON the front door of Ford's loft, needing to talk to her best friend, the one person in the world who could help her work through her messed-up feelings.

Instead, she got Charlie.

"Brooke! You're here!" he said excitedly, pushing the door open. His eyes skimmed over the skirt, blouse, and heeled sandals she'd worn into the office. "A little dressy for a barbeque, but we'll take it."

Brooke cocked her head in confusion. "Barbeque?" Then she remembered—oh, shit—the *barbeque*. Ford had sent her an e-mail about it two weeks ago, and she'd meant to respond, but then she'd gotten sucked into a project at work and the e-mail now was undoubtedly languishing at the bottom of her inbox.

"Right, the barbeque," she said, playing it off with a casual wave of her hand. "Ignore the work clothes, I didn't want to waste time changing after leaving work." Brooke stepped inside. "Wow. Full house."

She took a look around and saw people everywhere—all of them dressed casually. Feeling a little self-conscious in her business attire, Brooke followed Charlie into the kitchen. The counter was covered with hamburger fixings, pasta and potato salads, coleslaw, chips, and fruit.

Ah, yes, of course—she should've brought something to eat or drink. To the *barbeque* she hadn't even remembered.

She was the worst best friend ever.

"Brooke?"

She turned around and saw a woman with a sleek ebony bob smiling at her. "Oh my gosh, Rachel—hi!"

Rachel hugged her excitedly. "It's so good to see you!" She pulled back. "It's been, what, probably about three months, right?"

"Has it been that long?" Brooke tried to think when the last time was that they'd seen each other. Rachel was married to one of Ford's friends, and the two of them had independently become friends as well. "I guess since the last book club meeting I went to. When was that?"

"Hmm. What was the book?"

Brooke had to think. "The one about the woman who lost her memory every night when she went to sleep."

Rachel pointed. "Yes. Ooh, that was a good one. And, sweetie, that was *five* months ago." She laughed. "I remember now—you hadn't finished the book yet, and you kept covering your ears when we talked about the ending. That's not why you stopped coming, I hope?"

Brooke smiled. "No, I just had a hard time making the seven o'clock meetings, and I wasn't ever able to finish the books . . ." she trailed off, still surprised by something. "Has it really been *five* months?" She'd always enjoyed hanging out with Rachel. Actually, she'd enjoyed hanging out with all the book club girls, but the meetings had always seemed to come at a bad time with work.

"Ford keeps us up-to-date on all the great things you have going on at Sterling," Rachel said. "Any new deals on the horizon?"

"I've got a couple of feelers out with a few—" Brooke stopped herself, making a spur-of-the-moment decision. "No. Let's talk about something else. Anything else. For the rest of the evening, I don't want to even hear the name 'Sterling Restaurants.' "

"Okay, who are you and what have you done with my best friend?"

Brooke looked to her right and saw Ford approaching her, with his big, familiar grin.

"I can't believe you actually made—*oof.*" He was cut off as she half-tackled him in a hug.

She squeezed him tightly, oddly feeling as though it had been ages since they'd gotten together even though they'd just met for lunch last week.

"What was that for?" he asked with a chuckle, when she finally pulled back.

"Just glad to see to you," she told him.

Charlie and Tucker walked by right then, and noticed Brooke and Ford standing with their arms around each other. Charlie nodded slyly at Tucker, who opened his mouth to comment—

"*Still* not happening," Brooke and Ford said in unison.

AFTER THE LAST of the stragglers had left, heading either home or to the bars depending on marital status, Brooke picked up Ford's place. He'd gotten a call from his mother, and since Brooke knew how those calls could go, she figured she might as well do something productive to kill time.

Ford came out of his room just as she was wrapping up the rest of the potato salad. "You didn't have to clean all that up."

"I don't mind." Actually, it eased some of the guilt she felt about forgetting about the party. "How's your mom?"

Ford sat down at one of the bar stools in front of the island. "She says my dad is talking about going to rehab again. What'll that be, the sixth time?" he asked dryly. He ran his hand over his face.

"Maybe this time it'll actually work," Brooke said.

Ford peered up to give her a get-real look. "There's a better chance of both Charlie and Tucker getting laid tonight."

"Ouch. Those are not good odds."

That got a slight smile out of Ford. She walked around the counter and threw her arms over his shoulders in a backward hug. He squeezed her back. "Let's talk about something else."

She understood—Ford's father had never been his favorite topic of conversation. "Rachel told me she's pregnant."

"Good for them. Brandon told me they've been trying for a while."

"Something I probably would've known if I'd *seen* her in the last five months."

"Don't beat yourself up, Brooke," Ford said. "Work, family, whatever—everyone's busy these days."

"Maybe." She chewed on that, falling quiet as she began stacking the glasses in the dishwasher.

After they'd finished cleaning up, they sat outside on Ford's deck and looked out at the skyline while munching on leftover chips and taco dip.

"I think Charlie and Tuck were brokenhearted when Cade didn't come with you tonight," Ford said. "They have a bigtime man-crush on that guy."

"No kidding. They asked me four times if I would text him and ask him to stop by." Brooke paused. "Actually, though, I think I might cool things down with Cade for a while."

Ford looked surprised. "Really? I thought you guys were having fun."

"We were. We are. But lately, it seems like things are getting . . . complicated."

"Huh." Ford thought about that. "Because you have feelings for him, you mean?"

Brooke pulled back. "Is it that obvious?"

He shrugged matter-of-factly. "Yes."

"Well . . . why didn't you say anything?" she asked indignantly.

"I assumed *you* knew."

"No, I didn't know. Not until last night, anyway, when I got out of the bathtub and found him in my kitchen cooking dinner. It just looked so . . . *right*."

"Having a good-looking, six-foot-four, former football star turned hotshot prosecutor make dinner while you take a bath?

Yeah, I'm guessing that's an image a lot of women would say looks right."

Brooke shot him a wry look. "I meant that it *felt* right. The two of us being together."

"So maybe it is."

Brooke thought that over, and then shook her head. "I've been down this road. Three times in the last eighteen months. I know how it turns out. Things will be good, at first, but then slowly he'll start making comments about my job, and how many hours I work. And then the comments will turn into arguments, maybe even something about my success being 'emasculating'—"

"Who said that?" Ford demanded, cutting her off.

"Spencer. The Hipster Photographer who came before the Hot OB."

"An even bigger douche," Ford scoffed. "You know how Cade's different from those other guys?"

"He's not a douche?" she guessed.

"Exactly."

Brooke smiled, appreciating Ford's flash of protectiveness, before turning serious. "I like Cade. A lot. But there's so much happening at work these days, good things, and I need to stay focused. I'm pitching to the Bears on Monday, and I should be preparing for that, or working on the other 137 things on my to-do list, and not skipping out early on a Friday to relax. Because that's *not* something I can typically do, and soon enough he'll figure that out. And I don't want to start this, only to have Cade tell me in four months that I'm not a 'big-picture' girl or some other 'Sorry, sweetie, it really *is* you, not me' line like that." She shook her head. "I just can't hear that . . . from him."

Ford looked over and nodded. "Okay."

They both fell quiet, looking out at the skyline. Finally, Ford spoke. "You know you brought this on yourself by not following the Rules."

Smart-ass. "I did follow the Rules." Well, mostly. "But I somehow ended up here, anyway."

And, unfortunately, she knew what she needed to do about that.

Twenty-six

ON MONDAY AFTERNOON, Brooke spent the fifty-minute drive from Chicago to Lake Forest getting in the zone.

She was focused, determined not to be distracted by anything going on in her personal life, as she ran through the various points she wanted to make with Curt Emery. While her pitch varied somewhat depending on the potential client and their food service needs and facilities, what always remained constant was the fact that she one hundred percent believed in Sterling and the business they were growing.

Nevertheless, she remained pragmatic about the likely outcome of this meeting with the Bears. While Curt Emery may have been interested enough to hear her pitch, it was still a long shot given the team's long-standing relationship with Spectrum.

While driving, her phone chimed repeatedly with a stream of chatty text messages from Ian.

ARE YOU THERE YET?
HOW'S THE DRIVE?
THINK YOU'LL GET TO SEE THE PRACTICE FIELDS?
TOO BAD THE TEAM IS AT TRAINING CAMP.

I'M ALREADY PICTURING THAT SKYBOX ON THE FIFTY-YARD LINE. HA.

Clearly, Ian wasn't as down with the let's-remain-pragmatic approach.

Just before three o'clock, Brooke walked through the main entrance of Halas Hall, the modern glass and steel building that served as the Bears' headquarters. She checked in at the front desk, where the security guard handed her a visitor's badge and directed her to the elevators.

Curt Emery's office was located on the fourth floor, along with the rest of the team's front office. Brooke stepped out of the elevators and was greeted by a receptionist whose desk sat before a large, panoramic photograph of Soldier Field. Only a minute or so later, a man in his midforties, wearing khakis and a button-down shirt, approached.

He held out his hand and introduced himself. "Curt Emery. So nice to meet you, Ms. Parker."

"Please—call me Brooke," she said, shaking his hand. "Thank you for meeting with me."

He guided her down a hallway. "We're in a conference room this way." He smiled at her tentatively. "So about our meeting . . . this is rather unorthodox for me. As you know, we've contracted with Spectrum for nearly twenty years for the food service at Soldier Field. And in the interests of full disclosure, I have a good relationship with the senior manager there who handles our account."

"I understand," Brooke said. "I appreciate you giving me the opportunity to tell you about the things we're doing at Wrigley Field and the United Center—and the things we can do for your organization as well. But I promise, you won't get a hard sell from me. Not yet, anyway," she added.

Instead of laughing at the joke, Curt stopped in the doorway of the conference room and shifted uncomfortably. "Yeah . . . see . . . that's not exactly what this meeting is about."

Brooke cocked her head, having no clue what that meant. "Okay, what is this meeting about, then?"

"Here's the thing. I sort of mentioned to my contact at Spectrum that you'd called me. I was just joking around with him, saying that if he didn't keep me happy I might have to consider giving Sterling Restaurants our business, that kind of thing. But then I received a follow-up phone call from Palmer Green himself, the CEO of Spectrum North America. He was *very* interested in the fact that you were trying to pitch Sterling to me."

Brooke waited, trying to figure out where Curt was going with this. So Spectrum's CEO knew she was going after another one of their clients. So what? It was hardly a secret that Sterling was aggressively building its sports and entertainment division. "And how does this relate to our meeting?"

Curt gestured to the conference room. "Why don't you see for yourself?"

Confused, Brooke stepped inside and saw a man wearing a tailored navy suit sitting at the conference table. He stood up when she walked in.

Curt made the introduction. "Brooke Parker, this is Palmer Green. CEO of Spectrum North America."

Palmer looked her over with a sharp gaze. "So you're the one who's been stealing away my favorite clients."

Well. This was indeed a surprise.

Brooke looked back at Curt, beginning to understand why he'd insisted that she come alone. "Unorthodox? In your business, Mr. Emery, I'd think we'd call this a blindside."

Nevertheless, she walked over to Palmer and held out her hand. No clue what this was about, but if Spectrum's CEO had thought he could fly out here and intimidate her into backing off his company's business, he was in for a rude awakening. "What an interesting surprise, Mr. Green," she said while shaking his hand. "Let me guess. This is the part where you ever-so-charmingly suggest that I stay away from Spectrum's clients."

He smiled at that. "No, Ms. Parker. This is the part where I ever-so-charmingly offer you a job."

Twenty-seven

DESPITE BEING SURPRISED by Palmer's words, Brooke managed to give Curt a withering look as he smiled apologetically and quickly excused himself from the room.

"Don't be mad at poor Curt," Palmer said with a chuckle when the two of them were alone. "He was just following orders." He sat down at the conference table and gestured, the air of a man who was used to getting his way. "Please, have a seat. At least hear me out."

Brooke considered this for a moment, and then sat down. "Five minutes. But you should know that we're already off to a shaky start given the theatrics. Any reason you couldn't just pick up the phone if you supposedly wanted to offer me a job?"

"This isn't the kind of offer you make over the phone." Palmer eased back in his chair. "Besides, I wanted to size up the illustrious Brooke Parker myself." He cocked his head, taking her in. "Stealing Cowboys Stadium and the United Center was bad enough. But the Staples Center?" He whistled. "That was a dagger to my heart."

"I take it you're a Lakers fan."

"Born and bred in L.A."

That certainly explained the theatrics. "I think I need to clarify a misunderstanding," she said. "I'm part of a team at Sterling. My partners, Tony and Micah, were just as instrumental in landing those deals."

"Not according to my contacts at the Cowboys, the United Center, and the Staples Center." Palmer must've caught her look of surprise. "Oh? You think I didn't call them to ask why we'd lost their business?"

"I'm sure they told you it's because Sterling offers top-notch upscale hospitality service."

"They mentioned something to that effect. But they also said that you are a very convincing woman, Ms. Parker." He studied her. "It's remarkable, really, what you've accomplished for that company in two years. I hope Ian Sterling appreciates that."

"Ian Sterling appreciates it just fine."

The edges of Palmer's mouth curved in a smile. "You're loyal to him. I respect that."

"Thank you." She checked her watch. "You're down to three minutes, Mr. Green."

"All right, I'll get to the point," he said, appearing undeterred by her directness. "I want you on my team. You're smart, bold, and ambitious—and I've personally seen the fruits of that. You've stolen away three of my top clients in the past eighteen months, and now you're going after a fourth. I either need to shut you down—which I don't believe is possible—or get you to work your magic for *me*."

He folded his hands on the table. "You want me to be even more blunt? You are a rising star in the business world, Brooke. But you have a problem. There's nowhere for you to go at Sterling Restaurants. One man sits at the top—Ian Sterling. Think about that."

Brooke sat quiet for a moment, digesting everything Palmer had said. Frankly, his speech had caught her off guard. Of course, she was aware that the company had been getting a lot of good press. But she'd had no idea that people like Palmer Green, CEO of a billion-dollar-plus corporation, were specifically paying attention to *her*.

"What do you envision me doing at Spectrum?" she asked cautiously.

"Executive vice president of sales and business development."

Brooke blinked. She'd been thinking he planned to offer her an assistant general counsel position, but this was something else entirely.

"You seem surprised," Palmer said.

"Actually. . . yes," she admitted. "I've always considered myself a lawyer first, businesswoman second."

"Once you take the position, I'd be happy to have the legal department send a few problems your way," he joked. "But I think you'll be busy enough."

"You're really serious about this, aren't you?"

He leveled her with his gaze. "Very serious. I believe in striking while the iron is hot. I don't know what's driving you, and frankly, I don't need to know. I just want to tap into it. So I think you need to ask yourself something: are you ready to step up to the big leagues?"

What popped into Brooke's head right then was a similar meeting she'd had, two years ago, when Ian asked her to join Sterling Restaurants. She remembered the excitement and thrill she'd felt when first taking over as general counsel— feelings she still had to this day.

But she also remembered the promise she'd made to herself long ago: that she was going places.

"Just how big of a league are we talking?" she asked.

Palmer smiled, knowing that he had her attention now. "Seventy-five-thousand-dollar signing bonus. Three hundred thousand base salary, plus another one hundred and fifty thousand in stock via our equity incentive plan. You'll also receive a bonus of one hundred percent of your base salary, assuming you bring in the kind of deals you've been landing at Sterling."

After Brooke recovered from a split second of being absolutely dumbfounded, she pulled herself together and quickly did some math. If she did her job well, which—*hello*—of course she would do her job well—Palmer was talking about a compensation package, for the first year alone, that totaled $825,000.

Wow.

"Also, we'll obviously pay to relocate you to our headquarters in Charlotte," Palmer added.

That snapped Brooke out of the green haze of dollar signs floating before her eyes.

Right. Of course. She would need to relocate for this job. All the way to North Carolina.

"That's quite an offer, Palmer," she said.

"Trust me, you'll earn every penny. I won't sugarcoat it—you come to Spectrum and you'll work your butt off for me. I'm offering you a lucrative position, but also a demanding one. Lots of travel, schmoozing with clients, you know the drill. Although from what I hear, you're already putting in long hours. At least I can pay you more for it."

Certain parts of Palmer's speech were buzzing around in Brooke's head like annoying gnats. *Work your butt off. Demanding. Long hours.* She shook it off, remaining focused. "You've certainly given me a lot to think about." She saw Palmer raise an eyebrow, as if waiting for more. She chuckled. "You don't actually expect me to give you an answer on the spot, do you?"

He laughed. "No. Although I thought I had you for a minute there." He reached into the inside pocket of his suit jacket and pulled out a business card. "Call me after you've had a chance to think everything through. What I'd like to do is fly you out to Charlotte to meet the other executive officers, get a feel for us, get to know Spectrum better. Not sure if you're married or have kids, but the whole family is welcome. You could make a long weekend out of it and explore the city."

Brooke shook her head. "No husband or kids. Just me."

Palmer grinned confidently. "That makes things even easier, doesn't it?"

Twenty-eight

"SO AS IT turns out, your idea wasn't totally lame."

Cade looked at Zach, needing to squint in the noon sun. Belatedly, he realized he should've worn his sunglasses, although the decision to eat outside had been spur-of-the-moment.

They perched on one of the stone ledges in Daley Plaza, just a few feet away from the city's iconic fifty-foot Picasso sculpture, eating burritos from a restaurant across the street. Zach was downtown for the afternoon—some errand to run, he'd said—so they'd agreed to meet. While walking to the burrito restaurant, they'd heard a blues band playing a lunchtime concert in the plaza, and had decided, along with many other Chicagoans, given the size of the crowd, to grab a seat for a few minutes and enjoy the eighty-degree weather.

"What idea?" Then he noticed Zach's sneaky smile and remembered—the poetry book. "You talked to Paige, didn't you?"

"Sure did," he said slyly. "Got a date with her Friday, too."

"Way to go," Cade said, high-fiving him. "So? Tell me what happened."

"I decided to tweak your original idea. Instead of giving *her* the book, I figured I would pretend to read it myself at her dad's ice-cream shop, hoping that she would come up to me and ask about it."

"Coward."

"Ha. What you fail to understand is that, in this day and age, women *want* to take charge. So I was merely being supportive of Paige's natural feminist instincts by giving her the tools and the opportunity to approach me first."

"Nice try."

Zach grinned, conceding. "Okay, fine. Maybe I wussed out. Anyway, it was really busy in the shop that day, and I was getting bored waiting for everyone else to clear out, so I figured I might as well actually *read* the book I was pretending to be reading. And, you know, there was some stuff in there that was pretty cool."

Cade smiled at the kid's surprised tone. "Imagine that."

"So I'm reading some poem by Louise . . . something, I forget her last name, but it's about Hades and the underworld, and I don't even notice that Paige has come up to my table until she says, 'Doesn't everyone want love?' And I'm thinking, wow, that's a pretty deep question, but then again Paige is really smart, and this is my chance to finally show her that I'm not just a dumb jock. So *I* say, 'I heard this theory once that love means your subconscious is attracted to someone else's subconscious.'"

"Very deep," Cade said.

"Exactly. And I'm feeling proud of myself for that one, until she points to the book and says, 'Oh, that wasn't a question. I was just quoting a line from the poem.'"

Cade covered his mouth to hide his smile. "Well, that's . . . awkward."

"You think? I'm mortified at that point, and thinking that I'm never, *ever* listening to your advice on getting a girl again . . . but then she asks me what I think our football team's chances are of beating our rival, McKinley Tech, this year."

"She likes football? Sounds like this girl's a keeper."

Zach shook his head. "That's the thing—we started

talking and, dude, she doesn't know anything about football. But I think she wanted *me* to think she did."

Cade thought about this. "Let me get this straight—you secretly pretend to like poetry to impress the smart girl in your English class, while *she's* secretly pretending to like football to impress *you*." He paused. "That's gotta be the cutest fucking thing I've ever heard."

"I guess her subconscious finds my subconscious pretty irresistible," Zach said, all teenage confidence right then.

"You were lucky to pull that line off once, Garrity. I wouldn't push it."

Zach laughed, and then the two of them segued into a conversation about football, and what the chances were, in fact, that his team would beat their rival. They finished their lunch, and Cade checked his watch and realized he should get back to the office.

Zach cleared his throat. "Oh, hey, before you head out I wanted to mention that I've been thinking more about telling my dad that you and I have been hanging out."

Cade tried not to let the mention of Noah dampen his good mood. "That's your choice, Zach. I'm not telling you to lie to your father."

"*Our* father," Zach said pointedly. His expression turned more serious. "You can at least acknowledge him."

Cade could hear the frustration in his brother's voice. He'd suspected, for a while, that Zach secretly was angling for some heartwarming father-son reunion. But it had taken Cade a long time to get past the anger and resentment he'd felt over Noah's abandonment, and he wasn't sure he wanted to reopen the door to those emotions.

But before he could answer Zach, someone called his name.

"Cade—hey! I thought that was you."

Cade looked past Zach and saw a lanky guy in khakis and a short-sleeved polo shirt crossing the crowded plaza toward them. It took him a second to realize it was Brooke's friend, Charlie, whom he'd met at the Cubs game.

"Great minds think alike, huh?" Charlie said, holding up a carryout bag and gesturing to the blues band.

"Good to see you again, Charlie." Cade quickly made the introductions. "This is my brother, Zach Garrity."

When Zach looked over, Cade half-smiled because the significance of the moment had struck him, too. It was the first time he'd introduced Zach as his brother.

"Another Rose Bowl champ in the making, I hope?" Charlie said, shaking Zach's hand.

"Zach's a wide receiver. He also likes to wax poetic about love and has a thing for girls way out of his league."

"Story of my life," Charlie said, with an easy grin.

The three of them chatted for a few moments until Cade mentioned that he needed to get back to the office for a conference call.

"Bummer. I think I'll play hooky awhile longer," Charlie said, gesturing to the sun-drenched plaza.

"I didn't realize they let bands play here," Zach said.

"You can't beat this city in the summer." Charlie shook his head and sighed. "I don't know what Brooke is thinking with this Charlotte deal. It's sounds like a great job opportunity, but she can't be seriously considering moving to a city where she'll have to root for the *Panthers*." He shuddered, then looked at Cade. "You need to work your magic, Morgan, and convince her to stay."

Cade stood there, completely caught off guard as Charlie's words sunk in.

Brooke was thinking about moving, but she hadn't said one word to him about it.

A wave of disappointment rose up inside him, a sharp jab in the chest, but he immediately, fiercely crushed it.

That was . . . just fine.

Good for her. Really. If this job, whatever it was, was that great of an opportunity, she *should* take it. He'd seen her in action; she was an incredible lawyer—she deserved an opportunity like this.

Sure, obviously, this development came as a bit of a surprise to him, especially since he and Brooke seemed to be getting close lately. But it also served as a quick reminder that perhaps they'd been getting a little *too* close.

And he didn't do *too* close.

Too close, in his opinion, was for the naïve. *Too* close was for people who got caught up in a moment with someone, without acknowledging the very real possibility that all the feelings and emotions that made the moment so great and perfect were entirely one-sided. So if Brooke had somehow managed to get *in*, to be on the verge of *too* close, then that, unfortunately, meant one thing.

It was time for him to say good-bye.

He and Zach left Charlie to enjoy the concert, and then walked in silence for a few moments.

"You didn't know about the job offer, did you?" Zach asked quietly.

Cade stared at the stoplight ahead. "No."

And, being brothers, they left it at that.

Twenty-nine

BROOKE CHECKED THE clock and began to wonder whether Cade was going to show up after all.

She'd texted him earlier, asking if they could meet. He'd said he needed to work late, but that he would swing by her apartment afterward. That had been over three hours ago, and she hadn't heard from him since.

She planned to tell him tonight about the job opportunity with Spectrum. She was still shocked by Palmer's offer, and hadn't yet made any decisions. On the one hand, she hadn't been looking to leave Sterling, but on the other hand, they were talking about a position where she'd earn $825,000 a year. She'd have be a fool not to seriously consider that.

Since Monday, she'd done a lot of thinking about what to say to Cade, and in the end had decided to simply go with the truth. Unless she was completely misreading the situation, they'd crossed beyond just-having-fun territory and had wandered into true, genuine feelings, and so she owed him that much.

She liked Cade; she didn't deny that. But whether it was at Sterling—or more likely, Spectrum—her career needed to come first right now. After all her hard work, and with the opportunities available to her, she needed to stay focused on that. To keep her eye on the proverbial ball.

Knowing that, however, wouldn't make this conversation with Cade any easier. But he, too, was a logical person, and they'd been honest from the beginning about their relationship hang-ups. If they kept going down this path, it would only lead to bigger disappointment in the end.

This was for the best.

Just before nine thirty, Brooke heard a knock at her door. Cade flashed that charming grin of his when she answered, the same one that had caught her eye the moment they'd first met at Sterling.

"Sorry I'm so late," he said. "I got caught up in a witness interview that ran a lot longer than expected. Plus I had to make a stop on the way here."

"It's fine, I caught up on e-mail," she said with a wave. "You know me—always something to do."

He shut the door behind him. "I heard that congratulations are in order, Ms. Parker."

Brooke cocked her head, not sure what he could be talking about since she hadn't yet told him about her meeting with Palmer Green from Spectrum. "Congratulations?"

Cade reached into his briefcase and pulled out a bottle of champagne. "From what Charlie told me about your big job offer, I figured it was my turn to buy."

Brooke's hands fells to her sides. "*Charlie* told you about the job offer?" How the heck did he know? Then she realized that he must've heard about it from Ford.

"Sure did," Cade said, taking the bottle into her kitchen. "I ran into him at Daley Plaza yesterday, during my lunch break."

Brooke followed him into the kitchen, feeling horrible after hearing that. "Cade . . . I didn't mean for you to learn about it that way. I just got the offer on Monday, and I wanted to tell you in person. That's why I asked to see you tonight."

He gave her an odd look as he grabbed a corkscrew out of a drawer and went to work on the champagne bottle. "It's no problem. You don't owe me an explanation. Sure, I was surprised to suddenly hear you might be moving to Charlotte, but I'm really happy for you, Brooke."

He popped open the champagne, filled two glasses, and handed one over to her.

Brooke took the champagne flute. She'd been hoping Cade would understand what a great opportunity this job offer was for her, but she hadn't expected him to be *this* cheery about it.

"So. What are we toasting to?" he asked, raising his glass in celebration.

She paused before answering, remembering how she'd said the exact same words to him just two weeks ago, when he'd found out he would be the acting U.S. attorney. They'd had a good time together that night. Actually, they'd had a lot of good times together.

Her eyes met Cade's over their champagne glasses. For the briefest moment, she could've sworn she saw his smile falter, and she wondered if he was thinking the same thing.

But then the moment was gone, and his voice turned teasing. "You're speechless, Ms. Parker. It must be something really good, then."

"The CEO of Spectrum North America offered me the position of executive vice president of sales and business development."

"That's incredible." Cade tipped his glass to her. "Congratulations. It couldn't have happened to a more-deserving lawyer. Albeit one who once basically told me to stick my obstruction of justice threats up my ass."

Brooke laughed at that, and took a sip. This was how it should be, she reminded herself. No need for an angsty goodbye—they would end things on a good note, joking around and teasing.

Then she pulled her glass away, and when their eyes caught again she remembered what had happened the last time they'd toasted with champagne.

How is it?

Not bad. Have a taste.

I think I will.

"So tell me more about the job," Cade said.

Brooke blinked. Right. The *job.* "I don't have all the details about the position yet—the CEO wants me to fly down to Charlotte to meet with the rest of the executive team. But we discussed the compensation package, and it's—wow." She took a deep breath and exhaled, still unable to believe it.

"That good, huh?" Cade said.

"That good."

His next question got right to the heart of the matter. "Do you think you'll take it?"

Brooke rested one hip against the counter. "I don't know. I've been at Sterling for less than two years, and I've been so focused on developing the company that I hadn't given any thought to leaving. And I love the work I do there."

"But?"

"But . . . I'm not sure I can say 'no' to an opportunity like this. Spectrum is an eleven-billion-dollar corporation. To be an executive VP there would really launch my career into a different stratosphere." She paused. "It just seems weird, though, the idea of leaving Chicago."

They both fell silent at that.

Brooke set down her glass. "Speaking of which, I was thinking we should probably talk. About what this means for us."

Cade set his glass down as well. "I had the same thought. Since there's a good chance you'll be leaving, I was wondering if we should cool things down."

Brooke felt a pang of disappointment in her chest. Which was completely *silly*, obviously, since that was exactly what she wanted, too. "I was just about to say that."

"You were?" He spoke quickly. "I mean—good. Glad we're on the same page. Better to end things now, before the situation gets, you know, complicated."

Brooke nodded, quickly regrouping based on his reaction. "Right. Of course." Seemingly, she and Cade had not been on the same page—here she'd been thinking things already *had* gotten complicated—but there was no reason for him to know that now. As it turned out, they didn't need to have any messy "feelings" talk, after all.

Which was just . . . great. Absolutely. *Whew.*

She saw him watching her, and felt the need to say more. "I mean, we both knew from the start that this wasn't a permanent thing, right?"

"Exactly." He gestured between them. "It's not like either of us has had a lot of success when it comes to serious relationships."

"Very true." That silly pang of disappointment poked at Brooke again, but she ignored it and kept right on going. She even went for a joke. "And hey—there's always phone sex. Probably all I'll have time for, from the way Palmer described the job."

Cade studied her, then stepped closer. "Just tell me one thing, Brooke. You're sure that this is what you want?"

She assumed he meant the job at Spectrum. And that was an opportunity she just couldn't walk away from. "Yes." Her voice came out quieter than she'd expected, so she cleared her throat. "This is what I want."

He nodded. "So this is good-bye, then."

She exhaled. "I'm not good at this part." *Especially not with you*, she suddenly wanted to add.

But she didn't.

Cade's voice turned deeper. "Maybe we shouldn't say anything, then."

Falling silent, they looked at each other.

She reached for Cade at the same moment he pulled her closer, her lips parting eagerly as his mouth swooped down on hers. He edged her back against the counter, and she gasped at the feel of his hard, strong body against hers. The sound seemed to ignite him more—his tongue plundered her mouth demandingly as one hand cupped her bottom and pressed her against the hard length of his erection.

Yes. She may not have had the words to say good-bye, but she could have this one last time with him. She yanked his shirt out of his pants and smoothed her hands over the defined muscles of his stomach. She felt him tremble underneath her fingertips, and then he swung her up in his arms and carried her to the bedroom.

They peeled off their clothes and Brooke reached for him, wanting him inside her. Instead, Cade took his time, exploring nearly every inch of her body. He trailed his lips down her stomach, then gripped her thighs and held her open as he lowered his mouth between her legs.

He was relentless. He brought her to the peak, and then pulled back, and then brought her right there again, until she felt stripped bare with need. "Cade," she begged.

He hovered between her spread legs, rolling a condom on, then moved over her. Bracing himself on his elbows, he cupped her face and looked right into her eyes as he entered her.

"Brooke," he said, nearly a whisper.

It was the tender way he said her name, his face momentarily so open and unguarded that it literally took her breath away. He began to move inside her, lowering his head to kiss her as he continued his achingly smooth rhythm. She wrapped her arms around his neck, and her legs around his waist, holding on tight as she arched her hips to meet him. They shattered together, and afterward lay intertwined for several moments before she drifted off to sleep with her head on his chest.

IN THE MORNING, she woke up and saw the sun filtering in through the shades on her windows. Cade was sitting next to her on the bed, dressed in the suit he'd worn the night before.

He reached over and tucked a lock of hair behind her ear. "I need to get going," he said huskily. "I have to go home and change before heading into work."

"Okay." Brooke tucked her arm under her head and smiled softly at him, not quite sure what to say about last night. The sex had always been great between them, but *that* had been incredible. The way he'd said her name, the way he'd looked at her—she'd never felt that intimately connected with anyone before.

That is, until Cade leaned forward and kissed her on the forehead.

"Knock 'em dead in Charlotte, Brooke."

Then he stood up and walked out of her apartment.

Thirty

IT TOOK BROOKE almost two weeks to rework her schedule so she could fly out to Spectrum's headquarters. Granted, she was doing this on the sly, merely telling her secretary that she would be out of the office to attend to "personal matters." Since she'd only taken three other vacation days in the two years she'd been with Sterling, she figured she was due for the time off.

She did, nevertheless, feel guilty. She hated going behind Ian's back—although, obviously, she had no choice under the circumstances. She believed in loyalty, and she didn't relish the thought of having to tell Ian that she was leaving. But at the end of the day, it was *her* career. She worked hard, she was good at what she did, and she owed it to herself to explore this opportunity with Spectrum.

Thus, on a Friday morning Brooke found herself on a seven A.M. flight to Charlotte, North Carolina. After takeoff, she reviewed the questions she wanted to ask Palmer and the other members of the executive team, and ran through her vision for retaining market share and growing Spectrum's sports and entertainment division. She'd just begun perusing some articles she'd printed out about the city of Charlotte, when the first-class flight attendant came by to offer her breakfast.

"We have a choice this morning: blueberry pancakes or a Denver omelette," she said.

Brooke's mouth fell open. *Get out of here.* "A Denver omelette? Seriously?"

The flight attendant sighed, as if steeling herself for a two-hour ride with yet another fussy first-class passenger. "Yes, a Denver omelette. They're one of our most popular breakfast entrees."

"Oh, no—I wasn't criticizing," Brooke said quickly, trying to explain. "It's just this inside-joke thing. I mean, not with you, since obviously we've never met before, but with this other person who . . . you don't know and who isn't here and, actually, he isn't even really speaking to me right now, but if he *had* been here, trust me—he would've found this really funny."

The flight attendant gave her a no-more-coffee-for-you look. "Omelette or pancakes, ma'am?"

Right. "Omelette."

The flight attendant set the breakfast onto her tray and made a fast getaway. Brooke looked down at the omelette, knowing exactly what she would've done if circumstances had been different. She would've taken a photo of the omelette with her phone, and then texted Cade as soon as the plane landed with some sort of quip like, *Didn't realize you were moonlighting as a chef for United,* or—even better—*And I didn't even have to put out this time.*

Yep, that would've been a good one, all right.

A real good one.

Brooke looked out the window, trying very hard, as she had been for the last two weeks, not to wonder what Cade was up to. They hadn't spoken, texted, or e-mailed since that last night together, when they'd agreed that it was better not to see each other anymore.

That part had been harder than she'd anticipated.

She turned back to the Denver omelette, trying not to hear Cade's low, teasing voice in her head.

Nine o'clock it is. I'll pick you up at your place.

I'll have a Denver omelette waiting.
That's cute.
She should've just gone with the damn pancakes.

IT WAS A whirlwind day from the moment Brooke touched down in Charlotte.

A car met her at the airport and took her to the Ritz-Carlton for a quick pit stop to drop off her bags. From there, she was whisked away to Spectrum's corporate headquarters. She met first with Palmer, who then introduced her to several other company officers—she couldn't say how many; she lost count after ten. She learned all about Spectrum's mission to "transform the food hospitality industry," and there was no denying that they were indeed the Goliath to Sterling Restaurants' David: they were in hospitals, senior living facilities, schools, colleges and universities, corporate buildings, and, of course, sports and entertainment venues.

It was clear what Palmer was looking for in an EVP of sales and business development; in fact, he came right out and told her: someone aggressive and ambitious, someone who would do more than trot out the same old tired ideas and "corporate-speak." He spoke about the fairly extensive travel that would be involved, and made a comment about that not being a good "fit" for the former EVP of sales.

"Family man, really good guy," Palmer said. "We just needed someone who could step it up to the next level."

Brooke had lunch with two of the executive officers she'd been introduced to earlier, neither of whom she'd describe as the most *vivacious* person on Earth, but then again, there were a lot of stiffs in the corporate world. Luckily, she clicked better with the general counsel, whom she met after lunch.

About two minutes into her meeting with the general counsel, his assistant stuck her head into the office. "Sorry for the interruption. Randy Kemp wants to meet with you today. He says it'll only take five minutes."

The general counsel rolled his eyes. "Randy Kemp wants to talk about his deposition in the Kentucky FLSA case, and that is definitely more than a five-minute conversation. Tell him he can have twenty minutes at four thirty." He turned to Brooke after his assistant left. "How much are you *not* going to miss all this when you're EVP of sales?" he asked jokingly.

"You mean, having at least two conversations a day that start with 'So, um, how bad would it be, *legally* speaking, if I told you that . . .'"

The general counsel chuckled. "Exactly."

Brooke smiled. Weirdly . . . she thought she kind of would miss that.

At the end of the day, she met up with Palmer again, and he led her down yet another hallway to a corner office.

"Thought you might want to try it on for size," he said, with a wink.

"This would be mine?" she asked.

He nodded. "All you have to do is say 'yes,' Brooke."

She stepped into the large office, modernly furnished with cream marble and ebony wood furnishings. The view from her office at Sterling was better, but it wasn't the view that mattered—it was what the office represented. The money. The title. The fact that she'd be running the entire sales division of such a large corporation.

One simple word, and it was all hers for the taking.

All she had to do was say *yes*.

BY THE TIME Brooke finally made it back to the hotel around ten o'clock that night, she was exhausted. She'd been awake since five A.M., she'd had to be "on" for nearly twelve hours straight, and she was feeling somewhat . . . out of sorts.

Palmer and two of the VPs—luckily, not the two stiffs from lunch again—had taken her to dinner at a French-Italian "seasonal cuisine" restaurant located in the city's historic Elizabeth district. The conversation was good, and the food and wine were excellent, and all in all, she'd had an enjoyable evening. But something was off.

Never once had Palmer pressured her to accept the offer,

but she knew, understandably, that he was eager for her response. And several times during dinner, she'd been tempted to say that one word, *yes*, because *of course* she should accept the offer. It was an excellent opportunity, and by and large she'd liked the people she'd met at Spectrum. The pragmatic businesswoman in her had been shouting, *What are you waiting for?* all through the dessert course—but something kept holding her back.

She didn't know what, exactly, that something was. But she'd first noticed it that afternoon, when Palmer had shown her the office that would be hers at Spectrum. He'd needed to step out to take a phone call, and while he was gone she'd taken a seat behind the sophisticated ebony wood desk. To "try it on for size," so to speak.

It hadn't felt quite . . . right.

She'd ignored the sentiment, thinking it was nothing, that it was merely akin to buying a new house but not feeling like it was actually hers until she moved in. But that same nagging feeling had popped up again throughout dinner, whenever she'd been about to accept Palmer's offer, so in the end, she'd just stayed quiet.

Brooke decided to sleep on it, wondering if perhaps she was simply feeling off because she was tired. The next morning, she woke up refreshed, reinvigorated, and ready to check out Charlotte with an open mind. The driver was waiting for her when she got downstairs, and he came armed with a list Palmer's secretary had put together of places Brooke should visit while in town.

Charlotte was a big city, but she noticed that it had something of a small-town feel—which appealed to the midwesterner in her. After touring around all morning and early afternoon, she asked the driver to drop her off at an outdoor café by her hotel, one that the concierge had recommended. She ordered a Margherita pizza and a glass of wine, and then she settled in and waited for that moment to come when she knew that accepting the offer was the right way to go.

Then she waited some more.

The moment sure seemed to be taking its sweet old time.

When the waiter brought over the pizza she'd ordered and she was *still* waiting, she thanked him and happened to catch sight of the people at the table across from her: a little girl, about eight years old, eating lunch quietly while her mother typed away on her BlackBerry.

"Almost finished, I promise," the mother was saying. "I just need to get this e-mail out before my client drives me completely nuts."

Brooke watched them, able to identify with the woman's feeling all too well. In a minute or two, she would put down the phone, smile at her daughter, and say, "Sorry. Just had to finish that." Except it wouldn't be finished, because, really, no work problem urgent enough to require the immediate attention of a woman simply trying to enjoy lunch with her daughter, or, say, a barbeque with her best friend, or a book club meeting with some girlfriends, could ever be fixed with *one* e-mail. The work would still be there when the woman got home, or maybe another issue would pop up that required the woman's attention, because work was *always* there. And it wasn't that the woman was complaining—she actually liked her job, in fact— but lately she'd been wondering if her life had gotten a little . . . off balance.

Or, maybe Brooke was over-personalizing the situation. Just a bit.

She tabled that thought as she walked back to her hotel. In her room, she fired up her laptop and, naturally, turned first to work-related e-mails. After that, she checked her personal account and saw that Rachel had e-mailed her, saying how great it had been to catch up at Ford's barbeque and that she wondered whether Brooke wanted to get together for lunch anytime next week.

Brooke started to write back to Rachel, saying that next week was likely going to be busy. While she didn't specifically mention it, she was already thinking about how she needed to catch up on things at work after her three-day weekend, particularly since she very possibly was about to tell Ian that she was quit—

Midsentence, she stopped typing and took her hands off the keyboard.

She was so *sick* of writing those words.

Sorry. Too busy. Can't leave work right now.

Darn, I have a work thing that night.

Maybe after work.

Count me in tentatively, depending on work.

Work.

Work.

Work.

Brooke got up from the desk and walked over to the window. She looked out at the Charlotte skyline, which was pretty with the sunset. But it wasn't Chicago.

She took a deep breath, realizing that for the first time in years, she didn't have a clue what she wanted. It had been one thing when she'd accepted that her current lifestyle wasn't conducive to a long-term romantic relationship, but what about all her other relationships? She saw Ford, she'd managed to at least protect that one friendship, but what about everyone else? Rachel? The book club? Her former co-workers at her old law firm—they used to get together once a month for Friday happy hour. When had she stopped doing that?

She could hear Ford defending her, even to herself.

Don't beat yourself up, Brooke. Work, family, whatever—everyone's busy these days.

Yeah, but there was busy, and then there was crap-when's-the-last-time-I-called-my-parents *busy*.

Crap. When *was* the last time she'd called her parents? She e-mailed them fairly regularly, but an actual phone call? She could check her cell phone call log to find out how long it had been, but she was pretty sure she didn't want to know.

This EVP position at Spectrum sounded every bit as demanding as her job at Sterling, perhaps even more so given the travel involved. And Brooke knew herself, she'd be starting over at a new place, which meant she'd want to prove herself and succeed—the same thing she'd strived to do at Sterling, ever since Ian had taken a chance on her two years ago. Just like she'd always felt the need to do, the girl from the Quads who'd had to work her butt off for every opportunity.

But maybe it was time to stop feeling like she had to prove something.

Maybe it was time to take a breath, to slow things down a notch, and simply enjoy her success—and all the other things in her life, too.

Except . . . she wasn't sure she knew how to do that.

You're a smart woman. You'll figure it out.

Strange little tears sprang to Brooke's eyes, and she half-laughed at herself. Of course, even though Cade wasn't there, and they weren't even speaking, he'd still managed to have the perfect line.

He'd said exactly what she needed to hear.

Thirty-one

FRIDAY MORNING, CADE met with Cameron and Nick McCall, the special agent in charge of the FBI's Chicago office, to get him up to speed on the status of all open FBI investigations. It was the last agency they needed to cover—after this, Cade would be fully briefed and ready to take over as acting U.S. attorney.

They'd been going for over an hour when Cameron stood up from her desk. She took a deep breath and put her hands on her lower back, which parted her suit jacket over her very pregnant stomach.

Cade and Nick exchanged looks, speaking in silent man-code, as was necessary in such circumstances.

You've got this, right, if she goes into labor here?

You're asking me? No, I don't have *this.*

"You boys can stop staring at me like I'm a ticking bomb about to explode."

Busted.

"I just need to stand for a few minutes." Cameron marched on, turning to a Medicare fraud investigation into a large suburban home health care agency. "Next matter: Evergreen Healthcare. How are we looking there?"

"My agents tell me that we're set to make all ten arrests late next week," Nick said.

Cameron looked at Cade. "If I'm gone when that happens, make sure you keep SAC Lamont Johnson over at the Department of Health and Human Services in the loop."

He nodded. "Got it."

"And with that said . . ." Cameron checked the list on her desk, "I think that's it. You are officially up to speed." She smiled, as if relieved to have that out of the way, and then checked her watch. "Just in time for lunch, too. Jack and Sam are meeting with Rylann about the Arroyo homicide investigation. Maybe I'll pop in and see if he's almost done."

"I'll go with you," Nick said. "I can give Wilkins a ride back to the office."

As the three of them walked down the hallway, a young male paralegal saw Cameron coming with her power suit, heels, and stomach. His eyes widened and he quickly ducked into a cubicle, giving her a wide berth.

Cameron shook her head after they walked by, speaking under her breath. "You saw that, right? That's been happening for a week now. Whenever I walk down the hallway, people literally leap to get out of my way." She glanced at Nick and Cade. "I'm not *that* big, am I?"

"That's not it," Cade said with a laugh.

"What else would it be?"

"You might want to ask your husband about that," Nick said.

Cameron stopped in the hallway, nearly causing both men to run into her.

"What did Jack do now?" She gave them both her best don't-mess-with-the-U.S.-attorney look.

"He meant it as a joke," Nick assured her. Then he thought about that. "At least, I think he did. Sometimes, you can't tell with Jack."

"What was the joke?" When Nick hesitated, Cameron looked at Cade and raised an eyebrow. "Morgan?"

"I wasn't there. Inadmissible hearsay."

She glared at him, and then turned back to Nick.

The special agent in charge finally caved. "Jack was a little worried—you know, with the way you kind of storm through the hallways in your heels—that someone might bump into you and knock you over."

Cameron waited. "And?"

"He maybe, possibly, said that if he got word of anyone getting in your way, they'd find out whether there was any truth to that rumor about him knowing how to kill a man with paper clips."

"I see." With that, Cameron turned on her heel and began walking down the hallway again.

"He's toast," Nick whispered to Cade.

"Definitely."

They followed Cameron to Rylann's office, just in time to see two FBI agents leaving. The taller, dark-haired agent stopped in the hallway and watched with an unmistakably warm look in his eyes as Cameron approached.

"Madame U.S. Attorney," he drawled.

"Special Agent Pallas. Just the man I was looking for." Cameron went to fold her arms across her chest, then seemed to realize—nope, no room there. "What is this I hear about someone saying that my employees need to stay out of my way or risk an untimely death by paper clip?"

Next to Jack, Agent Sam Wilkins looked up at the ceiling, speaking under his breath. "I told you that would not go over well . . ."

Jack held up his hands. "It was a *joke*."

"A joke." Cameron's gaze went to Sam. "Agent Wilkins. Was Agent Pallas scowling or smiling at the time of this alleged joke?"

"I plead the fifth."

"A paralegal practically dove headfirst into a cubicle to get out of my way, Jack. So no more jokes. *Oh*." Cameron suddenly put her hands on her stomach, and then peered up at him. "I think I'm having my first contraction."

Jack's eyes widened, then he moved closer to Cameron and put his hand on her stomach. "Does it hurt?"

She covered his hand with hers. "I'd say it's only about a point two."

Jack smiled, tenderly touching her cheek. "I knew, when we were on that rooftop, that we'd be here someday."

Cade had no clue what a "point two" meant, and from the way Jack and Cameron were looking at each other, he wasn't supposed to. Clearly, an inside joke.

He headed back to his office, not wanting to intrude on the private moment, and also because he didn't want to be thinking about cute inside jokes—because that made him think about a certain green-eyed general counsel, and for the last two weeks his mission had been to *not* think about said certain green-eyed general counsel.

He shouldn't be hung up on this.

They'd both known it wasn't a long-term deal when they'd gotten together, they'd had a mutual parting of ways, and with Brooke likely now moving to Charlotte it had been the perfect time to say good-bye.

This was exactly how these things were supposed to end. No one was angry, they'd had fun while it had lasted, they still liked and respected each other. Hell, he could even envision having coffee with her sometime when she breezed into Chicago to visit Ford and her parents. It was all good.

Except . . . it didn't *feel* all good.

Rather, the thought of Brooke leaving, of him merely being some guy she'd once slept with, felt more like a punch to the gut.

Which was precisely the reason he was *not* thinking about her.

Once inside his office, Cade took a seat at his desk and resolved, as he had many times over the last two weeks, to focus on work. He managed to do a decent job of that, putting himself on autopilot until the end of the day, when a knock on his office door interrupted him.

Vaughn stood in the doorway. "Thought I'd see if you want to grab a drink at O'Malley's."

Cade rubbed his face, realizing that he'd been reading

audio transcripts for hours. "Sure." He blinked, and then cocked his head. "I didn't realize you had any meetings here today."

"I didn't."

Huh. "Then why are you here?"

Vaughn shrugged. "I just figured you might, you know, need a drink."

Cade frowned. "Why would you th—" Then it dawned on him. "Oh, no. You and I are not doing this. We are not having this conversation." The idea of him and *Vaughn* having some sort of best friend heart-to-heart about his relationship troubles was laughable at best.

"You've been brooding for two weeks, Morgan. So yes, we are having this conversation."

"I appreciate it, Vaughn. Really. But no offense—you suck at this stuff as much as I do."

Vaughn tucked his hands into his pants pockets, not looking offended in the slightest. "Yep. And that's why God made whiskey."

THEY WENT TO a bar a few blocks from the federal building and grabbed a table in the back. After the waitress brought their drinks, Vaughn led in.

"I'll take a wild guess. This new emo mood of yours has something to do with the fact that you're not seeing Brooke anymore."

Cade had shared that information last week, in a terse and abbreviated conversation, after Vaughn apparently had used his FBI powers of super perception to notice that he was *not* checking his phone all night. He could sense that tonight, however, he wasn't getting out of the conversation without giving the agent something more.

So he thought about how to best describe the situation. Things had started out just fine between him and Brooke, but somewhere along the way the hookups and the cute text messages had turned into something more—at least on his end.

Something that involved emotions, and him oddly feeling the need to share childhood stories, and him making dinner for her after a crappy day at work.

Which meant, basically, one thing.

"I pulled out too late with her," he said simply.

Vaughn nearly dropped his glass. "Oh, fuck. Brooke's pregnant?"

"Whoa, there. *No.* Nobody's pregnant. I meant that I pulled out of the *relationship* too late."

"Oh." Vaughn paused. "You know, you really might want to add that clarification next time."

"Thanks. And here I'd been worried we were going to suck at this," Cade said dryly.

Vaughn grinned. "Well, I would've brought Huxley along to handle the more sensitive parts of the conversation, but he's having dinner with *Addison* tonight." He gestured with his whiskey, getting back on point. "So. You think you ended things too late with Brooke. You mean . . . because you're totally crazy about her?"

When Cade shot him a glare, Vaughn gestured between them with his free hand. "Oh, are we still pretending that's not the deal? 'Cuz I can always wait two more drinks if you need time to ease into, you know, the *truth*."

"That's funny. Is this the good cop or bad cop routine?"

"A little combination I like to think of as the Agent Roberts special."

Cade shook his head. Just one non-FBI friend. That's all he was asking for. "The truth doesn't matter now, anyway. I'm pretty sure Brooke is moving to Charlotte."

Vaughn's expression turned serious. "Charlotte? What brought that on?"

"One of Sterling's competitors offered her some big executive VP position. It sounds like a once-in-a-lifetime opportunity."

"Wow. What did you say when she told you about it?"

"I said, 'Congratulations' and told her to knock 'em dead in Charlotte." He saw Vaughn frown. "What was I supposed to say? 'Don't go?' You've seen her in action; you know how good she is. If she wants this, she should take it."

Vaughn nodded. "You're right. She should."

Cade pulled back. That was . . . it? Granted, he was no pro at the heart-to-hearts, but he'd expected maybe a *little* bit more. "Glad we're on the same page."

"Absolutely. You and I—we are in total agreement." Vaughn leaned back in the bar stool. "Now if Huxley were here, *he*, on the other hand, would probably have an entirely different take on the matter."

When Vaughn said nothing further, Cade took the bait. "And what would *Huxley's* take on the matter be?"

"Probably something about how you should tell Brooke how you feel, regardless of whether she's moving to Charlotte. You know how Huxley's all into being honest and open like that." Then Vaughn met Cade's gaze straight on. "And after that, he'd probably tell you that if he ever finds a girl who fits him as perfectly as Brooke fits you, that he hopes you're a good enough friend to say, 'Dude, get over your shit, get off your ass, and go talk to her.'"

Cade blinked. This. . . from *Vaughn*. "Huxley sure has a lot to say."

"Yeah, he's always been a know-it-all like that."

That, at least, got a grin out of Cade. "Well, I will take *Huxley's* advice into consideration."

A comfortable silence fell between them.

"And, Vaughn?" Cade looked at his friend, speaking in all earnestness. "Thanks."

Vaughn tipped his glass in acknowledgement. "Anytime, Morgan."

Thirty-two

BROOKE STOOD BEFORE her closed office door, taking a few deep breaths before stepping out into the hallway—and the unknown.

She had no idea how this meeting with Ian would go, but since coming back from Charlotte she'd thought a lot about what she wanted, both professionally and personally. And she knew, in her heart of hearts, that it was time for a change.

She steeled herself and opened her door. The office was quiet; she'd deliberately scheduled her meeting with Ian at the end of the day when most of the other employees had already left.

Ian's door was open, and he sat at his desk reading the evening news on his computer. "Come on in." He rubbed his hands together eagerly. "I think I know what this is about. Curt Emery called you, right? He's decided he wants us to take over at Soldier Field."

Okay . . . this was going be a little awkward. "I haven't spoken to Curt since our meeting a few weeks ago. But, actually, I need to tell you something about that meeting. When

I got to Halas Hall, someone was waiting there: Palmer Green, CEO of Spectrum North America."

Ian frowned, obviously recognizing the name. "Palmer Green? What did he want?"

"The meeting was just a setup, a way for Palmer to meet me." Brooke looked Ian directly in the eyes. "So that he could offer me a job at Spectrum."

Ian's expression immediately turned somber. He exhaled, taking a moment. "What position?"

"Executive vice president of sales and business development."

Ian ran his hand over his mouth. "How much?"

"Eight hundred and twenty-five thousand dollars. Including stock options and bonus."

He cocked his head. "This last Friday. Your personal day."

She nodded. "I flew out to Spectrum's headquarters in Charlotte."

Ian said nothing at first in response to that. Then he peered at her across his desk, with sadness in his eyes. "Are you leaving me, Brooke?"

The moment of truth. "Well . . . that depends on you, Ian."

He sat forward in earnest. "Brooke, I would do anything I could to keep you. I hope you know that. But Sterling isn't Spectrum North America. I can't match that kind of package."

"I know that. And I hope *you* know that in many ways, I consider Sterling Restaurants to be like family to me. Which is why I'm hoping, Ian, that you can give me something Spectrum can't. Something that I've realized is more important than eight hundred and twenty-five thousand dollars a year." Brooke paused. She'd practiced this at home, actually saying the words out loud. She could do this.

"I want more balance in my life."

As soon as the words were out there, she felt . . . good.

Ian stared at her in surprise, as if waiting for another bomb to drop. When that didn't happen, he nodded eagerly. "Okay. Yes. Absolutely. What can we do to make that happen?"

As a matter of fact, she'd been prepared for just that question. "Glad you asked. I have a few ideas on that front." Brooke opened up the file folder she'd brought with her and pulled out the report she'd prepared.

"More charts and graphs?"

"Of course." She handed Ian the report. "The first problem we have is that I'm basically doing two full-time jobs: general counsel and VP of sales. The other problem is that our legal department is still the same size as it was two years ago, before we built the sports and entertainment division. As a result, we've been farming out more and more matters to outside counsel—in fact, we paid them over four hundred thousand dollars last year. And as I'm sure you are aware, because I know you *always* read the monthly summaries and open matter reports I send you,"—she gave him a pointed look, they both knew he never even opened the darned things—"seventy percent of that four hundred thousand was related to employment matters."

"I see that. Very colorfully illustrated on this pie chart here."

"What this means, however, is that we could substantially cut back our legal expenses if we brought in an in-house labor and employment lawyer to handle the less complex matters. Do you realize that we pay a Gray & Dallas associate four hundred and fifty dollars an hour every time we need to respond to one of those ridiculously onerous IDHR charges?"

"I did *not* realize that," Ian said indignantly. He held up a finger. "Question: what's an IDHR charge?"

"Seriously, if you would just *read* the summaries I send you . . ." Moving on, Brooke gestured to the report. "Now turn to page two. From what I've estimated, bringing in an in-house employment lawyer will save us roughly ninety thousand dollars."

"I like the sound of that."

"I would then like to apply that ninety thousand toward hiring a second in-house lawyer who will take on some of my responsibilities," Brooke continued. "Routine matters like reviewing our lease agreements, drafting the vendor contracts, et cetera, which will obviously lessen my workload. Given what I expect we'll have to pay to get two quality in-house counsel, this should cost Sterling, in total, about seventy thousand dollars more this year."

Ian stared at her. "That's . . . it? Seventy thousand a year is all it will take to keep you here? Done. *So* done. Where do I sign?"

"Actually, if you turn to page three, you'll see that I project, given the way the company is expanding, that by next year we'll nearly break even and in the year after that this will actually *save* us money."

Ian folded his arms over his chest, looking happy as a clam. "Sounds perfect."

"I also want my job title changed to executive vice president and general counsel."

Ian considered this. "I see no problem with that."

"And . . . there's one last thing."

Of *course* there was one last thing. This deal she'd struck with Ian, to hire two in-house counsel, would help her get back the balance she'd been missing in her personal life. But she'd also spent the last few days thinking about what she wanted, professionally speaking.

And there was just one thing.

Ian must've seen the gleam in her eyes. He put his hands on the desk, as if bracing himself. "This one's going to hurt, isn't it?"

"It might sting a little." Brooke met his gaze. "I want equity in the company."

Ian exhaled heavily and steepled his fingers, remaining silent. He was, and always had been, the sole owner of Sterling Restaurants.

"I could give you a long speech about what I've brought to Sterling Restaurants over the last two years, Ian. But I'm hoping you already know. So instead I'll just tell you that I believe in this company, and I know what I can do to continue building it. And I want to do that not as an employee, but as your partner."

She sat there, sweating it out while he said nothing.

"What percentage?" he finally asked.

Brooke exhaled. *Yes!* In her head, she was doing an imaginary dance in the end zone. "I'll tell you what. I've hit you with a lot of information this evening." She smiled charmingly. "Why don't you think everything over for a couple of days and get back to me with what *you* think is fair?"

"Always a negotiator," Ian muttered under his breath, shaking his head. But when he looked at her, there was a hint of a smile curling at the edges of his lips. "I should fire you for making me panic like that, you know."

Brooke smiled. "Well, seeing how you make me do all the firing, I'll be sure to get on that one right quick."

LATER THAT EVENING at Firelight, a bar Brooke had been meaning to check out for ages, Ford raised his glass of champagne in a toast. "Congratulations to the new executive vice president and general counsel and *part owner* of Sterling Restaurants."

Brooke grinned. "It'll be a long time before I get tired of hearing that." She clinked her glass to his and took a sip.

"So this means the job at Spectrum, the whole moving to Charlotte deal, is officially out of the running, right?" Ford asked.

"Yep. As soon as my meeting with Ian was over, I called Spectrum's CEO and let him know that I was declining the offer," she said. Palmer had been surprised, and disappointed, but the conversation had ended as amicably as one could hope given the circumstances.

"Any regrets?" Ford asked.

Brooke thought about that, then shook her head. "Not a one." In fact, she'd already begun step two of her plan to have more balance in her life. She'd e-mailed Rachel to say that, yes, she'd love to meet for lunch any day next week, and she'd also called her parents while walking home from work to tell them her news. She'd caught up with them for over an hour, undoubtedly the longest non-work-related phone conversation she'd had in about two years.

She looked around the bar, the *part owner* in her unable to resist checking out the competition. "So this is the place you, Charlie, and Tucker are always raving about." She gestured teasingly to the appetizer in front of her. "Must be the crab cakes." Actually, she was pretty sure it had a lot more to do with the all the attractive women dressed in jeans, heels, and camisole tops that showed lots of tanned skin.

Ford grinned mischievously. "Sure is. Love the crab cakes here."

Brooke could certainly see why. About a dozen of those "crab cakes" had been subtly checking out Ford since they'd sat down. She was about to make a joke about cramping his style, when something—or some*one*, rather—caught her eye. "This really is the happening place. Even the Twitter Terrorist is here."

She easily recognized Kyle Rhodes, an extremely wealthy computer genius turned businessman who'd originally shot to fame after hacking into Twitter when his then-girlfriend, a Victoria's Secret model, tweeted a video of herself cheating on him with a movie star. Like most Chicagoans, Brooke had followed all the media drama surrounding his arrest and conviction—not realizing that one day she would have a personal connection, of sorts, to the case.

Ford glanced over, then shrugged. "I've seen him here a few times. I think his friend owns the bar or something."

"And that must be Rylann," Brooke said, referring to the woman with long, raven-colored hair having dinner with him. She watched as Rylann shook her head at something Kyle said, and then laughed at whatever he said next.

Hold on. You're friends with a woman whose fiancé you sent to prison?

"You might want to stop drooling, Brooke," Ford said. "I'm pretty sure the Twitter Terrorist is already taken."

She blinked. "What? Oh, no—I was looking at her."

Ford raised an eyebrow. "Now this is getting intriguing."

Men. "I wasn't checking her out, Ford. I know her. Or at least, I know *of* her. She's friends with Cade. I was thinking about how he once told me that it's a weird situation since

he's the one who prosecuted her fiancé." She smiled, remembering their conversation that night. "I asked if he thought they
would invite him to their wedding, and we were laughing about
whether they made a card that said, 'So glad we've all gotten
past the time I called one of you a terrorist in open court.'"
She smiled, and then shrugged at Ford. "You probably had to
be there."

"Another inside joke."

"Yes." She felt her smile falter a bit, and exhaled. She
forced herself not to dwell on negative thoughts—this was a
celebration, after all. "Let's talk about something else. Like
the blonde in the pink shimmery shirt who's been eying you
all evening."

"Brooke." Ford looked at her in all seriousness. "Why don't
you call Cade? I get that you were holding back before because
of your work situation. But that's not a problem anymore."

She nodded, having realized this, too. And a part of her
was tempted to do just that.

But.

"I just . . . I don't know what he's thinking. When I told
him about the job offer from Spectrum, he wasn't exactly
begging me to stay in Chicago." To the contrary, really. *Knock
'em dead in Charlotte, Brooke.*

"Well, did you say anything that indicated that you were
considering *him* in your decision?"

Brooke took a moment, thinking through every word of
their last conversation. "Okay, no. Fair enough. But that's just
it. I've suddenly had this epiphany, this new outlook on what
I want in my life, but that's *me.* What if I go to him and tell
him everything that I've been feeling and he doesn't feel the
same way?" Potentially the one thing worse than having Cade
tell her she wasn't a big-picture girl, she'd decided, would be
having him tell her that she'd never been in *any* picture.

"That would suck balls."

She laughed, then realized Ford wasn't joking. "Wait,
that's your answer?"

"Yes, because it's the truth," he said.

"Well, I don't *want* the truth. I want to be pumped up, given a pep talk, the whole you-go-girl, you-can-do-this shebang. I want you to say, 'That's just crazy talk, Brooke. *Of course* Cade wants to be with you. You two are great together. In fact, I bet he's been moping around for the last two weeks, unshowered and barely able to leave his apartment because he's so depressed you haven't called.' Or something—anything—that gives me hope that I won't end up crashing and burning if I do this."

"That's what I was supposed to say?"

"Yes, *that* is what you were supposed to say, Ford Dixon," she said, all worked up now.

"Oh." He mulled this over. "On the upside, I do think there's at least a good forty to fifty percent chance that what you said is true. Well, not the part about him not showering and unable to leave his apartment. Guys don't do that. We avoid issues, we get drunk, sometimes we pick up another chick to forget the old one—" he must've seen the look of panic in her face—"*not* suggesting that's the situation here, I'm just talking, you know, about the gender in general, and . . . I'm thinking I should probably shut up now."

Brooke covered her face. "Thank you, Ford. And here I'd been worried before." She stared down, hands rubbing her temples as she tried really, really hard not to imagine Cade with another woman. Then something slid across the table and into her view.

Ford's Phone.

With a photo of a bare-chested Ryan Gosling.

Despite everything, she smiled.

"Sorry," Ford said with a sheepish grin. "Clearly, we've established that I'm not the best at the motivational pep talks. But can I say one more thing?"

"Just, please, try not to freak me out anymore, okay? I'm already far out of my wheelhouse just by considering this whole lay-everything-on-the-line scenario."

"The only way you'll know for certain what Cade is thinking is if you *ask* him."

Brooke considered this, and then nodded.

Reluctantly, she had to admit that her "best friend with the penis attached" had gotten that part right.

Thirty-three

CADE ASKED THE cabdriver to drop him off a few blocks from his apartment, thinking some fresh air would do him good. He wasn't drunk, but he'd had a few drinks and wanted to clear his head—especially after his talk with Vaughn.

The main issue he had with Vaughn's surprisingly non-terrible advice was that it didn't address the real problem. Brooke moving to Charlotte was not the real problem. Sure, it didn't make the situation any easier, but lots of couples dealt with job relocations and transfers, they made sacrifices for each other or they had long-distance relationships, and they figured it out.

The *real* problem was him.

The moment he'd heard from Charlie about Brooke's job offer, and he'd felt that stab of disappointment, he'd closed himself off emotionally. He'd gone into his hey-it-doesn't-matter mode, and had put on his nothing-fazes-me grin, and he'd told himself—and, essentially, Brooke, too—that it didn't matter if she left.

That was what he did. That was what he'd always done. He pushed things away that hurt, and then he moved on. His father? Don't want to think about the asshole. Football? Yeah, that was great back in the day, but let's talk about something else. Move on.

He remembered that very first morning with Brooke, watching her sleep in his bed and wondering if he could allow himself to get close to her. And slowly, he'd been doing that, whether he'd realized it at the time or not, but as soon as the other shoe had dropped and he'd felt foolish for thinking they were on the same page, he'd thrown on an easy smile and had walked away.

Typically, that was a good play for him. One that had always worked in the past. Noah's rejection had hurt, so he took all that anger and negative energy and he'd channeled it, positively, onto the football field. Then when fate had yanked football away from him, he'd gone to law school, and had funneled his ambition and drive into a successful legal career.

And he'd been doing just fine since then. Until everything had upended like the damn *Titanic* when a sixteen-year-old kid and a sassy lawyer had waltzed into his life. After that, it had suddenly become all *Oh, let's open up and share* and *Oh, isn't it cool having a brother* and *Oh, Brooke, it's so perfect with you* and there'd been voices in his head, and all these weird *feelings*, and now, for the first time in his life, he was a mess.

Cade took a moment to let that sink in as he turned onto his block.

Huh. Zach had been right.

It really wasn't that much fun being a mess.

He was in uncharted waters here, and he had a decision to make. He could keep doing his self-protective thing, and let Brooke walk out of his life, and continue on with his string of unfulfilling four-month relationships with women who didn't challenge him, didn't make him laugh over a simple text message, and didn't push him to be better. Or he could go find Brooke—a woman moving halfway across the country, a woman who'd specifically told him, in their very last conversation, that they'd both known from the beginning their relationship wasn't anything permanent—and lay it all on the line, and hope that he didn't look like a complete jackass in the process.

Cade waited for the annoying voices in his head to chime in with their opinions on that one.

Nothing.

This time, he was on his own, apparently.

As he opened the gate in front of his apartment building, he noticed someone sitting on the front steps. Whoever it was appeared to be waiting for somebody, and Cade smiled, thinking for a split second that maybe, coincidentally, it would be Brooke and—

Then he saw that it was his brother.

"Hey, Zach," he said, heading up the front walkway. They didn't have plans that night, so this was a surprise. "What brings—"

He stopped when he saw that Zach had been crying.

Instantly, Cade knew what was wrong—or at least, the source of whatever was wrong.

Noah.

The asshole had done something. Of course he had. Cade immediately went into protective mode. "What happened?"

Zach swallowed. "I kept thinking that you would come around eventually. I figured that once you got to know me better, you'd want to know more about our dad, too. But I don't think that's ever gonna happen."

Cade ran a hand through his hair and exhaled. He'd always suspected that Zach had been angling for some heartwarming father-son reunion between him and Noah, but he hadn't realized the kid was *this* serious about it. "I know you want that, Zach. And I want say that I'll try, but—"

"He's dying."

Cade pulled back, the words dropping like stones in the air. "What?"

"He's dying, Cade," Zach said quietly. "My father—your father—is dying."

Cade stared at him for a long moment. "How?"

"Cancer. Started in his lungs. I guess he used to be a big smoker before I was born. But we were—" Zach cleared his throat—"he was beating the lung cancer. Then an MRI scan came back about six weeks ago that showed a tumor on his brain stem. I knew it was going to be bad."

It was all coming together now. "Six weeks ago. That's

when you came to see me." And suddenly, a few things that had been nagging in the back of Cade's mind made sense. Why Noah wasn't helping Zach with football. A few odd, offhanded comments Zach had made here and there.

"After they did the biopsy, they told us that it's some really aggressive kind of tumor. I knew then that I had to find you. I needed to do that for him. And I hoped we would have more time, but . . . they did a follow-up scan and we found out today that the tumor's already grown." Zach's voice trembled. "They say that if we're lucky, he'll make it eleven months."

Eleven months.

Cade felt a pit in his stomach as Zach wiped the back of his hand across his eyes. It killed him to see Zach so upset. Maybe they hadn't found each other until six weeks ago, but it didn't matter. This was his *brother*. He reached out and put his hand on Zach's shoulder. "I'm so sorry, Zach."

Zach pushed Cade's hand away and stood up, suddenly going on the offensive. "You're sorry?" He stepped closer to Cade, raising his voice. "Really?"

Cade held his ground. "Of course I am. No matter what happened between us, I'd never wish this on Noah. And I'd certainly never wish this on you."

"Good. Then I want you to do something for me." Zach's jaw was set in determination. "I want you to go see him."

That was . . . not a good idea. "I understand what you're doing here, Zach. And it's an admirable thing. But I say this in all sincerity: I don't think Noah would want to see me. Especially not right now, with everything he has to deal with."

"That's a cop out."

"Does he even know we've been hanging out?" Cade asked.

Zach paused before answering. "No."

Christ. Before Cade could respond to that, Zach continued.

"I didn't want to tell him in case you refused to ever see him," he said defensively. "Look, I get it. You spent your whole childhood waiting for your dad to show up, this big hero you'd built up in your head. And then he let you down. You know why I get that? Because I waited my whole life for someone to show up, too. *You*. Cade Morgan, football star. I never forgot that day when I was watching the Rose Bowl and my dad told me you were my brother." His blue eyes snapped with anger. "When I was younger, I fucking *idolized* you. Whenever I got in trouble and my parents sent me to my room, I used to dream up these scenarios where you showed up and sneaked me out of my room, and we'd go on these crazy adventures together. So things didn't exactly work out the way *I'd* hoped either, did they?"

The words hit Cade right in the gut. "I didn't know, Zach," he said, nearly a whisper. "I didn't know anything about you."

Zach nodded. "But now you do. Now you know everything. And the question is, what are you going to do about it?" He held Cade's gaze. "He's at Northwestern Memorial Hospital. He'll be there until tomorrow afternoon. What you do with that information . . ." he said as he held out his hands, "is up to you."

CADE ENTERED HIS apartment and tossed his keys on the counter. He set his briefcase down, and sunk onto the couch, thinking about everything Zach had told him.

His father was dying.

Many thoughts ran through his mind, but the one he kept coming back to was, simply, *Why?* For years, he'd wondered what was so wrong with him that Noah hadn't wanted to be a part of his life. He'd forced himself to move on, but now that question had reared its ugly head again.

From what he could tell, Noah was a good father to Zach. For that, Cade was genuinely happy. And he would love to be able to say that knowing they were close wasn't a bitter pill to swallow, that he had no further feelings on the matter, and that after all these years he'd come to accept that Noah was just the guy who'd gotten his mom pregnant, nothing more. He wanted to fall back into the comfort of his routine, and be that blithe, that matter of fact. He wanted the *why* not to matter. He wanted to not care.

But after all this time, he thought maybe he still did.

Thirty-four

BROOKE PARKED HER car in a spot across the street from Cade's apartment, and killed the engine. She sat there, waiting for the moment when she knew this was a bad idea, when logic and reason kicked in and she realized that instead of a face-to-face conversation, she could just text Cade something simple like, "Not going to Charlotte. Dinner tonight?" Because that—ha, ha—would put the ball in *his* court, not hers, and then *she* wouldn't be the one . . . sitting outside his apartment looking like a stalker.

But the moment never came.

Crap.

So, fine, she was doing this. No clue what she was going to say to Cade—*Remember that part where I wanted to keep our relationship casual? Psych!*—but she figured she'd start with "hi" and go from there.

She got out of the car and crossed the street. It was hot outside, especially for eleven A.M. She'd wanted to wait a little longer to drop in on Cade, but she'd been driving herself crazy mulling over the various ways this conversation could go and had decided it was best to just rip off the Band-Aid and get it over with.

A teenager dressed in cargo shorts and a T-shirt was walking on the sidewalk, heading in her direction. They reached the wrought-iron gate in front of Cade's building at the same time, and he politely held it open for her.

"Thank you," she said.

She walked up the steps of gray stone, teenager in tow, and pushed the buzzer for "Morgan."

"Looks like Cade's a popular guy this morning," the teenager said from behind her.

Brooke turned around and saw that he was studying her curiously.

"You're the Niagara Falls girl," he said.

She had no idea what that meant, but after taking in his tall frame and familiar cobalt blue eyes, she was certain of one thing. "And you're the brother."

"Zach."

She smiled. His hair was lighter and shorter than Cade's, but he was cute and athletic-looking in a way that probably caught the eye of many a sixteen-year-old girl. "Brooke."

"You came to see Cade?" he asked, in a tone that hovered somewhere between a question and an accusation.

"I did." She gestured to the silent intercom. "Although . . . he doesn't appear to be home."

Zach seemed particularly interested in this. "Huh." He stared at the buzzer for a moment, and then looked back at her. "Aren't you supposed to be in Charlotte?"

She pulled back in surprise. "He told you about that?"

"I was with him when that guy Charlie told him you were moving. Something that Cade strangely didn't seem to know anything about."

Zach waited, clearly wanting a response from her.

"I think this is probably a conversation Cade and I should have, Zach. It's complicated."

He rolled his eyes. "You two are like a broken record with that."

Brooke's ears perked up. "Cade said the situation between us was complicated?" She paused. "Did he say anything else about me?"

Instead of answering, Zach looked her over with a wary expression, as if debating something. "You know what? It's been a really shitty couple of days, so I apologize if this comes out a little harsh. But . . . do you even like my brother? Because if he's where I think he is right now, this day is going to be pretty shitty for him, too. So if you're about to say good-bye, or do anything else that'll make things even worse for him, then you should go. Just send him a text message when you get to North Carolina, or an e-mail, or tweet him, whatever." He stopped and stared defiantly at Brooke, hands tucked into his pockets.

Brooke thought about how best to respond to that, since it sounded like there was a lot going on with Cade and Zach that she was out of the loop on. "I'm not here to say good-bye, Zach," she said gently. "I'm not moving to Charlotte. And yes, I do like your brother. Very much so. That's why I came here this morning—to tell him that."

"Oh." His face relaxed, some of the tension seeming to leave him. His expression turned sheepish. "Sorry. You'll probably be wanting your head back now." He pantomimed handing it back to her, a gesture that made her smile, then he took a seat on the first step.

He rested his arms on his knees and bowed his head, taking a deep breath. Brooke stood there awkwardly, not knowing what to do, and then sat on the step next to him.

They sat in silence for a few moments.

Brooke cocked her head. "Niagara Falls . . . from *The Breakfast Club*, right? Good to see you kids are keeping up on the classics."

Zach chuckled, then glanced over. "In answer to your question, yes—he talks about you. He says you're the smartest, wittiest woman he's ever met."

"He did?" Brooke's heart skipped a beat, suddenly filling with hope.

But first things first.

"About this shitty day you and Cade are having—is there anything I can do to help?" she asked.

Zach contemplated that. "Actually, maybe there is."

CADE PUSHED THROUGH the revolving door of Northwestern Memorial Hospital and walked up to the visitors' desk.

"I'm here to see Noah Garrity." He braced himself for the question he'd been dreading all morning. *Friend or family?*

"Sign in here," the front desk clerk merely said, pointing to a clipboard. "Name and time."

Cade did so, and then waited as the clerk typed something into the computer. She pulled out an ID badge and wrote a number on it. "Room 1502. Elevators are to your left." She handed him the badge.

"Thank you." Cade clipped the badge to his suit jacket and headed for the elevators.

He stepped into an empty elevator and pushed the button for the fifteenth floor. He stared straight ahead at the doors, refusing to toy with the cuffs of his sleeves, or run his fingers through his hair, or give in to any other kind of nervous gesture. He was doing this for Zach, and that was it. As much as a small part of him had questions for Noah, he had not come here seeking answers or closure. He was no longer a naïve ten-year-old boy, easily duped by a few pats on the back and a couple of nice moments.

And even if that small part of him still cared about the *why*, he'd be damned if he let Noah Garrity see that.

He didn't plan to be angry or spiteful. Just businesslike. Emotions would play no part in this visit today.

The elevator doors opened and Cade stepped out. The floor was quiet, the patients' rooms situated around the perimeter with a nurses' station in the center. He followed the arrows to room 1502, at the far end of the hallway.

He tucked his hands into his pants pockets, his strides purposefully unhurried as he passed by the other patient rooms. He'd deliberately chosen to wear a suit, skipping the tie since

it was Saturday, because he planned to get in and out as fast
as possible with an excuse about needing to get into work. But
he wouldn't lie—he also wanted Noah to see the man he'd
become. He may not have gone pro in football, but he'd done
well by himself regardless. Northwestern University. Rose
Bowl champ. Magna cum laude in his law school class. Assistant U.S. attorney. Today, he would wear those achievements
like a suit of armor.

I did it all without you.

He spotted room 1502 and slowed when he saw that the
door was open. One of the many things that had kept him
awake last night was this moment, when he saw Noah Garrity
for the first time in twenty-three years. He had a vivid image
in his head of a tall twenty-eight-year-old man looking cool
and tough in his leather jacket—a man younger than Cade was
today. Juxtaposed against that were the portrayals of gaunt,
bedridden cancer patients he'd seen in the movies and on TV.

He took a step closer to the door and saw that neither of
those images had been accurate. Sitting in one of the chairs
by the window, looking out at the view of the city, was a
normal-looking fifty-one-year-old man wearing faded jeans
and a navy sweatshirt. With the sunlight coming in through
the windows, Cade could see gray peppered throughout
Noah's dark hair. He wore gym shoes—not too-cool-for-
school work boots or even flashy running shoes—just regular
gray Nikes.

He looked like . . . a dad.

Cade watched as Noah stared out the window. He looked
lost in thought, and Cade realized then that his first instincts
had been right.

This was a bad idea.

The man had just found out he was dying; he undoubtedly
wanted to be alone. Now was not the time for a surprise, awkward visit from a long-lost son.

Cade took a step back to leave, but the heel of his leather
wing tip scraped softly against the tile floor. Noah blinked,
coming out of his reverie, and glanced over.

A look of shock crossed his face, and they both froze.

"Cade." Noah stood up from his chair, not saying anything for a long time. "How . . . did you know I was here?"

Cade kept his tone impassive. "Zach."

"Zach?" Noah's expression was confused at first, and then realization set in. "He came to you because of the tumor."

"Yes."

Cade was wholly unprepared for what happened next.

Noah's eyes welled up. "That's so . . . exactly the kind of thing he would do." His voice broke on the last word and he looked down. He said nothing for a moment, and then peered back up. "Sorry." He cleared his throat. "This has been an exhausting couple of days."

He gestured. "Please. Come in. Uh. . . maybe I can pull this chair over from here . . ." Moving awkwardly, as if nervous, he grabbed an extra chair from the corner and set it a couple of feet across from the one by the window.

After they'd both sat down, Noah rested his hands on his legs and looked Cade over. "So, wow. Assistant U.S. Attorney Cade Morgan, in the flesh."

Though he showed no reaction outwardly, this surprised Cade. He'd had no clue Noah knew he'd become a prosecutor. "How are you feeling?" It seemed like the kind of question one should ask in a hospital.

"Well, it's been a roller-coaster ride, all right," Noah said. "But actually, I feel pretty good this morning. They started me on some new steroid yesterday—told me I needed to stay for observation for twenty-four hours to make sure there aren't any side effects." He waved in the direction of the hallway, managing a smile. "I think the nurses are pissed that I won't wear the hospital gown. I told them they'll have plenty of chances to see me in one of those soon."

"What about chemotherapy or radiation?"

"I start radiation next week. They say it won't shrink the tumor, but they're hoping it might slow how quickly it grows."

An awkward silence fell between them.

Cade figured he might as well get right to the point. There was one thing, at least, he wanted to say. "Noah, I—"

"I read about your big promotion in the news," Noah cut

in eagerly, before Cade could finish. "Acting U.S. attorney, that really is something. Will you still be able to try cases when you take over that role? Sounds like the Sanderson trial is shaping up to be a real dogfight."

Cade carefully studied the man across from him. Noah sure seemed to have a *lot* of information about him. "You follow all the news related to the U.S. Attorney's Office that closely?"

Noah met his gaze, his voice quiet. "No. Just the news related to my son."

All the anger that Cade had been pushing down for years suddenly came boiling right up to the surface.

My son.

Noah Garrity had lost the right to call him that a long time ago.

Jaw clenched, Cade took a moment. He calmed himself before speaking. "I didn't come here to talk about my job."

"I'm sure you want an explanation from me. I know I sure as hell would."

"No." Cade locked eyes with him. "I don't want anything from you."

"Humor a dying man, then."

Cade felt a mixture of emotions at the poor attempt at a joke. He said nothing further and . . . waited.

Noah took a deep breath, as if steeling himself. "I was a screwup back then, Cade. I couldn't keep a job, I drank, I got high, and I didn't give a shit about anyone except myself. When the landscaping business I'd started with my brother folded, I came back to Chicago to live off my parents. That gave my father plenty of opportunities to tell me how useless I was— and trust me, he had no problem taking every one of them."

Father issues? Was that what Noah was blaming everything on? Cade almost laughed at the irony. *Join the fucking club.*

"I called your mother about a month after getting back in town," Noah said. "I thought that seeing you would help me get my act together."

"Didn't exactly work out that way, did it?" Cade said sarcastically, before he could stop himself. *Keep emotions out of this, Morgan.*

"I was immature. And stupid. I thought it would be fun to see my kid, someone I could take to a ball game or play video games with. I wasn't thinking about all the responsibility that came with it." Noah paused. "But when I saw you that day, it suddenly become so . . . real. I kept thinking that you were already ten times smarter than me, and stronger, too, with the way you stood up to me and asked me straight-out why I hadn't been around." He smiled ruefully. "But you also had such a good heart. I could see how much you wanted me to be your fath—"

"Don't." Cade spoke in a low tone. "Don't say it." He knew the exact moment Noah was talking about—when he'd called him *Dad*.

A flash of sadness crossed Noah's eyes. "I know there's no excuse for what I did." His eyes met Cade's, the same shade of blue. "But you need to understand—I would've messed you up, Cade. Despite what a jerk I was back then, even I could see that your mother had gotten it so *right*. Staying out of your life was the best thing I could've done for you."

Cade stared out the window, shaking his head. "That's . . . such bullshit."

"Is it?" Noah gestured to Cade. "Look at you. Think you would've gotten this far with a deadbeat dad bringing you down?"

"Bit of a shame those were my only two options, don't you think? No father, or a deadbeat one?"

"Yes, it is," Noah said, without any trace of sarcasm. "It took me thirty-five years to learn how to be a father. And I will go to my grave being ashamed of that."

Cade turned back to the window, having nothing to say to that.

"I used to go to your football games, you know," Noah said.

Cade slowly looked over. "When?"

"At Northwestern. First game I saw was your sophomore year, against Penn State. After Zach was born, I'd begun to think about you a lot. A real lot. I knew they were starting you that game—your first time—and I wanted to be there."

"I remember that game."

"I'm sure you do. You were up against the number-one team in the Big Ten, it was your first year as starting QB, and *nobody* expected you to pull out a win. But you showed them all."

Cade stared at him stoically. It was a little late for fatherly pride.

"I hung around the parking lot after the game," Noah said. "You came out of the stadium, and there was this moment when I got to see you for the first time in years." His voice grew thick with emotion. "I remember hoping so badly that you'd see me standing there. That maybe . . . I don't know, we could talk or something. But then everyone swarmed you. Friends, fans, your mother, and your grandparents—even reporters. They were all cheering for you, and you looked so proud." He paused, clearing his throat. "I realized then that I had no place there. You were grown up, a man with a very bright future ahead of you, and I had lost my chance to be a part of that."

The room went quiet after that.

Finally, Noah mustered a smile. "Wish I could've been a fly on the wall when Zach somehow convinced you to see me."

The mention of his brother, at least, helped to ease the tension. "Zach is quite persuasive. The kid could be a lawyer someday."

Immediately, Cade realized that was the wrong thing to say.

"Maybe he will be," Noah said softly. "I'm sure, whatever he does, that he'll grow up to be a really good man. Like his brother."

Cade watched as his father struggled to maintain his composure.

He might not be able to forgive, but there was, at least, one thing he could do for him.

"I'll take care of him, Noah. Whatever he needs. Zach . . . will be okay."

Noah closed his eyes. His bent his head, going quiet for several moments before he pulled himself together and wiped his eyes. "Thank you."

Cade felt the stinging in his own eyes. The hospital room suddenly felt too small, the air too thick and heavy. "I need to get going."

Noah stood up. "Cade, wait. Please. You have no idea how much it means to me that you came here. I know I have no right to ask, but I'd still like that second chance." He reached out tentatively and put a hand on Cade's shoulder. "At least think about it, Son."

The hopefulness on Noah's face brought Cade back to that moment, so many years ago, when he'd wanted nothing more than to be this man's son. But he'd shut that door long ago, and he didn't think he could open it again.

Not when that would mean losing his father all over again.

Cade felt the tightness in his throat, his voice coming out hoarse.

"Good-bye, Noah."

CADE PUSHED THROUGH the hospital doors and kept walking. He spotted an alley up ahead and turned into it.

Once alone, he pressed his hands against the brick wall of the hospital and closed his eyes.

So much *fucking* time wasted.

He hit the wall hard with the side of his fist, the pain a welcome distraction from the ache in his chest. He felt angry and lost and so goddamn raw he wanted to climb out of his own skin. No amount of charm or jokes or quips could protect him now—this was real and it was hard and it was rough. His estranged father was dying, and he was furious about that, at Noah for being a dickhead for so much of his life, and for laying all this on him now. But he couldn't just feel anger, because he'd seen the genuine look of regret in Noah's eyes, and also the desire to make things right.

Cade did not want to be that man.

If he took one thing from this screwed-up experience, it was that he didn't want to look back on his life at the end of his days and regret the actions he'd never taken and the words he'd never said.

The hell with his hang-ups. The hell with holding back. He was going for the win on this one.

He was going to find Brooke.

His decision made, he turned away from the wall, not caring if she was at home, at work, or in goddamn Charlotte. As soon as he pulled himself together, he was going to—

He stopped in his tracks.

Brooke stood there, at the end of the alley.

"Hi," she said softly.

Cade wiped his eyes, not understanding how her being *there* was possible. "Why—how—are you here?"

"I went to your place and ran into Zach. He told me you were here." She gestured in the direction he'd just come from. "I was waiting in the lobby, and when I saw you walk out, I thought maybe you—" She stopped, shifting hesitantly, and then walked over to him. "When I heard about Noah, I wanted to be here. With you."

Cade was trying to process this, wondering what that might mean, when she pointed to his hand.

"You're bleeding." She reached out and took his hand in hers, tenderly turning it over.

He looked down and saw that he'd split one of his knuckles. "I punched a wall."

"I caught that part." She reached into her purse and pulled out a tissue.

Cade watched as she gently dabbed at the cut, blotting the blood. He felt no pain anymore, just the warmth of her hand around his.

So much he wanted to say to her. But really, it came down to one thing.

"I love you."

Brooke paused with the tissue and looked up at him with surprise in her eyes. "Cade. You're obviously having a very intense day. I totally under—"

He pressed his finger to her lips, cutting her off. Maybe she didn't want to hear it, and maybe he was indeed going to look like a jackass at the end of this. But he was going to say what he needed to say regardless. "I love you. On intense days. On good days. On long, exhausting workdays. On really strange days when I find out that I have a long-lost brother. And most of all, on days when you make me smile, which happens to be every day I'm with you." He gazed deep into her eyes. "You are not just a big-picture girl for me, Brooke Parker. You're the *only* picture."

She touched his face, her eyes turning misty. "Cade—"

"You've got this job offer in Charlotte. I know. But if you want, that's something we can figure out together. I made a commitment to Cameron, so I need to stay in Chicago until she's back from maternity leave. But after that, I can—"

"I didn't take the job in Charlotte."

"Oh. Right." He exhaled, trying to catch up to speed. "Well. You should know that I had at least two minutes left on that speech. Really quality stuff."

"Sorry. I just thought this might be a good time to mention that I love you, too." She made a rolling gesture. "But, please—carry on."

He grinned. *Sassy as ever.* He took her hand, armed with this information, and backed her against the brick wall. "You love me?"

With a smile curling at the edges of her lips, she gazed up at him. "Yes. These past two weeks, I've been doing a lot of thinking about what I want in my life. And somehow, you ended up at the top of that list."

He lowered his head. "It's because your subconscious finds my subconscious irresistible," he said huskily.

"I have no clue what that means," she murmured against his mouth.

"For starters, it means I'm going to kiss you."

And that's exactly what he did.

They kissed for a long time in that alley, the rest of the world bustling by on the sidewalks and streets just a few feet away, but for that moment, pressed against the bricks, it was just the two of them. Nothing else mattered.

Afterward, they walked the five blocks to Brooke's apartment, where Cade told her about his conversation with Noah.

"Do you want to see him again?" she asked, putting a Band-Aid on his split knuckle.

"No." Cade sighed, and then nodded. "Yes."

Later, they lay wrapped around each other on the couch, and Brooke told him about her trip to Charlotte and her subsequent discussion with Ian.

"Afterward, when I was celebrating with Ford, I kept thinking that you should've been there, too." She shifted, sitting up halfway so that she could look him in the eyes. "I missed you these past two weeks. So much."

It was the heartfelt way she said it, the way her voice turned throaty with emotion. As much as he loved the quips and the inside jokes, it was this moment, when her walls were down and he saw her softer, vulnerable side, when she just *melted* him.

He reached up and touched her cheek. "Let's not do that again."

"Be apart for two weeks?" She slid her arms around his neck. "I agree."

Well, yes. But he was talking about something more than that. "No, I mean what got us to that point." He held her gaze. "No more tough-girl or tough-guy routines. At least, not between us. I want to be in the inner circle, Brooke." He realized what that meant—that he'd be letting her in, too.

And as he lay there with her, he knew there was nothing he'd ever wanted more.

In answer, she took his hand and placed it on her chest. Right over her heart. "You're in, Cade Morgan. Only you."

Yep, that pretty much made it official.

When it came to Brooke Parker of Sterling Restaurants, he was a goner.

Thirty-five

Three weeks later

"SO, UNFORTUNATELY, THE concession stand did not have beef tenderloin, shrimp kabobs, or that fancy Sterling Restaurants dessert cart. But, fret not, because I was able to snag you . . ." With a flourish, Cade pulled two things out from behind his back. "This lukewarm, rubbery hot dog and this Reese's Peanut Butter Cup—the *twin pack*. How's that for fine dining?"

"Yes on the twin pack," Brooke said. "No on the bun-wrapped trip to the emergency room to get my stomach pumped."

"My, somebody's quite a hot-dog snob."

"An occupational hazard when one is part owner of a pre-miere restaurant company with a rapidly expanding and increasingly lucrative sports and entertainment division," Brooke said, with a proud flick of her ponytail.

"Still subtly slipping that in there, I see."

"You betcha." She was in a particularly good mood tonight, seeing how, just this afternoon, she'd hired the in-house law-yer who would be taking on some of her responsibilities. He wouldn't start at Sterling for another two weeks, but change was on the horizon. She'd left work at six o'clock on a Friday night—possibly with a few heart palpitations on her way out the door, but she'd persevered—and now she had the whole night free to spend with Cade.

Or, rather, with Cade *plus* five hundred rabid high school football fans dressed in maroon and gold.

Brooke's eyes scanned the stands. "Wow. I didn't expect it to be so packed."

"Zach said that the team they're playing tonight is his school's rival," Cade said.

They spotted Noah and his wife, Tracy, about halfway up the bleachers. Cade linked his fingers through Brooke's and headed in that direction.

Over the last three weeks, Cade and his father had made progress in getting to know one another. The initial step had been the most difficult and awkward, with neither man knowing exactly how to make the first move. Fortunately, Zach had intervened once again, suggesting the three of them meet for dinner at a restaurant not far from the Garritys' house—and then had remembered at the last minute that he had a "late practice," and had suggested that Cade and Noah carry on without him.

"I like this kid's style," Brooke had said, chuckling, when Cade had told her about the obvious setup.

When Cade had finished grumbling, he'd admitted the dinner wasn't "too terrible."

"In some senses, it was easier not having Zach there," he'd said. "We just talked about him the whole time." He'd paused. "And about how Noah's treatment is going."

The bitter part of this bittersweet reunion, of course, was that it was finite in duration. Although Noah was currently asymptomatic, the doctors had explained that the radiation and steroid treatment was only buying them time and that, in the not-too-distant future, the tumor on Noah's brain stem would grow and begin to impair his motor skills and respiratory functions. Nevertheless, Noah had laid down the law: people weren't going to spend every moment dwelling on his cancer—they were going to enjoy the time they had left together, for as long as they could.

"Noah, Tracy, good to see you again," Brooke said when

they reached their row. She and Cade took the open seats next to them, and everyone made pleasant—even if still a little awkward—chitchat. Noah asked Cade about work, and Brooke saw the look of pride on his face when Cade talked about his new responsibilities as acting U.S. attorney, a transition that had taken effect earlier in the week when Cade's boss, Cameron, had gone into labor in the middle of a Potbelly Sandwich Shop—and, nine hours later, had delivered a healthy baby boy named William "Will" James Pallas.

Not too long after Brooke and Cade had arrived, the game started. And from that moment on, all work chatter stopped, the outside world ceased to exist, and football became life itself.

As Brooke sat in those stands that night, she was reminded of something Ian had told her—*while watching a game, we could hang out and yell and cheer and just be a father and son again*. Cade and Noah might not have been at that point, but talking about football certainly helped bridge the gap between them. At times, in fact, they actually seemed to be having fun together.

And beyond that, *wow*, did she ever see a new side of Cade that night. He paced, he was on his feet nearly the entire time, and he had this really intense game face that was . . . kind of hot.

Late in the third quarter, Zach got tackled four yards behind the line of scrimmage, and apparently this was the last straw for Cade.

"A reverse on fourth and one? Come on!" He threw up his hands in exasperation. "The defense hasn't stopped a single slant pass to Zach all night. Or if you're going to run the ball, at least go up the middle." He gestured to the field. "Hell, I could coach these kids better than that."

"Maybe you should, then."

The words came from Noah, sitting next to Cade.

Cade half-chuckled at that. "Yeah, right." He looked over at Noah and then pulled back. "You're being serious?"

Noah shrugged casually. "Just seems like you're getting a little twitchy up here in these stands."

"I'm just excited about the game, like everyone else here." Cade threw Brooke a look. *Can you believe this guy?*

"Actually, you do seem a little twitchy," she said.

He glared. "*Et tu*, Ms. Parker? I'm a prosecutor. I don't have time to coach a football team."

"Maybe not full-time," Noah said. "But I'm sure that any Chicago public school would be more than happy to have a former Rose Bowl champ come in occasionally and talk to the team."

Cade fell quiet at that, and Brooke could see the spark of interest in his eyes. She smiled to herself, thinking that Noah may have been onto something.

Perhaps it was time for Cade Morgan to get back on a football field.

AFTER THE GAME, Cade found a parking spot on a side street a few blocks from Brooke's place. Hand in hand, they leisurely walked in the direction of her apartment.

She looked over at Cade, curious about something. "I saw you talking to Zach's head coach in the parking lot. Congratulating him on his victory, I assume?"

He smiled, busted. "Okay, okay. Noah's idea about coaching stuck with me. It's no big deal—I'm just going to work with the quarterbacks for a couple of hours on Tuesday afternoons. Assuming there aren't any emergencies I need to handle at work."

"Will the kids have to call you 'Coach Morgan'?"

"They will if they don't want to run sprints and do bag drills the entire practice."

Brooke chuckled at that. Then, out of the blue, she remembered something. "I can't believe I forgot to tell you this. You'll never guess what they served for breakfast on my flight out to Charlotte. A Denver omelette."

Cade laughed. "Well, they are quite tasty." He glanced at her sideways, his tone coy. "Now, did you ask if they always serve Denver omelettes, because that's their thing, or if they tailor the breakfast to the *specific* passenger?"

"Ha, ha. You had that coming. Do I even want to know how many women before me enjoyed one of Cade Morgan's Denver omelettes?"

"I can tell you who the last one will ever be."

Brooke paused, quip raring to go, when the significance of those words hit her.

Oh.

Well, then.

She tugged Cade closer, then stood up on her toes and kissed him. "Nice save."

They linked their fingers together, walking along Michigan Avenue, passing through the tree-lined courtyard adjacent to the historic Water Tower. It was a gorgeous late-summer night, with a warm breeze coming off the lake.

"Should we grab a late dinner?" Cade asked. "It's Friday night, but I'm sure there's some restaurant filled with over-caffeinated jackrabbits who would be more than happy to find a table for the illustrious Brooke Parker."

"True. Although, it's so nice outside tonight. Maybe instead we can find a wine bar with outdoor seating."

"We could take my carriage there, Cinderella," Cade joked, pointing in the direction of the horse-drawn carriages lined along the Water Tower courtyard, waiting with their tops down for passengers willing to shell out for a thirty-minute ride.

Brooke chuckled. Romantic, yes, but that was a little too touristy for their tastes.

Then it struck her.

"I just realized something," she said. "*We* are one of those couples, walking hand in hand along Michigan Avenue, with no plans at all." For two years she'd watched everyone else from her office window.

But now, here she was.

"So we are." Cade let go of her hand and put his arm around her. He pulled her close, kissing the top of her head. "How does it feel?"

She turned and peered up at him, having only one answer to that.

"Perfect."

Keep reading for a sneak preview of
another irresistible contemporary romance
from Julie James

Something About You

Available now from Berkley Sensation

One

THIRTY THOUSAND HOTEL rooms in the city of Chicago, and Cameron Lynde managed to find one next door to a couple having a sex marathon.

"Yes! Oh yes! YES!"

Cameron pulled the pillow over her head, thinking—as she had been thinking for the past hour and a half—that it had to end *sometime*. It was after three o'clock in the morning, and while she certainly had nothing against a good round of raucous hotel sex, this particular round had gone beyond raucous and into the ridiculous about fourteen "oh-God-oh-God-oh-Gods" ago. More important, even with the discounted rate they gave federal employees, overnights at the Peninsula weren't typically within the monthly budget of an assistant U.S. attorney, and she was starting to get seriously POed that she couldn't get a little peace and quiet.

Bam! Bam! Bam! The wall behind the king-sized bed shook with enough force to rattle her headboard, and Cameron cursed the hardwood floors that had brought her to such circumstances.

Earlier in the week, when the contractor had told her that

she would need to stay off her refinished floors for twenty-four hours, she had decided to treat herself to some much-needed pampering. Just last week she had finished a grueling three-month racketeering trial against eleven defendants charged with various organized criminal activities, including seven murders and three attempted murders. The trial had been mentally exhausting for everyone involved, particularly her and the other assistant U.S. attorney who had prosecuted the case. So when she'd learned that she needed to be out of her house while the floors dried, she had seized on the opportunity to turn it into a weekend getaway.

Maybe other people would have gone somewhere more distant or exotic than a hotel three miles from home, but all Cameron had cared about was getting an incredibly over-priced but fantastically rejuvenating massage, followed by a tranquil night of R&R, and then in the morning a brunch buffet (again incredibly overpriced) where she could stuff herself to the point where she remembered why she made it a general habit to stay away from brunch buffets. And the perfect place for that was the Peninsula.

Or so she had thought.

"Such a big, bad man! Right there, oh yeah—right there, don't stop!"

The pillow over her head did nothing to drown out the woman's voice. Cameron closed her eyes in a silent plea. *Dear Mr. Big and Bad: Whatever the hell you're doing, don't you move from that spot until you get the job done.* She hadn't prayed so hard for an orgasm since the first—and last—time she'd slept with Jim, the corporate wine buyer/artist who wanted to "find his way" but who didn't seem to have a clue how to find his way around the key parts of the female body.

The moaning that had started around 1:30 A.M. was what had woken her up. In her groggy state, her first thought had been that someone in the room next door was sick. But quickly following those moans had been a second person's moans, and then came the panting and the wall-banging and the hol-lering and then that part that sounded suspiciously like a butt cheek being spanked, and somewhere around that point she had clued into the true goings-on of room 1308.

WhaMA-WhaMA-WhaMA-WhaMA-WhaMA-WhaMA . . .

The bed in the room next door increased its tempo against the wall, and the squeaking of the mattress reached a new, feverish pitch. Despite her annoyance, Cameron had to give the guy credit, whoever he was, for having some serious staying power. Perhaps it was one of those Viagra situations, she mused. She had heard somewhere that one little pill could get a man up and running for over four hours.

She yanked the pillow off her head and peered through the darkness at the clock on the nightstand next to the bed: 3:17. If she had to endure another two hours and fifteen minutes of this stuff, she just might have to kill someone—starting with the front desk clerk who had put her in this room in the first place. Weren't hotels supposed to skip the thirteenth floor, anyway? Right now she was wishing she was a more superstitious person and had asked to be assigned another room.

In fact, right now she was wishing she'd never come up with the whole weekend getaway idea and instead had just spent the night at Collin's or Amy's. At least then she'd be asleep instead of listening to the cacophonous symphony of grunting and squealing—oh yes, the girl was actually *squealing* now—that was the current soundtrack of her life. Plus, Collin made a mean cheddar and tomato egg-white omelet that, while likely not quite the equivalent of the delicacies one might find at the Peninsula buffet, would've reminded her why she'd made it a general habit to let him do all the cooking when the three of them lived together their senior year of college.

Wheewammawamma-BAM! Wheewammawamma-BAM!

Cameron sat up in bed and looked at the phone on the nightstand. She didn't want to be that kind of guest that complained about every little blemish in the hotel's five-star service. But the noise from the room next door had been going on for a long time now and at a certain point, she felt as though she was entitled to some sleep in her nearly four-hundred-dollar-per-night room. The only reason the hotel hadn't already received complaints, she guessed, was due to the fact that 1308 was a corner room with no one on the other side.

Cameron was just about to pick up the phone to call the front desk when, suddenly, she heard the man next door call out the glorious sounds of her salvation.

Smack! Smack!

"Oh shit, I'm cooommmminnnggg!"

A loud groan. And then—

Blessed silence. Finally.

Cameron fell back onto the bed. *Thank you, thank you, Peninsula hotel gods, for granting me this tiny reprieve. I shall never again call your massages incredibly overpriced. Even if we all know it doesn't cost $195 to rub lotion on someone's back. Just saying.*

She crawled under the covers and pulled the cream down duvet up to her chin. Her head sank into the pillows and she lay there for a few minutes as she began to drift off. Then she heard another noise next door—the sound of the door shutting.

Cameron tensed.

And then—

Nothing.

All remained blissfully still and silent, and her final thought before she fell asleep was on the significance of the sound of the door shutting.

She had a sneaking suspicion that somebody had just received a five-star booty call.

BAM!

Cameron shot up in bed, the sound from next door waking her right out of her sleep. She heard muffled squealing and the bed slammed against the wall again—harder and louder than ever—as if its occupants were *really* going at it this time.

She looked at the clock: 4:08. She'd been given a whopping thirty-minute reprieve.

Not wasting another moment—frankly, she'd already given these jokers far too much of her valuable sleep time—she reached over and turned on the lamp next to the bed. She blinked as her eyes adjusted to the sudden burst of light. Then she grabbed the phone off the nightstand and dialed.

After one ring, a man answered pleasantly on the other end. "Good evening, Ms. Lynde. Thank you for calling Guest Services—how may we be of assistance?"

Cameron cleared her throat, her voice still hoarse as her words tumbled out. "Look, I don't want to be a jerk about this, but you guys have got to do something about the people in room 1308. They keep banging against the wall; there's been all sorts of moaning and shouting and spanking and it's been going on for, like, the last two hours. I've barely slept this entire night and it sounds like they're gearing up for round twenty or whatever, which is great for them but not so much for me, and I'm kind of at the point where enough is enough, you know?"

The voice on the other end was wholly unfazed, as if Guest Services at the Peninsula handled the fallout from five-star booty calls all the time.

"Of course, Ms. Lynde. I apologize for the inconvenience. I'll send up security to take care of the problem right away."

"Thanks," Cameron grumbled, not yet willing to be pacified that easily. She planned to speak to the manager in the morning, but for now all she wanted was a quiet room and some sleep.

She hung up the phone and waited. A few moments passed, then she glanced at the wall behind the bed. Things had fallen strangely silent in room 1308. She wondered if the occupants had heard her calling Guest Services to complain. Sure, the walls were thin (as she definitely had discovered firsthand), but were they *that* thin?

She heard the door to room 1308 open.

The bastards were making their escape.

Cameron flew out of bed and ran to her door, determined to at least get a look at the sex fiends. She pressed against the door and peered through the peephole just as the door to the other room shut. For a brief moment, she saw no one. Then—

A man stepped into view.

He moved quickly, appearing slightly distorted through the peephole. He had his back toward her as he passed by her room, so Cameron didn't get the greatest look. She didn't know what the typical sex fiend looked like, but this particular one was on the taller side and stylish in his jeans, black corduroy blazer, and gray hooded T-shirt. He wore the hood pulled up, which was kind of unusual. As the man crossed the hallway and pushed open the door to the stairwell, something struck her as oddly familiar. But then he disappeared into the stairwell before she could place it.

Cameron pulled away from the door. Something very strange was going on in room 1308 . . . Maybe the man had fled the scene because he'd heard her call Guest Services and was abandoning his partner to deal with the fallout alone. A married man, perhaps? Regardless, the woman in 1308 was going to have some serious 'splaining to do once hotel security arrived. Cameron figured—since she already was awake, that is—that she might as well just sit it out right there at the peephole and catch the final act. Not that she was eavesdropping or anything, but . . . okay, she was eavesdropping.

She didn't have to wait long. Two men dressed in suits, presumably hotel security, arrived within the next minute and knocked on the door to 1308. Cameron watched through the peephole as the security guards stared expectantly at the door, then shrugged at each other when there was no answer.

"Should we try again?" the shorter security guard asked.

The second guy nodded and knocked on the door. "Hotel security," he called out.

No response.

"Are you sure this is the right room?" asked the second guy.

The first guy checked the room number, then nodded. "Yep. The person who complained said the noise was coming from room 1308."

He glanced over at Cameron's room. She took a step back as if they could see her through the door. She suddenly felt very aware of the fact that she was wearing only her University of Michigan T-shirt and underwear.

There was a pause.

"Well, I don't hear a thing now," Cameron heard the first guy say. He banged on the door a third time, louder still. "Security! Open up!"

Still nothing.

Cameron moved back to the door and looked out the peep-hole once again. She saw the security guards exchange looks of annoyance.

"They're probably in the shower," said the shorter guy.

"Probably going at it again," the other one agreed.

The two men pressed their ears to the door. On her side of the door, Cameron listened for any sound of a shower running in the next room but heard nothing.

The taller security guard sighed. "You know the protocol—we have to go in." Out of his pocket he pulled what presumably was some sort of master key card. He slid it into the lock and cracked open the door.

"Hello? Hotel security—anyone in here?" he called into the room.

He looked over his shoulder at his partner and shook his head. Nothing. He stepped farther in and gestured for the second guy to follow. Both men disappeared into the room, out of Cameron's view, and the door slammed shut behind them.

There was a momentary pause, then Cameron heard one of the security men cry out through the adjoining wall.

"Holy shit!"

Her stomach dropped. She knew then that whatever had happened in 1308, it wasn't good. Uncertain what she should do, she pressed her ear to the wall and listened.

"Try CPR while I call 9-1-1!" one of the men shouted.

Cameron flew off the bed—she knew CPR—and raced to the door. She threw it open just as the shorter security guy was running out of 1308.

Seeing her, he held up his hand, indicating she should stop right where she was. "Ma'am—please get back in your room."

"But I heard—I thought I could help, I—"

"We've got it covered, ma'am. Now please step back into your room." He rushed off.

Per the security's guard order, Cameron remained in her doorway. She looked around and saw that other people in the nearby rooms had heard the commotion and were peering into the hallway with mixed expressions of trepidation and curiosity.

After what seemed like forever but what was probably only minutes, the shorter guy returned leading a pair of paramedics pulling a gurney.

As the trio raced past Cameron, she overheard the security guard explaining the situation. "We found her lying there on the bed . . . She was nonresponsive so we began CPR but it doesn't look good . . ."

By this time, additional staff had arrived on the scene, and a woman in a gray suit identified herself as the hotel manager and asked everyone to remain in their rooms. Cameron overheard her tell the other members of the staff to keep the hallway and elevator bank clear. The thirteenth floor guests spoke amongst themselves in low murmurs, and Cameron caught snippets of conversations as a guest from one room would ask another if he or she knew what was happening.

A hush fell over the crowd when the paramedics reappeared in the doorway of room 1308. They moved quickly, pulling the gurney out into the hall.

This time, there was a person on that gurney.

As they hurried past Cameron, she caught a glimpse of the person—a quick glimpse, but enough to see that it was a woman, and also enough to see that she had long red hair that fanned out in stark contrast to the white of both the sheet on the gurney and the hotel bathrobe she wore. And, she saw enough to see that the woman wasn't moving.

While one of the paramedics pushed the gurney, the other ran alongside it, pumping oxygen through a handheld mask that covered the woman's face. The two security guards raced ahead of the paramedics, making sure the hallway was clear. Cameron—and apparently several of the other hotel guests as well—overheard the shorter guard saying something to the other about the police being on their way.

At the mention of the police, a minor commotion broke out. The hotel guests demanded to know what was happening.

The manager spoke above the fray. "I certainly understand that all of you have concerns, and I offer you our sincerest apologies for the disturbance." She addressed them in a calm, genteel tone that was remarkably similar to that of the man from Guest Services who Cameron had spoken on the phone with earlier. She wondered if they all talked that way to each other when no customers were around, or if they dropped the charm routine and that vague, quasi-European-even-though-I'm-from-Wisconsin accent the minute they hit the lunchroom.

"Unfortunately, at this point I can tell you only that the situation, obviously, is very serious and may be criminal in nature," the manager continued. "We will be turning this matter over to the police, and we ask that everyone remain in their rooms until they arrive and assess the situation. It's likely the police will want to speak with some of you."

The manager's gaze fell directly upon Cameron. As the crowd fell back into their murmurs and whispers, she walked over. "Ms. Lynde, is it?"

Cameron nodded. "Yes."

The manager gestured to the door. "Would you mind if I escorted you back into your room, Ms. Lynde?" This was Polite-Peninsula-Hotel-speak for "You might as well get comfortable because your eavesdropping ass isn't going anywhere."

"Of course," Cameron said, still somewhat shell-shocked by the events that had transpired over the last few minutes. As an assistant U.S. attorney, she'd had plenty of exposure to the criminal element, but this was different. This was not some case she was reviewing through the objective eyes of a prosecutor; there were no evidence files neatly prepared by the FBI or crime scene photos taken after the fact. She had actually *heard* the crime this time; she had seen the victim firsthand and—thinking back to the man in the blazer and hooded T-shirt—very possibly the person who had harmed her as well.

The thought sent chills running down her spine.

Or, Cameron supposed, maybe the chill had something to

do with the fact that she was still standing in the air-
conditioned hallway wearing nothing but her T-shirt and
underwear.

Classy.

With as much dignity as one could muster while braless
and without any pants, Cameron tugged her T-shirt down an
extra half-inch and followed the hotel manager into her room.

Two

SOMETHING WASN'T RIGHT.

Cameron had been trapped inside her hotel room for nearly two hours while the Chicago Police Department supposedly conducted their investigation. She knew enough about crime scenes and witness questioning to know that this was not standard protocol.

For starters, nobody was telling her anything. The police had arrived shortly after the hotel manager escorted her back into her room. A middle-aged, slightly balding and extremely cranky Detective Slonsky introduced himself to Cameron and took a seat in the armchair in the corner of the hotel room and began to take her statement about what she had heard that night. Although she had at least been given two seconds of privacy to throw on yoga pants and a bra, she still found it awkward to be questioned by the police while sitting on a hastily made hotel bed.

The first thing Detective Slonsky noticed was the half-empty glass of wine that she had ordered from room service still sitting on the desk where she'd left it hours before. That, of course, had prompted several preliminary questions regarding her alcohol consumption over the course of the evening. After she seemingly managed to convince Slonsky that, no, she was not a raging alcoholic and, yes, her statement at least had a modicum of reliability, they moved past the booze issue and she commented on the fact that Slonsky had introduced himself as "Detective" instead of "Officer." She asked if that meant he was part of the homicide division. If for no other reason, she wanted to know what had happened to the girl in room 1308.

Slonsky's sole response was a level stare and a curt, "I'm the one asking the questions here, Ms. Lynde."

Cameron had just finished giving her statement when another plain-clothes detective stuck his head into the room. "Slonsky—you better get in here." He nodded in the direction of the room next door.

Slonsky stood and gave Cameron yet another level stare. She wondered if he practiced the look in his bathroom mirror.

"I'd appreciate it if you would remain in this room until I get back," he told her.

Cameron smiled. "Of course, Detective." She was debating whether to pull rank in order to start getting some answers, but she wasn't quite at that point. Yet. She'd been around cops and agents all her life and had a lot of respect for what they did. But the smile was to let Slonsky know that he wasn't getting to her. "I'm happy to cooperate in any way I can."

Slonsky eyed her suspiciously, probably trying to decide whether he heard a hint of sarcasm in her voice. She got that look a lot.

"Just stay in your room," he said as he made his exit.

The next time Cameron saw Detective Slonsky was a half hour later, when he dropped by her room to let her know that, due to certain "unexpected developments," she would not only have to remain in her room longer than anticipated, but that he was posting a guard at her door. He added that "it had been requested" that she not make any calls from either her cell phone or the hotel line until "they" had finished questioning her.

For the first time, Cameron wondered whether she personally was in trouble. "Am I considered a *suspect* in this investigation?" she asked Slonsky.

"I didn't say that."

She noticed that wasn't officially a "no."

As Slonsky turned to leave, she threw another question at him. "Who are 'they'?"

He peered over his shoulder. "Excuse me?"

"You said I can't make any calls until 'they' finish questioning me," Cameron said. "Who were you referring to?"

The detective's expression said that he had no intention of answering that question. "We appreciate your continued cooperation, Ms. Lynde. That's all I can say for now."

A few minutes after Slonsky left, Cameron looked out her peephole and—sure enough—was treated to the view of the back of some man's head, presumably the guard he had stationed outside her door. She left the door and went back to sitting on the bed. Cameron glanced at the clock and saw that it was nearly 7:00 A.M. She turned on the television—Slonsky hadn't said anything about not watching TV, after all—and hoped that maybe she would see something about whatever was happening on the news.

She was still pushing buttons on the remote, trying to figure out how to get past that damn hotel "Welcome" screen, when the door to her room flew open once more.

Slonsky stuck his head in. "Sorry—no television either."

He shut the door.

"Stupid thin walls," Cameron muttered under her breath. Not that anyone was listening. Then again . . .

"Can I at least read a book, Detective Slonsky?" she asked the empty room.

A pause.

Then a voice came through the door, from the hallway. "Sure."

And indeed the walls were so thin, Cameron could actually hear the faint trace of a smile in his answer.

* * *

"THIS IS GETTING ridiculous. I have rights, you know."

Cameron faced off against the cop guarding the door to her hotel room, determined to get some answers.

The young police officer nodded sympathetically. "I know, ma'am, and I do apologize, but I'm just following orders."

Maybe it was her frustration at being cooped up in her hotel room for what was now going on five—yes, *five*—hours, but Cameron was going to strangle the kid if he ma'am-ed her one more time. She was thirty-two years old, not sixty. Although she'd probably given up the right to be called "Miss" somewhere around the time she had started thinking of twenty-two-year-old man-boy police officers as kids.

Deciding that throttling a cop was probably not the best way to go when presumably dozens more stood right outside her door (she couldn't say for sure; she hadn't been permitted to even look out into the hallway, let alone step a toe out there), Cameron tried another tactic. The man-boy clearly responded to authority, maybe she could use that to her advantage.

"Look, I probably should've mentioned this earlier, but I'm an assistant U.S. attorney. I work out of the Chicago office—"

"If you live in Chicago, what are you doing spending the night in a hotel?" Officer Man-Boy interrupted.

"I'm redoing my hardwood floors. The point is—"

"Really?" He seemed very interested in this. "Because I've been trying to find somebody to update my bathroom. The people who owned the place before me put in this crazy black and white marble and gold fixtures and the place looks like something out of the Playboy Mansion. Mind if I ask how you found a contractor to take on a job that small?"

Cameron cocked her head. "Are you trying to sidetrack me with these questions, or do you just have some weird fascination with home improvement?"

"Possibly the former. I was under the distinct impression that you were about to become difficult."

Cameron had to hide her smile. Officer Man-Boy may not have been as green as she'd thought.

"Here's the thing," she told him, "you can't keep me here against my will, especially since I've already given my statement to Detective Slonsky. You know that, and more important, I know that. There's clearly something unusual going on with this investigation, and while I'm willing to cooperate and give you guys a little leeway as a professional courtesy, I'm going to need some answers if you expect me to keep waiting here. And if you're not the person who can give me those answers, that's fine, but then I'd like it if you could go get Slonsky or whoever it is that I should be talking to."

Officer Man-Boy was not unsympathetic. "Look—I know you've been stuck in this room for a long time, but the FBI guys said that they're gonna talk to you as soon as they finish next door."

"So it's the FBI who's running this, then?"

"I probably wasn't supposed to say that."

"Why do they have jurisdiction?" Cameron pressed. "This is a homicide case, right?"

Officer Man-Boy didn't fall for the bait a second time. "I'm sorry, Ms. Lynde, but my hands are tied. The agent in charge of the investigation specifically said I'm not allowed to talk to you about this."

"Then I think I should speak to the agent in charge. Who is it?" As a prosecutor for the Northern District of Illinois, she had worked with many of the FBI agents in Chicago.

"Some special agent—I didn't catch his name," Officer Man-Boy said. "Although I think he might know you. When he told me to guard this room, he said he felt bad for sticking me with you for this long."

Cameron tried not to show any reaction, but that stung. True, she wasn't exactly buddy-buddy with a lot of the FBI agents she worked with—many of them still blamed her for that incident three years ago—but with the exception of one particular agent who, fortunately, was miles away in Nevada or Nebraska or something, she hadn't thought that anyone in the FBI disliked her enough to openly bad-mouth her.

Officer Man-Boy looked apologetic. "For what it's worth, I don't think you're so bad."

"Thanks. And did this unknown special agent who allegedly thinks he knows me have anything else to say?"

"Only that I should go get him if you start acting fussy." He looked her over. "You're going to start acting fussy now, aren't you?"

Cameron folded her arms across her chest. "Yes, I think I am." And it wouldn't be an act. "You go find this agent, whoever he is, and tell him that the fussy woman in room 1307 is through being jerked around. And tell him that I would appreciate it very much if he could wrap up his little power trip and condescend to speak to me himself. Because *I* would like to know how long he expects me to sit here and wait."

"For as long as I ask you to, Ms. Lynde."

The voice came from the doorway.

Cameron had her back to the door, but she would've recognized that voice anywhere—low and as smooth as velvet.

It couldn't be.

She turned around and took in the man standing across the room from her. He looked exactly the same as he did the last time she'd seen him three years ago: tall, dark, and scowling.

She didn't bother to mask the animosity in her voice. "Agent Pallas . . . I didn't realize you were back in town. How was Nevada?"

"Nebraska."

From his icy look, Cameron knew that her day, which had already been off to a most inauspicious start, had just gotten about fifty times worse.

Fate has thrown two sworn enemies into each other's arms.

FROM NATIONAL BESTSELLING AUTHOR

Julie James

Something About You

Staying overnight in a luxury hotel, Assistant U.S. Attorney Cameron Lynde overhears a high-profile murder involving a U.S. senator. Special Agent Jack Pallas is assigned to the investigation—the same Jack Pallas who still blames her for nearly ruining his career three years ago. Now the pair will have to put their rocky past behind them, focus on the case at hand—and smother the flame of their sizzling-hot sexual tension.

"Julie James rocks! You'll laugh out loud and wish you had an FBI agent of your own."
—Sandra Hill, *USA Today* bestselling author

penguin.com

"Julie James writes books I can't put down."

—Nalini Singh, *New York Times* bestselling author

FROM *USA TODAY* BESTSELLING AUTHOR

Julie James

THE FBI/US ATTORNEY SERIES

Something About You

A Lot Like Love

About That Night

Love Irresistibly

juliejames.com
facebook.com/Authorjuliejames
facebook.com/LoveAlwaysBooks
penguin.com

M1211AS1112